D0494954

Praise for Elizabeth Chadwick

'Picking up an Elizabeth Chadwick novel you know you are in for a sumptuous ride. Beautifully strong characters and a real feel for time and place'
Daily Telegraph

'Blends authentic period details with modern convention for emotional drama'
Mail on Sunday

'Enjoyable and sensuous'
Daily Mail

'Meticulous research and strong storytelling'
Woman & Home

'Chadwick's research is impeccable, her characters fully formed and her storytelling enthralling . . . The best writer of medieval fiction currently around'
Historical Novels Review

'Chadwick has excelled herself. This terrific novel is packed with action, emotion, politics and passion'
Sunday Express

'Elizabeth Chadwick is an excellent chronicler of royal intrigue . . . an author who makes history come gloriously alive'
The Times

'One of Elizabeth Chadwick's strengths is her stunning grasp of historical details . . . Her characters are beguiling and the story is intriguing and very enjoyable'
Barbara Erskine

Also by Elizabeth Chadwick

The Wild Hunt series
The Coming of the Wolf
The Wild Hunt
The Running Vixen
The Leopard Unleashed

The William Marshal series
A Place Beyond Courage
The Greatest Knight
The Scarlet Lion
The Time of Singing
To Defy a King
Templar Silks

Eleanor of Aquitane trilogy
The Summer Queen
The Winter Crown
The Autumn Throne

The FitzWarin series
Shadows and Strongholds
Lords of the White Castle

Other novels
Daughters of the Grail
Shields of Pride
First Knight
The Conquest
The Champion
The Love Knot
The Marsh King's Daughter
The Winter Mantle
The Falcons of Montabard
Lady of The English
The Irish Princess

A MARRIAGE OF LIONS

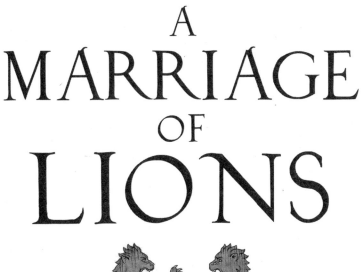

ELIZABETH CHADWICK

sphere

SPHERE

First published in Great Britain in 2021 by Sphere

1 3 5 7 9 10 8 6 4 2

Copyright © Elizabeth Chadwick 2021

The moral right of the author has been asserted.

All characters and events in this publication, other than those
clearly in the public domain, are fictitious and any resemblance to
real persons, living or dead, is purely coincidental.

All rights reserved. No part of this publication may be reproduced, stored
in a retrieval system, or transmitted, in any form or by any means, without
the prior permission in writing of the publisher, nor be otherwise circulated in
any form of binding or cover other than that in which it is published and
without a similar condition including this condition being imposed
on the subsequent purchaser.

A CIP catalogue record for this book is
available from the British Library.

Hardback ISBN 978-0-7515-7758-7
Trade Paperback ISBN 978-0-7515-7757-0

Typeset in BT Baskerville by Palimpsest Book Production Ltd, Falkirk, Stirlingshire
Printed and bound in Great Britain by Clays Ltd, Elcograf S.p.A.

Papers used by Sphere are from well-managed forests
and other responsible sources.

Sphere
An imprint of
Little, Brown Book Group
Carmelite House
50 Victoria Embankment
London
EC4Y 0DZ

An Hachette UK Company
www.hachette.co.uk

www.littlebrown.co.uk

For my father, Robert 'Bob' Chadwick,
22 January 1928 – 27 March 2020.

Remembering 'Crispin's Capers'.

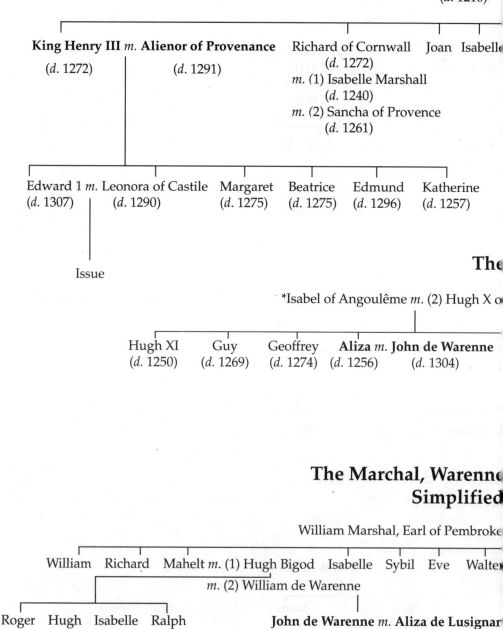

King John
(*d*. 1216)

King Henry III *m*. **Alienor of Provenance**   Richard of Cornwall   Joan Isabelle
(*d*. 1272)   (*d*. 1291)   (*d*. 1272)
                                                    m. (1) Isabelle Marshall
                                                        (*d*. 1240)
                                                    m. (2) Sancha of Provence
                                                        (*d*. 1261)

Edward 1 *m*. Leonora of Castile Margaret Beatrice Edmund Katherine
(*d*. 1307)   (*d*. 1290)   (*d*. 1275) (*d*. 1275) (*d*. 1296) (*d*. 1257)

Issue

The

*Isabel of Angoulême *m*. (2) Hugh X o

Hugh XI   Guy   Geoffrey   **Aliza** *m*. **John de Warenne**
(*d*. 1250) (*d*. 1269) (*d*. 1274) (*d*. 1256)   (*d*. 1304)

The Marchal, Warenn
Simplified

William Marshal, Earl of Pembroke

William Richard Mahelt *m*. (1) Hugh Bigod Isabelle Sybil Eve Walter
                        m. (2) William de Warenne

Roger Hugh Isabelle Ralph   **John de Warenne** *m*. **Aliza de Lusignan**

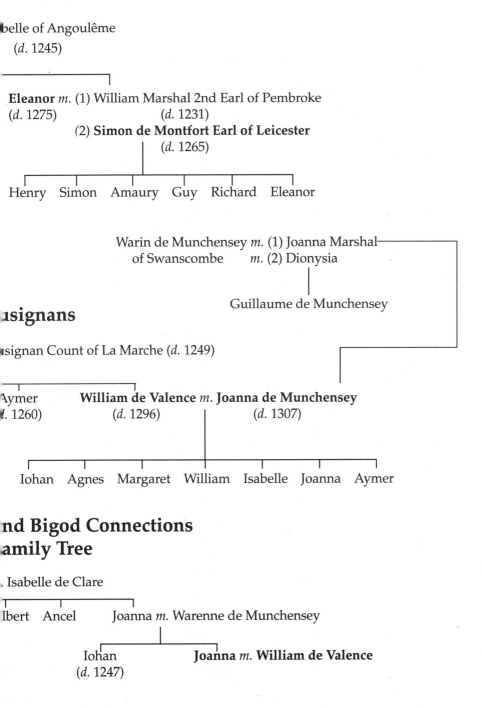

belle of Angoulême
(*d*. 1245)

Eleanor *m*. (1) William Marshal 2nd Earl of Pembroke
(*d*. 1275)   (*d*. 1231)

(2) **Simon de Montfort Earl of Leicester**
(*d*. 1265)

Henry   Simon   Amaury   Guy   Richard   Eleanor

Warin de Munchensey *m*. (1) Joanna Marshal
of Swanscombe   *m*. (2) Dionysia

Guillaume de Munchensey

ısignans

ısignan Count of La Marche (*d*. 1249)

Aymer   **William de Valence** *m*. **Joanna de Munchensey**
l. 1260)   (*d*. 1296)   (*d*. 1307)

Iohan   Agnes   Margaret   William   Isabelle   Joanna   Aymer

nd Bigod Connections
amily Tree

Isabelle de Clare

lbert   Ancel   Joanna *m*. Warenne de Munchensey

Iohan   **Joanna** *m*. **William de Valence**
(*d*. 1247)

A Cast of Characters

In order of appearance on stage

Joanna de Munchensy
Eight-year-old granddaughter of the great William Marshal, former regent of England. She is being raised at court and trained in the Queen's household

Madam Biset
A lady of Queen Alienor's household

Mabel
Joanna's nurse and servant

Cecily de Sandford
Joanna's tutor and mentor. A noble older lady of the household

Sausagez
A fluffy white dog lapdog owned by Dame Willelma

Dame Willelma
Queen Alienor's nurse. An older lady of the household who has been with the Queen since her childhood

Mistress Roberga
One of Queen Alienor's ladies

Henry III, King of England
Son of the notorious King John but very unlike him and an artistic family man – not a warrior

Gilbert Marshal, Earl of Pembroke
Joanna's maternal uncle

Sybil Giffard
Another of Queen Alienor's ladies and an accomplished midwife

Alienor of Provence, Queen of England
Sixteen years old when the novel opens

Iohan de Munchensy
Joanna's brother, two years older than Joanna

Simon de Montfort
Earl of Leicester, married to Eleanor the King's sister

Eleanor de Montfort
Simon de Montfort's wife and also sister to King Henry III and half-sister to the later-mentioned Lusignans

The Lord Edward
Henry III and Queen Alienor's son. Heir to the throne

Richard of Cornwall
King Henry III's brother

Isabelle Marshal
Richard of Cornwall's first wife, and Joanna's maternal aunt.

Mahelt Marshal, Countess of Surrey
Mother of John de Warenne and also Roger and Hugh Bigod. Joanna's maternal aunt

John de Warenne
Joanna's cousin and heir to the earldom of Surrey

Margaret
Daughter of Henry III and Alienor of Provence

Warin de Munchensy of Swanscombe
Joanna's father

Peter of Savoy
The Queen's uncle and Earl of Richmond. Guardian of John de Warenne

Isabel of Angoulême
Mother of King Henry III, Richard of Cornwall and Eleanor de Montfort. Also by her second marriage, mother of the Lusignans including William de Valence

Aliza de Lusignan
Half-sister of Henry III through their mother Isabel of Angoulême. Later wife of John de Warenne

Guy de Lusignan
Son of Isabel of Angoulême and half brother to Henry III

Geoffrey de Lusignan
Son of Isabel of Angoulême and half brother to Henry III

William de Valence
Youngest son of Isabel of Angoulême and half brother to Henry III. Eventual husband of Joanna de Munchensy

Beatrice
Daughter of Henry III

Edmund
Son of Henry III

Henry of Almain
Son and heir of Richard of Cornwall and his first wife Isabelle Marshal. Joanna's cousin

Elias
Servant to William de Valence

Aymer de Valence
Son of Isabel of Angoulême and half brother to Henry III. Destined for the priesthood, becoming Bishop Elect of Winchester

Master Peter
Physician of the royal household

Adam Marsh
A friar in the royal household

Jacomin
English serving man of William de Valence

Richard de Clare
Joanna's cousin. Son of her aunt Isabelle from her first marriage

Robert
Joanna's cook

Boniface
Archbishop of Canterbury and another of Queen Alienor's uncles.

Iohan
Joanna's firstborn son

Dionysia
Joanna's stepmother

Guillaume de Munchensy
Joanna's half-brother from her father's second marriage to Dionysia

Agnes
Joanna's eldest daughter

Emma
Country serving girl and later mistress of Aymer de Valence

Eustace de Lenn
An official in the employ of Archbishop Boniface

Isabelle
Second daughter of John de Warenne

Louis IX
King of France and brother-in-law to Henry III

Marguerite
Wife of King Louis, Queen of France, sister of Queen Alienor of England

Katharine
Youngest daughter of Henry III and Queen Alienor

William (Will)
Second son of Joanna and William de Valence

Leonora of Castile
Wife of the Lord Edward

Albricht
A London pie seller

Henry de Montfort
Eldest son of Simon and Eleanor de Montfort

Nicolas
Joanna's chaplain

Isabelle
Joanna's youngest daughter

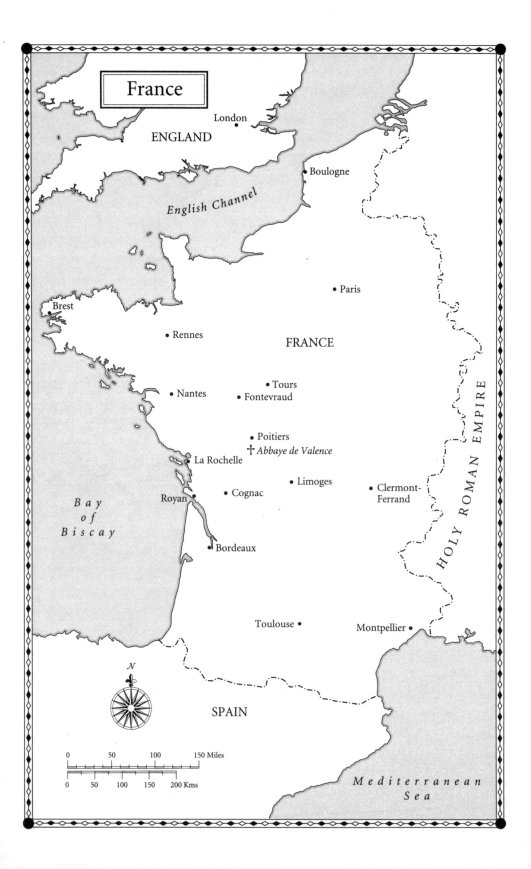

1

Awakening to darkness in the soft feather bed she shared with her nurse, Joanna gasped as she surfaced from the grip of her dream. At her side, Mabel's familiar, warm weight dipping the mattress anchored her to comforting, blessed reality. Grainy light from the night candle outlined the other beds in the room and the slumbering forms of the Queen's ladies mounded like foothills before the inner chamber where the King was sleeping with his wife.

The dream was already fading, but it had been about her home at Swanscombe, and her mother – her dreams always were. Rolling on to her back, she gazed at the painted gold stars on the chamber ceiling, gleaming in the dim flicker of the candle light. Six months had passed since she had arrived at court on her eighth-year day to be raised and trained in the young Queen's household. With scarcely a backward look, her father had left her here and returned home to his new wife and child.

Joanna had a vivid memory of touching her mother's cold

tomb slab, knowing that she lay beneath the stone, wrapped in her shroud, inches away but unreachable. The marriage vow said no man should separate a couple whom God had joined, but God himself had sundered her parents' bond, and a new wife had taken her mother's place and borne a son. The past, herself included, had been swept aside as of little consequence – a failed effort. Her father said a place in the royal household was a great honour and a magnificent opportunity for a daughter who possessed better connections than prospects of wealth, but Joanna knew it was because neither her father nor stepmother wanted her at Swanscombe under their feet.

Thirsty, she eased from the bed and tip-toed, agile and bare-foot, around the sleepers to the flagon of spring water standing on the sideboard. Dame Willelma's fluffy white lap dog Sausagez raised his head to watch her, and then curled around again, nose to tail in his cushioned bed.

From behind the closed inner chamber door, Joanna heard Queen Alienor's light voice, and the King's rumbled reply, ending on a throaty chuckle. He had visited his young wife almost every night since their arrival at Woodstock and Joanna had lost her initial shyness and grown accustomed to his presence. Her tutor, Dame Cecily, said it was the Queen's duty to bear children now she was old enough, and King Henry's to beget them.

Joanna liked the King. His skin smelled of roses and incense. Sometimes he would pat her head and enquire with a kindly smile how her lessons were progressing. He was always giving the Queen thoughtful little gifts and surprises and clearly doted on her. To Joanna it was a magical thing – a man who loved and paid court to his wife.

Drinking her water, Joanna noticed that the outer door was a crack open with a glimmer of light beyond, which meant that Madam Biset was at her prayers again. Perhaps she might like a drink too. Joanna carefully poured a fresh cup and, slipping into the vestibule, approached Madam Biset who was kneeling at a small table counting her rosary beads before a figurine of the Virgin Mary. Joanna's arrival shadowed the candle flame and Madam Biset looked up, two thin, vertical lines creasing between her eyebrows.

'Child, what are you doing out of bed in the middle of the night?'

Joanna curtseyed and held out the cup. 'I woke up, and I was thirsty, madam. I knew you were at prayer and I thought of you.'

The frown relaxed. 'Bless you for your kindness, child.' Madam Biset took the drink. 'The Queen has asked me to pray for her fruitfulness, so that she may conceive an heir for England tonight. Come, you may say a prayer with me.' She patted the folded cloak at her side.

Joanna obediently knelt upon the cloth. Clasping her hands, she focused her gaze on the exquisite little statue. The Virgin's robe was blue and she wore a delicate golden crown. The baby Jesus sat in her lap, one arm extended to the world. The Queen was so anxious to bear the King a son. Only this morning she had been consulting a treatise on conception from the medical school at Salerno, and tonight Joanna had helped to prepare the tub containing special herbs and rose water in which the Queen had bathed before retiring to bed with her lord.

Madam Biset implored the Virgin to grant the Queen succour and grace regarding the matter in hand, counting a bead on each plea, but suddenly stopped in mid-flow as angry shouts rang out, followed by several loud crashes that sounded like furniture being smashed.

A drunken voice roared, 'Where is he? Where is the man who has stolen my crown? Where is the liar who calls himself King! I will cut out his beating heart and feed it to the crows!'

A man shambled out of the darkness towards Joanna and Madam Biset, his clothes in stained disarray, one leg of his hose wrinkling around his calf, exposing a hairy thigh. He swiped the air with a long knife, slashing wildly at an invisible foe.

Joanna screamed and grabbed Madam Biset's arm.

'You, woman, where's the King?' He bared his teeth and Joanna caught the stench of sour wine and vomit from his open mouth.

Madam Biset, on her feet now, pointed to the small chamber used by the clerks. 'In there,' she said. 'He went in there a moment ago.'

He turned and stumbled towards the room, knife poised.

Madam Biset dragged Joanna into the bedchamber, slammed the door and rammed the draw bar across. 'Go to Cecily,' she commanded. 'I will rouse the King.'

The ladies were stirring, shocked out of sleep, wide-eyed and alarmed. Mistress Roberga hurried to bring more light. Joanna ran to her bed where her nurse, Mabel, was groping for her clothes. Dame Cecily was already gowned and securing a veil over her long, grey plait. Sausagez dashed around the room, yapping at full volume, indiscriminately attacking ankles.

'There's a man with a big knife outside.' Joanna's voice quavered. 'He . . . he said he was going to cut out the King's heart. I was bringing Madam Biset a drink and he came at us out of the dark . . .' She shuddered, remembering the gleam of the blade stabbing the air. The open, stinking mouth.

Cecily took Joanna's cloak from the foot of the bed and swept it around her trembling shoulders. 'Just one man?'

Joanna nodded. 'He s-said the King had stolen his crown.' She shrank in alarm at more violent sounds from outside the door – shouts, swearing and scuffling.

Cecily pressed Joanna's shoulder in firm reassurance, and moved protectively in front of her. Dame Willelma had managed to grab her dog and tuck him under her arm, where he continued to lunge and yap.

Someone blasphemed outside the barred door. 'The King will die! The King will d—' The last word ended on a blow, a wild yell, and then a thud. Eyes wide, Joanna huddled against Cecily.

Behind them, the inner chamber door flung open and the King emerged, white-faced, a sword tightly clenched in his right hand. He had thrown a cloak over his undershirt, and his legs were bare.

Outside, a fist struck the door, and Joanna flinched. 'Sire, madam, it is Gilbert the Marshal – we have taken the felon.'

The King gestured and the women drew the bar to admit Joanna's uncle, Gilbert Marshal, Earl of Pembroke, a wide-shouldered man with heavy brows and watchful dark eyes. He and Henry were of a similar height, but the Earl looked taller because of his breadth.

'Sire,' he said, bowing, 'we have caught and disarmed an intruder intent on doing you harm. He awaits your interrogation.'

Henry nodded stiffly. 'How did he get in?'

'Climbed in through your chamber window, sire – so I believe.' The Earl pushed one hand through his thinning hair. 'I was retiring to bed when I heard the commotion and rallied the guards. If you had not been visiting the Queen . . .' He let what he did not say speak for itself.

Henry exhaled hard. 'Have the rest of the palace searched – every room, every chest and cupboard. Check behind the hangings and curtains. Leave nothing to chance. Let me dress and I will speak with him. Thank God, my lord Marshal, that you keep late hours.'

'Thank God indeed, sire,' Earl Gilbert said, and bowed from the room.

Henry turned to the women and Joanna noticed he was shaking, just like her, and the night was not cold. Was the King afraid? But he had possessed the courage to face the danger with his sword, as had her uncle. She clenched her fists, determined to be as brave as they were.

'Ladies, all is well,' the King said tremulously and gestured with his free hand. 'Our thanks are due to Madam Biset – her quick thinking has saved us all. Pray settle yourselves and return to bed when you are ready.' Handing the sword to his squire with a grimace of distaste, he retired to the bedchamber to dress.

The hearth maid poked the embers to life and Lady Giffard set about preparing hot spiced wine to calm everyone's anxiety.

Dame Cecily kissed Joanna's cheek. 'Come, child, it is over and no harm done. Indeed, we may benefit from this because we are warned now to take better precautions. There are remedies for any situation if you ask for God's help and use the wits He has given you.'

Joanna nodded wordlessly. Fear still churned in her stomach like indigestion, but Cecily's words comforted her.

The King re-emerged from the bedchamber fully clothed, followed by Queen Alienor, a cloak covering her chemise and her hair a loose brown cascade down her back. 'Be careful, sire,' she entreated, touching his arm.

Taking her hands, he raised them to his lips. 'I promise I shall, have no fear. I will return later, and in the meantime, take succour from your ladies. Your door will be safely guarded for the rest of the night.' He kissed her forehead and took his leave.

The Queen watched him close the door, and then with a sigh, sat down by the fire.

Cecily gave Joanna a few sips from her cup of spiced wine before sending her back to bed with Mabel. 'Go to sleep,' she said gently. 'In the morning all of this will be behind us.'

Joanna climbed between the sheets, drew her knees towards her chest and faced the fire and candle light to watch the women gathered at the hearth. Listening to their low-voiced conversation as they sat over their wine, she put her thumb in her mouth – something she had not done in many weeks, but tonight she needed that security. When Sausagez leaped up beside her and curled up nose to feathery tail, she did not push him off.

'Thank God the King was with me,' the Queen said. 'He might have been killed. Indeed, but for Dame Margaret's quick wits we could all have been murdered in our beds.'

'You should not dwell upon it, madam.' Dame Cecily's voice was soothing. 'God has seen fit to preserve us all.'

Alienor gathered her loose hair over one shoulder and ran her fingers through it, rich, dark-brown in the firelight. 'But we should not make it more difficult for God than it has to be. I will insist that my lord puts bars at all the low windows tomorrow.'

Joanna's eyelids fluttered down. Bars at the windows. Would they too be like prisoners? In her mind's eye she saw the man running at them again, ready to do murder, and shivered, but she remembered too Madam Biset's swift reactions to the crisis and Cecily's calm protection. She thought of the King holding his sword, ready to fight, although he had been afraid. She was safe in her bed, watching the women share companionship and reassurance by firelight. The lesson here was to rise to the challenge, face it, and never let fear take control no matter how scared you were.

In the morning Queen Alienor spoke to the King about fitting bars to all the low windows in the palace. Joanna's brother, Iohan, was among the attendants of the courtiers who had gathered to discuss the night's disturbance, and Joanna brought him a cup of buttermilk. He was eleven years old to her eight, and a page to their uncle Gilbert, Earl of Pembroke, a great and powerful lord, well positioned to advance his nephew. Iohan was heir to Swanscombe with a bright future, and he regarded Joanna with a superior air, for her prospects in comparison to his were modest and of small consequence.

'The man Uncle Gilbert caught had already come before the

King yesterday, claiming he was the true heir to the throne, but the King dismissed him as a madman to be pitied,' Iohan said, taking the buttermilk. 'Uncle Gilbert says he should never have been set free. He stole one of the big knives from the kitchen to murder the King and would have done so if we hadn't arrived.' He expanded his chest and spoke as if he had played an active part in the arrest.

'Yes, I saw him.' Joanna related her own part in last night's events.

'Well, it's a good thing we caught him,' Iohan said, peeved at having his glory stolen. 'We saved all your lives for certain.'

Joanna said nothing. She was learning from Cecily which battles were worth fighting, especially with males. 'What will happen to him now?'

Iohan shrugged and drank the buttermilk, leaving a white moustache on his upper lip. 'He's confessed to plotting the King's murder so he'll be put to death. He's going to be tied to two horses and torn apart, and then beheaded as a warning to others.' His voice rang with relish and bravado.

Joanna shuddered at the image.

'It does not do to be a traitor,' he added, folding his arms and regarding her sternly. She recognised his attempt to maintain his superiority by intimidating her. She would never be a traitor in thought or deed, but it would be terrible for someone to think such a thing when she was innocent.

'I am glad you and Uncle Gilbert are here to keep us safe,' she said to mollify him. Words cost nothing, and she was indeed glad to be protected. Cecily said the instinct should be encouraged and directed in men.

Iohan preened and looked supercilious.

The King and Queen moved into the room from their conversation by the window and Joanna swiftly curtseyed as they crossed her path.

Henry stopped and gently raised her to her feet, tilting her chin on his forefinger. 'An eventful night, little demoiselle,' he said ruefully. 'I hope you are none the worse for your ordeal.'

Joanna shook her head. 'No, sire.' The King's eyes were warm blue, and the morning light made his beard sparkle like gold. He smelled of incense.

'I am glad to hear it.'

'Joanna has a sensible head on her shoulders for one still a child,' said the Queen, who was not yet sixteen years old herself. 'She serves me well and often runs errands for Willelma. Cecily is well pleased with her progress.'

'Well then, continue as you are, and who knows what shall grow from such diligence.' Henry patted her head and unfastened a delicate round silver brooch from his tunic. 'There,' he said, pinning it to her gown. 'Wear it always in token of that service.'

'Yes, sire.' Joanna curtseyed again, overwhelmed with pleasure and embarrassment.

The Queen smiled warmly and she and the King went on their way arm in arm, trailing scents of incense and flowers.

Her uncle Gilbert, following them, paused and smiled at her too, his complexion ruddy with tiny thread-veins in his cheeks. 'I am glad to hear good news of your progress, niece,' he said. 'Well done, and long may it continue.' He beckoned to his youngest squire. 'Iohan, come with me and wipe that moustache off your lip, there's a good lad. I've work for you.'

Iohan hastily scrubbed his mouth with the back of his hand, made a face at Joanna, ensuring that their uncle did not see, and followed Gilbert out.

Joanna looked at the shiny silver circlet pinned to her gown and with a full heart vowed to do exactly as the King commanded.

2

Royal Palace of Woodstock, October 1238

Joanna stroked the pony's muzzle and presented him with half an apple on the flat of her palm. Ears pricked, he lipped the treat from her hand and crunched with enjoyment while Joanna watched him with pride. Usually when the court took to the roads, she travelled in a covered cart, but her uncle Gilbert had given her this pretty dappled grey gelding with a red bridle and saddle. He said good riding skills were important, for her mother had been a Marshal, and every member of her maternal family was born to horsemanship.

Her new mount was from her uncle's estate at Goodrich on the Welsh borders, and his name was Arian, which meant 'Silver' in the Welsh tongue. She had ridden him for the first time today and he had been swift to respond to her voice and her touch on the reins. She could scarcely believe her good fortune.

'He's a beauty,' Iohan said with reluctant admiration, leaning against the stable door, arms folded. Sausagez snuffled around in the straw, hunting for rodents, Joanna having brought him with her for exercise.

'Yes, he is.' Brimming with happiness, Joanna patted Arian's warm dappled neck.

The last rays of evening sunlight tinted the trees beyond the palisade with burned gold. A man led a donkey towards the kitchens, two side panniers mounded with chestnuts from the woods.

'Of course, he is far too small for me,' Iohan said condescendingly. 'Uncle Gilbert lets me help with the destriers.' It wasn't strictly true. He was allowed to polish the harnesses and mix the feed, but the head groom and the older squires saw to all the close work on the big stallions.

A fanfare announced the arrival of visitors, and moments later horses came pounding into the yard, their hides steaming and streaked with sweat. There were serjeants and knights, squires and heralds, one bearing a banner blazoned with a fork-tailed lion on a crimson ground.

'Simon de Montfort, back from Rome,' Iohan said knowledgeably. 'His harbingers brought the news to the King this morning.'

Joanna eyed the men on their big, stamping horses with trepidation. Their open mouths and laughter, the boldness and colour, vivid in the burnished light. She had heard several tales in the bower about the clandestine marriage between the King's sister, Eleanor, and the French knight Simon de Montfort. The marriage had happened shortly before she came to court. Her uncle Gilbert's brother, William, had been Eleanor's first husband. After he died, suddenly, the lady Eleanor had taken a vow of chastity, but had broken that vow for love of de Montfort. They had conducted a clandestine courtship – discreet, but not discreet enough, and rumours abounded that they had shared a bed out of wedlock. The King had agreed to let them marry and their hasty, secret wedding had taken place in his private chapel at Westminster. Almost immediately that secret had come undone and when the news broke in public, the scandal and upheaval had been enormous.

Eleanor had retired to Kenilworth to await the birth of the child, so swiftly conceived that many whispered she had already been pregnant on her wedding day. Simon de Montfort had journeyed to Rome to obtain a papal dispensation for the match amid much cynical grumbling about bolting the stable door after the horse had gone, and remarks louder than whispers about newcomers shouldering their way up the ranks through dishonourable and ribald behaviour. The King's brother, Richard, and Joanna's uncle Gilbert had protested furiously because of the implications to their own families and status, and although peace had been made it was fragile. She had overheard her uncle Gilbert grimly telling one of his lawyers that if de Montfort thought to pursue claims to his new wife's rights from her former marriage, he would be sadly disappointed, for he would not receive a single penny.

Joanna called Sausagez to her side and leashed him, deciding it was time she returned to the Queen. Iohan watched the dismounting men, admiring their equipment, but stiff with tension.

Joanna took his arm. 'Will you escort me back to the bower?'

His irritated look was superficial and she saw the relief in his eyes. 'Very well, but only because you are my sister and you need protecting. Don't think I am your servant.'

Joanna curbed the retort that Cecily said all men should serve ladies courteously. She gave Arian a final pat and left the stable, Iohan at her side and Sausagez dragging on his leash.

De Montfort, wearing a fine fur-lined cloak, reined his pawing sorrel stallion across their path, amusement brightening the hard planes of his face. 'What have we here?' he asked. 'Are you both not a little young to be attending a tryst?'

Joanna's cheeks flamed. Sausagez bared his teeth and began a shrill yapping that caused the horse to put back its ears.

'I am escorting my sister to the Queen,' Iohan said stoutly, although his voice wavered.

'Your sister?' De Montfort looked him up and down. 'Remind me who you are.'

'Iohan de Munchensy, son of Warin de Munchensy of Swanscombe, sire,' Iohan said, jutting his chin.

De Montfort's smile lost some of its humour. 'A Marshal by maternity,' he said. 'Well, your mother's family came from the stables, I suppose.' He looked round at his companions and laughed, and then pressed his heels into his mount's sides. The horse surged towards Joanna, hooves dancing. She sprang backwards, feeling sick, and scooped the hysterical Sausagez into her arms. Iohan stepped in front of them, his body a rigid shield. De Montfort smiled and pranced closer again. The palfrey's hot breath gusted and the shod hooves flashed. Joanna whimpered. De Montfort made a contemptuous sound and pulled the big chestnut back. 'What a fine little hedge knight you are, Iohan of Swanscombe,' he said. 'Begone to your nursemaids. I do not make war on milksops and mongrels.' Abruptly he reined the horse away and clopped across the courtyard to his waiting groom.

Joanna blinked, determined not to cry. Iohan wrapped his hands around his belt. 'Don't worry, de Montfort won't be staying long.'

'How do you know?'

'Because his wife is great with child. He'll be going to Kenilworth for the birth as soon as he has reported to the King.'

Joanna shuddered. The dying blood-red light in the west, the steaming horses and the raw masculine power seemed like a weight dropping across her shoulders, heavy with threat.

'He doesn't frighten me,' Iohan said.

She didn't believe him. She had been terrified, and he was no braver than she was.

*

That night the court gathered in Woodstock's great hall to enjoy conversation, music and games of chess and dice. Simon de Montfort had been welcomed back into the royal household now that his match with the King's sister had received the Pope's sanction. Henry was being conciliatory towards his new brother-in-law, and the Queen was effusive, for Simon's wife was soon to bear her first child and she harboured hopes of her own fruitfulness.

While the King was occupied to his personal delight with the artists and craftsmen who were designing a new mural for the Queen's bedchamber, de Montfort stood at the fire with a cluster of knights and courtiers, roasting chestnuts on the wide, flat blade of a serving knife. Their mood was convivial and the jests and laughter increased in volume as the wine sank in the flagons.

The blaze from the hearth heated Joanna's cheeks, and almost seemed to connect her with the red-faced laughing men. Their strength and vital masculinity intimidated and fascinated her. She looked around, seeking reassurance, but Cecily had discreetly retired to empty her bladder, and Lady Giffard and Madam Biset were on the other side of the room, playing chess.

De Montfort caught Joanna's gaze and fixed her with his stare. 'Come here, child,' he said, beckoning.

Joanna's stomach churned, but courtesy brought her to her feet and towards him, like the chicken charmed by the fox.

'Ah, my little mistress of Swanscombe,' he said with a vulpine smile. 'You did not give me your name earlier. What would it be now?'

Joanna swallowed, for anonymity was protection and she hated being singled out. 'Joanna, sire.'

'Well then, Joanna of Swanscombe, would you like a nice roast chestnut?'

She gazed at the nuts jumping on the flat blade of the knife, and then looked into his eyes, and they were steely like the metal.

14

He winked at her and stooped to a pile of blackened shells in a shallow cup on the hearth. 'Here, have this one – it's cooling down.' He held it out on his palm. His fingers were thick and powerful, muscular from controlling spirited horses and wielding weapons.

Joanna stood transfixed, her fists clenched at her sides. The men with de Montfort chuckled, watching her.

'Take it,' he urged. 'I promise it won't hurt.'

Against her will, she held out her hand, but dropped her gaze. The nut was still hot, although not enough to burn.

'Eat it, young mistress, it's good.'

They watched her with an avid pack hunger that made her terrified to be the focus of their attention. She raised the chestnut to her mouth and bit into the burned shell, before spitting it back into her hand and throwing the fragment on to the hearth; and then fled, her eyes blurring with tears. An acrid taste soured her tongue and she was mortified by the sound of the laughter trailing in her wake. She was so distraught, she did not see Dame Cecily until she ran into her.

'How now, child.' Cecily took her by the shoulders and held her fast. 'Come, come, this is not my steady, sensible Joanna. What is wrong?'

Joanna gulped and dashed her sleeve across her eyes.

Gently but firmly, Cecily took her hand and examined it. 'What is this?'

'The men . . .' Joanna's voice hitched. 'They are roasting chestnuts and . . . and Messire de Montfort made me take one.' The story sounded feeble when spoken aloud, but her humiliation was intense.

Cecily tightened her lips. Taking a firmer grip on Joanna's hand, she marched back into the hall and, going up to the laughing men, addressed them fearlessly as if they were recalcitrant youths.

'What are you doing that you have nothing better in your minds than teasing a child?' She fixed de Montfort in particular with a gimlet stare.

He bowed to her, smiling. 'Madam, I but offered the girl a roasted chestnut, and not even a hot one at that. It is no fault of mine.'

'It never is, my lord,' Cecily retorted in a voice that Joanna had never heard her use before, for although quiet, it cut like a whip.

De Montfort bowed. 'I shall give your kind regards to my wife, Lady Sandford.'

'As you wish,' Cecily said. 'Tell her that she is constantly in my prayers.'

She departed the hall, one arm protectively around Joanna's shoulders. 'When men gather in groups to drink and feast, they become a pack,' she said with distaste. 'The King is not like that of course, but others are made of coarser stuff and you would do well to be wary.'

Once in their chamber, she took Joanna to the stone sink set in the wall, and poured cool water from a jug standing at the side. 'Come, let us clean you up.' She tenderly wiped the sooty marks from Joanna's face and hands. 'Learn from this experience, child. Do not ever let men tell you what to do, for they are not worthy of your soul – none of them. Indeed, you should be teaching them worthiness.'

Joanna bit her lip, for she could not imagine doing such a thing. Dame Cecily could stand up to anyone without fear, and she longed to be like her, but how could she hold her ground against grown men when they were wolves and she was a small deer?

'Come with me,' Cecily said, 'and we shall pray.'

Taking Joanna's hand, Cecily led her into the Queen's intimate private chapel. The beeswax candles gave off a honey light before the altar, and a red glass lamp illuminated an exquisite statue of the Virgin with the Christ child perched on her knee. As they knelt, Cecily squeezed Joanna's hand. 'Make your peace,' she said. 'Be still, and ask God's Holy Mother to guide you. She will listen, for she is a woman, and she will always answer another such.'

Joanna pressed her hands together and closed her eyes.

Cecily's smooth wooden rosary beads clacked together as she unfastened them from her belt and clasped them between her fingers.

Gradually, the peace and the silence filtered their way through Joanna's jangled being and her breathing calmed. The humiliation and the panic of being singled out diminished to an uneasy flicker. Cecily's support and tuition had increased her resilience over the past months, but the incident had revived her anxiety about how powerless and expendable she was. A vulnerable little girl to be teased for sport. She opened her eyes and prayed to the Virgin for the wisdom and strength to be like Cecily and to face every trial with grace.

Eventually, Cecily lifted her head. 'You must not let incidents like this destroy you,' she said firmly. 'Let them increase your strength. You shall grow in yourself as you grow in your body and such things will become trivial in time. Never forget, but do not be troubled. Leave it here with God and bring your prayers and fortitude instead.'

'Yes, Dame Cecily,' Joanna said, and lifted her head, bolstered with new determination.

'That's better.' Cecily patted her hand. 'Come, we shall have some sweetmeats and Eunice shall play her harp for us.'

Joanna nodded, keen to put the moment behind her and go forward with her new learning.

3

Royal Palace of Woodstock, November 1238

On a grey morning in late November, the Queen was queasy for the third day in a row, and the royal physician pronounced what everyone had begun to suspect – that Alienor was with child.

An ecstatic Henry visited his young wife and lavished her with gifts and tender attention. The Queen, wan but proud, delicately sipped a ginger tisane prepared by Lady Giffard, the midwife, and basked in her husband's approval.

Watching their shoulders touch, seeing their absorption with each other, made Joanna feel warm and secure – safe at the heart of a family. Moreover, news had just arrived that Henry's sister, the lady Eleanor de Montfort, had given birth at Kenilworth to a healthy baby boy. The infant was to be called Henry in honour of his royal uncle, and the joyous new parents had asked the King to be the baby's godfather.

Alienor took Henry's hand. 'It would be generous of you to stand in that role to their child,' she said, 'and healing too.'

Setting her other hand to her waistline, she gave Henry a shy smile.

'You are right, my dear; matters should be mended,' Henry agreed. 'I shall ride over to Kenilworth and visit my sister and my new namesake.' He raised her hand to his lips. 'So young to be so wise!'

Alienor blushed coyly, but the look, half hidden by her eyelids, was knowing and strategic.

Joanna had heard that Eleanor de Montfort and the Queen had been good friends before the scandal of the clandestine marriage with Simon de Montfort had torn the court apart. Joanna had often seen messengers being sent to Kenilworth with letters and small gifts for the King's sister as the Queen played the delicate role of peacemaker and tried to mend the holes in the family fabric.

Henry's face lit up. 'I shall bring them the good news that even as I have a new nephew to celebrate, come the summer, they shall be making acquaintance with the heir to the throne.' He beamed at his wife. 'What shall they have as a gift do you think? An engraved silver cup perhaps?' He was off, deciding what offerings to take with him, his enthusiasm like a bright light, as it always was when it came to celebration and gift-giving.

Joanna was glad for everyone's joy, but privately hoped Simon de Montfort would keep his distance even if ties were being mended.

Three months later, in February at Winchester, the court celebrated the feast of Candlemas, to commemorate the purification of the Virgin Mary, forty days after Christ's birth. Queen Alienor, resplendent in blue silk, her belly now a proud curve, drew everyone's eye as she progressed gracefully up the cathedral nave towards the altar, clasping her lighted candle. Joanna loved the smell of incense and the ceremonial and sacred atmosphere – of taking part in a ritual that was holy and ancient and centred around women. The singing of the choir raised gooseflesh on her arms.

Following the mass, King Henry officially invested Simon de Montfort with the title of Earl of Leicester. Safe and anonymous amid the congregation, Joanna was lost in the wonder of the event – the rituals, the textures and colours. She admired the magnificent jewelled belt that the King fastened around Simon's waist, and the Earl's coronet with finials of golden roses which he placed upon de Montfort's wavy dark hair, adding a regal touch to the new Earl's already impressive height and breadth.

He had been back at court since Christmas, but Joanna had managed to avoid him. She was learning how not to be seen. If he attended on the Queen, Joanna found excuses to be absent, or else performed her duties with quiet diligence, staying within the group, never putting herself in a position where she could be picked off – staying safe.

Once the public feasting and fêting were over, the Queen retired from the hall, but her private chamber was still filled with bustle. De Montfort's investiture had brought many barons and their families to court and a line of ladies waited to pay their respects to Alienor. Joanna was run off her feet serving drinks and sweetmeats and fetching and carrying.

Joanna had only glimpsed the King's sister Eleanor, the new Countess of Leicester, in the cathedral, but now came into closer proximity. She was a beauty, with dainty, almost sharp features and blue eyes as clear as glass. Small double-tailed lions danced in golden thread along the hem of her silk gown and Henry had presented her with a precious jewelled belt too, which gleamed at her waist. Joanna knew from talk in the chamber and Cecily's own circumspect information that Cecily had tutored the Countess and been her companion for several years between her marriages.

Having greeted Alienor, the Countess made a point of embracing Cecily and presenting her with a small carved box containing a little gold cross with blue and green enamels.

Cecily's eyes moistened as she gently touched the gift. 'My lady, you have no need to give me such a fine thing,' she said softly.

'I would give you a dozen such.' The new Countess fiddled with her wedding ring and a red flush stained her throat and cheeks as Cecily's attention fell upon the gesture.

'I thank you with all my heart, but a simple prayer would have sufficed. You are faring well? And the little one?'

'Yes, indeed. Our son is flourishing,' the Countess said with a brittle smile.

'I am pleased to hear it, and hope to see him. I shall always hold you in my prayers, my dear, you know that.'

Joanna had been waiting to present Cecily with a cup of boiled spring water, and managed to curtsey without spilling the contents.

'This is Joanna de Munchensy of Swanscombe,' Cecily said, presenting her to Eleanor. 'You will not know her since she has been here less than a year.'

The Countess's glass-blue gaze fixed on Joanna, assessing and cool. 'No, but I knew her mother, and of course I am well acquainted with her kin. You are fortunate to have this position, this education,' she added, addressing Joanna directly.

'Yes, madam.' Joanna looked down, feeling awkward, knowing she was being measured and somehow found wanting through no fault of her own. The words 'her kin' had been laden with meaning.

The Countess departed to speak to another lady, and Joanna served the spring water to Cecily, who smiled reassuringly. 'The

Countess is right: you are indeed fortunate, but so am I. Seldom have I had such an apt pupil.'

Cecily's gaze was troubled and a little sad as it rested on Eleanor de Montfort's graceful figure. Joanna was confused by Eleanor's coldness towards her, but decided she would avoid her too, just as she avoided her husband.

'Uncle Gilbert says that with de Montforts it is all about money and land,' Iohan told Joanna when they had a moment's leisure together the next day in the great hall. 'He says that is why the Earl of Leicester and his wife do not like us.'

They were standing side by side looking at the recently completed mural of the Wheel of Fortune, ordered by the King, depicting how a man might rise to sit on a throne on one turn of the wheel, and on the next rotation be toppled off the crest and replaced by an ambitious rival. Joanna gazed at the golden crown tumbling from the king's head towards the ragged man at the foot of the cycle, reaching out to catch it as Fortuna, robed as a queen, rotated the handle.

'But we have no money,' she said.

'De Montfort's wife was once married to our uncle William.'

'Yes, I know.'

Iohan puffed out his cheeks at having to explain. 'When he died, she stood to inherit a third of his property in dower as his widow, but it was a vast amount. No one ever expected our uncle to die without a son, but he did. Our uncle Richard inherited, and agreed to pay her an annual sum of money instead of giving her the lands. Now he is dead too and the duty has fallen to Uncle Gilbert. De Montfort says the agreement took unfair advantage of the lady Eleanor when she was distraught with grief and the payment falls far short of her just due. He's demanding more with interest, but Uncle Gilbert said yesterday that hell would freeze over before that happened.' He screwed up his face. 'You don't have to do anything to annoy the Earl and Countess of Leicester except be a Marshal by connection. They hate all of us.'

'But that's not fair!'

Iohan shrugged. 'But that is how it is. They say it isn't fair to them and that Uncle Gilbert should pay a lot more. De Montfort is in debt up to his ears. He had to give a huge amount to the Pope to have the marriage recognised – he even had to borrow money from the Queen's uncle.'

'How do you know all this?' Joanna demanded.

He looked nonchalant. 'I pour wine, I run errands. I hear things.' He eyed her sidelong. 'I bet you do too, sitting at the Queen's feet.'

Joanna said nothing and continued to study the Wheel of Fortune – the king and the fallen king.

'Well, don't you?' Iohan prodded. 'What does the Queen tell you?'

'Cecily says that things overheard are like gold coins cast into a well,' Joanna replied primly, 'and that the person hearing them should make sure they stay at the bottom of the well for ever and not dredge them up for gain.' She gave him a hard stare. 'I would not repeat what the Queen says to anyone. It would be wrong. How would anyone trust me if I did?'

Iohan reddened and clenched his fists. 'Well, I trust you, and what I tell you is for the good of our family, but I shan't tell you anything ever again.' He stalked off.

Joanna sighed; she did not want to lose his support, but she could not let him undermine her integrity.

Returning to the women, she picked up her sewing and sat quietly out of the way in the corner where she was less likely to hear things that she had to drop in the well and keep secret.

23

Cecily joined her and gave her a discerning look. 'What is the matter, child?'

Joanna executed several small, neat stitches. Cecily's bond with Countess Eleanor made her hesitate, as did her knowledge of Eleanor's high connections and friendships. On the other hand, she trusted Cecily who had her own wells of knowing and silence. 'My brother asked me about things I heard in the Queen's chamber,' she said at last. 'I refused to tell him because it was breaking a trust.'

Cecily's expression softened. 'You have a wise head on very young shoulders. Often people will ask you to break faith, and you must always resist them – doing so will only add to your lustre. Never be ashamed.'

Joanna smoothed her sewing. 'He told me things too – things he had overheard.'

'Then I hope your refusal to join in will make him think twice next time. I am glad you had the strength and maturity to withstand him. There are too many wagging tongues at court.'

Joanna's voice sank to a whisper. 'He said the reason Countess Eleanor does not like me is because I am part of the Marshal family.'

'Tush, child!' Cecily said sharply. 'The Countess of Leicester does not dislike you. Indeed, she does not know you. Pay no heed to what others say – always trust your own judgement.'

Joanna swallowed. The trouble was that her judgement told her that Eleanor de Montfort disliked her, and Iohan had given her a reason for it.

Cecily said briskly, 'Returning to court is an adjustment for the Countess of Leicester. She will settle with you – you will see. She may be in dispute with your uncle Gilbert, but these are legal matters far removed from your sphere and have nothing to do with you – I hope you understand.'

'Yes, madam,' Joanna said dutifully, although for the first time she was not sure if she believed Cecily.

'I am always watching out for you, remember that,' Cecily said firmly. 'Now, go and take your sewing to the window seat. You cannot see to stitch in this dark little corner, nor should you dwell there from choice. Always seek the light.'

Over the next few days, Iohan got over his sulk and the air of constraint between brother and sister gradually thawed, although Iohan made a pointed show of not talking about court business at all. In the Queen's chambers, the Countess of Leicester often summoned Joanna to perform tasks and dance attendance on her. Eleanor was autocratic and abrupt, firmly putting Joanna in her place as a subordinate. Cecily observed and said nothing, but quietly gave Joanna tasks that kept her out of Eleanor's way whenever possible. Sausagez enjoyed twice as many walks as usual.

If Joanna had to be in the Countess's vicinity, she was unobtrusive and obedient, which seemed to calm Eleanor's critical regard. When the Countess departed home to her baby son at Kenilworth three weeks later, riding a black Spanish palfrey and laden with gifts from the King and Queen, Joanna breathed a sigh of relief. Simon de Montfort, however, remained at the King's side and dominated the court with his ebullience and charisma. He was easier to avoid than his wife, and Joanna made sure that she did, and although she was wary, life returned to a more comfortable routine.

One of her regular tasks was to rub the Queen's feet. 'You have the tenderest touch of all my ladies,' Alienor said, leaning back against her pillows. 'You remind me of my little sister Sancha – I miss her so much. Your hair is like hers with those chestnut lights in the sun, and so thick and smooth too.'

Embarrassed, Joanna concentrated on her task. She had sometimes peeked into the Queen's ivory mirror, but pretty women were golden-haired and blue-eyed like her aunt Isabelle or the Countess of Leicester. Her own eyes, like her hair, were brown, and she had freckles.

The Queen smiled. 'When you are grown up and married, you will still be my favourite and I shall keep you at court with me. I shall have the King find you a fine and worthy husband. Won't that be wonderful?'

The Queen's words were like an extension of one of the stories read aloud in the bower during leisure time, but Joanna was already sceptical. Choices concerning her life were always made by others, no matter what Cecily said. What if the 'worthy husband' was like Simon de Montfort or one of the other forceful barons at court, striding about in their assured arrogance. She would be eaten alive. If he was like the King, it might not be so awful, for she had observed that Henry was generous, kind and thoughtful, but such traits were rare and never considerations when it came to arranging a marriage.

'Yes, madam,' she said meekly. 'Thank you.' She made the correct reply, but without enthusiasm.

'You are still very young,' Alienor murmured, opening one eye. 'Do not worry. When the time comes you will be ready, I promise.'

4

Palace of Westminster, London, June 1239

In the anteroom to the birthing chamber Joanna was folding the linen napkins and swaddling clothes ready for the new baby's arrival. Lady Sybil Giffard had given her the task to keep her busy while they waited. The Queen had been labouring since dawn, and now the western sky was deep teal with new stars pricking through like silver pins. Joanna had lit the candles as dusk encroached and they blazed in every sconce and holder.

Joanna prayed as she folded. Her mother had died giving birth to a stillborn son, and she was worried for the Queen's safety even while knowing that Lady Sybil was a highly respected and experienced midwife. The King was holding a prayer vigil in his private chapel and kept sending servants to ask how matters were progressing and they received the same patient answer despite Lady Sybil's exasperation at the constant enquiries. All was well; the birth would happen in due course; just let the women do their sacred work.

Joanna stopped folding and her heart began to race as she

heard a long, agonised groan from the inner chamber. Then another, and the voice of Lady Sybil, calm, encouraging and urgent all at the same time. And suddenly, another sound – a baby's wail, heralding the arrival of a new soul into the world. The other ladies waiting in the antechamber with Joanna exchanged glances, crossing themselves, casting looks at the door.

The wails grew stronger. Willelma opened the door, her creased face bright with joy and relief. 'The Queen is safely delivered of a fine son!' Her smile was wide and beautiful despite several missing teeth. 'Send the news to the King and let him rejoice. Praise God, a healthy prince is born!'

Within moments of receiving the tidings, Henry rushed into the chamber, his face flushed with emotion. The ladies curtseyed at his arrival but were disconcerted at the irregular etiquette for a man had no place in the confinement chamber, even if he was the King and this his firstborn son. 'Ladies.' He swept them with a single bright look before entering the inner sanctum and closing the door.

Everyone started talking at once, filled with excitement, and a little shock at the King's defiance of propriety. Roberga poured wine, and they toasted the new prince and his parents. Joanna wanted to jig and twirl, and it was an effort to maintain her decorum and keep her feet still. Sipping wine from one of the cups being passed around, she wondered eagerly when she would be able to see this new little person.

The bells began tolling from the abbey, ringing out the birth of the royal heir in exultant peals that spread across the night sky and resonated through Joanna's body, touching her soul.

Eventually, the bedchamber door opened and the King emerged, tear tracks shining on his cheeks. 'I have a son! Praise God, I have a son! Ladies, thank you all for your care and devotion to the Queen. I shall not forget. You shall all have gifts!' He gazed towards the open shutters. 'Do you hear the bells?' He paused to listen, his expression beatific, and then he smiled at all of them. 'I shall remember this moment for ever,' he said, and left the room, wiping his eyes.

Joanna went to the window and leaned into the open air. The sound of shouting filled the warm June evening and torches were being waved about in wild sweeps of flame as the inhabitants of the Westminster complex celebrated the birth of a future king born on the cusp of midsummer. He was to be named Edward after a long-ago King of England who had been a godly man and a saint. A pious, peacemaker king. Henry wanted to renew that bond like a golden chain, connecting the past to the present via a son bearing an English royal name of ancient descent.

Listening to the revellers, to the bells, and to the cries of the new-born child, Joanna's eyes filled with tears of joy.

In the morning, Joanna attended mass with the other ladies before breaking her fast on bread and cheese. The church bells were still ringing, and the palace flurried with activity as messengers were sent out far and wide bearing the news of Prince Edward's birth. In the ladies' chamber there was talk of nothing else.

Joanna took her sewing to the bright window embrasure, now and then pausing her work to watch the river sparkle under a cloudless sky. Trading vessels plied their way under oar and sail between the various wharves, and red cattle were drinking at the waterside across the river.

The door to the Queen's chamber opened and Lady Sybil emerged, cradling a swaddled bundle. Immediate warmth flooded Joanna's heart. She had never connected with her baby stepbrother at Swanscombe, for, in her eyes, his mother was a usurper, but this infant she could love with pure, unalloyed joy.

Sybil sat down in the sunlit embrasure and the ladies gathered to take their first look at him, cooing and exclaiming. Joanna tip-toed forward. He was bound from head to toe in swaddling and snuggled in a soft, creamy blanket. She could see a little face, the closed eyelids, delicate as tellin shells lined with fair lashes of coppery gold. Yesterday he had been hidden inside the Queen's womb but now he was here, whole and himself. The face and the little body all wrapped up. 'It is a miracle from God!' she whispered.

'Indeed.' Sybil smiled at her. 'You may touch his head for luck and remember this day all your life.'

Hardly daring, Joanna set a light fingertip on the baby's forehead where his soft skin met the band of his cap. He screwed up his face and opened his mouth in a gummy yawn. 'He's beautiful,' she whispered. A fierce, protective yearning filled her heart, and in that instant, she fell overwhelmingly, irrevocably in love.

Over the next several weeks the Queen recovered from the birth and settled into her role as a new mother. Baby Edward grew plump and thrived. Joanna was given permanent charge of folding the napkins to line his swaddling and was very proud of the task. She observed closely as Sybil or the wet nurse, Alice, changed him and wiped his bottom with rose water, and she loved to watch him suckle at Alice's breast. The entire process of Edward's nurturing and tending made her feel whole and nourished too.

Gifts for little Edward poured into Westminster – cloth and gemstones, silver cups and plate, jewelled reliquaries, ivory rattles, boxes of spice, goblets and drinking horns. Henry presided over the gift-giving, weighing the prestige of each one with a judgemental eye. His heir was the most precious thing on earth and deserved presents to reflect that preciousness. If an offering fell short of his exacting standards, Henry returned it as being unworthy and demanded better. After he sent back a cloak to a furrier because the ermines were of inferior quality, Joanna overheard a court clerk remark to his companion that Richard the Lionheart had once said he would sell London if he could find a buyer, but Henry, it appeared, was selling his son for as much as he could obtain. Joanna quashed the thought that the King was being ungracious and even foolish; he had been carried away by his pride in his son and his desire to surround him with the best of everything, that was all. He was the King; she owed him her loyal gratitude, and surely it was wrong to criticise him.

The Queen remained in her chambers recovering as high summer closed over the city. The river glistened in the sun and the air ripened with the stink from the privies and wharves lining the bankside. But at Westminster there were gardens and closes too, perfumed with flowers and graced by the shade of trees. Taking Sausagez for his daily walk around the complex, Joanna soon came to know all its corners and enclaves.

A constant stream of visitors flowed into and out of the Queen's apartments, especially haberdashers and seamstresses as they prepared the Queen's wardrobe for her churching ceremony where she would give thanks for the safe delivery of a healthy infant and celebrate her return to court. She would also welcome the King back to her bed.

The court tailors fashioned Alienor a magnificent gown of patterned gold silk with a matching ermine-lined cloak. The King had presented her with a delicate jewelled crown, twinkling with sapphires. All the ladies had new robes for the occasion too. Joanna's was of blue silk embellished with a hem-strip of gold left over from the cutting of the Queen's robes, and she loved it; never had she owned such a gown before and it made her feel important and valued.

On the eve of the churching ceremony, Henry held a social gathering in his beloved great painted chamber. The Queen was still in confinement but Henry had little Edward brought to him in his cradle to show him off to his courtiers, with Alice his wet nurse and Lady Sybil's husband Hugh Giffard keeping watch over the baby.

Growing increasingly anxious about Edward's exposure to so many people, Alienor eventually told Sybil to go and bring him back. Sybil curtseyed and summoned Joanna to accompany her.

'One day you will be training and leading young ladies of your own on such errands,' she said as they walked, and gave Joanna a shrewd look. 'Dame Cecily thinks highly of you and I am inclined to agree with her.'

Joanna warily eyed the people spilling outside the buildings on to the gravel walkways. The air was convivial, a little raucous, the raised voices and exaggerated gestures revealing how freely the wine had been flowing. It was all part of her education in resilience, so she would know how to comport herself in every situation. She hoped she would not disappoint such expectations.

They entered the King's painted chamber through the ornate doorway, over which strong black lettering proclaimed *ke ne dune, ke ne tine, ne prent ke desire* – 'he who has and does not give, will not, when he wants, receive'. Walking beneath those words into the chamber always filled Joanna with a sense of destiny and awe. She loved it too and knew it was the King's pride and joy.

The walls were painted to resemble green curtains secured with golden rings, and the work was so skilled it was difficult to tell that it was plaster not cloth. At the room's far end, protected by depictions of King Solomon's armed guards, the King's bed had the same hangings but of actual green wool, heavy and thick, and the bed posts were gilded with stars. A quatrefoil window at the side of the bed gave a view into Henry's private chapel.

Pages and squires moved among the gathering, serving wine and small dainties. An immense hubbub of voices talking all at once filled her ears. Men said that women were the greatest gossips, but this crowd of mostly males was making a fair effort to disprove it. One of the loudest voices belonged to Simon de Montfort, who was holding forth on the matter of the best way to wield a lance in combat. Men gravitated to de Montfort's charisma like the moths that gathered to the candle flames in the hall. Joanna felt the draw of his powerful energy, but unlike the moths, she knew to keep her distance.

Henry's gaze kept flicking with displeasure to the boisterous knot of men surrounding his brother-in-law. He turned a sharp look on Sybil and Joanna as they made their obeisance.

'Sire, the Queen is asking for the lord Edward,' Sybil said. 'May I take him?'

'I am not yet ready,' Henry said petulantly. 'I would have sent a summons if I was.'

Joanna had never seen Henry in such a mood before; to judge from his flushed complexion, he was not sober.

Sybil stood her ground with quiet dignity. 'Sire, the Queen will not settle until the lord Edward is returned to her side, and I am only concerned for her wellbeing and that of your heir.'

Henry tightened his lips and continued to scowl, but her appeal had pierced the veil and he heaved a martyred sigh. 'Very well.' He cast his gaze around the room until it landed on his sister, and he called her to him, raising his voice. 'Eleanor, your nephew is retiring to the nursery. Let his favourite aunt bid him farewell before he departs!'

The Countess, who had been standing beside her husband while he held court, left the group and came to Henry, her silk gown shimmering. 'If I am his "favourite aunt",' she said, leaning over the crib, 'then he is my most cherished nephew.'

'I am pleased to hear it, sister,' Henry said, and relaxed a little. 'He shall be a great king one day.'

Edward crowed as if agreeing with his father. A group of courtiers followed the Countess's lead and gathered around to admire the baby. Simon de Montfort wandered over, and Joanna saw his expression harden as he observed his wife cooing over the crib.

He cleared his throat. 'Eleanor, we should be going too,' he said.

She straightened and went to him as if tugged by a string, turning her back on Henry. Simon took her hand and kissed it, claiming his right. Joanna gasped, shocked that Eleanor would turn from Henry without a proper obeisance.

Henry's expression darkened with growing anger. 'You would whisk my sister away under my very nose yet again, my lord of Leicester, and without my leave?'

Little Edward sucked his fist and made small sounds of impending hunger. Sensing a storm, Sybil exchanged glances with Alice the wet nurse, who started to rise from her stool.

De Montfort raised his brows. 'Then I beg your leave, sire,' he said, with laboured courtesy, and continued to keep firm hold of his wife's hand.

'Either come or go hither as you choose, for it seems to me that is your custom,' Henry said curtly.

De Montfort bowed. 'Then with your given consent, we shall depart and not disturb you further.' He left on the instant with Eleanor and his entourage.

Henry lifted his cup in a trembling hand and took several swallows. The baby, no longer content with his fist, commenced bawling into an uncomfortable silence.

'If I may take your son to the Queen, sire,' Sybil reiterated, deferential, but insistent.

'Yes, go,' Henry snapped. 'Everyone else deserts me after all.'

Sybil curtseyed and stooped to pick up the swaddled baby, her expression neutral. Her husband lifted the cradle and Joanna and Alice followed the couple from the painted chamber, walking with heads down and hands clasped. Joanna had not understood all the nuances, but the friction between the King and de Montfort had been palpable and frightening.

In the Queen's apartments, nothing was said. Alice settled Edward at her breast and Joanna fetched clean napkins and swaddling to change him. The Queen, wearing a loose robe, sat on a stool by the bed while Willelma combed her hair in long, smooth strokes, applying rose water to the tines. The churching gown lay across a long trestle, the rich silk gleaming in the candle light.

Joanna had just handed a towel to Alice because Edward had burped a milky trickle when Henry stormed into the chamber like an agitated whirlwind and everyone knelt in haste. The Queen stood up and faced him, her eyes wide with shocked surprise. 'Sire, what is it?' she asked.

'My sister's husband!' Henry was almost choking on his words. He shook the piece of parchment clutched in his fist. 'Never have I known such arrogance and ingratitude.'

'Come, my lord, sit down.' Alienor kissed his cheek and drew him to the bench. 'You should not upset yourself. Willelma, fetch the King some wine.'

'Should I not? Your uncle Thomas has written saying he needs funds for his pilgrimage to the Holy Land. De Montfort owes him five hundred marks and has had the gall to tell him I will honour the debt out of my own treasury, when he has neither told me of the arrangement nor sought my permission. Instead I learn about it now, in this letter!' He waved the parchment under her nose. 'After everything I have done for that man, he pushes his debts on to me behind my back while upstaging me in my own chamber on the eve of your churching! I will not stand for it!'

Willelma returned with the wine and Alienor presented it to him herself. 'Calm yourself, sire, anger avails you nothing,' she said gently.

'I will not be made a fool of in this way!' His eyes shone with angry tears. 'Simon de Montfort will not take advantage of my goodwill and outdo me like this. When all is said and done, he seduced his way into my family. I have tried to embrace him as my sister's husband. I have given him every privilege and benefit of the doubt and all he sees is an opportunity to take still more. If you had seen him tonight, posturing and swaggering, with never a word to me about this debt of his. He should read that motto above my chamber door and apply it to himself!'

Joanna shrank into the shadows, frightened by the King's rage. She looked to Cecily for reassurance, but Cecily's lips were tightly pursed.

'You must not allow such things to upset you,' Alienor soothed, kissing his cheek. 'You should manage them with diplomacy. I hope you do not hold this against Uncle Thomas.'

Henry shook his head and cuffed his eyes. 'No. He is bound on a holy cause and he is indeed owed the money. It is not he who has given offence.' Abruptly he set his cup aside and stood up. 'Simon de Montfort will learn that he cannot ride over me rough-shod and escape the consequences.' He raised Alienor's hands to his lips. 'I am the better for seeing you, but I should not be here.'

'No, you should not,' she replied, smiling. 'You should go to bed, my lord – all will seem better on the morrow.'

'I know where I wish I could sleep,' Henry said, causing Alienor to blush. 'I know where I want to lay my head.'

She gave him a coy look. 'Well, that is for tomorrow too. You are truly not angry with my uncle?'

'Truly not, my displeasure lies in other directions.' He went to look at Edward, now replete and sleepy in his cradle. 'Perfect little man. I will give you the world.' He stooped to kiss the baby's brow, and then left.

Alienor sighed. 'I thought everything was settled between

them, but it seems that the Earl of Leicester has overstepped the bounds again – likely they were both in their cups. I will try and find a way around, but they are men at different ends of a line. Keeping them apart is better than having them close.'

The household prepared for bed. Remembering what she had seen in the hall, Joanna shivered. The court was a place of beauty and grace, but it could be dark and dangerous too. Like a forest full of sunlit dells and deep undergrowth.

As she knelt at her bedside to say her prayers, Cecily touched her shoulder. 'Put your faith in God, child,' she murmured. 'Whatever troubles you, He will always answer.'

'But what if He does not?'

'Then you have not been listening hard enough.' Cecily tenderly smoothed Joanna's hair. 'God always answers. Sometimes He does not give you the answer you desire, and then you deny it, but He is always there.'

Comforted by Cecily's voice as much as her words, Joanna finished her prayers, promising God she would listen harder from now on. Settling in bed beside Mabel, she watched as Roberga extinguished the candles one by one leaving a single lamp burning; a light in the darkness.

Together with the other girls from the Queen's household, supervised by Cecily, Joanna stood near the altar in the abbey church, holding a tall candle, as yet unlit. Golden morning light streamed into the cathedral nave, illuminating the drapes and decorations the King had ordered for the Queen's churching. Joanna felt very grown up. The trimming from her new gown sparkled in the sun's rays and Mabel had woven her hair in an intricate plait with a light veil over it, secured with little golden pins.

Waiting at the altar for the Queen's entry, King Henry looked tense and tired. Joanna thought he probably had a headache.

His younger brother Richard, Earl of Cornwall, was at his side – tall, fair-haired and handsome, with a jutting jaw and harder features than Henry's. His wife was Joanna's maternal aunt, although Joanna barely knew her. Countess Isabelle was a beauty with lustrous flaxen hair coiled under her headdress. Her hand rested protectively on her belly, swollen with yet another pregnancy. Her brother, Joanna's uncle Gilbert, stood beside her, the light glistening on his scalp under his thinning hair. Iohan, wearing a green and gold tunic, was in attendance as part of his entourage. So many of Joanna's Marshal relatives were present, she could barely mark them all.

A sudden flurry at the back of the church heralded the late arrival of Simon and Eleanor de Montfort. Their matching robes of scarlet and gold and the manner of their entrance in all their tardiness and magnificence was like the appearance of the royal couple at the heart of the event.

Joanna glanced at Cecily for guidance, but her tutor gave a minute shake of her head, her lips tight.

Grooves of tension deepened in Henry's cheeks and his expression was livid as the de Montforts pushed their way forward to the altar. 'How dare you force yourselves to the forefront as if this is your occasion, when nothing could be further from the truth,' he said, almost grinding his teeth. 'Your ill manners and arrogance are not welcome at the Queen's churching.'

De Montfort started to open his hands to explain, but Henry gave him no opportunity.

'You,' he said, stabbing an accusatory finger that stopped a fraction from de Montfort's chest. 'You! Let all hear the truth for what it is, since you so desire fame and notoriety! Let everyone witness that you took my sister away from me and from the heart of her family. You pursued her in shameful secrecy; you seduced her so that she broke her sacred vow of chastity. You dishonoured her for your vile ambition after others had refused your suit. You have changed my sister so that she no longer gives honour to her natural family – to her own brother! You have stolen away treasure from beneath my nose and sworn me to honour debts that are yours, not mine. You are the root cause of all this ill. Get out, for I do not want to see your face!'

A collective gasp shivered through the congregation and Joanna covered her mouth in shock. Richard of Cornwall reached out to Henry, who shrugged him off hard.

De Montfort said nothing, remaining still and upright. Then he bowed and swung round to leave.

Eleanor started to follow, but Henry seized her arm in a biting grip. 'No, sister, you stay. He should never have had you. I was fool enough to turn a blind eye and even wish you well, but I was never more wrong.'

She wrenched free, a flush blooming under the powder whitening her cheeks. 'You are beside yourself, brother, and do not know what you are saying. I am lawfully married, a mother like your own wife, and in the charge and good care of my husband.' She turned and pressed into the shelter of Simon's outspread arm. 'Dear God, I pity you.'

'We shall leave as you wish, sire,' de Montfort said, his tone steely. 'We are both aggrieved at your treatment, but we shall not stay to argue.'

'Do so,' Henry answered, his voice rising and growing shrill. 'I will speak to neither of you again until you have mended your ways.'

Richard of Cornwall tried again to intervene but Henry rounded on him. 'You complained of the marriage at the time and I pacified you, but you were right, brother, and nothing you say or do now will change my mind for he has sullied my wife's churching.' He closed his eyes and drew a shuddering breath. 'The matter is closed. I will not have him further destroy the occasion.'

Joanna felt queasy both at the de Montforts' brazen arrival and the King's response; it was like watching a parent become the child. Where was the gentle, kindly man who patted her head, praised her learning and considered her welfare?

'Be calm.' Cecily touched Joanna's shoulder. 'We are in the sight of God for the Queen's churching as the King says, and that is our concern now. Let this be a lesson in how to behave, and how not to.'

Joanna gathered herself and stood upright, strengthened by Cecily's guidance. The Queen entered the church, bearing a lighted candle, her expression smooth and calm, her step measured. Joanna admired her, for she must know what had just happened, yet she was performing her role with focused dignity. Henry, pale and tense, played his part and gave his full attention to his wife and to the ceremony, like a man trying to banish a bad taste by rinsing his mouth with sweet wine.

However, the moment they left the church, Henry ordered his knights to evict the de Montforts from the Bishop of Winchester's palace, where they were lodging.

'Is that wise, brother?' asked Richard. 'Some might accuse you of being vindictive.'

'Let "some" say as they will,' Henry retorted, still tight with anger. 'The Earl of Leicester has gone too far, so let me send him a little further – and my sister shall learn her lesson too. I do not want them here. Let them consider their manners in exile for a while.' He shook his head at his brother. 'I am more than half minded to put Simon de Montfort in the Tower to show him exactly where he stands, but let exile suffice as lenience. They have insulted me and the Queen beyond forgiveness. Let them reap what they have sown.'

*

That night, the King slept in the Queen's bed with the door firmly shut on the servants in the antechamber. The heavy summer air smelled of thunder and the atmosphere permeated the household. The ladies cast glances at each other, but no one broached the subject of what had happened at the churching ceremony because the magnitude of it was too enormous.

Joanna knelt with Cecily to pray. She could tell her tutor was upset from the way she pressed her rosary tightly between her clasped hands, leaving small round impressions in her skin. Joanna bowed her head and asked God for peace in the household – and if it pleased him, to keep the de Montforts in exile for ever.

Cecily sighed and raised her head. 'Soon it will come time for you to marry,' she said to Joanna. 'You are nine now and many girls are brides at twelve and must wed to the dictates of their family and their overlords.'

'Yes, Dame Cecily,' Joanna said dutifully. Her father was paying to have her trained at court so she could make the best marriage possible with the resources at the family's disposal.

'Some may become brides of Christ if they have a vocation, and their families agree, and a few will continue in service, unwed, but for most, their future lies in matrimony.' Cecily took Joanna's hand. 'I never had any girls, only sons, but I have raised many men's daughters and I have taught them well. The Countess of Leicester was my pupil. I educated and protected her as best I could, but I was no match for the wolf when he came prowling around the fold in search of the most delectable of my lambs.'

Joanna eyed Cecily in surprise for usually she was more circumspect in her opinions.

'What happened today was disrespectful to the King and a disgrace to all,' Cecily said. 'A wife should obey her husband, but it is also her duty to try and turn him from folly and dishonourable behaviour, for a husband dishonoured puts that reflection on his wife. Even if it is not her fault, it becomes her dishonour too.'

Joanna solemnly dipped her head, absorbing the lesson and feeling afraid. It must be terrible to be the wife of a husband who could not be turned towards sense.

'I am sad for the Countess,' Cecily continued. 'Some men are hard of hearing and difficult to manage. It would not have happened had she heeded my advice and remained true to her vow of chastity, but she was rash, I am sorry to say, and gulled by blandishments and lust. I do understand her yearning for offspring and a family life and I shall always love her – she was my charge for too long that I could let go so lightly – but I worry for her wellbeing.' Cecily patted Joanna's arm. 'You are a sensible girl. I want you to think on what has happened today, and try always to stay true to your path whatever temptations you face. Never listen to the blandishments of men, and trust your own heart. Promise me you will do that.'

'Yes, I promise,' Joanna replied fervently. She could not imagine being married to anyone. Whatever Cecily said, it was a distant land. She knew several girls of her age who were already betrothed, but it might not happen to her. Her dowry was modest and she was no great heiress to be married the moment she came of age. If her life continued at court in service to the King and Queen, it was enough for all her days.

5

Palace of Westminster, January 1241

Snow had fallen earlier in the day, covering the ground in white smocking, and flakes still drifted through the early winter dark, softening edges, melting into the deep glitter of the Thames. The buildings blazed in the gloom, lit by lamps and candles and firelight.

Within Westminster's great hall, seasoned logs burned in the hearths, dark-scaled on the surface, cracked and red-bellied beneath. Everyone wore their fur-lined cloaks against the cold, but under their winter weight, silk and cendal gleamed, embroidered with gold in honour of the Feast of St Edward the Confessor, beloved of King Henry's heart.

Joanna wore her best blue gown and the silver brooch the King had given her two years ago. Earlier, the court had crowded into the abbey, braving the snow, first to worship the saint, and then to witness the King knighting several lords, barons and young men, among them the Queen's uncle Peter of Savoy who had arrived to take his place at court and be granted a lifetime title of Earl of Richmond.

Between the evergreen swathes decking the great hall, the shields of the attendant barons proclaimed their owner's lineage. The lions of Marshal and Bigod, the blue and gold chequers of de Warenne, the horseshoes of Ferrers, the bold red chevrons of de Clare. Many of her mother's relations were here, the majority of whom she did not know, even if she recognised their powerful, firelit blazons.

Her father was here from Swanscombe and stood talking to Iohan and her uncle Gilbert. Joanna had barely spoken to him because he had been busy with 'important' matters. He had provided a purse of money for her upkeep and enquired after her welfare, but with the air of a stranger undertaking a duty.

'You look so like your mother when she was a girl.'

Joanna turned and curtseyed to the woman who had spoken. Her aunt Mahelt was a handsome woman with high cheekbones, a firm jaw, and watchful dark eyes. Her mouth had a bitter curl directed at life in general. She was the widow of the Earl of Surrey and Warenne and Dowager Countess of Norfolk. Joanna's mother had been her youngest sister. Her second husband, thirty years her senior, had recently died and she had come to court to settle the matter of her dowry and her children's future.

'I am often told that, madam,' Joanna replied. She was unsure what to make of her aunt Mahelt and her razor-sharp gaze that pared everything and everyone to the bone.

'But you are yourself too, remember that, child. You are privileged to be raised at court, although I have never cared for its madness and falsehood myself.' Her aunt gave a mordant smile. 'You have your mother's eyes, for she would look at me as you do – dutifully, but guarding her thoughts. Your mind is alive, child, and it needs to be.'

'Did you know my mother well?' Joanna ventured, hoping for crumbs.

Her aunt held out her empty cup to a passing servant to be refilled. 'I was married with a child before she was born, but I saw her sometimes and I grew to know her better when our father was dying. We sang to him, your mother and me. She was young and shy, but he took great delight in it and it was a moment of light and blessing amid his pain.' A shadow crossed her face. 'Our mother died less than a year later and I cared for your mother until she came to be wed. That is why I say you are like her for I knew her well when she was your age. I miss her. I miss all of my sisters. I am the last one. None have made old bones.'

'I am sorry, madam,' Joanna said. Her aunt Isabelle, Mahelt's sister, had died bearing the child she had been carrying at the Queen's churching – a stillborn son. Her husband, the King's brother, Richard, had since departed on crusade with Simon de Montfort who was making good use of his exile. 'I am sorry for the loss of your husband too.'

'Him I do not miss,' her aunt said brusquely. 'Marriage is a bargain, and you make the best of your circumstances. If you are fortunate you will bear sons and daughters to nurture and shape, who will be your consolation and make you proud.'

She beckoned to a junior squire who had been attending on the newly knighted Peter of Savoy.

The boy joined them, and bowed. Joanna eyed him curiously. He had glossy crow's-wing hair and dark-brown eyes set under slanted brows. He was of about her own age and she recognised his guarded expression from her own repertoire. Her aunt introduced him as her son, John de Warenne, who was entering the household of the newly knighted Peter of Savoy as his squire and ward, where he would be trained to knighthood.

The boy bowed again and gave Joanna an evaluating, slightly wary look. She could almost see prickles bristling on him like a defensive hedgehog. She understood his tension for she had reacted in the same way when she first arrived at court.

'I will be glad to have another cousin to talk to,' she said.

He inclined his head and was obviously relieved when Cecily summoned Joanna to help prepare the Queen's chamber for her retiring.

Her aunt Mahelt gave her a cool, dry kiss on the cheek. 'You do your mother proud and I am glad to be reminded of her,' she said, her expression almost wistful.

Joanna curtseyed dutifully. Her cousin John bowed and darted her another look from under his fringe.

Joanna perched little Edward on her knee and fed him small squares of rose-water sweetmeats from a silver dish. The young heir to the throne was thoroughly enjoying himself, lunging forward to catch each cube in his mouth and grabbing her hand to pull it towards him. 'More,' he cried, 'more!' and kicked his chubby legs. She gave him another and ate one too. The sweetness burst on her tongue, tasting of roses. Edward flung his arms around her neck and branded her cheek with a big sticky kiss. Joanna wrestled him round to wipe his mouth with a moist cloth. 'You little tyrant!' Laughing, she hugged him.

He wriggled off her knee and dashed to the cradle to look at his baby sister, Margaret, who had been born in September, a year after the Queen's dramatic churching ceremony. She was golden-haired and blue-eyed like Edward, but a sweet little thing rather than a force of nature.

Joanna ruefully eyed the sticky fingerprints on her gown but she was smiling, for Edward was so loveable and their connection was mutual and strong. She had folded his napkins and rocked his cradle; had soothed his hot gums when he was teething; had helped him form his first words. She had supported his wobbly little legs as he learned to walk. The women, teasing, called her his little mother.

She was cleaning her gown when a page arrived to say that her father was preparing to leave and wanted to bid farewell. Immediately, Joanna's stomach lurched with tension. Cecily rose to accompany her, and touched her hand in reassurance as they made their way to the great public hall beyond the King's painted chamber.

Cloaked and booted ready to leave for Swanscombe, Warin de Munchensy exuded an air of impatience. A soft paunch rolled over his belt, mounding his tunic.

Joanna approached him and curtseyed deeply. 'My lord father.'

He raised her to her feet, and kissed her cheek, then drew back and wiped his lips with a slight grimace. Setting her hand to her face, Joanna was dismayed to feel a lingering residue of Edward's sticky kiss: her father must think she had been gobbling sweetmeats in the bower.

Other than their brief meeting yesterday they had barely spoken, and now he was leaving. Iohan had already departed with Gilbert Marshal, so had clearly made his own farewells earlier.

'You have grown, daughter,' he said with strained pleasantry. 'You are a fine lady now, eh?'

'Joanna is a valued member of the Queen's household,' Cecily intervened. 'The lord Edward dotes on her, and she is most helpful to Dame Willelma the Queen's nurse, now that her hips are so stiff. She is a conscientious girl and never shirks her lessons.'

Joanna flushed, and her father cleared his throat. 'I would expect no less of my daughter.' He looked her up and down as though assessing the points of a horse. 'I may not visit often, but your stepmother and I receive news of your progress and we are very pleased.'

Joanna lowered her gaze at the empty platitudes. Their interest in her was only because of the connections she was making at court. 'I pray for you both and my stepbrother every day,' she replied. It was true. Cecily had taught her all about her Christian duty, but sometimes she prayed through gritted teeth.

Cecily touched her sleeve. 'Joanna, go and bring that piece you have made for your father. I think you have finished it.'

He cleared his throat impatiently.

'It will not take a moment, my lord,' Cecily said. 'I know you are anxious to leave.' She shooed Joanna. 'Quickly, child.'

Joanna curtseyed and hurried back to the Queen's chamber, wiping her cheek, knowing Cecily wished to have a private word with her father; she hoped it was all to the good.

'I had not expected my daughter to look so fine and grown up,' Warin said to Cecily. 'She is almost of marriageable age.'

Cecily eyed him sharply.

'As her father I must consider such matters.' He hitched his belt officiously.

'She is very young still,' Cecily replied with composure. 'It will greatly benefit her to continue her education at the court.'

'Yes, for now, but that time is coming.'

'Indeed, my lord, and the ties she is forming in the Queen's household will stand her in good stead.' Cecily had received the impression from his occasional visits to court that his daughter was a loose thread to be woven in somewhere useful on the tapestry, but of no immediate consequence – a girl with a high maternal lineage, but no lands to accompany that prestige. 'Joanna will make a fine wife and I am sure a worthy husband will be found for her in due course,' she added diplomatically. 'Unless you are considering her for the Church?'

Warin shook his head. 'Not at the moment.'

'Well then, let her continue here for now. She is trustworthy and a favourite with the Queen, and her skills will only improve with further education. It takes four years to train a page to become a squire and seven years further to bring him to knighthood. Joanna is quick to learn and sensible for her years, but she is not yet a woman. There is time, my lord.'

'Indeed, indeed,' he said gruffly. 'I am pleased to hear she is making such excellent progress and I am grateful to you and the King and Queen for your efforts.'

'You should be very proud of your daughter. Seldom have I taught such a rewarding pupil. Ah, here she is.'

Cecily turned as Joanna arrived, flushed and a little breathless. Performing a curtsey, she presented her father with a small linen package.

'What is this?' He unfastened the ribbon tie and opened the cloth to reveal a pouch, embroidered with a white swan sailing upon three blue waves.

Joanna blushed bright red. 'I made it for you, sire.'

He looked at her in amazement, and then at Cecily. 'This is your own work?'

'Yes, sire.'

'That is what I mean about your daughter's accomplishments,' Cecily said, pressing her point. 'Before long she will be one of the finest seamstresses in the court.'

His own face reddened with pleasure and hubris. 'I am blessed indeed that my seed has engendered such a skilled daughter.'

Joanna's heart filled with pleasure at his praise, dulled by a touch of disappointment. He had taken away the shine of the moment by turning the glory upon himself as her begetter. She had expended many hours on that little pouch and he would never think upon the meticulous care and attention she had put into it.

He tied the gift to his belt and kissed her cheek again, this time on the opposite side. 'Continue to do well for me, daughter,' he said. 'I shall look forward to hearing more of your progress.' And then he was gone, hurrying from the hall and summoning his squires for the return to Swanscombe.

'You have done yourself proud, child.' Cecily gave her a quick, maternal hug. 'You are a lady of the court, and your father now understands how much you are valued, and how accomplished you are.'

Raising her chin, Joanna tried to behave as if all was well and normal, but deep inside there huddled an insecure little girl whose mother was dead and who had her father's duty, but not his love.

Six months later, Joanna sat at her sewing, one eye on her needle, the other supervising the lord Edward and his companions who were playing in their father's painted chamber. Edward was galloping around on his toy hobby horse, his hair a flaxen nimbus, his dexterity and balance astounding for his age. His nurses were laughing at his antics as he urged on his mount with high-pitched commands to go faster and faster. His two small friends galloped with him – boys of a similar age who were the sons of two soldiers from the garrison. In later years their rank would separate them, but for now they were just infants romping together.

At the far end of the chamber, a painter, his apprentices and workmen sat on high planks of lashed scaffolding where they were working on a frieze of royal golden lions in a long panel intended to run the length of the chamber. They had completed several feet already and had paused to eat a noon repast of bread and cheese, perched like hawks overlooking all. Joanna often came here to watch them.

The King was busy speaking to the tiler from whom he was commissioning a pavement for the chamber floor. The decoration of this room where he spent so much time when in Westminster was his passion and his joy.

Iohan arrived with John de Warenne, the latter bearing a heaped bowl of cherries, and sat down with her in the window seat. Joanna immediately set her sewing aside for cherries were her weakness and she did not want to spoil her work with their juice. The orchards running down to the river were laden with them just now.

'I hope you had permission,' she said.

Iohan grinned. 'Of course we did. We said we had been sent by one of the Queen's ladies.'

She gave him a reproving look.

'We were just anticipating your desire, and anyway, it means less for the pigeons.' Iohan offered her the bowl. Abandoning her censure, she delicately took four of the glossy fruits, their red so dark that they reminded her of the shiny hide of one of the King's palfreys.

Her brother and their cousin John had struck up a friendship, and although they had different lords and duties, they would seek each other's company if they were at court together. They were riding and wrestling partners – friendly, highly competitive rivals – and comrades in mischief. John, taciturn on the outside, was gradually emerging from his shell.

Joanna popped a cherry in her mouth and worked her teeth around the stone, then delicately spat it into her cupped hand. The boys competed, seeing how far they could spit their own stones. They seemed cheerful today and none the worse for their ordeal a month ago, when they had witnessed the death of their uncle Gilbert the Marshal at a tourney held at Hertford.

The trial of arms between the English barons and the Queen's

Savoyard relatives had been presented as a friendly gathering to test out new horses and prove valour rather than as a tourney, because the King was deeply concerned about the disruptive and dangerous potential of such gatherings which often escalated into full battles and riots. But everyone had known it was a tourney by a less volatile name. Their uncle Gilbert had been chosen to lead the English barons and Peter of Savoy the foreign lords, and thus Iohan and John had been in attendance.

Uncle Gilbert had been showing off the paces of his new spirited Lombardy stallion, charging him up and down, when the horse's reins had suddenly broken and Gilbert had been thrown. His foot had caught in the stirrup and he had been dragged for several minutes along the hard, dry ground until someone managed to catch the horse, by which time their uncle was already dying from his injuries. His body had been borne back to London for burial in the Temple Church beside his father and brother.

The King had been so furious on learning of Gilbert's death that he had refused to grant Walter, Gilbert's brother and successor, his inheritance, although Joanna expected he would in time – for a price. Iohan had been taken into Henry's entourage for now.

She prayed for her uncle's soul every day, and remembered him each time she rode Arian. She had not known him well, but he had always been kind to her and she was sad to think she would not see him again. Even the King, through his anger, had grieved. 'We had our differences,' he said, 'but he was a stalwart tree in the forest and now he is gone I can no longer call upon his shelter and support.'

John spat out his last cherry stone and declared himself the winner, and Iohan protested, which resulted in a bout of elbowing and half punches, causing Joanna to roll her eyes and wonder why boys and men had to behave like this. She gave a small sigh, and turned her gaze to the painters who had finished their own food and were preparing to resume work. One man was working below the frieze, mapping out the figures of Faith, Hope and Charity in deft charcoal strokes.

John was summoned away by an older squire, for the Earl of Richmond desired him to run an errand.

'You have cherry stains round your mouth,' Joanna told him, and with a helpful smile handed him a scrap of waste linen from her sewing basket.

'Hah, "cherry lips"!' Iohan quipped, referencing a common name for a lady of dubious repute and easy favours.

John thumped him with amiable violence, then wiped his mouth with the cloth and departed, waving assent over his shoulder to Iohan's shouted invitation to play dice later.

With his friend gone, Iohan folded his arms and looked at Joanna. 'They say Uncle Gilbert was murdered,' he said.

Joanna hastily looked round, but no one was within earshot. 'Who says?' she whispered.

Iohan shrugged. 'People. Servants gossiping in corners.'

'Why would they say such things?'

'Because Uncle Gilbert was always talking about foreigners forcing their way into court circles and having too much influence. He had many enemies.'

Joanna dropped her gaze. Iohan had still not learned to be circumspect, and perhaps never would, but she could only admonish him so far.

'The horse was a new Lombard stallion and hard to control, so it might have happened anyway, but someone must have cut his reins because they do not just break.' Iohan lifted his chin. 'He was a Marshal – he knew the importance of caring for equipment.'

'Do you believe it?'

'It may just have been a servant with a grudge – but you never know what is waiting round the corner, do you?' He shivered. 'I do not think I will ever forget the sight of him being dragged across the ground with his foot caught in that stirrup.'

She laid her hand on his arm to comfort him and he gave her a wan smile and rose abruptly to his feet. 'I should go too,' he said.

'Thank you for the cherries.'

He smiled at her. 'I spat the furthest stone whatever John says,' he said, and took his leave.

Joanna noticed he had left the bowl, which would have to be returned to the kitchens. She thought of the madman in the palace at Woodstock, and how they all lived with bars on the windows now. She was glad that her place in the world was not exalted. Better to be a pawn on the edges, or not on the board at all.

6

Palace of Westminster, May 1242

Under Willelma's watchful gaze, Joanna carefully folded one of the Queen's gowns and laid it in a travelling coffer, layered with sweet-smelling herbs. The blue silk robe was loosely cut, and light for a hot southern summer and the last months of pregnancy. The court was moving to Gascony for the King had disputes to settle with the French and other business to conduct. The Queen was accompanying the King, for they both desired their third child to be born in Gascony to further their claim to the lands. Edward and his little sister were remaining behind with Sybil Giffard and her husband. Joanna had half expected to stay too, but the Queen wished her to perform tasks and run errands for those less agile. 'No one else folds as quickly and neatly as you do, or reads with such a sweet voice,' she had said.

'You have never crossed the Narrow Sea and seen the lands of France, have you, Joanna?' the Queen asked. She was sipping a tisane and sitting with her feet propped up on cushions.

'No, madam.'

'This will be a true adventure for you then.' Alienor's eyes glinted with mischief. 'Cecily is a fine tutor but she cannot teach you all you need to know about womanhood.'

Joanna's cheeks burned. The Queen enjoyed matchmaking and adored tales of valiant knights and virtuous ladies. Of hidden smiles and the whisper of a silk gown slipping through a doorway. Of great deeds and courtly pleasures.

'What you are told is well and good,' the Queen continued, 'but you must have practical experience too.'

She beckoned to Willelma who came stiffly to her, rubbing her sore hip. She was a good ten years older than Cecily with a crop of silver whiskers sprouting on her chin. Her faculties were sharp though, and she missed nothing that went on in the Queen's chambers, even if she could no longer see well enough to thread a needle. Caring for the Queen was her sole reason for life, and she was protective, always observing the other ladies in the chamber to ensure they did not shirk their duties. In her charge, hanging from her belt were the keys to the household coffers, the linen press, the spice box and the Queen's jewel casket.

'Now,' Alienor said to Joanna, 'I have decided to entrust you with some of my keys. I have had duplicate ones made to Dame Willelma's so that if a lady requires linen from the fabric press, or needle and thread, she need not trouble Willelma if she is busy, but may come to you. I expect you to note who asks and what is taken, but the duty shall be yours. I am depending on you to do it well and honestly.'

A sunburst of delighted surprise expanded inside Joanna, and she dropped in a deep curtsey. 'Thank you, madam! I will do my best!'

'I know you will, and that is why I am recognising and rewarding your service.' The Queen picked up an embossed leather belt, to which was attached a chatelaine's ring holding three new, shiny keys. 'Do this well for me and you shall have more authority in due course. You shall answer to Dame Willelma. Do as she tells you and ask if you have any concerns.'

Striving not to appear flustered, keenly aware of the sharpness underlying Willelma's smile, Joanna took the belt and curtseyed again, accepting her new obligations with a feeling of deep seriousness bordering on the sacred.

Joanna was kept extremely busy over the next few days as the packing continued apace and she had to be everywhere – folding garments, checking boxes and baggage, dealing with servants, running errands, answering questions. Several ladies came to ask her for access to the fabric chest and linen closet and she had then to report faithfully back to Willelma. She suspected the first few were deliberate tests of her ability to perform the task, but she accomplished the duty well, and it gave her the confidence to become more assertive.

The court and contingents of troops arrived in Portsmouth to cross the sea and there was more supervision to do as servants loaded the baggage on to the anchored ships. Joanna gazed at the banners flapping from the masts of the moored vessels as the sailors hefted packages and barrels on board. Her stomach tightened with apprehension when she looked at the wide stretch of water glittering under the sun to the horizon, but excitement filled her too. The Thames at Westminster often carried the salt tang of the sea, and her childhood home at Swanscombe lay on the estuary, but travelling across miles of ocean on a ship was a new experience.

The King's famous grandmother Alienor of Aquitaine had ridden to Jerusalem with an army and crossed great mountain ranges as an old woman. The young Queen herself had been

Joanna's age when she left her homeland to marry, and Joanna bore their inspiration in her heart as the ship cast off. She gripped the keys at her belt and fixed her gaze, not on the diminishing coastline of England, but on the sparkling sea-road to Gascony.

The hot May weather more resembled the middle of July as Queen Alienor rested on her bed in her chamber at the royal camp in Pons while the King met the barons of the Lusignan to discuss and deal with French encroachment upon English Crown interests. War, it seemed, was inevitable.

Joanna looked up from rubbing Alienor's swollen ankles and feet with a lavender unguent as a squire arrived to announce that the King's mother and the Countess of Leicester were here to pay a social visit.

Caught by surprise, Alienor hastily bade Joanna wipe and dry her feet and help her put on her embroidered shoes. Roberga hurried to bring refreshments and another maid set about plumping the cushions and smoothing covers. The musicians were summoned. Joanna retreated to the background with her sewing, ready to be called too, but hoping not to attract the attention of the Countess of Leicester now she had returned to court.

Since their return from crusade, Simon de Montfort and his wife had been staying with the Count of Burgundy. Henry, desperate for military expertise, had summoned de Montfort who had agreed to join him – for a payment of six hundred marks, citing the King's injustice to him in the past, and his own difficult financial circumstances. Henry had acquiesced and they had patched up their quarrel, their need of each other for the moment being mutual.

The King's mother, Isabel, once Queen of England, now

Countess of La Marche, poised as the herald announced her, and then entered Alienor's chamber, bearing herself regally as though she still wore a crown. Rising from her curtsey, Joanna saw a long-limbed, slender woman with the loosely rounded belly of someone who had borne numerous children. Her features were fine with high cheekbones and slanted dark-blue eyes. Lines of weariness and strain grooved her face, giving it a harsh aspect, although her beauty still shone through. Joanna noted the strong resemblance between her and Eleanor de Montfort, their relationship as mother and daughter clearly defined.

Isabel waved her hand as Alienor started to curtsey. 'No, my dear, sit and rest. I know what it is like to be heavy with child in the last weeks of carrying – although my youngest is thirteen now.'

Alienor relaxed on to the bed and Willelma plumped the pillows at her back. Cushioned chairs and settles were arranged at the bedside for the visitors.

Isabel introduced her attendant ladies, presenting a lithe young woman with glorious warm-bronze hair woven in a long plait, topped by a gauzy veil. 'My daughter Aliza,' she said.

The girl curtseyed modestly to Alienor, but her vivacious smile hinted at concealed mischief.

Joanna and Roberga served wine and small pastries to the Queen and her guests in a slightly strained atmosphere, for the women were strangers, their common ground being Henry, who had had no contact with his mother since childhood. Isabel had returned to the Limousin soon after the death of Henry's father, King John, and had married Hugh de Lusignan, Count of La Marche, bearing another nine children to add to the five she already had from her first marriage.

The attending younger ladies were dismissed to a different part of the chamber out of earshot while the Queen spoke with

Henry's mother and sister. Joanna settled down beside Aliza de Lusignan.

'How long have you been attending on the Queen?' Aliza wanted to know.

'Four years,' Joanna replied. 'My brother is at court too and a royal ward. Our mother died and our father remarried and he has a second son, but I do not see them often.' She surprised herself, for usually she was more circumspect, but she had felt an immediate, instinctive rapport with Aliza.

Aliza did not pry, but volunteered information in exchange. 'We are here because my mother greatly desired to see her other family again. She had to leave Henry and Richard and my sisters behind when she returned to Angoulême and it has always haunted her. Four of my brothers are here too, with the men.'

Joanna shook her head. 'You have many brothers and sisters.'

'Sometimes it is like living in a litter of puppies! There's Aymer too, but he's at home.' She rolled her eyes. 'My brothers think they know it all, but women have the better awareness. I love them to the marrow of my bones, but I shall never let them think for me.' She glanced towards her mother, deep in conversation with Alienor, and grew more serious. 'It has been difficult for Mama. She had to leave England after King John died – there was no role for her, no purpose, and no acceptance; some wounds do not heal even when a fresh start has been made.'

'Indeed,' Joanna said, thinking of her own mother and how much she missed her. 'How long are you staying?'

'No, only a couple of days. A battle muster is not the best place to gather and we would not have come save to meet our kin. And you?'

'South, to La Reole and then to Bordeaux for the baby's birth, depending on the Queen's health.'

Aliza nodded. 'It is good for my half-brother to have a child born on Gascon soil,' she said. 'But tell me about England, what is it like?'

That evening the King presided over the family gathering with pride. The hostilities with the de Montforts had been put aside if not forgotten, and the rift bandaged over. Toasts were raised and brimming cups sent around the table. Alienor sat at Henry's right hand and his mother at his left with Henry's brother Richard beside her, full of bonhomie. Arrangements for his match with Queen Alienor's younger sister Sancha were being finalised, and he would soon be a married man again.

Joanna quietly observed King Henry's half-brothers. She remembered what Aliza had said about them being a litter of puppies, but to her mind they more resembled lean young wolves. Hugh, the oldest, was a grown man, tall and strong. Guy and Geoffrey had not attained full manhood, but were not far off – brash, self-assured young men. The youngest, William, was just entering adolescence. He had a mass of tight brown curls flashed with gold, and intelligent eyes, flecked like grey agate. He and Aliza shared the same sun-bright smile.

Later, there was informal conversation and music. Tables were set up for games of chess, dice and merels. Joanna introduced Aliza to her brother, and to her cousin John de Warenne.

'I would never guess you were kin,' Aliza said to the youths. 'One so fair and one so dark. Who is the oldest?' Her gaze lingered briefly on John.

'I am.' Iohan puffed out his chest. 'I am fourteen.'

Aliza smiled. 'My youngest brother is almost your age.' She sought among the gathering, and waved to catch the attention of the curly-haired youth, who left his companions and joined them. 'This is William,' she said as introductions were made. 'I try to keep him out of mischief, but I don't always succeed.'

The youth rolled his eyes. 'Do not believe her – it's usually the other way round!'

Aliza laughed. 'Well then, we know each other's deeds well enough to look innocent and promise to say nothing.'

He inclined his head. 'As you say, sister.'

'I have to go.' John stood up in response to a summons from Peter of Savoy and concealed a grimace. 'We are leaving for Provence at first light and the baggage must be ready or I'll be to blame.' He nodded to William and bowed to Aliza. 'We shall meet again.'

'I hope so. Godspeed and a successful mission,' Aliza said graciously.

Bereft of a partner, Iohan invited William de Valence to play chess and the youths went off together to find a table and a board.

'I do love William,' Aliza said. 'He will have no great wealth unless he marries a rich heiress but he will inherit a few castles and our brothers will look out for him and keep him employed.' She looked over to where William and Iohan were now sitting over a chess board arranging the pieces. William said something that made Iohan laugh. 'He puts his whole heart into everything he does. He wants to do well; he wants to belong. If you keep poking him, he will eventually round on you, but mostly he's well mannered – unless he's up to mischief.'

Joanna raised her eyebrows and Aliza laughed. 'I remember him sitting in a tree dropping green apples on the people passing beneath, including a bishop. Our mother was so cross with him! If he's not kept constantly occupied, he causes trouble, but he starts his full training once we're home and then he'll have no time for pranks.'

Joanna shook her head and wondered at the propensity of males for behaving thus. It would never have entered her head to do such a thing.

'I wish we could spend more time together,' Aliza said, 'but we are leaving in the morning. I truly hope to see you again.'

'I hope so too,' Joanna said, for her heart had warmed to Aliza de Lusignan and she felt as if she had known her for much longer than a day. 'Perhaps we could write.'

Aliza gave her a broad smile. 'Yes, I would like that.'

The afternoon sun was so hot that the sky was white and shimmering waves rose from the land, although the walls of the Ombrière Palace in Bordeaux kept the burning light at bay. Joanna paused to wipe her brow, and then carried a fresh bowl of rose water into the birthing chamber where Alienor had been in travail since dawn. They had been a month in Bordeaux and the midsummer heat had burned the grass into dormancy. The King was on campaign in the field against the French, accompanied by his brother Richard, his Lusignan stepfather and Simon de Montfort.

Joanna entered the chamber as the Queen gave a drawn-out groan of effort, and was in time to see Sybil Giffard lift a blood-streaked baby from between Alienor's parted legs, attached by a writhing bluish cord. 'A fine little girl!' Sybil laughed as the baby started to bawl. 'Just listen to her lungs!'

Joanna's heart expanded with relief and happiness. She had been so anxious for the Queen and the baby because Alienor had been unwell and they had been forced to move swiftly from La Reole to Bordeaux when war had threatened their refuge.

Lady Giffard cut the cord with a little pair of shears and carried the baby away to be cleaned and bathed.

'Joanna, don't just stand there like a ninny, bring the rose water,' Eleanor de Montfort snapped.

Concealing a twinge of resentment, Joanna brought the bowl to the bedside. The Countess took it from her, wrung out the cloth, and wiped the Queen's brow. 'You may go,' she said imperiously.

Joanna retreated to watch the baby being washed and then gently dried before her little limbs were rubbed with scented unguent. She had a quiff of gilt-gold hair and already a look of her father in the way she pursed her lips. Clean and swaddled, the new princess was brought to her mother who took her with tearful joy.

Joanna tidied in the background, watching and smiling. She had been involved in a royal birth three times now, and still the novelty and miracle enthralled her. A new life, a new little person. She decided she would write back to Aliza today, sending her an embroidered napkin and the joyful news of the baby's birth. Last week a letter had arrived from Aliza with the gift of a pretty braid belt, and this news would be a fine way to reciprocate.

Joanna gave Iohan a cup of watered wine and watched him down it in a few swift gulps, the liquid spilling from the sides of his mouth. In the month he had been gone on campaign he had grown yet again and his throat showed the apple swelling of an adult male.

He gasped and returned the cup to her with a nod of gratitude as she refilled it. The great hall of the Shadow Palace heaved with the commotion of a returning army. The pungent smell of sweat from men who had ridden hard in summer heat filled the room. There were wounded among them; the worst affected were being tended in another part of the complex, but there were superficial injuries aplenty among those gathering in the hall. The King had gone straight to the Queen's chambers, ostensibly to see the new baby and speak to his wife, but also to avoid the unsettled melee.

The Queen, still in confinement following the birth, had sent several of her ladies including Joanna to help where they could. Joanna had heard the gist of what had happened from the heralds who had ridden in ahead of the dust-smothered troops. The campaign against the French had been a calamity and they had lost swathes of land, including the ground they had come to safeguard. The King's stepfather, Hugh, Count of La Marche, on whose behalf they were here, had turned tail when put under pressure and yielded to the French to preserve his hide. The English had been saved from full disaster because the French troops were suffering badly from the flux and had drawn back, reluctant to pursue Henry all the way to Bordeaux.

'The King promised Gascony to Earl Richard if he could effect a truce between us and the French,' Iohan said. 'Earl Richard went to the King of France and begged him to allow us time to withdraw. But the Earl cannot have Gascony because the lands are the lord Edward's inheritance, so who knows what will happen now.' He screwed up his face. 'The Earl of Leicester was raging when we had to flee. He's behind us, but not far – he'll be arriving soon.' He gave her a warning look. 'It is not good for the King. He has suffered a harsh defeat and the best we can do is negotiate a better truce than the one granted to allow us to retreat.' He returned the cup. 'I have to go, I have duties.'

'I am glad you are safe,' she said.

'So am I.' He kissed her cheek in a rare gesture of affection. 'I'm going to be saddle-sore for days after the pace we had to set!'

When he had gone, Joanna moved among the crowd, serving more watered wine, making sure the jugs were replenished and directing the servants. Then Simon de Montfort arrived, striding into the room, shouldering people aside, his expression thunderous. His garments were filthy with dust and battle stains, including ominous red-brown splashes on his surcoat. He slammed through the hall like a mighty wind and disappeared in the direction of the chamber that had been made ready for him.

Returning to the Queen's apartments, Joanna had to step aside for Eleanor de Montfort, who was hurrying to join her husband. She ignored Joanna, taking her curtsey as a given.

Within the chamber, Henry sat on a bench, hands covering his face. The Queen, dressed in a loose linen robe, stood over him, calm but purse-lipped.

'You have done your best in trying circumstances,' she was saying. 'It is not your fault that others have let you down and deserted. You are safe now, and we shall manage affairs between us. All is not lost. You should not have told Richard he could have Gascony, but you made that choice in the need of the moment and we can change it. If he is to wed my sister, he will agree to relinquish the lands even if he complains.'

Henry raised his head and gave her a sheepish, relieved look. 'I wish I had had you with me at the time to give me counsel.'

'I wish I could have been there too,' Alienor said, looking exasperated.

He departed to deal with his courtiers, but Alienor wanted to know what was being said and, since she was still in confinement, sent Joanna and two other ladies to stand in the background and listen. Joanna found an unobtrusive place at the side of the chamber, near the door, and stood quietly with her head bowed and her hands clasped.

Simon de Montfort appeared as the last courtiers were assembling in the chamber. A sombre brown tunic had replaced his stained armour and he wore soft leather shoes and a plain belt. Ever since the King had castigated him at Queen Alienor's churching, he had affected a much simpler mode of dressing, although his wife remained wedded to her silks and cosmetics.

Stony-faced, he gave Henry a perfunctory bow. 'Sire,' he said. 'We have turned away from battle with no credit and no honour. We have lost Saintes. We have been pushed back by the French from every place we were supposed to hold and secure. All of it gone, and they would be at our doors now had the bloody flux not struck them down, and had the Earl of Cornwall not begged for a truce. Hugh of Lusignan has turned traitor and submitted to the French like the vermin he is. We shall be pushed from the map when there was barely a place for us before. It is the worst defeat we have ever experienced!'

De Montfort's words were like fists and Joanna kept her eyes down, fearing to meet that devastating rage full on. His bold, forceful voice and the way he stared into the audience as he spoke made it personal while being a speech for all. His plain garments stood in direct contrast to the King with his golden garland and green silk robes, but it seemed as though de Montfort should be sitting in Henry's stead.

His complexion flushed as the King said nothing. 'What do we have left?' he demanded. 'This shameful thing has been brought on the entire English court, by following this man.'

Henry drew himself up. 'How dare you speak to me in such a wise!'

De Montfort's top lip curled. 'How dare I? When I see what we have lost in following your foolish enterprise? When I see that your supposed Lusignan allies have deserted you? Their respect for you is obvious by their deeds, but I do not hear you saying "How dare they?" By Christ, you should be locked up with bars at your windows like Charles the Simple. I do wonder if you are "Henry the Simple" for you could not make a more bungled fist of this matter if you had tried.'

Joanna gasped at the blatant disrespect verging on treason. De Montfort stared around, seeking and expecting agreement. People murmured and exchanged embarrassed glances. There were even some dour smiles, but no one spoke up in support for it was too stark an accusation.

'This man is no better than any one of you, and he should not be allowed to dictate our defeat!' De Montfort was almost grinding his teeth.

'Yet again, you forget yourself, my lord of Leicester,' Henry retorted, his voice quivering. 'I could have done nothing else. There was no other outcome, and if you say there was, then I am but one man. I have to go by what my advisers and my soldiers say. You should have given me the benefit of your wisdom before we got into this position rather than turning with a sneer on your face and criticising me now and causing further division. How does this help us, my lord?' Henry waved his hand. 'You are dismissed. Be very careful what you say to me, or you may find yourself looking through a prison grille, whether you are married to my sister or not.'

'This is not finished by a long way,' de Montfort said, almost choking, and having flourished a savage bow he stormed from the room.

Henry drew a breath down his larynx like a drowning man fighting for air. 'I am the King.' His voice quivered with strain. 'I am God's anointed, and I will have respect for that position.'

Joanna bit her lip. The King should be more forceful. He made errors of judgement and had suffered misfortune too, but de Montfort's outburst had undermined him before all, and not for the first time.

Although visibly shaken, Henry rallied, and encompassed his

barons with an imperious look. 'Now is not the time for discussion, my lords. We will deal with matters in the morning when we have rested. Gentlemen, you may take your leave.'

By the time Henry returned to the Queen, Joanna and the ladies had made their report, and Alienor was fully apprised of the situation.

'That man is outrageous!' Henry said tearfully, approaching her as if she was the mother and he the child. 'Did you hear him? If he thought he could do better then why did he not advise me? He is the one who has reneged on his duty to his king.'

'I know, my love, I know,' Alienor soothed, putting her arms around him. 'Do not worry, we shall find a solution. Let those who have the fighting skill fight, and those who have the diplomatic skill weave their threads. I shall write to my sister and she shall speak to Louis. Women are after all the peacemakers.' She stroked his hair, calming and gentling him. 'The Earl of Leicester should never have spoken as he did, but that is his way and it did not reflect well on him. Tomorrow, when the dust has settled, we shall see what is what. Perhaps because he is your brother-by-marriage he thinks he has the leeway to speak bluntly; there are even times when such a thing is useful. You are his king. He owes you his allegiance and his respect, but do not disown him because of his behaviour, even if that is your first instinct.'

Henry lifted his head and looked at her, wide-eyed.

'If he wants to put his fist in a soldier's glove then let him,' Alienor said. 'Why should a man have a guard dog and bark himself? If he has military advice then let it become deed, not word after the event. If he succeeds, reward him. If he fails, then it shall be his fault, not yours.'

Henry relaxed a little and kissed her cheek. 'You are wise beyond your years, my love.'

'I look and listen and learn.' She signalled Joanna to come and pour wine. 'You are the King, do not let men use you, save that it be to your advantage.'

Joanna curtseyed after she had presented the filled cups. 'Sire, madam, you shall always have my service,' she said, wanting to give something to heal what had happened, and she touched the silver brooch pinning the throat of her gown.

The King gave her a harassed smile over the rim of the goblet. 'You are a treasure, my dear,' he said. 'Whatever happens, bless you, I know you will be steadfast.'

7

Windsor Castle, Berkshire, December 1245

It had snowed overnight, the first full fall of the year, and the children in the royal nursery were engaged in a competitive snowball fight. Six-year-old Edward, cheeks and lips as red as scarlet cloth from the cold, was determined to win. His voice shrilled as he aimed and threw, striking Joanna's brother on the side of his cloak. Iohan laughed and retaliated, but Edward ducked and the ball exploded against the wall.

Joanna and Edward's little sister Margaret had joined the fray, hurling snowballs at the boys. Powdery white smudges patterned Joanna's cloak where she had protected the little girl from the boisterous attacks of the boys. Margaret, despite her haphazard aim, was resolute and Joanna was taking the brunt. Her thick brown braid had straggled loose and she was breathless with laughter. Her cousin John de Warenne lifted Edward up piggyback and Iohan did the same with another of their cousins, Henry of Almain, and the boys indulged in a snow-joust, jostling, shoving each other, grunting and struggling. Sausagez danced around them, barking. Grey-muzzled and middle-aged he might be, but his terrier enthusiasm remained undampened.

Joanna moulded another mitten full of snow, but paused before throwing as one of the King's chaplains, Brother Thomas, approached the group. She dropped her missile and dusted off her hands and the boys ceased their rough and tumbling. The friar studied them from under bushy silver brows before addressing Iohan, who was brushing snow from his tunic. 'Master Munchensy, the King wishes to see you and your sister, and you, my lord,' he added to John de Warenne. He turned to encompass Joanna in his stare, and she hastily tidied her hair back under her cap, wondering what had happened or what they had done. 'Come,' the friar said, his gaze sombre. 'We should not keep the King waiting. He has important news.'

Henry, clad in a mantle lined with squirrel fur, sat by his hearth, surrounded by clerics, barons and administrators. He was busy dictating, but looked up as Joanna and the two youths were ushered into the room. A gesture and a word dismissed those around him, including Simon de Montfort, who regarded the three youngsters with fierce eyes. He and Henry had again patched up their differences and made a bygone of the words exchanged in Gascony, but they disliked each other; however, since they were kin-by-marriage, they existed in a state of uneasy truce, bolstered by their wives.

Joanna's frozen fingers started to tingle as she stood near the fire, and her stomach churned with tension because Henry looked so serious. Everyone had retreated, but the clerks lingered, distant enough to give space but sufficiently close to be summoned, and the nearest stood clutching an assortment of parchment sheets, their seals dangling.

'I am afraid I have some sad and serious news for all of you.' Henry fixed them with a sorrowful gaze. 'I am sorry to tell you that your uncle Ancel has died at Striguil. He was coming to court for the Feast of St Edward to be invested with the earldom of Pembroke, but he has succumbed to illness.'

Shocked, Joanna made the sign of the cross on her breast. Last month their uncle Walter had died of a flux and now his last remaining brother was also dead. A whole generation of her Marshal male relatives had been extinguished. It was like standing between sheltering trees and suddenly have a gale blow them down.

'I shall have prayers said for his soul in the chapel of St Edward,' Henry said, 'and naturally I shall ensure all the business concerns of the earldom continue as usual.' He regarded them with genuine sadness. 'I knew your uncle Ancel when we were boys, and we played together as you have been playing today. We have not been close for a long time, but still it was a memory made.'

Others saw the King's sensitivity as a failing, but Joanna regarded it as a sign of his goodness and sincerity, and she loved him for it. However, the enormity of the news hit her as he spoke again.

'This will make a difference to your inheritance, my boy,' he told Iohan. 'Lawyers will be employed on your behalf because now your uncles have all died without issue, the lands come to their sisters and to the heirs of their sisters. Since you are your mother's male heir, you stand to inherit her portion when you come of age. Others have details of what that entails, but it is considerable.'

Iohan stammered out a flustered response and Henry responded with a sympathetic smile. 'Your uncle's death is a sad shock, I know, and your changed circumstances will take a great deal of adjustment. Go and sit in the embrasure and I will have a servant bring you some wine. And then light candles in my chapel and pray for your uncle's soul.' He raised his hand. 'All of you, together. Be each other's comfort and support. I will talk to you again when I have finished my other business.'

Sitting in the embrasure, warmed by heat from a charcoal brazier, Joanna curled her hands around her cup of hot spiced wine and looked at Iohan. He was flushed and bright-eyed, for now instead of receiving an ordinary baronial inheritance from Swanscombe he stood to gain castles and lands that would vastly increase his status.

'All of our Marshal uncles are gone,' said John de Warenne. 'There is no longer an Earl of Pembroke – unless the King gives you the title.' He nudged Iohan. Ancel was John's uncle too, but he had living older brothers who would inherit their mother's share of the Marshal lands in due course, so the news for him was not as immense.

Iohan shook his head in bemusement. 'I do not know what to say. Who would think that my Marshal uncles would die without begetting heirs? I would wish my uncle Ancel still alive, although I never knew him beyond a word. I want to grieve for him, but I cannot feel the sorrow.'

'I never knew my father,' John admitted with a grimace. 'I never saw him. He and my mother were . . .' He paused. 'Not close. When he died, though, I wanted him back and I was angry that he could leave me and my mother without protection.' His eyes were dark with pain. 'I will never get to face him in manhood and show my worth before him. He failed me. I honour my bloodline, but I do not want to be him.' He gave Iohan a shrewd, cynical look, far older than his sixteen years. 'You are important now. Your lands will have a steward and a great marriage will be arranged for you.'

Iohan shook his head again: it was too much to take in.

'And a greater marriage for you too,' John said to Joanna.

She returned his look calmly, although she was not calm inside. She was more resilient to change these days, but this new alteration in status unsettled her for it meant moving into the foreground instead of service behind the curtain. 'Perhaps,' she said. 'Who can tell? We should pray for our uncle's soul.'

The three of them repaired to the King's magnificent private chapel, gleaming with gold, ornaments and precious jewels, the air perfumed with incense. Iohan looked bemused and Joanna pressed his hand supportively. He replied with a strained smile and a slight shake of his head.

Joanna's breath escaped in a cloud of cold vapour and she bowed her head and prayed dutifully for her uncle's soul, for her mother's, for those who were gone from this world and were with Jesus; and for those still treading their path on this earth, that they might find succour and healing. And with herself and Iohan in mind, that they might find the strength to face whatever lay beyond the horizon.

8

Fontevraud Abbey, France, May 1246

Clad only in his linen breeches, William de Valence stretched and inhaled a deep lungful of morning air through the open window of the abbey guest house. The scent of fresh grass beaded with dew called to him with all the promise of spring. He was eighteen years old, bursting with life, and whatever his tribulations, nothing could suppress his instinctive response to the season.

The birds had started singing before the stars had set, and the chorus now resounded like a cathedral choir. Blackbird and robin, starling, sparrow and thrush. Going to the jug and bowl standing under the window, he poured water and sluiced his face, torso and hands, drying the latter by pushing them through his thick curls, sleeking his hair into a semblance of order. Ablutions complete, he took a clean shirt from his baggage. The sleeves were a little short on his long wrist bones, for he had grown again since the winter and now stood a head taller than any of his brothers. Indeed, it amused and delighted him that he was bigger than Geoffrey, although Geoffrey insisted it was only William's unruly hair that made the difference.

His stomach growled but he knew he should pray before he broke his fast. There was no sign of his servant Elias, whom he assumed was tending to the horses. His brothers were absent too. William was bursting to be out in the glorious morning, cantering his horse along sun-dappled woodland paths, but such delightful earthly pursuits were not the reason they were here at Fontevraud, five days' ride from home.

The sunlit doorway darkened as his brother Aymer entered the room. 'Our lady mother is asking for you,' he said. Aymer, older than him by two years, was studying for the priesthood.

'How is she this morning?' William threaded his knife on to his belt.

'Weak, but she has eaten a little bread and milk and she has her wits about her.' Aymer squeezed William's shoulder. 'She wants to see you.'

William tugged his tunic straight. His gut tightened and his joy sank beneath a layer of dull anxiety. Following their family's humiliating defeat by the French, and his father's surrender to the inevitable, his mother had renounced her marriage and her life as the Countess of La Marche and retired to the abbey at Fontevraud. She had kissed him a tender farewell and bidden him become a man to make her proud. Now, she was dying, and about to take the veil.

He walked quietly through the leafy spring morning to the cell where she lay on a plain wooden bed made up with a coarse linen sheet and an undyed blanket. A crucifix hung on the sparse white wall facing her bed. Nothing about the diminished, gaunt-cheeked woman lying under the thin blanket indicated she had once been Queen of England, wife to King John, and was the mother of the reigning King. Her life had been filled with rumours, slander and scandal put about by enemies and detractors, but whatever the world said about her, she was his mother; he was her youngest son, and all he had ever received from her was love. His sister Aliza sat at her side holding her hand, but as he arrived she yielded her place, touching his arm in passing before leaving the room.

William knelt at the bedside, awkward because of his gangly height. 'My lady mother,' he said and, taking her hand, kissed her dry, febrile cheek.

She turned her head on the pillow and smiled at him. A simple linen cap covered her hair and her white chemise emphasised the yellow hue of her skin. Her breath was sour. 'My William,' she said. 'So much the man.'

Seeing his beautiful mother so wasted and weak filled him with grief. He remembered her cuddling him when he was little, and the way she had teased him when he was fourteen and fussing over his appearance before a feast, and how she had tenderly pinned a brooch at the correct angle on his hat and kissed his cheek.

'I have thought about you often,' she whispered. 'Some say I should not have come to Fontevraud, but there was nothing left for me beyond the purging of my soul.' She gestured at the cup on the bedside, and he gave her a sip of boiled spring water. 'I am tired,' she said, 'so very tired.'

'I will pray for your recovery and good health, Mother.'

She shook her head, and an impatient frown twitched her brow. 'I shall have no more good health in this life. Pray for my soul if you will, for my time is short.'

William flinched. He did not want to believe she was dying even though the evidence was before him. 'Yes, from my heart.'

'You and your siblings must take courage and strength from each other,' she said. 'Stay united in all you do. Remember your duties and obligations to yourself and to others.' She squeezed his hand, and with her other, touched his head in blessing. 'My curly-haired beautiful boy, now you must be a man in all you say and think and do – ask what will be said of you when you make your own end.'

She paused and indicated her cup, and William helped her sip a few mouthfuls until she raised her hand and told him enough.

'There are things in my life that people have forced upon me, and other things I have done that I deeply regret,' she continued in a weak voice. 'But there are also things that make me proud, even if pride is a sin, and one of them is my children. You are the part of me that stays behind, and when you go out in the world you are representing me. You embody your ancestors and in turn you will become someone's ancestor when you have offspring of your own.'

William bowed his head, apprehensive at the weight and responsibility of her expectation.

'I have asked your brother in England to help all of you. You have a small portion here, but Henry sits on a throne and you are born of the same womb. I have said my farewell to the world, but I can still strive to give my children what their father cannot.'

William did not reply. His father was a distant figure. He had provided him with protection and education. He had supplied him with horses and servants and training. But William had always been the child trailing in his wake, the last son, the one with the fewest prospects. Essentially his older brothers had raised him, the youngest cub in the pack. He might be the least in the hierarchy, but they had looked out for him. He had always been certain of his mother's love, even in the dark days, but his father's for a last-born son was less certain.

'You are mine,' she said, as if reading his mind. 'My womb gave life to the King of England just as surely as it gave life to you and your brothers and sisters.' She briefly closed her eyes. 'I did not ask you here to embroil you in such matters. I have set in motion what is needful. Now you must seize whatever opportunity is offered with a whole heart, and listen well. Your father was often deaf, and I do not wish that trait for you.'

'No, Mama.' He raised her hand to his lips and kissed the bird-fragile bones.

'Then it is settled. For my many sins I have left instructions that when I am buried, my grave shall be outside the church. I do not have the grace to lie within it. I shall take the veil and pray for God's mercy on my soul . . . I am glad to have seen you again and I give you my blessing. Live your life well, and if God grants you lands and a family, care for them with diligence and honour in remembrance of me – my sweet boy.' She touched his hair again.

'Mama . . .'

'Do not be sorrowful,' she said, suddenly sharp. 'Be joyful. That is a command.'

He swallowed manfully, although the lump in his throat seemed enormous. He left the cool, austere cell and entered the warm May sunshine, but then had to lean against the wall and let the dammed-up tears run down his face.

Aliza rose from the bench where she had been waiting and came to put her arms around him. 'I know,' she said soothingly. 'I know.'

William's shoulders shook with silent sobs, but he mastered himself and pushed her gently away. 'I am not weeping for our mother,' he said. 'She bade me not to. I am weeping for myself, for not having her in the world. Even if we were parted from her, I knew she was here and I could reach her if I had need.'

'She will still be here for us,' Aliza soothed. 'We can still speak to her and tell her things, and we still have each other.'

'She says she wants to be buried outside the church; did she tell you that?' He blinked hard to empty his eyes.

'Yes, she did,' Aliza replied in a more subdued voice. 'I would not wish it for her, but it is her choice.'

'I know she will go to Jesus in Heaven,' William said fiercely.

'Yes, she will – for everything she had to endure in this life.'

'She said she had written to our brother in England.'

'Yes, she told me too. I think Mama has had this in mind for us for a long time. She has never forgotten that she was England's queen, even if she had to leave. I am sure she mooted it to Henry when she met him in Pons.'

'What do you think about going?'

'Why not?' she said brightly. 'It will be an adventure and it will be interesting to see the land where she was a queen. We are Henry's close kin and will be useful to him. He has lands here, and that makes us valuable for his rule of Gascony. His wife has all her relatives at court and in high positions, it is only right that our brother, as King, should have his.' She gave him a meaningful look. 'His family matters a great deal to him – and it should matter to us too.'

William returned to the guest house, his mind churning with all the changes being thrown at him, not least the knowledge that he was about to lose his mother. Another life in England. What would it be like?

Elias had returned from tending the horses and was breaking his fast on a loaf of warm bread and a hunk of cheese. He was a personable dark-haired youth, the same age as his master. His mother had been William's wet nurse, and the boys had grown up together, although Elias's status meant that he would remain a man at arms and body servant, rather than rising to knighthood.

'I have saddled Jasper,' he said. 'I thought you would want to ride him.'

William gave him a grateful look. 'Yes,' he said. 'Thank you.'

Elias served William with the bread and cheese and poured him a cup of buttermilk. William took the food out to his palfrey and ate and drank while adjusting the tack. Jasper had been a gift from his mother before she entered Fontevraud, together with harness and equipment. The sorrel gelding was William's pride and joy. He was good-natured and responsive and also, for a palfrey, strong and tall. William could use him for light battle practice with his brothers and pretend Jasper was a warhorse.

Leaving his empty cup on a tree stump, he dusted crumbs from his hands and, setting his foot in the stirrup, swung into the saddle. He always thought better on horseback, or when in motion of any kind. He could be still if the occasion demanded, such as in a church or before his superiors at formal occasions, but that discipline had been hard-won.

For a while he absorbed himself in training with a pole the length and thickness of a lance but without an edge. He had begun learning to joust at fourteen and was becoming adept through daily practice. Turning the pole this way and that, manoeuvring, balancing, using his body to guide the horse. Everything smooth and controlled.

He wanted to prove his valour and manhood, but all the training in the world would not prepare him for the actual shock of a real tourney, and with every fibre of his being he wanted to engage with it and have it over and done – like losing his virginity, the memory of which still made him hot with embarrassment but had not dented his enthusiasm one whit. Once something had been accomplished for the first time, the second time became easier, and the third even better as anxiety diminished.

If they were called to England, then so be it. He would make his way at his half-brother's court and become an Englishman, and make his mother proud.

*

Two days later his mother died, having taken the veil in her last hours, and become a nun of Fontevraud. She was buried as she had stipulated outside the precincts of the church to atone for her sins. Deeply saddened, William did not understand her decision, for she was more sinned against than sinning. He had seen the effigies of Henry's grandparents and uncle, Queen Eleanor, King Henry II and King Richard, inside the abbey with all their richness, gilding and gold, and it seemed a terrible thing that his mother should not be graced with the same honour, even if she desired this burial outside the church. She had no more sins upon her than those lying in state before the choir.

His brother Guy put his hand on William's shoulder. 'It is an end and a beginning,' he said. 'I am sure our brother in England will soon summon us to his side.' Guy was preparing to take the cross and embark on a military pilgrimage to the Holy Land where their ancestor had once been King of Jerusalem. William knew Guy was hoping their royal half-brother would fund his travel expenses.

Geoffrey joined them. The sun slanting into his eyes gilded their warm brown with tawny lights. 'Let us hope so.'

William swallowed and looked at the mound of freshly turned soil covering the grave. A worm wriggled on the crumbly brown surface. This came to everyone. All the striving. All the hopes and fears and joys and sorrows, stoppered and silenced and turned to worms.

Aliza touched his arm. 'We have each other. Come, Mama said we should live our lives to honour her and we must do it. That is the best gilding she could ever have.'

9

Windsor Castle, Spring 1247

Joanna lifted the ring of keys at her belt and approached the Queen's jewel cupboard. She had been instructed to fetch Alienor's favourite ruby brooch. Joanna had more keys to sort among these days for at almost seventeen years old she was a fully fledged damsel of the household, entrusted with many duties and responsibilities. She had girls herself these days to train, and was expected to go about her business without close supervision.

Joanna unlocked the jewel cupboard and picked up a coffer fashioned of marvellous blue and gold enamel panels depicting a summer scene of a lord and lady flying their hawks. Joanna stroked the little box because she loved it so much. Inside were numerous brooches fashioned mostly in gold, but also a few silver ones set with precious gems or engraved with inscriptions. The lozenge-shaped ruby brooch was one of many gifts from the King at the time of the Queen's churching following the birth of their second son, Edmund, two years ago. Joanna carefully placed it on a small silk cushion, locked the coffer and returned to the Queen.

Alienor thanked her warmly and leaned forward so that Joanna could pin the ornament to her gown. 'You know the exact place.' She fondly patted Joanna's cheek, and Joanna smiled, feeling proud and valued.

With a little time before the dinner horn sounded, she took the opportunity to read the letter that had arrived from Aliza with a messenger from the Limousin that morning. Aliza said that she and her half-brothers were making their final preparations to come to England, and would arrive before midsummer, joining the court at Woodstock. Joanna's heart warmed at the thought of seeing her friend again and spending more time with her than the moments of a letter. As always, Aliza had included a gift with her note, this time some small enamelled robe decorations. Joanna touched the beautiful little embellishments and decided she would stitch them around the cuffs of her new blue court dress.

Everyone gathered in the Great Hall for the midday meal. At the lower end, a hundred poor people had assembled at several trestles to receive bread and pottage as charity from the King. Joanna often worked with Cecily, serving food to the people as a work of humility and Christian charity, but today she was helping the royal nursemaids and had custody of the lady Beatrice, a delightful little girl almost five years old, with brown-gold ringlets and huge blue eyes.

At the high table, Iohan was performing service duties, an embroidered dapifer's towel over one shoulder as he carried a bowl and a jug of rose water for the guests to wash and dry their hands between courses. The royal children sat apart from their parents at a table nearby, attended by servants and learning their manners, observed by but not interrupting the adults.

Joanna helped Beatrice with her food and while doing so cast her eye over the other children with a proprietorial eye. Edward, coming up to eight, was very conscious of his status as the golden prince and heir to the throne. He could be autocratic and demanding but Joanna still loved him unconditionally. He had enormous charm and would often give her a spontaneous hug and kiss. Last year at the consecration of Beaulieu Abbey he had been seriously ill with a fever but had eventually made a full recovery. Nevertheless, the scare he had given everyone had made him even more precious.

Beatrice wriggled back and forth on the bench, and when Joanna touched her arm to settle her down, Beatrice whispered to her and wriggled some more. Without fuss, Joanna took her hand and led her from the chamber to the nearest latrine. She helped her lift her skirts and sat her on the wooden seat over the hole. Beatrice swung her legs and hummed a little tune and then wrinkled her nose. 'It smells in here,' she said.

It would be surprising if it did not, Joanna thought, but Beatrice had her father's sensitivity about such matters – Henry was always complaining about the noisome privies.

Beatrice finished, and as she hopped off the seat, Joanna's brother barged past them, tearing down his braies in haste. Throwing himself down over the hole, he voided his bowels in a violent explosion. If the latrine smell had been noxious before, now it was overpowering. Iohan leaned forward and vomited a puddle at his feet.

Alarmed, Joanna hastily returned Beatrice to the hall, gave her into Roberga's care and, begging her excuses, sped back to her brother. He was still sitting on the seat, groaning.

'Iohan?'

He raised his head to look at her. He was red-faced, sweating and glassy-eyed.

'What have you eaten?' Joanna demanded.

'Nothing. I wasn't hungry this morning. I had a chicken pasty yester-eve from a pie seller.'

She cast her gaze heavenwards. Hungry young men often bought pasties and the like from the traders and opportunists who hung around the court, sometimes with disastrous consequences. 'Go to your pallet and I will come to you when I can,' she ordered him.

'I can't. I have to serve at table!'

'Not like this you cannot! I will make it right with the King.'

He started to rise off the hole but had to sit down again as another spasm tore through his bowels. The stench made Joanna retch.

'I will fetch a physician.'

She fled the latrine. Before returning to the hall she washed her hands and face to banish any miasma that might linger over her person. She sent word to the King of Iohan's illness and begged leave of the Queen to go and tend to him.

'Of course,' Alienor said, concerned. 'Go to your brother. You have my full leave and I will send you my physician.' She cast an anxious glance towards the children, for any malaise was a threat to their wellbeing.

Joanna raced back to Iohan who had collapsed on the latrine floor. She found two valets to pick him up and bear him to his bed and had them strip him to his undershirt. His soiled hose and braies she kicked aside for the laundry maid before fetching a bowl of lavender water and a cloth.

Iohan groaned and clutched his stomach. His skin burned like a furnace under her hand, but his teeth were chattering. She wrung out the cloth and set it upon his brow. He looked at her fearfully.

'You will be all right,' she soothed. 'See, here is the physician now. This will teach you to eat pasties from the door, no matter how hungry you are.'

The physician, Master Peter, was a small, bright-eyed man with quick movements that still managed to be unhurried. He examined Iohan carefully and got him to piss into a glass vessel. Then he swilled the dark yellow urine around in the light and compressed his lips. 'Your sister is right,' he said, giving Iohan a stern look. 'No more chicken pasties, young man.' He prescribed boiled water to be drunk from a silver cup.

Iohan drank the first dose once a cup had been found, but soon after, vomited it back up. Joanna made him some more, this time ensuring he took small sips, and it stayed down. Following which, he fell into a restless, febrile slumber.

'I will come back later,' she said, and smoothed his damp hair with a tender hand.

He nodded faintly without opening his eyes.

When Joanna returned to the ladies' chamber Cecily came to her straight away. 'How is Iohan?' she asked. 'We have all heard he is unwell.'

'Sick,' Joanna replied numbly. 'Burning and shivering with fever and voiding his belly and bowels. Probably a bad chicken pie. He was well yesterday – he pulled my braid and teased me because I was in a hurry and he wouldn't let me pass, and I called him a nuisance. I shouldn't have.'

'Do not start laying that upon yourself, my girl,' Cecily said. 'I have taught you better than that.'

Chastened, Joanna bit her lip, and Cecily hugged her.

'You should keep him cool and quench his thirst,' said Sybil Giffard. 'Young men of that age often have too much choler in their humours. I will come and see him myself if it will help.'

'Thank you,' Joanna said with heartfelt gratitude. 'I would be glad of your opinion.'

When the women arrived at Iohan's bedside, he had woken from sleep but had been sick again and his fever was raging. Cecily and Sybil exchanged glances and Joanna's heart clenched with terror.

'I fear that he is very unwell, poor boy,' Sybil said. 'But we must do what we can to make him comfortable. And pray for him. Prayer is always of great value.'

Joanna sat with Iohan for the rest of the day and throughout the night. At first he continued to purge and sweat, but then the sweating stopped and his mouth became very dry. He lost the power of speech, and she cradled him in her arms and prayed desperately to God to spare his life, knowing that while God was always listening, sometimes it was not part of His plan to fulfil the desperate need of the supplicant.

She stroked her brother's lank hair and listened to his harsh breathing. 'Don't leave me,' she whispered, 'please, please don't leave.'

'How is he?'

Turning, she met the worried gaze of her cousin John de Warenne, Iohan's close friend at court. She shook her head at him and swallowed.

John crouched at the bedside and took Iohan's hand in his. 'Cousin, come back to us,' he said. 'Who will go out riding with me or challenge me at wrestling if you are not here? You must not leave.'

Iohan gave a deep, shuddering sigh. 'Too far,' he whispered through cracked lips.

Joanna told him about the pie, and John grimaced. 'I was going to buy one myself,' he said, 'but changed my mind. I wish I had stopped him too . . .' He lifted his gaze to Joanna, and they looked at each other for a long moment.

Abruptly he broke the contact and fled the chamber at a

near-run, leaving Joanna startled and a little hurt that he would desert in a moment of such extremity. Perhaps he could not deal with sick-beds. Some people, even grown men, could be squeamish.

However, a short while later he returned with Brother Adam, a friar who was a familiar visitor to the royal household and a confidant of both the King and Queen. Brother Adam stooped over Iohan, putting his palm to his brow, and spoke comforting words, and then he nodded at John who took Joanna's hand.

'He must be shriven,' John said. 'We should leave the good friar to hear his confession.'

'He is not going to die,' Joanna said, trembling. 'He can't. I won't let him.'

'No, of course, this is just for comfort.' John's expression was very different from his words. 'When Brother Adam is finished, we shall sit with Iohan and keep vigil.'

He drew her from the chamber and gently sat her down on a bench outside, and then fetched a cup of wine, which they shared in silence, for there were no words.

In the deepest part of the night, Iohan exhaled his last breath in Joanna's arms without regaining awareness of where he was, although she had heard him whisper 'Mama' a few minutes earlier. Joanna's own breath caught when she realised that his chest had ceased to move. 'Iohan, wake up!' She kissed his brow and patted his cheek.

Brother Adam gently touched her shoulder. 'Come, child, his soul is in the hands of God. It is over for him now.'

'But he can't be dead, he can't!' Panicking, she surged to her feet. 'He's my brother! He cannot die!'

John said softly, 'Joanna, he has gone. God has made his will known. Come . . .'

She let out a wail of grief and John pulled her into his arms and held her close. She started to fight him off, and then reversed her action and, gripping the soft wool of his tunic, pressed her face against his chest. It couldn't be true; she would not allow it. She didn't want to think about being alone in the world with yet another tree in the forest cut down.

John brought her to Cecily who gently took over and led Joanna to her chamber and sat her before the hearth while she prepared a hot tisane sweetened with honey.

'Why him?' Joanna demanded, lifting desolate eyes to Cecily. 'Why not me? I would have given my life for his.'

'I know you would.' Cecily came to embrace her. 'But that is not what God intended for you. For now, you remain among the living and you must reconcile yourself with His will. It is never easy, but you are strong, and you have a duty to your brother and to your kin both living and dead to go forward and make the most of your life. It is right that you mourn, but do not drown yourself in grief, for that is a sin.'

Joanna barely heard what Cecily was saying, because she was already under water.

Joanna picked away with dainty stitches at the altar cloth she was embroidering in Iohan's honour. She had been working on the piece for several weeks before his death, but had changed its purpose, and as she stitched she added her thoughts and memories to the piece. The King and Queen had been very kind and solicitous following Iohan's death and had wept with her, but there had been some constraint. At a stroke, Joanna had become the King's ward and a young woman of substantial means with an inheritance that included vast swathes of land throughout England, Ireland and Wales. Suddenly she had villages, mills and castles to her name, as rich as they were diverse. Courtiers who had barely glanced at her before now deferred to her. She had a higher place at the dining trestle and finer clothes, and dealing with the situation sometimes left her overwhelmed.

She pressed her lips together, and a tear blot fell on to the linen. Cecily, observant as always, swiftly came to her side and set a tender arm around her shoulders. 'What is it, my dear?'

Joanna shook her head. 'Iohan should not have died,' she said miserably. 'I saw it in my father's eyes when he stood at the graveside. He wished me dead in his stead. It is all my fault.'

Cecily gave her a swift shake. 'None of this talk! God decided that you should be female and it is an honoured position, not a lesser one. Straighten your spine and face the future head on. I will hear no more of this foolish nonsense! God has chosen you for this position just as He has chosen to take your brother to his bosom. You must stand in your brother's stead and do as he would have done.'

Chastened, Joanna nodded and wiped her eyes on her sleeve.

'You may not be a warrior with sword and shield, but you have your wits,' Cecily continued. 'I hope I have taught you well and your time at court has not been wasted. You can do many useful things with what has fallen to you – indeed it is a great opportunity. Few are given such privilege and you can do much good. Raise yourself to be worthy in God's eyes. Do you understand me?'

Joanna struggled to meet Cecily's gaze, which blazed with fierce passion, but she tried. 'Yes, madam.' She raised her chin to show that she had rallied.

'I am glad to hear it. Your future is yet to be written, and if you are the clever young woman I know you to be, you shall have a part in the writing.'

Cecily's homily ceased as Edward arrived holding a writhing cloth bag by its drawstrings.

'I don't want you to be sad,' he said to Joanna, mischief dancing in his blue eyes, 'so I have brought you a gift.'

Cecily regarded him with a raised brow while Joanna was wary. 'That is most kind of you, sire.' She eyed the bag askance, wondering what he was up to this time.

Smiling like a cherub, he unfastened the drawstrings and tipped out a spitting golden tabby kitten with four white mittens. 'The groom was going to drown it,' he said. 'There have been too many born this spring already.'

Joanna stared at the little creature, now backed up against the embrasure wall, furiously lashing its fuzzy ginger tail. Its eyes were still blue, but it was not a new-born for its ears were unfurled and it was up on its toes. Her heart melted at the sight of the little creature which was very sweet even in the midst of its ire. Edward did not possess the tender sensibilities of his father; she knew he would quite happily assist the groom to be rid of surplus cats and see it as a practical and even interesting thing to do. Therefore, this was a genuine gift born of thought-fulness, and if she refused the kitten, it would probably suffer the same fate as its siblings. Sausagez had died of old age in the winter and her heart was vulnerable and in sore need of comfort.

'It is indeed a kind thought, my lord,' she said, feeling tearful all over again. 'I shall make him a collar and give him a name.'

Edward beamed with pleasure. 'He's called Weazel.'

Joanna lifted her brows at the name, which was a term for a foolish fellow, although it might also refer to the swift, supple little carnivores that preyed on rats and mice, the same as cats. 'Why do you call him that?'

Edward shrugged. 'Because the groom said he must be a "weazel" himself for letting me have him.'

Joanna cautiously reached to the kitten which had calmed

from its original high dudgeon and was busy grooming its ruffled fur. 'Weazel.' She tested the name. It curtailed its ablutions and rubbed its head on her hand, a rumble vibrating from somewhere deep in its chest.

'He likes you,' Edward said. 'I hope you like him because I will then have saved his life and made yours better.'

Joanna smiled at him. 'Bless you, sire, for your kindness,' she said, wondering what she was going to do with her sudden new responsibility.

Edward beamed at her and ran off to play with Henry of Almain, his good deed done and the kitten safely bestowed.

Weazel climbed into Joanna's lap and continued to groom himself, stroking his rough pink tongue down his shoulders. Joanna looked helplessly at Cecily whose eyes were brimming with amusement. 'I have no sage words for you on this,' she said, 'but you acted wisely in accepting the lord Edward's gift. Things always happen for a reason.'

Joanna shook her head. 'It will pounce on my needlework silks and run up the wall hangings.' She tickled it under the chin.

'It will catch mice and rats,' Cecily said equably, 'and it will take care of itself once it is grown. You only need to be its mother for a little while.'

The kitten curled up in a ball on Joanna's knee and closed its eyes, still purring, and as it did so it took a little piece of her heart.

Standing on the deck of the ship, William watched the port of Royan become a collection of miniature buildings as the gap between the land and sea turned from a narrow blue hem to a wide border, and then to a rippling blue cloth. He had splashed and sailed in the waters of the Tarn and the Garonne all his life, but he had never been to sea, and the swelling tide under the hull seemed like the muscles of a great creature, filling him with exhilaration and fear. He licked his lips, tasting salt, and listened to the scream of the gulls harnessing the wind.

His brother Aymer joined him at the prow and clapped his shoulder. 'Well,' he said, 'it is done. I shall become a bishop and you will be a knight.' Aymer's eye corners crinkled as he smiled. Quick and intelligent, he had a love of secular things, but possessed a spiritual side too. He had yet to be ordained.

Eager to have the qualification of manhood that being knighted would convey, William returned the smile. His mind filled with images of fast horses and glittering armour, of knighthood and of proving himself among men.

'Of course, some factions at our brother's court won't be overjoyed,' Aymer said. 'Henry has not invited us purely from the goodness of his heart, generous though he might be.'

The ship plunged into a trough and spray tossed over the strakes, making the brothers recoil. Aymer laughed. 'Kissed by a mermaid,' he said. 'That has to be good fortune surely! He wants his family around him. His queen has promoted her uncles and protégés and Henry needs us to balance the scales. Just bear in mind that what he gives to us will be diverted from the hands of others, who will resent us.'

William frowned, for he had not given that aspect much consideration.

Aymer shrugged. 'I am warning you in advance. No man goes into battle without his armour. Find your friends and cherish them, and be wary of your rivals. Others will be pressing the King for favour against our advantage, but if we stay loyal through thick and thin, he will protect us in our turn.'

'Aymer, stop lecturing the lad and let him be.' Guy, the oldest of the brothers, invited to England, joined them. His light-brown hair, in direct contrast to William's, flopped forward over his forehead. A pilgrim's cross was prominently stitched to his cloak symbolising the vow he had taken to campaign in the Holy Land – the expedition he was hoping their royal half-brother would help to fund. 'Let us hope that charm of his will snare both our royal brother and a rich heiress.' He too clapped William's shoulder. 'Geoffrey and I are counting on you and Aymer to keep everyone afloat – the Churchman and the courtier.' He ducked as another surge of spray hissed over the strakes.

William cuffed his wet face. The expectations being heaped upon him were daunting. He glanced over at Geoffrey who was puking into a bucket and not weathering the crossing well – strange for someone so bold and sure on dry land. He too was seeking money from their royal brother – to further his interests in the Limousin, rather than settling permanently in England.

They were all on edge and reacting in their different ways. Aymer was concealing his worry by talking too much, Guy by lecturing the lecturer. Geoffrey would have been pacing the deck like a caged lion if he wasn't so sick – and probably picking a fight. And William was stuck in his thoughts as they turned and turned like a wheel of fortune, buoyed and anxious, high and low and high again as they embarked on the biggest gamble of their lives.

Leaving his brothers, he joined Aliza where she sat on a bench protected from the wind and spray by a canvas awning. She was nibbling on candied ginger to calm her stomach, and appeared quieter than usual.

'Are you well?' he enquired.

She offered him a piece of the ginger, which he took because he liked it rather than to stave off mal de mer. 'A little queasy,' she said, 'but not about to join Geoffrey's endeavours.' She sent him a sidelong glance. 'England will be a different world – a different life.'

'Yes.'

'When we return – if we do – even if the land remains the same, we will be changed.'

William did not always understand his sister; her thoughts were sometimes convoluted and deep. 'Do you not wish to go then? You know we will all look after you and protect you.'

'I know you will.' She sighed pensively. 'After Mama died, I considered taking vows and joining her at Fontevraud. There is such order and certainty in convent life.'

William eyed her askance. 'I'm not sure how good you would be at obeying orders. You have the will, but I doubt you have the patience to wear a habit.'

She pinched him, making him yelp.

'You see! Would a nun do such a thing?'

'Of course she would, if being tested by a devil!' she replied, laughing, but then folded her arms across her waist in a gesture of self-comfort. 'I might pinch you and you might tease me, but I can trust you and the others with my life. But in England, the King becomes our guardian and our sponsor. I do not know him, nor what lies in store – other than marriage, and that is a far greater risk than taking vows and becoming a bride of Christ.'

'That is true, but it is also a great opportunity. Think of all the suitors you will have!'

'And what a pot of mixed luck that might prove to be!'

'Do you not wish to go?'

She screwed up her face. 'I did not say that. I am very aware of the honour and opportunities being extended to us. I am looking forward to sharing company with Joanna again. It is just that nothing will ever be the same.'

'It is not that far,' he said, trying to cajole her out of her strange, fey mood. 'Who knows, we may return with our fortunes made – and perhaps with some little Lusignans to swell the family.' He waggled his eyebrows suggestively.

Aliza pushed him. 'Oh you!' she said crossly, although her eyes sparkled with exasperated humour. 'It is all a game to you isn't it, Will? A vast, shiny tournament, and you the untarnished knight.'

'I know life is not like that.' On his dignity, he withdrew a little. 'But there is nothing wrong in striving, is there?'

She puffed out her breath, but then her expression softened. 'No,' she said, and touched his hair gently. 'No, there is not. I shall embrace England with open arms, but you and your brothers had better behave.'

'Of course we will! Why would you expect anything else?'

'Why indeed?' She cast her gaze heavenwards.

10

Royal Palace of Woodstock, May 1247

The ladies of the court had taken their needlework into the palace gardens to enjoy the glorious late May weather. Joanna was appreciating the soft spring day, with the sun warm on her shoulders and the daylight so beneficial for sewing. The altar cloth was nearing completion.

'Your stitches are always so neat,' the Queen praised. 'I used to watch you work when you were a child and was amazed at your skill for one so young.'

Joanna flushed with pleasure and tried not to feel too proud.

'How are you faring these days?' Alienor asked gently.

'I am well, madam,' Joanna said without looking up.

Her heart ached when she thought of Iohan. The sap had risen, the trees were in leaf, the animals all had young at heel, while he rotted in his grave. One of the Queen's musicians was singing a song of merry springtime in the background and she had to stop sewing because her eyes had blurred with grief. Alienor sympathetically touched her arm.

The younger royal children, Margaret, Beatrice and Edmund, were playing around their nurses' feet, but Edward had drifted away and was intently occupied over a flower bed in the corner of the garden.

'Go and see what my son is doing, and bring him to me,' Alienor said to distract her. 'I fear he is up to mischief of some sort – as always.' Her sigh was exasperated but indulgent.

Joanna left her sewing and went to Edward, wiping her eyes on the side of her hand, annoyed at her sudden stab of emotion. The gardeners had been busy gridding out seedlings in heraldic patterns in the soil beds and there were delineated squares marked out with small sticks. Edward was using one of the sticks to flick the others away and the little plants had been flattened, uprooted and scattered.

'Sire, what have you done!' Joanna was aghast. 'Now there will be no flowers to enjoy later in the year.'

He slanted her a look from vivid blue eyes. 'I am confusing the enemy, and I have won the battle!'

'But these are not the enemy,' Joanna remonstrated. 'These are seedlings trying to grow.'

He deliberately flurried his hand over the bed, further disturbing the soil. 'There! I'm the winner!'

'Your mother wants you.' Edward could be a tyrant at times, and as his eighth birthday approached he was becoming increasingly difficult despite his undeniable charm. She reached for him and he backed away.

'I'm too big to sit with women and little children,' he said mutinously, and stamped off towards the garden gate.

Joanna chased after him and caught him as he lifted the latch. 'You cannot go out there.' She tried to take his hand.

'I can go where I want!' Edward shoved her off. 'I'm the King's son!'

'All the more reason to behave as a king should,' Joanna retorted as he struggled.

Cecily had noticed the altercation and arrived to help. 'Come now, sire,' she said firmly, 'you should not be so vexatious. You would not want to be bled for an excess of choler. A king must learn control of himself so that he may control others.'

Edward gave her a narrow look, his eyes vivid blue in his scarlet face, but he ceased to fight.

A fanfare of trumpets blared from beyond the garden gate, heralding the arrival of a bright array of nobles and attendants, with hawks and dogs and baggage-laden sumpter horses. Joanna recognised Aliza de Lusignan with a flash of pleasure, and then her brothers, no longer youths but grown men. One sported a pilgrim's cross on his cloak, another was clad in clerical robes, and a striking young man wearing a shallow-brimmed hat fluttering with peacock feathers rode at his side, whom she thought from memory must be William.

'Your father's kin have arrived,' Joanna said.

Edward's flush had receded and he studied the newcomers with interest.

'Come, we must tell your mother and wash off all this soil.'

She took his hand, and Edward capitulated now because here was something new and interesting, and the only way through to it was by being agreeable.

On receiving the news, Alienor gathered her ladies together. 'I had not realised they would be here so soon!' Although she smiled, irritation marked her brows. 'Ah well, let the King greet them while we make ready – especially you, young man.' She pinched Edward's cheek. 'I shall know who to blame when there are no flowers in my garden.'

'But I will protect you, Mama,' Edward said practically. 'Flowers can't do that.'

She laughed and shook her head. 'Your father named you after a peaceful king who did not know what a sword looked like, but you cannot thwart God's will.'

She had a swift word with the gardener, giving him instructions concerning the ruined flower bed, and a small purse of coins to rectify the damage and mollify the upset.

Grumbling, Edward was scrubbed and made to put on a clean tunic. The Queen changed into a sumptuous gown of gold silk and called for her jewels, selecting several ruby rings, an ornate gold brooch and her favourite embroidered belt. Once Alienor was satisfied, her household made its way to the great hall and were announced by another fanfare of trumpets. The King hastened to greet his wife and escort her to her chair on the dais. Joanna moved quietly to one side with the other ladies, her hands modestly clasped before her. But she raised her eyes to look across at the group waiting to be presented to Alienor and briefly caught Aliza's glance, and exchanged a smile.

Guy and Geoffrey, the two oldest Lusignan brothers, were first to kneel before the Queen – strong, wide-shouldered men in their twenties, with the swagger of warriors. Then Aymer, the priest in training, who had softer features but quick, intelligent eyes that took everything in. Henry had a bishopric in mind for him, and Joanna had heard mutterings about the King's half-brother being far too young, and not the right choice for a role that demanded a serious, scholarly approach. The youngest brother, William, now stood on the cusp of manhood. His hair was still the mass of burnished tight curls she remembered and his eyes, with the light in them, were the grey-gold of field flints. He had high cheekbones that set his eyes at a slight slant, a chiselled, sharp nose and a wide smile. He had carefully folded his feathered hat through his belt and now he knelt to Alienor.

She extended her hand. 'The King has spoken often of having

you come to dwell with us and I am glad to welcome you to court,' she said.

'I am pleased to be so warmly greeted, madam,' he replied in a voice light with youth, but holding the promise of richness, and bowed over her hand. Then he stood straight and turned, arm extended to Aliza, and brought her forward to curtsey to the Queen, who gave her a kiss on either cheek, greeted her as a sister, and indicated that she should sit on a stool at the side of her chair. Before doing so, Aliza presented Alienor with sweetmeats, contained in an exquisite enamelled box worked in the jewel-colours for which the Limousin was so famous.

Alienor's face brightened with pleasure. 'How thoughtful of you, and how beautiful.' She handed the box to Joanna for safe keeping, and then introduced Edward to his aunts and uncles whom he was eyeing with critical interest.

'My liege lord.' William bowed deeply, a twinkle in his eyes. 'I am looking forward to being of service. We have a gift for you also.' He presented the boy with a decorated red leather belt from which hung a small ivory-hilted knife.

Smiling with delight, Edward took the belt and drew the knife from its patterned sheath to examine the strong little blade, and thanked his uncle with enthusiasm.

'You have found the way to my son's heart,' Henry said with amusement. 'He is a proper little knight.'

'I've started my training.' Edward jutted his chin.

'Then I hope to ride at your side in the fullness of time, sire,' William said gravely.

Edward stepped back but insisted on wearing the belt rather than handing it to an attendant. He gripped the knife sheath possessively.

The formal greetings completed, attendants served wine to the gathering, and the Queen sent Joanna to put the little enamelled casket away in her chamber. Joanna loved the decoration of tiny jewel-coloured cloisonné flowers, and the confectionery within gave off a wonderful scent of rose and spices. She unlocked the Queen's jewel coffer and placed the little box within, thinking that the gift was very clever, and suspecting it had been Aliza's idea. She was so glad she had come to court with her brothers.

Returning to the hall, she went straight to Aliza who was talking to Cecily and Sybil Giffard. Aliza's eyes lit up as she saw Joanna, and she immediately embraced her with open arms. 'I am so pleased to see you again!'

'And I you. I hope you fared well on your journey.'

Aliza's hair smelled of nutmeg and roses and her gown of exquisite deep-pink silk had put a flush in her cheeks. Several of the younger male courtiers were eyeing her covertly.

Aliza laughed. 'I was not so keen on the sea voyage, but at least I wasn't like Geoffrey – he was sick all the way over. I am so grateful to the King and Queen for inviting us to court. I hope you will show me what to do.'

'Yes, of course,' Joanna said, delighted to have Aliza for company – perhaps even a little overwhelmed.

Leaving Cecily and Sybil, the young women drew aside to an embrasure to talk.

'I was so sorry to receive your letter about Iohan,' Aliza said, touching Joanna's hand. 'When I think of losing one of my brothers, I know it would be terrible, but knowing is not the same as having the pain in your heart.'

'No,' Joanna said, swallowing. 'I do grieve for him deeply. He had his life before him – and now he does not.' She looked down for a moment, collecting herself, then raised her head to Aliza's concerned, sympathetic gaze and managed a tremulous smile. 'And now everything has changed in ways from which there is no return – indeed, for both of us, since you have come such a long way to the court.'

'I did consider taking the veil,' Aliza said. 'Perhaps at Fontevraud like my mother.'

Joanna eyed her in surprise. 'I cannot imagine you wearing the garb of a nun unless it be that of an abbess when you are old,' she said.

Aliza gave a wry laugh. 'That is almost exactly what William said to me. Bride of Christ or bride of man, I decided I could best serve my family by taking the second path – indeed that is why I am here.' She smiled brightly at Joanna, concealing her anxiety. 'I hope our half-brother chooses my new husband well.'

'The King is always kind and well meaning,' Joanna reassured her. 'He has been anticipating your arrival for his own delight above all, and that is the truth.'

'I think I shall become very fond of him,' Aliza said, 'but I know there are plans afoot.' She looked across the room. 'William seems to have made a friend already.'

Joanna followed Aliza's gaze to the two young men conversing over their wine. 'That is my cousin John de Warenne, future Earl of Surrey – you met him in passing in Gascony.'

'Yes, I remember.' Aliza's gaze was thoughtful. 'William needs to make friends in England. It is difficult when you are an outsider, but with God's help and by our own efforts we shall succeed.'

Next morning, emerging from her sleeping chamber, Aliza met William making his way purposefully towards the courtyard, wearing leather riding hose, a pair of gloves tucked through his belt.

'Where are you off to so early?' she asked, smiling.

'John de Warenne has invited me to go riding and has offered to lend me a horse while mine recover from the journey,' he replied, eyes bright with enthusiasm.

'I am glad you are making friends so swiftly.'

He shrugged. 'We seem to have plenty in common. How are you faring?'

'Well enough. Everyone has been kind, especially Joanna de Munchensy. I slept well with the Queen's ladies last night, but I know we are a little on trial.'

He gave her one of his disarming grins. 'Is that a way of warning me to be on my best behaviour?'

'What do you think?'

'I always am, you know that.' He winked at her, and strolled off, whistling.

Aliza rolled her eyes but smiled after him. She loved her youngest brother with a pang that hurt, and part of it was fear for their future. They stood as newcomers in a highly competitive arena and were as likely to be savaged as welcomed, except by Henry. They had to be so careful, and she worried for her brothers, especially William. Loyal and brave he might be, but he was also impetuous and inexperienced. The King had called him 'my boy' and William, for his own sake, needed to become a man, and swiftly.

Arriving at the stables, William found John de Warenne already waiting and petting a courser with charcoal dappling on its rump and shoulders.

'What a beauty,' William said admiringly.

John flashed him a smile. 'This is Neddy,' he said.

William raised his brows. 'Neddy?'

John's grin became sardonic. 'Usually men give their horses the most glorious and warlike names, but I chose to be different.'

William flushed, for the first would have been his instinct. He thought it a little demeaning to give such a fine horse a common name; however, he held his peace.

'He's from a line bred from a Spanish mare given to my mother's grandsire by Empress Matilda. They're always greys. I have had him since he was foaled. By the time he is ten he will be almost white.'

William examined the horse, patting its neck, running his hands down its shoulders and checking its legs. He was aware of John de Warenne assessing him closely too. They had formed a rapport last night in the hall but it was still fragile. Aliza thought him naive, but he was not entirely wet behind the ears. He gave people the benefit of the doubt, but he could stand up for himself if they proved to be false. He suspected that John's overtures were coming from a direction of self-interest at the moment. The King had signalled his intention of lavishing his new kin with favour, so it behoved the future Earl of Surrey to extend a friendly hand. Whatever the motive, however, William instinctively liked John de Warenne and was prepared to see where events took them.

John gave him the bridle. 'Here, see what you think of him.'

'You are not riding him yourself?' William asked, surprised.

John smiled and shook his head. 'I can ride Ned any time, and you are the guest. I have a good second horse.' He signalled to the groom who brought forward a glossy liver-chestnut with a wide stripe from brow to muzzle. 'This is Blaze.' John slapped the horse's neck.

William tried not to look too impressed, although both animals were magnificent, and he and John de Warenne were of a similar age. Clearly his companion shared his enthusiasm and had the resources to indulge his passion.

'England is a fine land for horse flesh,' John said. 'The grazing is good and there are no difficult extremes of weather.'

William took the reins and swung across the grey's back. Neddy stood still, ears flickering. He rubbed his neck and told him how fine he was.

'I will keep you company the best that I can, but I may not be able to stay with you,' John mounted and gathered the reins. 'Neddy knows the Woodstock circuit well and will take you of his own accord. Let him have his head and he'll bring you safely back.'

The grey tossed his head as if in agreement and pawed the ground, eager to be off.

William noted John's amused, slightly superior expression, and his mettle rose to the challenge, although he reminded himself that he was a guest on a borrowed animal and needed to exert courtesy.

They trotted through the open gate into the park, the morning mist shredding away before them. The grey moved smoothly and William appreciated the coordination and power of his muscles and the instant response to his guidance. He urged him to a gentle trot and used leg commands to weave him one way and then the other, to prance and sidestep.

They arrived at an open grassy area, and William gave the courser his head. The grey struck out in a ground-devouring gallop that remained as fluid as water even as the speed increased until William felt as though he was flying. He could hear the chestnut thundering up behind, but Neddy stretched further and kept ahead by several lengths. As the field ran out and they approached a hazel coppice, William reined him down and turned him side on, so exhilarated he wanted to whoop aloud.

'What a magnificent horse!' he declared as John pulled up beside him.

John's eyes were bright with pleasure, but his face wore an expression of respectful reassessment. He had not expected the King's half-brother to be so good – a natural horseman, unlike the King, who was average at best. 'You ride very well yourself.'

William flushed at the compliment. 'We were all put on horses the moment we were out of swaddling,' he said, 'but I suppose you were too.'

John inclined his head. 'While still in the womb,' he responded with sardonic humour.

For a while the young men rode companionably side by side, deepening their acquaintance, regaling each other with tales of their backgrounds, William's in the Limousin and John's in Norfolk and Surrey.

'I suppose you will live in the royal household most of the time,' John said as they rode through the coppice, winding through the lopped trees and following the meander of a stream. 'Even if the King finds you lands, he will want your presence and support.'

'I suppose so,' William answered.

'The King will be glad to have his family around him. The Queen has hers – her uncles and sister. I think the King feels threadbare of supporters at times.'

William detected a slight edge in John's tone. 'Is the Queen not his ally?'

'Of course she is, but her relatives are only the King's kin through marriage, not blood. You are a link to his past through your mother. You preserve that bond for him now that she has gone to God,' John said shrewdly. 'You stand in her stead.'

'Yes, if you put it in those terms,' William replied. 'He has invited us to court, and to make our homes in England, but we have no means of support lest it be from his hand and none of us knows yet what he will provide. He has not said.'

'No, but it will be a bargain that benefits both sides,' John said with cynicism beyond his years. 'The King will give you a wealthy marriage to provide you with funds.'

William smiled at John. 'Anyone you can recommend?'

'I would not presume to pre-empt the King,' John answered neutrally. 'I am sure whoever he chooses will suit you well.'

'But you must have some notion.'

John shook his head, refusing to be drawn, for which William respected him. The thought of wedding an unknown heiress constricted his chest and he had to gallop Neddy again to work off his tension.

People were assembling to dine in the Queen's chambers and savoury aromas wafted as valets hurried to and from the kitchens bearing bread and dishes of meat and sauces, pottage, rabbits and salmon. Joanna had been coaxing a tired and fractious Edmund. His nurse had a heavy cold and Joanna and Cecily had been caring for him for the day.

Crossing the room, William de Valence diverted to pull out the bench for her and Cecily to sit down at the trestle. 'Ladies,' he said with a bow and a smile. 'Who is this little one?'

'The lord Edmund,' Joanna replied, 'the King's youngest son. His nurse is unwell and I am caring for him today.'

'So, this is my youngest nephew?' William stroked Edmund's cheek. 'I can see my lady mother in him for sure, and he has our family chin.'

'I am sure he will be very well pleased if that is the case,' Joanna replied politely.

He bowed and moved on.

'An interesting young man,' Cecily said. It was not entirely a compliment.

'Why do you say that?' Joanna fussed with Edmund to settle her tension.

'He is the King's brother, and handsome to be sure. His smile is fine coinage and he has a way with courtesy and the easy remark.'

'You do not like him?' Joanna looked at the King's table, where William had engaged Henry in conversation. Both men were smiling.

Cecily shook her head. 'I do not know him, but what lies on the surface is not always the same as what you will find beneath, as you should know by now if you have listened to anything I have taught you. I reserve my judgement. He is barely out of boyhood. Girls are always swifter to mature. Which reminds me, did that official from the chancery speak to you today about the division of your uncle's lands among the heirs?'

Joanna nodded. 'Yes, the documents are with the treasury, and he is speaking with my lawyers later.' She made a face. 'Settling an inheritance seems to me like untangling a huge knot of embroidery threads where more keeps being added and pulled tighter. And I have to write to the steward at Goodrich about the wool clip and decide with his advice how much to keep and how much to sell.'

'You have learned from your lessons in estate management,' Cecily said equably. 'Now is the time to put it all into practice.'

'Yes.' Although apprehensive, Joanna felt a frisson of excitement at making decisions about her land and her property. It was a reaching out, an awakening of power.

Following the meal there was dancing. Joanna watched and cuddled a sleepy Edmund in her lap. All of the Lusignan brothers were fine dancers, even Aymer the bishop in training. William in particular had the grace of a cat. Aliza shone like a jewel, catching many a young man's eye.

'Go and join them,' Sybil Giffard said, taking Edmund from Joanna. 'We will look after him.'

111

Almost reluctantly, Joanna handed Edmund to Sybil, for his warm weight was a security, keeping her safe on the river bank rather than joining the flow. As she started to rise, a laughing Aliza darted over, grasped her hand and tugged her to the floor where a new carol-dance was about to start. 'You should dance every opportunity you have,' Aliza cried. 'You can sit in the shadows when you are an old woman and your legs will no longer do your bidding!'

'I thought you were considering becoming a nun,' Joanna said with amusement.

'Do you not think that nuns dance too?' Aliza tossed her head and pulled Joanna into the circle.

Once she became involved in the movements, creating chains and patterns, heel and toe and heel and turn, Joanna began enjoying herself. She danced round the King who smiled at her, and then the Queen, who was laughing like a girl. Next came her cousin John, followed by Aliza, and then William de Valence. They bowed and wove forward and back, with a fleeting moment of eye contact, a half smile and a swift hand-clasp before moving on. No words were spoken, but Joanna experienced a brief frisson as their fingers touched.

When the dancing finished, William and John retired to a table to play a game of chequers. Edward joined them, leaning on William's shoulder to watch the moves. William said something and affectionately tousled Edward's thick blond hair. Joanna observed from her bench across the room with the women and thought that the presence of the de Lusignans had certainly enlivened and refreshed the court.

Next day the entire court went out riding in the park, taking hawks and hounds. William still lacked a horse, but Henry gave him a fine black palfrey with a white star from the royal stables.

'I know you want to choose your own horses,' he said, benevolently, 'but Nuit here will tide you over for now and you may keep him or sell him on as you choose.'

'Thank you, sire,' William said, delighted by his good fortune. 'I am honoured by your generosity.'

'You are my brother,' Henry replied. 'Your presence alone does me more good than you can know – you mend my family and my heart.'

William was unsure how to respond as he caught a suspicion of tears in Henry's eyes. 'Sire, we are all grateful to be here,' he said awkwardly. 'We never thought to receive the welcome you have bestowed.'

Henry waved his hand in negation. 'Our mother would have wanted us to be close, and by taking care of you, I respect her memory. I could not do it without you.'

Edward trotted up on his pony. William noted that he rode remarkably well for his age. Henry was competent but lacked the enthusiasm of a born horseman. He clearly took great joy in the pleasure of others, but for him, this outing was of minor interest. Edward, however, showed off, galloping his mount in little surges of speed and watching William with alert eyes. Acknowledging the clue, William gave Edward a short race, allowing the boy to lead and encouraging him, holding his palfrey back to let Edward in front – 'Go on, go on!' – and then suddenly spurting out ahead of him, before slowing down, and finally manoeuvring the black back into place so that Edward now rode next to his father.

Henry looked quizzically at William.

'I know what it is to be the youngest in a group and how a child can be overlooked by the adults, sire.'

Henry snorted, but regarded William with affection. 'Edward will never be overlooked, and from now on, neither will you, but you are perceptive, and I am glad to see you already have a rapport with my boy.'

'He is a fine young knight,' William replied, experiencing a surge of anticipation at Henry's words.

Edward puffed out his chest at the description. He was a little beside himself to have been winning, at least for a time, against his wonderful new uncle. 'Are you good at tourneying?' he asked William eagerly.

'I train when I can, sire,' William answered.

'Are you going to train here, in England?'

'In a while, when I have a horse – and it is for the King to say.' He darted a glance to his royal half-brother whose lips had tightened at the mention of the word 'tourney'.

'We shall see,' Henry replied in the tone of a parent kicking a request into the long grass. 'There is much to accomplish first. I have plans in hand, my boy, never you fear.'

On returning from the ride in Woodstock Park, Henry sought solitude in his private chapel. Communing with God in beautiful surroundings always soothed his heart and soul. He had enjoyed the delight others derived from the exercise and it pleased him to please them, but he had little enthusiasm for it himself. His own pursuit was of beauty, of creating jewelled settings and perfect moments with everything smooth, orderly, and as rich as silk. All life should be expressed with beautiful dignity, especially the worship of God.

To him, reaching out to his half-siblings from the Limousin was like bringing fragments of his mother back into the family. Once trained, Aymer would enter the Church and become a bishop. Alienor's uncle Boniface was Archbishop of Canterbury so she could hardly complain if he raised Aymer's status. Guy would have money and resources for his crusade. Geoffrey would liaise between England and the Limousin, and Henry would give him money to support his endeavours. For Aliza he was considering a marriage that would suit both parties well, although he had yet to make the final decision.

Henry regarded his hands and twisted a ring on his finger. He had saved William for last in order to savour the moment. There was something very appealing about his youngest half-brother. He had handled Edward this morning with a perfect blend of good humour and courtesy, while demonstrating an ability to connect at Edward's level.

Henry harboured a deep yearning to nurture William. His full brother Richard was close to his own age and shrewd and powerful. Richard would look at him in exasperation and cast his gaze to the ceiling if he thought Henry was being foolish, whereas with William, Henry could be the older, benevolent mentor, full of wisdom, kindness and largesse.

William needed a good marriage to set him up for life, and Henry knew exactly who to choose – a young woman of sense, practical and efficient like his own dear wife. She would keep William steady, and William would be grateful for such a magnificent gift and would not abuse it. He was bound to fall for her, for she was delightful as well as being a wealthy heiress. William would be enriched in all senses of the word and his bride would become part of his family by marriage.

Uttering a sigh of satisfaction, he rose from his knees and signed his breast, thanking God for helping him to think the matter through. It was all so wonderful – he felt like a gardener planting seeds.

Sleeves rolled up to her elbows, Joanna was helping the royal nurses to wash the children after they had finished their morning bread and milk. Edward, true to form, ran away and had to be caught, and he screwed up his face as she wiped his mouth with a cloth.

'I don't get dirty in the night,' he protested. 'I had to wash before I went to bed.'

'But it honours God to wash in the morning,' Joanna said firmly. 'You are the oldest and should set a proper example to your brother and sisters. Come now, nearly done.'

Edward submitted, scowling but resigned. He had flashes of temper when there was no reaching him, but mostly, if a reason was framed in logical terms he would listen and at least digest what was said, even if he sometimes still chose to go his own way.

As soon as she released him, he ran off, leaving her to deal with Edmund, who lifted his face and giggled at her, a sunny, easy little boy. Task finished, Joanna rolled down her sleeves and prepared to join the Queen who was chatting animatedly over her needlework with Cecily and Sybil Giffard.

The King arrived, embroidered robes swishing and giving off the scent of incense. Apart from two attendants he was alone, when normally an entire troop of courtiers would follow in his train. He approached Alienor and made a courtly obeisance, before leading her aside to an empty embrasure, where they sat down to talk.

Joanna disposed of the washing water down a drain at the end of the room and finished tidying up.

'Joanna, come here,' the Queen called to her.

Joanna's stomach lurched, for this too was unusual, and she wondered if she had done something wrong.

Henry smiled reassuringly and gestured at the cushioned seat beside the Queen. 'Come, sit. I want to talk to you, my dear.'

Feeling tense, Joanna perched on the cushion and folded her hands in her lap.

Henry cleared his throat. 'I would not have you think I have come to this lightly,' he said. 'But I have sought God's help, and I am content that I have made the right decision.'

Joanna's stomach continued to wobble. Henry was studying her with an expression compounded of mischief and pleasure. The Queen was smiling, but with slight irritation lining her brow.

Henry crossed one leg over the other, artfully displaying his red silk hose and an embroidered soft shoe. 'As your sovereign and guardian of your welfare I have been pondering the matter of your marriage for some time, and I am delighted to tell you that my choice has fallen on my dear brother William de Valence. I believe he will suit you well – as I also believe you shall suit him.'

Joanna could only stare at him. His words had taken her breath in shock, for although she had known this moment would come, she had not imagined it would happen so suddenly, like this. Between pushing up her sleeves and rolling them down, her life had changed.

Henry's eyes twinkled. 'Do not worry, I have chosen wisely. I have known you since you were a child serving at the Queen's hearth. You shall have your heart's desire and you shall be my sister-by-marriage – is that not a fine thing?'

Joanna's mind was solid, like a wedged door. The King watched her with kindly amusement, and the Queen with quizzical interest. 'Thank you, my liege lord,' she managed in a constricted voice. 'I am . . . I am honoured you should think of me with such diligence.' She was overwhelmed and struggling. 'I beg your leave, I am sorry!' She stood up, mangled a curtsey in Henry's direction, and fled.

Seeking refuge, she ran into the Queen's wardrobe chamber, closed the door, and leaned against it. Surrounded by rich fabrics, furs, bags and chests, she put her face in her hands and fought for breath. She had known ever since Iohan's death that she would be married. She was a wealthy heiress, seventeen now, which was old for a daughter of the nobility to wed; but even so she was not ready. Everything was turning and changing and she could do nothing to prevent it. No longer would she sleep with the Queen's ladies, except on rare occasions. She would have her own household and would have to accommodate the tastes, ways and habits of a young male she barely knew.

William de Valence seemed pleasant enough, but he was not even knighted yet, and she had been expecting the King to present her with a husband of staid experience. How could someone who was a younger son barely older than herself administer a household and a barony? He was not qualified in military matters, diplomacy or in running estates. How could he be a safe pair of hands? But he was the King's brother, which meant he would be in line for privilege and preferment. She would remain close to the royal family and doubtless they would live at court. She would always have the King's protection.

They would have a marriage bed. Her mind darted to what happened in a bed beyond sleeping and she almost whimpered, but then pressed her lips firmly together. This would not do at all. She must be resilient and strong. She could not be 'little Joanna' for she would not survive.

There was a knock on the door. Swallowing, wiping her eyes, Joanna opened it and then dropped in a curtsey as the Queen entered, followed by a servant bearing a tray with a flagon and cups, which she put on a chest before withdrawing.

'I am sorry, madam,' Joanna said in a stricken voice. 'I should not have run away – it was inexcusable.'

The Queen waved away Joanna's apology and drew her to her feet. 'I do not blame you; I blame that foolish husband of mine. I am as surprised as you are, for the King told me nothing of his intent either until now. Here, let's dry those tears. All women come to this moment.' She wiped Joanna's eyes with a square of linen purloined from one of the fabric shelves, and directed her to pour wine. 'I know you must be shocked at having this announcement sprung on you, but it is not so bad. The King acted from the best of intentions.'

Joanna swallowed. 'I do not want to leave you or the King,' she said from the place of the 'little' Joanna.

Alienor took the cup from Joanna's hand. 'Ah no, you shall not, save for small morsels of time. You will still be part of our family and dear to us.' An amused glint entered her eyes. 'We shall have more children to fill the nursery, and how wonderful that will be.'

Rendered speechless, Joanna stared down at her drink, heat scorching her cheeks.

'Come,' Alienor said, 'what do you think of him really? He is handsome and a good dancer, no? And strong legs for all that he is as lean as a hound.'

Joanna gave a silent nod, unable to make a full reply.

'And what magnificent hair!' Alienor continued, enjoying the moment. 'It shows his vigour. He will give you many robust and handsome children, and they will bring you great happiness as mine have to me.'

Joanna gasped, and the Queen laughed at her embarrassment. 'Just you wait and see! Of course, he is still a youth, and girls grow into women far sooner than boys become men, but no matter. You will do well together I am sure, and you may come to me and ask me anything – anything at all.' She gave Joanna a meaningful look.

Joanna swallowed at the notion of approaching the Queen on any such matters of intimacy. 'Does he know?'

Alienor shook her head. 'The King has gone to tell him now. He wanted you to be first, and I am glad. Women should be put first by their menfolk more often, I think – we are eminently more sensible than they are.' She beamed at Joanna. 'We have a wedding to plan. Drink your wine and let us give the other ladies the glad tidings!'

Joanna did as she was bidden, and accompanied the Queen with her head high, although she was still numb with shock. Everything had changed in an instant, but adapting to the new reality was going to take much longer.

11

Royal Palace of Woodstock, May 1247

Standing outside the Queen's chamber, feeling sick, William wiped his hands down his tunic, not wanting them to be clammy and create a bad impression. He had been at court barely a week and Henry's swift decision in arranging a wealthy marriage for him was an unexpected push from the side. Joanna de Munchensy was a great heiress with lands throughout England, Wales and Ireland as her portion of the great Marshal inheritance. They had exchanged only a handful of words but would be husband and wife by midsummer. He had known from her status that she would be a strong candidate when it came to Henry's choice, but receiving the news had still been a jolt. Henry could easily have given him money and other entitlements as an interim arrangement.

William turned to John de Warenne. 'What shall I say to her?' he demanded. 'You are her cousin and know her best.'

'I would not say I know her best – what male understands the mind of a woman?' John replied wryly. 'But she is clever and conscientious, and dutiful. Her tutor is Cecily de Sandford and she is formidable.' He gave William a pitying look.

'Is that supposed to reassure me?' The elderly woman who chaperoned Joanna always looked at him in a way that made him feel threadbare and unworthy.

John flashed a dour smile. 'Forewarned is forearmed. Just be open and tell her what is in your heart. Joanna values truth and honesty above all else, but she is susceptible to sweetmeats as most women are.'

William raised his brows. 'Meaning?'

John shrugged nonchalantly. 'Pay her compliments. No amount can be too many – spoken sincerely, of course. Joanna will not be taken in by flattery. Present her with some little gifts and fripperies. Women set great store by such things.'

William eyed him narrowly. John was younger than him, but either he had a wealth of living under his belt or he was repeating words he had heard from someone more experienced.

John frowned, and said more seriously, 'Joanna is dearly loved by the King and Queen, but no one could have foreseen that so much wealth and status would come her way and change her destiny. Perhaps you would do well to honour her by seeing her as she truly is and praise her for it.'

William rubbed his hands down his tunic again. 'And what will she think of me?'

John gave him a lop-sided smile. 'That, my friend, is up to you.' He looked round. 'Here is the King now.'

Warm golden bars of morning light shone on the tiled floor of the Queen's antechamber. Joanna stood very still in one of them while the ladies fussed around her twitching and smoothing. Her new gown, a gift from the Queen, was of dark-red damask, tightly laced at the sides to emphasise her figure. A white veil covered her coiled braids, secured by a delicate circlet of silver-gilt, intertwined with little enamelled blue flowers and green leaves. The Queen had given her that too, throwing herself into the arrangements. Not so much to please the King, with whom she was still a little annoyed, but for her own romantic gratification. She had bestowed a litany of advice, most of which had swept straight over Joanna's head because she was too overwhelmed to absorb it.

'It will be all right,' Aliza said. 'It is wonderful that you are to wed my brother and become my sister. William had better know how fortunate he is or I shall box his ears!'

Joanna smiled wanly at her friend. She felt queasy and feared she might be sick. She hated being the focus of everyone's gaze and just wanted this public agreement to the marriage to be over.

'William is just as anxious as you are,' Aliza said. 'It is a great moment for him too and he has to come and propose to you. You have the power to decline his suit, or look upon him with disfavour.'

'But if I declined him I would be refusing the will of the King and my position would become untenable. I have no choice, although I do not find him distasteful.' Her cheeks burned with embarrassment.

'I sat with him last night and he told me he could not believe his good fortune and he fears it might all be a dream. You are not alone in having qualms.'

Joanna raised her brows. 'But he must have known the King would afford him a fine marriage as a means of remaining here.'

'Perhaps, but not taken for granted,' Aliza replied. 'We are on probation, indeed on trial, and our every movement is observed and judged at court. We have no security other than the King's will.'

A herald arrived to announce that the King and his brother, William de Valence, awaited admittance. Alienor gestured assent and rested her arms along the sides of her great chair. Joanna came to stand at her left, with the other ladies behind. A chair for the King had been placed at Alienor's other hand and her chaplain, Brother Thomas, stood by it, representing the Church in bearing witness.

'Bid my lord and the seigneur de Valence enter,' the Queen said.

Joanna dug her fingernails into her palms. Her stomach was so tight she felt as if it was clamped to her spine.

The King entered the room, pacing slowly to give a heightened sense of occasion. William de Valence walked behind at his shoulder, followed by his brothers and John de Warenne. Advancing to the Queen's chair, Henry bowed to his wife, and then took his place at her side, smiling. 'This is a happy and auspicious moment,' he said, and then extended his hand in an open gesture to William.

Doffing his hat, with a flourish, William made a deep obeisance. 'Madam, I thank you for this opportunity and audience.'

Alienor graciously gestured him to rise. 'You are welcome as my dear lord's brother,' she said. 'And we are both delighted to oversee and bear witness to this moment of betrothal.' She indicated Joanna with a graceful gesture.

William turned to Joanna, knelt again and bowed his head. He wore a tunic of fine dark-blue wool, and deep, reddish-brown hose, set off by ankle boots patterned with gold lions. Breathing shallowly, Joanna tried to take it all in and make the moment real, but felt as if she was standing inside an illuminated picture in one of the Queen's romance books, created by someone else.

He raised his face and looked at her with his striking grey-gold eyes. 'My lady, I hope you will do me the greatest honour of accepting my offer of marriage as conveyed to you by my brother the King, and I humbly ask that you might look on my suit with favour.'

His ears were scarlet and Joanna knew her cheeks must match, for they felt as hot as fire. She wanted to cover her face with her veil and hide. 'You also do me a great honour, sire,' she replied formally, her voice hoarse with tension. 'I only ask that you treat fairly with me and I will do due diligence to you and gladly accept your proposal.' She attempted to smile, but it was like trying to draw a tightly strung bow.

The Queen prompted her with a look and a small gesture, and Joanna realised, mortified, that William was still on his knees. Hastily she gestured him to rise.

He stood up and smiled at her with relief in his eyes. 'My lady, I swear I shall treat you with all the honour, deference and respect that is your due. Indeed, I would stay on my knees for ever if you so bid.'

Joanna lowered her gaze. 'That will not be necessary.'

'I am mightily relieved, and glad for your lenience.'

She was too tense to respond to the flash of humour in his voice, but heard a soft grunt of amusement from the King.

'I ask you to accept this ring as a token of our betrothal,' he said, and produced a delicate gold ring set with a disc of exquisite Limoges enamel depicting a flower in blue and gold. 'I hope it will be the first of many jewels and gifts with which to express my esteem.'

Joanna's sense of unreality increased. Feeling ever more like a figure in illuminated parchment, she whispered her assent and extended her left hand so that he could slip the ring on to her third finger. It fitted perfectly, making her wonder if the Queen had been consulted about the sizing. He drew her hand to his lips, kissed the ring but not her skin, and then took a step back, but still holding her hand. Joanna looked down, blushing.

It was done. The Queen clapped, and waiting attendants brought drinks and refreshments for the guests. William took a cup of wine, handed another to Joanna, and they stood awkwardly side by side as they were congratulated and feted. Joanna lost count of how many kisses and embraces she received, although none from her betrothed, who did not yet have that right.

The moment came when they stood alone and Joanna had to fight the urge not to flee as she had done when first told of the marriage. 'It is another fine day,' she said to fill the awkwardness, and was utterly chagrined because the comment was so inane to mark a moment of such enormity.

'It is certainly an auspicious one,' he replied, and looked towards the window where the shutters were open to a jewel-blue sky.

She gave him a covert look, taking in the delineated masculine features, the sharp nose, the curly hair. What would it feel like under her fingers? She remembered what the Queen had said about it being a sign of vigour and a shiver ran down her spine composed of fear and anticipation. She was going to share her life with this man and be intimate with him. He would be the father of her children, and she the mother of his. She had always known she would have no choice in her marriage and would have to accept whatever dish was set before her, but this was like expecting a chunk of meat and being given a platter of rare confectionery instead.

'I meant what I said a moment ago,' he said quietly. 'I swear I will honour and protect you, and treat you with respect.'

She inclined her head. 'I meant what I said too.'

He drew her to the window, and she was stiff, knowing how avidly they were being observed. 'Will you tell me about your family?' he said.

Henry would have informed him of her circumstances, but William's request and the genuine interest in his eyes helped to ease her tension and it was a step more intimate than talking about the weather. However, she had no wish to dwell on her parents, or the death of her brother. 'My grandsire had ten children,' she said, 'so I have many cousins. I do not know all of them well, but John is dear to me.' She gestured towards John de Warenne who was talking to Aliza and the Queen.

'John has already become a good friend,' he replied. 'I know your grandsire was lord of Pembroke, and his tenure was through his wife, as mine shall be, so I am following tradition. I hear he had a reputation as one of the greatest tourneyers of his day.'

'I believe so.' Joanna noted the gleam in his eyes. 'Do you tourney?'

'When I have the opportunity. I would enjoy proving my valour in your honour.'

She tried not to think about what had happened to her uncle Gilbert.

'Have you ever been to Pembroke?'

Joanna shook her head. 'I grew up at Swanscombe and then at court. My lands and affairs are being managed for me while I am the King's ward, but I should like to see them.'

He nodded. 'You should know what you have beyond names in a ledger. You need to know who you employ and that you have their loyalty.'

'I speak often with my lawyers and stewards,' she said. 'I would not have you think I am ignorant of my lands. I know what is mine.'

His ears reddened again. 'Indeed not, I would never think that, but I would like us to view them together when we have the time and to see for ourselves. Then it becomes real.'

'I would like that too.' She met his eyes briefly before looking down. They were the colour of field flints but clearer and brighter.

'Then we are already of one mind.'

He had to take his leave then with the other men, because

both the King and Queen had other appointments and duties. William bowed over Joanna's hand again. 'Perhaps I shall see you in the hall later – with the Queen's permission.'

Joanna curtseyed. 'Perhaps,' she answered with a demure smile.

He withdrew gracefully, backing from the room with a flourish. Joanna shivered when he had gone and sudden tears pricked her eyes as she released the emotion she had been holding at bay.

The Queen came and enfolded her in a warm hug. 'Come, come, my dear, this is a happy occasion. You must not be upset.'

Cross with herself, Joanna wiped her tears. 'I am not upset, madam. It is just that everything is so changed. I came to court after you and the King granted that favour to my father following my mother's death. I had no fortune and I imagined a very different future for myself from this.' She swallowed, her throat aching. 'You and the King have been my family and my solace. I have no other duty. I take on this marriage willingly and with gratitude.'

The Queen's expression softened. 'Bless you, child, and I hope this will be a good match for both of you. That is a very beautiful ring.'

Joanna looked down at the sky-blue flower set in delicate gold. 'Yes, it is,' she said.

Alienor's lips curved in a mischievous smile. 'Would I be right in suspecting you might already have given him your heart?'

A reply was beyond her. Had she given her heart? Was that the reason for the hollow hunger she felt inside? Or was it fear and trepidation?

The Queen laughed softly. 'Ah, you will know soon enough. Everyone gives their heart in their own way and you will do it as only you can, with courage and honesty. I admit I am looking forward, with your help, to bringing your young man into my fold.'

Joanna blushed again at the notion of William de Valence being 'her' young man. 'I hope not to disappoint you, madam.'

'I know you will not,' the Queen said with a meaningful smile. 'Indeed, Joanna, I am counting on you.'

William breathed out and let his tension go as the door to the Queen's chamber closed behind them. He could still hardly believe that he was going to marry the blushing, beautiful young heiress to whom he had bent the knee barely an hour since, and he wondered with self-doubt if he was up to the task. Joanna might be sweet and shy and delightful, but the women surrounding her were more daunting prospects. The formidable Cecily de Sandford had stared at him like a mother hen protecting a particularly delectable chick from the fox, and his half-sister Eleanor de Montfort had eyed him with near-contempt, as if he were an impostor wearing borrowed clothes to cover rags. The Queen had been warmly accepting on the surface, but she had been weighing him in the balance nevertheless. Even his own sister had been glued to his every move.

'Well done, my boy!' Henry declared, cupping William's shoulder, his eyes bright with pleasure. 'Our mother would have approved. You are precious to me because of her, but also because of yourself.'

William was unsure how to respond to Henry's emotion. His softness was a constant surprise and not quite how he envisaged the estate of manhood or kingship. 'I will strive to serve you honourably all my days,' he said diplomatically.

'I do not doubt it – and it was one of the reasons I asked you to come to England.' Henry smiled wryly. 'Affinities are stronger when the ties of loyalty and duty are bound by affection and blood. I am not as fond or foolish as some would have me.'

'I would never think that, sire,' William said hastily.

'I am glad to hear it.'

William cleared his throat. 'I was wondering if I might have leave to go and train with weapons for a while.'

Henry eyed him with indulgent humour. 'You truly have the restlessness of youth. Very well, be off with you. If I am going to knight you then you must be worthy of your sword.'

William's eyes widened, and Henry laughed. 'I have in mind to perform the deed on the Feast of St Edward. I have a most precious relic to bestow on his abbey and it will be an auspicious occasion. Of course, your nuptials come first and that is our concern for now, and there is the matter of settling lands upon you so you have an income and a proper place at court.'

'Thank you, sire!'

Henry waved his hand in dismissal. 'Go, we shall talk later. I have little interest in the military arts, but if you have an aptitude then away and develop it, my boy.'

William bowed and departed, his stomach churning with so much excitement that he wanted to leap and run to burn off the excess. Marriage to a beautiful, modest young woman, an heiress beloved by the King and Queen whose vast lands would become his at the church door – that alone was a banquet; but now he was to be knighted too, and at Westminster on the Feast of St Edward! All his life he had been the younger son, following his brothers around, loved but patronised. But when he became a great lord, they would have to depend on him to keep the King's goodwill and largesse. That prospect filled him with anticipation, a hint of fear, and a wild burst of exhilaration.

Joanna sat by the window in the warm afternoon and stroked the curled-up kitten at her side while she struggled to adapt to the notion of being married. This time next year she might have a baby in her arms; this time next year she might be dead. Hastily she pushed that thought aside. The will of God could not be altered and what would be would be. She would have a husband to protect her and share her burdens, which might be a good thing, but her lands were a means to an end – as her mother had been a means to an end for her father. Smiles and easy words, especially for a courtier, often masked the language of truth, and she did not want to be paid in false coin.

Through the open window she could see the tilting ground and the young men of the household at their training. William arrived with John de Warenne and some young knights and older squires, including another cousin of hers, Richard de Clare, with his conspicuous bright auburn hair. She drew a short breath and her stomach gave a strange, pleasurable twist. William had borrowed another of the King's horses, a fine bay, and was rubbing its nose and offering it titbits on his palm. His behaviour towards the horse suggested he might be kind to his wife and his children, more so than someone who brought a whip to the meeting.

He mounted the bay in a single lithe movement, ignoring the mounting block, and drew the reins through his gloved hands. He made the horse sidestep and then rear. Shouts floated up to her on the breeze – the laughter, the banter of young men – and she smiled, responding to their joy. He raced with his companions, chasing and weaving. In fierce competition with de Clare, he held his own with assurance, despite de Clare being ten years older.

Once warmed up, they turned to lance work. William took his turn at catching on his lance rings suspended from a pole and succeeded every time, even when the hole size diminished, and despite riding an unfamiliar horse. Joanna admired his accuracy, his seat in the saddle and the controlled force. While not powerfully built, he was strong and supple like a good bow.

He took another run at the quintain rings and looped a row of them on to the end of his lance, before turning towards the window where she watched. Joanna gasped and pulled back from the chained casement as he levelled the lance to the horizontal, holding the tip steady before raising it in salute. And then he reined around to rejoin his companions.

Aliza came over to the window. 'William is mad for the tourney,' she said. 'Every chance he had when we were at home he would be out practising.'

'He has great skill.' Joanna put her hand against the strange twist in her stomach.

'It is woven into his soul. When you take him as your husband, you will be wedding the sport too.'

'Is that a warning?'

Aliza laughed. 'Perhaps, but I do not mean it in a spiteful or critical way. I confess I should not have favourites, but I love William the best of all my brothers – and I hope you will come to love him too.'

Joanna blushed. 'I will try,' she said, and thought that it would not be difficult.

Golden evening light warmed Woodstock's great hall. Sitting in the embrasure sewing with Cecily, Joanna saw William slip into the room and stand looking around, searching, and her heart leaped. She had been expecting him for a while, and had begun to doubt his earlier sincerity. He was holding a small parcel wrapped in purple silk and tied with a gold ribbon. Catching her eye, he smiled and made his way around the room to her side.

'My lady, I am sorry to be late. I did not expect to be so long, and I crave your pardon.' He bowed very correctly to Cecily, who raised one eyebrow at him, but acknowledged him and gathered her sewing together.

'I shall leave you to talk for a short while,' she said, and went to join Madam Biset in the next embrasure, having cast a warning look over her shoulder at William.

William looked rueful. 'She does not think well of me,' he said.

Joanna shook her head. 'It is her duty to guard and protect me until I am wed, and she is rightfully cautious.'

'And I suppose I must prove myself worthy and she does not know me.'

'Neither do I . . . are you worthy?' His tardiness had set her on edge.

He gave her a wry look. 'I want to be,' he said. 'I would have been here sooner, but I wanted to bring you a gift.' He presented her with the small silk package.

She took it from him and unfastened the ribbon and opened the cloth, expensive in itself, to reveal a little trinket pot, enamelled like her ring in rich blue and gold, with small touches of green and red too. Dainty heart-shaped curves joined each other around its perimeter and it had a hinged lid with a gold knob on the top. She could put her rings in it, including her betrothal one, or anything else she chose. It contained a small scroll of parchment secured with gold thread, and when she unfastened and unrolled it, written upon it in exquisite lettering was a brief note: 'Lady, you shall have me faithful, henceforth I will think only of you. This stands as a symbol of my captured heart, and it is in your keeping for ever.'

Joanna swallowed, thoroughly unsettled. The gift and the words were so beautiful that they were beyond reality, and even dreams. 'I am deeply moved by your gift and the honour you do me, but do not be so swift to give me these things unless they are true and more than courtly trifles.'

He looked wounded and a little indignant. 'I would never tell you a lie, my oath on it.'

She searched his open, clever face. 'I do not take what is on the surface for what exists beneath.'

His smile remained, but grew a little taut. 'It is my honour. When I say you have captured my heart, I mean it, and if I am being too eager or presumptuous, then forgive me. I can wait on yours. Whatever is given in grace, you should cherish and nurture.'

Joanna shivered. It was like standing on the edge of a fire and being told that she could walk into it without being burned, when she had seen so many others come to grief and she did not trust the person who was encouraging her to take that step. 'Thank you,' she said, looking at the exquisite little pot. 'I shall think on what you have said and I shall cherish your gift.'

'The first of many – you may hold me to my word.'

She found a smile. 'I saw you earlier,' she said, 'when you were training.'

His face brightened with enthusiasm. 'I hoped you were watching. It gave me encouragement to think you might be. Perhaps I will be able to ride in a full tourney later and break a lance in your honour.'

Not wanting to dampen the moment, she did not say that the King strongly disapproved of tourneys.

'Do you like to ride?' he asked.

'Yes, on occasion.'

'Then we must do so together.'

A summons from the King who had been speaking with a group of clerks and advisers ended their conversation, and together they went over to join him.

'Ah,' Henry said with a twinkle as they made their obeisance to him. 'You are already becoming soul mates, I see.'

Joanna flushed.

'We are both very grateful for your kindness, sire,' William said.

Henry smiled benevolently and waved his hand. 'Come, I want to talk to you together and detail the lands that shall be

134

yours to govern as soon as you are wed.' He indicated the trestle at his side, covered with documents and scrolls, and proceeded to enumerate the lands that were Joanna's by right of inheritance. Pembroke in South Wales, Goodrich in the Marches, Tenby, Sutton, Brabourne, Wexford, Fearns. A tapestry of manors, castles and estates running through England, Wales and Ireland. There were also lands Henry intended granting to William in his own right – Bampton and Swindon, Newton and Collingbourne, with the promise of more to come. Henry touched the charters and parchments as he listed them, flicking his gaze between Joanna and William, hungry for their response.

Joanna had had the lands explained to her soon after Iohan's death, but this was different because now they were being enumerated for the benefit of her future husband. She smiled to please the King, but to her this bestowal carried an immense and serious responsibility. More than a table full of parchments indicating wealth, property and importance, this was heritage, duty and custodianship. She wondered how much William understood such things, or if he was just looking at it in terms of destriers, rich clothes and personal aggrandisement.

'I expect in the fullness of time you will enjoy some of them as your homes, although for now, I treasure your company by my side,' Henry said. 'Some of the household might transfer from the Crown to your employ but you will need to build up your personal staff of clerics and stewards and servants to take care of yourselves and your estates – people you trust who are honest and competent.'

Joanna nodded seriously. Finding the right people for the task was an underpinning of such an inheritance, for without the right wheels, the cart would not move at all.

William picked up one of the parchments referencing the land that Henry was bestowing on him personally. 'I desire them to be men of English birth,' he said, 'for they understand the customs and laws, and will better relate to them. If I am to settle here, I must begin as I mean to go on.'

'Admirable, my boy.' Henry pressed William's shoulder by way of approval.

Joanna had been observing William's astonishment and pleasure at the extent of the King's generosity, but she saw that his mind was at work too and that he was looking beyond the initial dazzle of all this largesse.

'I shall help you to furnish and improve what you have, of course,' Henry added. 'And I shall look forward in the fullness of time to visiting you – and the nieces and nephews you will give me to indulge.' His eyes twinkled.

Joanna looked down, and William's ears reddened.

'God willing, sire,' he said.

On the day before her wedding, Joanna tried on her gown for a final fitting. The deep-blue silk was set off by a crimson cloak lined with blue and cream squirrel fur. Eyeing her train, Joanna wondered how she was going to walk in all this and manage the fabric when she had so much else to think about. She bit her lip, close to tears, feeling overwhelmed. Since May the court had moved from Woodstock, to Clarendon, to Windsor, and she had been constantly packing and unpacking amid preparations for the wedding, and her tension was knife-sharp.

Cecily arrived bearing a bunch of blooms from the garden – daisies, marigolds and gilly flowers, their stems wrapped with a green silk ribbon.

'What am I to do about all this cloth?' Joanna demanded, swallowing a sob.

Cecily clucked her tongue, her eyes alight with humour and compassion. 'My dear, you must look to the future and watch where you are going, not what is behind you, for the latter will do you no good at all. Let those following you manage what is there. Trust to your maids because that is what maids are for, and if they do well, you may reward them fittingly afterwards.' She gave the ladies a meaningful look.

'You are right, of course,' Joanna said, blinking hard. 'It is just . . .'

'I know,' Cecily sympathised. 'So much change, so much to do – so much expectation when you are untried. You want everything to be perfect and you think only you can do what must be done. But you must trust others and delegate. You know this.'

Joanna nodded in chagrin. She allowed the maids to unlace and remove the gown and accoutrements, and wearing a simple linen undergown, her hair left uncovered, allowed Cecily to draw her to the window and sat down on a cushioned seat. Cecily eased down beside her and gave her the flowers.

Joanna inhaled their delicate, dewy scent. 'You always know when to come to my aid and rescue me – often from myself,' she said. 'What will I do without you?'

Smile lines crinkled Cecily's cheeks. 'It is only experience, my dear. You will manage very well on your own, I promise you.'

Joanna gently touched the petals. 'These are beautiful.' She wondered what was coming, for with Cecily, flowers and ribbons were never just flowers and ribbons. There was always a lesson.

'They are from the Queen's garden, but you have seen them often enough in their bed as you pass.' Cecily took a large daisy from the bunch and stripped the white petals into her lap one by one until only a golden dimpled heart remained, dusty with pollen. 'A woman becomes an inviting bed for her husband to lie upon when she has been deflowered,' she said. 'She becomes his resting place and for him alone.'

Curious, interested and embarrassed, Joanna eyed her tutor. She did not need a lesson in marital chastity, but Cecily clearly had more to say on the matter.

'She will fulfil the role of confidante and adviser. It is her duty to protect the family from gossip and keep it strong and principled. She will know not to gossip herself, and be wise in all she says and does, and she will let no one, man or woman, play her for a fool.'

'Of course not,' Joanna said, beginning to feel irritated for she knew all this.

'If you must confide in anyone beyond your husband, then let it be to God alone,' Cecily said, bending her a stern look. 'There are those who will give you away, like the bee that lands on each flower and goes to each in turn. Some will be well meaning, and some will assuredly not.'

'I understand,' Joanna said stiffly. 'I hope I have learned discretion in service to you and the Queen.'

Cecily gave a firm nod. 'You had that even before you came to us, but a man is different and you must be careful. I know you think I am being an old hen, but I am a wise one too, who knows the world. Young men are often irresponsible and you will need to have good sense for both of you.'

'I know you want the best for me,' Joanna said. 'And truly, I value your advice . . . but I do like him,' she added defensively, for she had noticed the way Cecily looked at William, as if she thought him not good enough for her.

'And that is a good thing,' Cecily replied. 'But there is a difference between walking in joy and stumbling because you have not seen the path under your feet. He is charming and handsome, I grant you, but what lies beneath the gilding will be the true test. Is he worthy of your love? Do not let any man sweep your feet from under you – and especially not your husband.'

Joanna realised with a sudden glimmer of understanding that Cecily was bound to be cautious after the scandal concerning her last important charge, the King's sister, who had married Simon de Montfort and caused upheaval and rebellion at court. 'No,' she said with quiet determination, 'you may be assured that it will not happen.'

'I am pleased to hear it, but I expect no less from you. You will meet whatever comes your way with courage.' Cecily took Joanna's hand. 'I remember what it was like, even if I no longer have that appetite and Christ is my solace. On your wedding night, be ready to know your husband in a full and carnal way, because that too is part of your flowering and womanhood, and your duty as a wife. Do not turn away, but meet him in honour and partnership.'

Joanna's cheeks grew hot, but she met Cecily's candid, compassionate gaze with resolve. Her tutor's eyes were faded grey, frosted with the weight of years, but they held the wisdom of the world. 'Thank you,' she said, and impulsively threw her arms around Cecily's neck and kissed her soft, wrinkled cheek. 'You are my mother when I have no mother to ask these things. I am ready to be a true and loving wife – but I heed your advice, and thank you for it.'

12

Windsor Castle, Summer 1247

Escorted by a smiling Henry, Joanna came to the King's chapel of St Edward the Confessor on her wedding day, wearing her blue gown and crimson vair-lined cloak. A headdress of plain white silk covered her rich brown hair, held in place by a gold circlet encrusted with pearls and sapphires. The maids bore her train with practised care, and with Cecily's words in mind Joanna made a determined effort not to look behind, but to go forward with her head carried high.

She could still hardly believe she was about to wed the King's brother. Her father stood at the forefront of the crowd gathered at the chapel door to witness the marriage, but since Henry was her guardian in respect of her Marshal inheritance, the responsibility fell to him to bestow her on William, for which Joanna was glad. She regarded the King as close family, and her father as a distant relation.

Waiting for her before the chapel door, William wore blue and white, with jewelled red swifts embroidered on his tunic.

The fine morning light enhanced the mica glints in his eyes and put gleams of gold in his tight curls. His brothers stood with him, almost shoulder to shoulder, and they too were robed in the blue and white of Lusignan.

The bright expression on William's face filled Joanna's heart, for it was all focused on her. Only once did his glance flicker around the congregation, daring anyone to snatch this from him at the last minute.

Henry's chaplain conducted the marriage ceremony. Oaths of endowment and property were sworn, and of faith and obedience. Having pledged their willingness, William slipped a gold wedding ring onto Joanna's finger beside the enamelled flower one, and then they processed into the chapel for a wedding mass and prayers.

The chaplain preached a sermon on the sanctity of marriage – the duties of a good husband and the compliance of a diligent wife. Joanna risked a glance at William, but his expression was straight and bland – apart from a slight, natural smile. There was no indication of his thoughts on the matter.

The choir sang 'Christus Vincit' and then the company processed solemnly out of the chapel where the waiting crowd showered the bride and groom with grains of wheat and flower petals – symbols of fertility. Henry kissed Joanna and William heartily. 'I wish you lasting joy and many children to bring to their fond uncle's feet,' he said mischievously, making Joanna blush.

'You are the most beautiful woman I have seen in my life,' William murmured to her as they processed, her arm on his, to the great hall for the marriage feast. 'We are two halves of one whole, and I know how fortunate I am. I will serve you day and night as it pleases you, I promise.'

Joanna looked at him sidelong. He had just sworn to protect

and honour her, as she had sworn to honour and obey him. But what that might mean lay in the future, and who could say that it would hold true?

'What?' he said with a quizzical smile.

'I was thinking that together we can write our own future,' she said. 'When I was a child, I never imagined such a day.'

'Then what did you imagine?'

She lowered her lashes. 'Certainly not this. And if I had, and the reality was less, then it would have been a foolish dream. And if I imagined less, then how much less should I settle for?' She swallowed. Laughter and tears. Both sides of the same coin, and she was dangerously close to both.

'I will give you the reality,' he said. 'You should dare to dream. We both should.'

Entering the bedchamber that had been prepared for the wedding night, Joanna inhaled a perfume of spices, rose water and incense. The quilted white coverlet, a gift from the King and Queen, had been strewn with rose petals, and sumptuous matching curtains were hooked back in two swathes. A lamp of tawny glass hung from the canopy on delicate chains, the oil within infused with musk and incense. Food had been set out on a table covered by a white cloth as well as a flagon and delicate glass goblets. A painted chest crouched under the window, decorated with the arms of Lusignan and England, of Marshal and de Munchensy, all gifts from Henry and Alienor. Joanna was taken to silence, and William spoke hoarsely for both of them. 'Sire, madam, I do not know how to thank you, but our hearts are full.'

'You are thanking me just by being here,' Henry replied, his eyes glistening with tears. He swayed slightly, the worse for drink. 'My family is of the greatest joy and importance to me. I wish

I could give both of you much more – I swear I shall do in the fullness of time.'

The Queen raised her brows, as did several other courtiers, and taut glances were exchanged.

Henry took the hands of the newly-weds, making himself the link between them, and fixed William with an owlish stare. 'I wish you the joy that has been mine and the Queen's,' he declared. 'You have a veritable princess for your wife. She is very dear to me and I expect you to treat her with consideration. We all want to be friends on the morrow.'

Mortified, Joanna dared not look at William, who cleared his throat and bowed. 'Sire, you have my word on it.'

'Then that is good enough for me.'

The Queen stepped forward, and taking Joanna from Henry, enfolded her in a perfumed embrace. 'You have all my love, dear Joanna.' She turned to William. 'And no less than my husband, I expect you to make her a happy woman in this marriage – not just for tonight.'

'That is my intention, madam,' William said with another deep bow, maintaining his aplomb, although his ears were scarlet.

Joanna kept her eyes modestly lowered as the maids removed her train, her headdress and her outer wedding gown, leaving her standing in her under-dress of embroidered cream silk.

William's new valet, a Londoner named Jacomin, divested him of his wedding finery as far as his shirt and hose. The chaplain joined their hands and gave his blessing with a wish for fruitfulness and fine offspring, while an acolyte scattered them with water from a silver aspergillum. The bed too received a thorough sprinkling.

Joanna had heard of boisterous wedding ceremonies full of bawdy talk, but even with too much drink inside him the King was pious and proper in that respect, and with the blessing complete, he started ushering everyone from the room. 'Come, there is wine and supper in the hall,' he cajoled. 'The finest musicians from Gascony shall entertain us while we take our final repast. Let us leave the bride and groom in comfort and peace.'

Full of drunken bonhomie, William's brother Geoffrey brought a heavy hand down on his shoulder while giving him a smacking wine-sodden kiss. 'Good fortune, little brother!' he cried. 'Don't mess this up, for any of us. Acquit yourself with honour!'

Aymer and Guy dragged him away and out of the door.

Aliza kissed William and Joanna on the cheek. 'Pay no heed,' she said. 'I wish you both well and will see you on the morrow.'

Finally, the last guest departed, closing the door, although the servants remained in the room – Mabel and Nicola, Joanna's ladies, and William's servants Elias and Jacomin.

The women completed Joanna's toilet, combing her hair and removing her undergown to leave her clad in her chemise. Jacomin neatly folded William's clothes and then attended to the refreshments, pouring wine into the delicate cups.

'That will be all, you may go,' William said, and then hesitated and looked at Joanna. 'Unless you have any more need of your ladies?'

Joanna appreciated his asking her rather than dismissing them out of hand. She was battling her fear, for when the servants departed, she and William would be alone for the first time that day and with the expectation that they would consummate the marriage. Thus far they had been players in a pageant, two among many, but now the role had become real and personal. Soon they would take part in an act of the utmost intimacy while still being little more than polite strangers. 'Yes,' she said, and nodded to the women. 'You may go – and thank you.'

As the door closed behind the servants, Joanna shivered. Nothing she had been taught by Cecily, for all her advice about meeting her husband frankly, had prepared her for this moment. Intensely aware of his every movement, thoughts flashed through her head faster than a guttering flame. She looked at the bed; the fresh linen sheets and bolsters; the embroidered pillows that she had worked on as part of her trousseau. Which side might he wish to sleep? How would it feel to lie beside him?

'Do you want some wine?'

Joanna did not particularly, but tactfully accepted a cup. It was Gascon, sweetened with sugar and lightly spiced.

'I am forever in the King's debt,' William said. 'I fear that either I am going to awaken and discover it is all a dream, or else that it is true and I am not worthy of the responsibilities set upon me. I do not know if I am enough.' He took another gulp of wine, but then put the goblet aside, and Joanna suspected he was trying to dissipate his tension rather than slake a genuine thirst. An attempt to normalise something that was not normal.

'I have felt that too,' she said. 'The King and Queen have been so good to me and I do not want to disappoint them – or you. I was not born to what I have now. It has come to me because members of my family have died untimely – my mother, my brother, my uncles.' She took a shuddering breath. 'I too do not know if I am enough for this.'

'Then we are as one.' The light from the glass lamp trembled as a moth blundered around the flame, and his face and hair were illuminated in gold. 'You make me a proud man,' he said huskily, 'and a proud husband, and even for all I have been given, you are the most precious gift of all.'

She put her cup down and faced him, determined to claim her own power. 'Then let it be more than words. Let it be more than the coin of the courtier. Let it be true and real and honest. That is what I desire from you most of all.'

'I give it to you freely,' he said. 'Openly and honestly.' He

145

reached across the divide between them to touch a strand of her hair that had fallen forward over her shoulder. 'I never realised there were so many colours in brown – chestnut and hazel and gold.' He raised the strand to his face. 'It smells of roses.' He ran his fingers delicately through the tress, and Joanna stood, breathing shallowly. Her maids combed her hair every day. Sometimes Cecily would do so in a tender, maternal moment, but now it was her husband on their wedding night and the feelings and sensations were very different, and intense. She wanted to reciprocate and touch his hair with its thick, vigorous curls, but she hesitated, thinking it too bold a move.

He stroked her cheek with the back of his hand and then her neck in a slow, hypnotic movement, as if reading her by touch, and she quivered at the intimacy. 'The King settled you upon me because of your wealth and lands and I need those to live in this country, but he also drew us together because he thought we would suit each other. He treasures you, and I will treasure you also, as my dearest friend and companion and love, and that, I swear, is the honest truth.'

Joanna looked at him, absorbing his words but still unsure. 'You do not know me,' she whispered.

He took her by the shoulders. 'Not yet, but what little I have learned in the weeks since we made our agreement has led me to want to discover more, and I do know that I am already fond of you. It can only deepen. I hope you have at least some regard for me.'

She nodded shyly, feeling hot and cold all over.

'We are bonded together for life by our marriage vows. I for you and you for me, and I pray come what may that it shall always be so.'

He took her hands, raised them to his lips, and drew her to the bed. He laid her down on it, and knelt over her, kissing her, and

Joanna remembered Cecily's advice and kissed him in return. A first time for everything, she thought as her senses opened to him, the feelings rushing through her excitement and fear. She raised her hand and did what she had wanted to do from the moment he had come to court, and ran her fingers through his hair.

Joanna lay against William feeling the thunder of his heart, listening to his rapid breathing. She was overcome. No advice or guidance from Cecily or the other women could have prepared her for this. It was like the times when she had become dizzy and disorientated from drinking too much wine. The sore feeling between her legs was a background discomfort, although more noticeable now that the overwhelming physical sensations had diminished. He had stroked every inch of her body. Parts that no one else had touched; parts that she could not even reach herself. The experience had been new, intoxicating and strange, but she felt utterly bonded to him because all the boundaries had been swept away by their shared experience. No one else would ever have this intimacy and not only in physical terms. She had never let anyone this close before.

When he moved, she followed, not wanting to lose the contact, and he reacted by putting his arm around her, pulling her close and kissing the side of her head. 'Now we are truly man and wife,' he said, 'and I could not be more blessed.'

Joanna hesitated, for giving her heart made her vulnerable and to admit to giving it even more so, but she seized her courage. 'Neither could I,' she said, and buried her face against his smooth chest.

Joanna awoke to find the covers flapped back and William putting on his clothes. She murmured his name as a question, and when he turned and smiled, her heart somersaulted.

'I didn't want to wake you,' he said. 'It is still very early but I am always up with the dawn.'

'So am I, usually,' she answered, 'but this morning is different.'

He finished fastening his hose to his braies. 'Indeed. I have never woken up with a wife in bed beside me. I watched you sleeping as the sun rose and thought again how fortunate I am.'

'So where are you going if that is the case?'

'Only to see what is afoot and then I'll return, I promise. I won't be long.'

He leaned over to kiss her, quickly put on his shoes and left the room, pausing on the threshold to look over his shoulder and grin at her.

Joanna sat up and clasped her hands around her folded knees, feeling pensive. Their wedding night might have been the most intimate of experiences, but she had awoken to find him on the verge of stealing out. She wanted to talk and share her thoughts with him as well as her body. However, she recognised his restless energy, his need to be busy. She only had to look at his hair to know his character.

In the hall, servants were setting up trestles for people to break their fast, although few were about because everyone had drunk and danced to their utmost the previous night. William was hoping to avail himself of sustenance without being noticed, but unfortunately his brothers Geoffrey and Guy were already awake – if they had been to bed at all – and so was John de Warenne.

'Little brother!' Geoffrey struck William a hefty blow on the shoulder. 'What's all this? Away from your duties so soon?'

'Leave him alone,' Guy replied. 'He's clearly ravenous after the night he's spent. Being a bridegroom is like a joust. Lance work takes a lot out of a man. He needs all the nourishment he can get!'

William shook his head at them, but took the joshing in good part. In truth he had been surprised there had not been more of it last night but then the King had been overseeing the proceedings. 'Thank you for your concern,' he said. 'I assure you that all is well and I am both very happy and very hungry. Nor am I being dilatory in my attendance on my beautiful wife.' He purloined a tray from a passing servant and loaded it with bread, cheese, a dish of honey and slices of cold roast meat. He plucked three roses from a jug of flowers standing on one of the trestles and arranged them on the tray.

Geoffrey raised his brows and shook his head, but John watched with interest. 'Nice touch,' he said.

'Just be careful you don't contract love-sickness, little brother,' Geoffrey warned. 'It is unwise to be in thrall to a woman's skirts – to what lies under a woman's skirts.'

William returned the raised brow. 'It does no harm to be courtly to one's wife on her wedding morn. Do not worry, I am my own man.'

'Yes, and a wise one.' Aliza arrived to join her brothers. 'A contented wife is a valuable weapon in a husband's armoury.' She stood on tip-toe to kiss William's cheek. 'Pay them no heed. If I was a new wife and this was my first morning, I would love you for ever if you brought me roses.'

Geoffrey gave an exaggerated sigh and Aliza pinched him hard, making him yelp. John looked on, grinning. 'I would certainly bring my wife roses if I had a wife,' he said, looking at Aliza.

'See,' she said to Geoffrey, making him shrug his shoulders in baffled disgust.

William took his leave to resounding cheers. Turning at the foot of the steps, he flourished a bow before making his escape.

*

Joanna was dressed in her chemise and undergown and Mabel was combing her hair when William returned, bearing the tray. He had been gone a while and she had decided she might as well rise, but now she looked at the food and the flowers, and her heart blossomed at his trouble and consideration. She was chagrined too, for thinking he had been about his own concerns rather than organising this. He set down the tray in the window embrasure and Joanna dismissed her maids.

'How thoughtful.' She gave him a soft look and picked up a rose to sniff the delicate perfume while he poured wine and arranged the food on one of the King's silver-gilt platters. 'Will it be like this every morning?' She gave him a teasing smile.

William laughed. 'It is your turn tomorrow.' He pushed the predatory, inquisitive Weazel away from the plate. 'I hope we shall often talk like this. I know it will be difficult to manage at court – there are always people listening at keyholes and behind the curtains – but even so, these moments will be ours, and precious.'

She struggled not to melt in a complete puddle. 'I hope that too,' she said.

He took her hands. 'You will always have my respect and honour and I will do nothing deliberate to shame you, and that is my vow.'

Tears filled Joanna's eyes for she had never expected this kind of consideration in a marriage. To be courted with fair words and gestures was a gift beyond measure, but still she clung to caution. Fair words and gestures could be like attractive silk ribbons that you might covet until they wound around your limbs and tied you in knots. This had to go much deeper than words before she yielded. She needed to know him beneath the mask of the courtier and suitor he projected so well. She needed to discover his measure and find out how steadfast he truly was.

'I will hold you to it,' she said. 'And I mean it.'

'So do I.' He kissed her again. 'Come, we should eat.'

The young cat mewed and twined around his legs. Joanna put some meat on a small platter and set it on the floor. William looked at her askance. 'Should you be encouraging it?' he asked dubiously.

'His name is Weazel.' She gave him a look. 'He was a personal gift from the lord Edward. A good mouser is worth his weight in gold and I am very fond of him.'

'Then I suppose he should stay,' he said, although without enthusiasm.

'You will come to love him, for my sake if nothing else,' she answered with a smile.

He made a wry gesture. 'I shall apply myself, although I make no promises.'

They sat down to eat. Weazel finished his breakfast and went to wash his paws in a pool of sunshine.

Joanna and William spent the morning together planning their future. They examined their estates in more detail and discussed prospective employees – lawyers and stewards, scribes and clerks and chaplains, cooks and foresters. Not everything would be accomplished in a day or even a week, but they made a start. William's serious application to the task impressed Joanna; she had expected him to lose interest, but he remained sharply focused and clear. He continued to insist that most of his administrators should be men of native birth. 'They know the business of the land and they speak the language easily,' he said. 'If I am to dwell here, I should employ such people.'

At the noonday meal, Joanna and William continued to be feted as newly-weds and were given the place of honour at the high table beside the King and Queen.

Alienor touched Joanna's hand in a solicitous gesture. 'Are you well, my dear?' she asked gently.

Joanna blushed at the Queen's veiled but intimate question. 'Quite well, madam,' she replied. 'Truly.'

'I am glad.' Alienor gave Joanna a meaningful look. 'You know I am here if you have need.'

'Thank you, madam, you are very kind.'

'You are a lady of my household, and that means you are mine to me.' Alienor kept her hand over Joanna's. 'And by your marriage you are my dear sister too.' She turned to William and spoke in a firm voice. 'Treat your wife well, my lord, or you shall answer to me.'

William bowed to her. 'Madam, I have been blessed many times over in crossing the Narrow Sea to England, but my wife is my greatest treasure, and you will find me diligent in caring for her wellbeing.' Taking Joanna's hand, he raised it to his lips.

'I am pleased to hear it.' Alienor relaxed, although she continued to watch William and Joanna with a keen but indulgent eye.

Following the meal, William took Joanna for an afternoon on the river in a boat so that they could be away from everyone. Joanna watched the clouds of midges swirl above the slow-moving water, listened to the lazy plash against the boat's sides, and her happiness overflowed, making her want to weep, for surely nothing would be this perfect ever again. William lay with his head in her lap and she ran her hands through his hair, loving the feel of it under her fingers and the way she could leave wavy tracks like the ripples in the water. Perhaps last night they had conceived a child who would have that hair, and she blushed a little. She took in his eyebrows, the fine line of his nose, the glint of stubble on his jaw.

'The Queen seems very solicitous of your welfare,' he murmured with eyes closed. 'It seemed to me she wanted to know everything about last night.'

'I have been in her household since childhood, and she is concerned for me,' Joanna said, feeling uncomfortable.

'Yes, but you have nothing to remark upon to others if you do not wish to do so. What is between us, is for us alone. You may be one of the Queen's ladies, but now you are a married woman and that changes matters.'

Joanna frowned. She did not want to evade the Queen but neither did she want her prying into her intimate life with William. She had a new loyalty now, to her husband, but at the same time she still owed her full duty and service to the Crown, and felt torn.

William had brought some little balls of marchpane wrapped up in a cloth, and they shared them companionably. Snack in one hand, Joanna continued to run the other one through his hair.

'Do you think we will have children?' she asked after a moment, her mind on the night before and her body languorous with the pleasure of touching him and of having this intimate moment to themselves.

'If God is good, I see no reason why not.'

'Do you think they will look like you or like me?'

His lips parted in a smile. 'Me if they are boys, but of course you if they are girls.'

She narrowed her eyes, considering the remark. 'Do you really think so? A little girl with your hair tied in silk ribbons would look beautiful.'

He gave her an indignant look. 'Are you saying I have hair like a woman?'

She laughed and shook her head. 'It would not be exactly like yours, and I would love to bear you sons in your image too, but I was thinking of a daughter with ripples like that to her waist.'

'Who knows what the future will bring,' he said, 'but we can strive our best to prepare the ground and give it every opportunity to happen.'

He rowed them in to shore, to a grassy bank in the concealing, whispering shade of a willow tree, and there they made love in the dappled afternoon. His masculine strength and the beauty of his lean young body intoxicated her, and the gentleness of his hands, and his kisses tasting of marchpane, as her lips must taste to his.

Afterwards they lay side by side, fingers entwined, listening to the lap of the river, the call of a coot, the plop of a vole. They dabbled their feet in the water. She made a daisy chain and William chewed on a sweet stem of grass and watched the sun-coins glitter on the water.

'I suppose they will be looking for us,' she said reluctantly at last.

'Yes, we should go, but . . .' Sighing, he reached for his shoes. 'We shall soon be immersed in duties at court and on our lands. But I want us to have time together like this, always. Just us; no attendants, no one watching. And even if we have cares, time to set those cares aside, if only for a moment. I want it for always – until the end of our lives, no matter what. Promise me.'

Joanna almost pinched herself in disbelief. This was the King's brother, vital, handsome, and at her feet, asking her for reassurance. 'We shall promise each other,' she said. 'Wherever we are, whatever the circumstances.'

They kissed again, tenderly, and returned to the boat. He had to work harder at the oars now as they made their way against the stream to the original mooring.

'Of course, everyone will surmise what we have been doing,' William said ruefully, 'but that is between us, and we are man and wife. There is no cause for embarrassment.'

'No.'

Amusement filled her because his ears were red again. She dipped her hand over the side and lightly flicked water at him. He ducked, and Joanna felt light and golden with love for him because he was hers, and she would not have flicked water over any other man with such spontaneous daring.

13

Windsor Castle, September 1247

The practice on the tilting ground had been hard work in the sultry, thunderous weather of early September. Hot and sweaty from the exertion, William stripped to his braies and scrubbed his body with a cloth steeped in cool, herb-scented water. One of Joanna's numerous cousins, Richard, Earl of Gloucester, wanted to organise a tourney against him and his brothers and had approached the King for permission. Henry had procrastinated and not yet given an answer, but William hoped he would consent, for he and John de Warenne were to be knighted on the Feast of St Edward next month.

Joanna was occupied with the Queen this morning, but William would see her at dinner in the hall. He sometimes resented the time Joanna spent with Alienor, but he had to attend similarly on Henry, and maintaining royal patronage was necessary. Sometimes he would catch the Queen's gaze on him when he was with Henry, and although she would smile, her eyes were speculative and assessing, which made the hair prickle on the back of his neck.

Jacomin was helping him with the laces of his court tunic when John de Warenne put his head around the door. A week ago, the King had announced to the court that John and Aliza were to wed, much to William's delight. He could think of no better alliance, and it would be wonderful to have his best friend as his brother too. There had been some angry grumbling in the royal circle about how the best English heirs were being married off to various hungry interlopers, but William ignored the complaints as mere jealous griping.

'I am almost ready.' William grinned at John. 'We did well today. I'm hoping the King will let us tourney against Richard of Gloucester's party once we are knighted.' He pointed to the rectangular cloth bundle tucked under John's arm. 'What have you got there?'

'This?' John unwrapped the cloth to reveal a leather-bound book and handed it to William. 'You are always reading, and this might interest you.'

William ran his forefinger over the ornate brass clasps.

'It's a history of my grandsire, William the Marshal, who was Earl of Pembroke and regent of England when the King was a boy,' John said. 'My uncle commissioned copies so that our family could listen to his story on the anniversary of his death. It's not until May, so you can have the book for the winter. No one could best him in the tourneys – he defeated five hundred knights in single combat.'

William whistled. Five hundred was like numbering the trees in a forest, and probably exaggerated, but it still whetted his appetite.

'When we have children, his blood will run in their veins,' John said. 'I wish I had known him but he was more than ten years in his grave when I was born. I do not believe Joanna's mother had a copy, for she was still a child at the time, so Joanna might like to hear the story too.'

'Thank you,' William said with heartfelt gratitude. 'I promise I will take great care of it.' He went to his personal coffer, and locked it inside with his crystal and jasper chess pieces. Then he turned to John and smiled. 'I am glad we are going to be related by marriage, for I can think of no one I would rather call brother, even my own.'

Following the evening repast, William sat to play dice with his brothers and a few companions. Aymer was leaving the next day to study in Oxford. Henry had given him funds for his upkeep, and had promised him a bishopric to the great annoyance of many, who considered the King's generosity to his siblings wasteful and foolish.

Edward joined his uncles around the dice table to watch. In the warm September evening his hair was dark with sweat and his eyelids were heavy.

William glanced at the boy. Edward was chafing against the ties that his mother had bound around him. He understood the lad's need for masculine camaraderie and his avid curiosity about the world of dicing and banter – experiences he would receive from neither parent. A coterie of high-spirited young uncles was a different matter entirely.

Edward leaned against the table and desultorily flicked at a pile of silver, caught William's eye on him in amused reproval, and with a sigh, propped his chin on his hands. William presented him with the dice cup. 'Here, throw for me,' he said.

Edward immediately brightened and cast the dice into the middle of the table, scoring a winning throw. Chuckling, William scooped up the coins and handed three to Edward. A glance at the Queen showed him narrowed eyes and pursed lips. William turned back to the game, feeling a glimmer of resentment.

*

Seated near the Queen, Aliza and Joanna were busy with their sewing and conversation. Aliza's mind was largely focused upon John de Warenne, whom she was imminently to marry.

'What colour do you think would suit him best for our wedding?' Aliza asked.

'Dark red for sure,' Joanna answered, 'with gold edging. He takes rich colours well.'

'Yes, he does.'

Aliza sighed softly, and Joanna gave her a fond look, for she recognised the yearning and had it in her own heart, stomach and loins for William – although currently he, and the others, were foolishly indulging Edward as they played dice. The Queen had noticed and was not impressed.

There was a sudden flurry of action from the gaming board and with a gleeful yell Edward ducked away from William, the dice cup in his hand, and ran around a trestle where two scribes were playing chess.

'Can't catch me!' Edward sang out, his eyes alight with mischief.

William pursued him but Edward was as lithe as a little monkey in the spaces between the tables. A cup of wine went flying and drenched someone's expensive tunic. A dog joined in, barking and attacking ankles. Joanna put her hand to her mouth. The Queen sat up straight, her jaw taut with anger.

William finally caught up with Edward, his reach being longer, and after a bear-hug tussle removed the shaker from his hand. The dice went flying and landed on the floor.

'Hah!' cried Edward. 'Two sixes, I win, I win!' He capered, waving his fist in the air.

William stooped to pick up the dice and shook his head, although he was laughing. 'Sire, I concede you the victory,' he said, 'but I believe you are summoned elsewhere.'

Edward's face fell as he beheld Walter Dya, the master of the boys in the royal household. 'Sire, your lady mother says it is time that you retired but she wishes to speak with you first – you also, sire,' he added to William.

Joanna watched Edward and William approach the King and Queen, looking sheepish, but eyeing each other sidelong like fellow conspirators. She was mortified, for this was not the way she had envisaged her husband being singled out for royal attention.

The Queen fixed Edward with a stern gaze. 'One day you will rule over all these people in the hall as your father rules now and this unseemliness is not the behaviour of a future king. If you cannot behave in a civilised fashion in company, you shall have to stay in the nursery with the little ones. Is that understood?'

Mutiny filled Edward's eyes, but tempered by calculation. 'Yes, my lady mother,' he said. 'I am sorry.'

'I hope you are. Now, come kiss me; it is time you retired.'

Edward dutifully kissed her cheek, the same to his father, and departed with Master Dya, but threw a look over his shoulder at William on the way. 'Will you take me riding tomorrow?' he asked with an irrepressible grin.

'If your lady mother permits, sire,' William replied, bowing.

Joanna thought it highly unlikely.

The Queen turned her attention and her wrath on William. 'My son is eight years old and I do not expect such conduct from him in the hall, but you do not have the excuse of childhood to defend your behaviour. We are doing our best to make a king of him and you are encouraging him to act in unruly ways. I will not tolerate such wild pranks.'

William bowed again. 'I apologise, madam, I did not think, or if I did, it was of my childhood days with my brothers. I intended no malice.' He flicked a glance at Henry, but the King said nothing, content to let Alienor deal with the matter. 'I should have come to you to ask you to intervene.'

'That would have been the better plan,' she said frostily. 'I shall pay my own heed to this incident and keep him away from your gaming in future.'

'I will strive not to let such a thing happen again,' William said. 'I am truly sorry.' He gave her a beseeching look from under his curls.

'Make sure you do not. You are a grown man, a married one with responsibilities, and soon to be knighted. The time for unruly behaviour is over.'

'It got out of hand,' William said to Joanna as they lay in bed. 'Edward was bored and snatched the dice shaker. What could I do?'

Joanna shook her head. 'The Queen is right. You should have considered how it would look to others. You are the King's brother. People will not listen to you in counsel if they see you behaving like a child.'

He tossed his head irritably and turned on to his back.

'It reflects on me too,' Joanna continued. 'People will see you as a bad influence and blame me for not holding you to reason. In God's name, William, think before you act or speak.'

'I do not need a lecture,' he said, sulky because he had been looking for support.

'Then what do you need?'

'Sleep.' He rolled over, dragging the bed clothes with him.

Joanna dug her fingernails into her palms and suppressed the urge to pummel him with her pillow. Silence fell between them, filled with thorns. He heaved a sigh, sat up, and by the light of the night candle pulled on his shirt and braies, draped his cloak over, and stamped from the room.

Joanna too sat up, angry and tearful. He made her feel like an ungenerous scold. Cecily was right: young men took a long time to grow up, and tonight she had a man-child on her hands, one who put both of them in danger.

She hoped he had not gone off to continue drinking and dicing with his brothers and the other young rakes of the court, or even to seek another woman's bed. Some courtiers kept mistresses or made use of the whores, although the King frowned on such behaviour. She thumped the pillow and buried her face in it, telling herself she did not care where he went; but it wasn't true and she was heartsick.

Weazel leaped on to the bed and butted her, his purr vibrating his whole body, and she took comfort in his warm, tactile presence. After a while, she left the cat and went to sit on the bench by the window to think. She would have to channel William's energies into less troublesome areas, but without henpecking him. Perhaps engage him in a few projects dealing with their lands. His brothers Aymer and Guy would soon be gone from court, but that still left Geoffrey for William to spark off, not to mention Richard de Clare and John de Warenne.

Still agitated, she was pacing the room when William returned. She was relieved to see him, but unsure whether to be cold or welcoming. And then she saw the look on his face.

'Edward is sick,' he said. 'I went for a walk and came upon Master Dya running to bring the physician.'

Alarm flickered through her. 'What's wrong with him?'

'Purging, burning fever and sweat. He was all right just a few hours ago.' He looked at her with a glint of fear. 'The King and Queen are both with him.'

'No, not Edward.' She shook her head. There had been reports of the deadly sweating sickness in the city, and the pox, which often left terrible scars even if the afflicted person survived.

William pulled her into his arms. 'I know you think I behave foolishly at times, but life is too short not to seize it.' He buried his face in her hair, and she felt him shudder. 'If he dies . . .'

'Don't say that! Dear Christ, William, do not!' She pushed away, showing him her own fear. 'He cannot die!' All the terror, guilt and anguish associated with her brother's death washed over her. All the pain of loss. 'We must light candles and pray for his recovery.'

William swallowed and drew himself together. 'That is what the King has asked – for prayers.' He touched her cheek. 'Joanna, forgive me . . .'

She raised her hand to close over his. 'I am sorry too,' she said. 'We shouldn't quarrel.'

Side by side they knelt at the small, portable altar near the bedside. Joanna lit every candle and lamp she could find, and vowed her weight in wax if God would only spare Edward's life.

'I am very sorry to see the lord Edward so ill,' Joanna said as she curtseyed to the Queen. 'If there is anything I can do.'

She and William had snatched a couple of hours' sleep at the end of the night and this morning they had prayed again. Her eyes were sore and her head thick with tiredness.

Eleanor de Montfort was present, comforting Alienor, and she eyed Joanna coldly.

The Queen looked up from Edward's bedside, her face haunted and ravaged. 'Pray, for my boy,' she said. 'The King has sent to every church in the land to hold vigils for his recovery.'

'Madam, you need to rest.' Willelma hobbled to the bedside. Her wrinkles were deep furrows this morning.

'I will stay awhile,' Joanna offered. 'Let me wipe his brow and watch him for you.'

'It is all my fault,' Alienor said. 'I should never have let him wander among the men and join their foolish games.' She flashed a glance at Joanna filled with hurt, bordering on accusation.

Joanna recoiled at the unfair implication. Edward had probably been sickening well before then. To her knowledge none of the men who had been playing dice had been taken ill. 'With God's will, the lord Edward will make a good recovery, madam, I am sure,' she said quietly. 'He is strong.'

The Queen's chin wobbled. 'I cannot lose him,' she whispered.

'No, madam. I pray you will not. Please, let me be of service. I want to make amends for any folly on my husband's part.'

Alienor bit her lip, then nodded, and stood up to allow Joanna to take her place, by which Joanna understood that she was not entirely banished from favour.

The Countess of Leicester put a comforting arm around Alienor's shoulder, and Joanna saw genuine concern in her expression, one woman to another for the life of a sick child. The Queen indicated the bowl and cloth to Joanna. 'Just for a short while then.'

The Queen retired to her bed. Joanna wrung out the cloth in the rose-scented water and tenderly bathed Edward's brow and neck. 'Come, my little lord,' she said softly. 'You are as strong as a lion – as three golden lions indeed.'

Edward responded with a moan and his eyelids fluttered. She remembered watching Iohan die, and being helpless to save him. It mustn't happen to Edward.

'You are going to get better,' she told him fiercely. 'You have been a fighter since the day you were born.' She wiped him and soothed him with soft words, and she prayed.

A new candle had burned halfway down on the pricket when Eleanor de Montfort returned to the bedside. 'The Queen is sleeping,' she said. 'I will take over now.'

Joanna had no recourse but to yield her position to the Countess of Leicester.

'I know what it is like to watch over a sick child,' Eleanor said as she laid the cloth upon Edward's brow. 'When my son had spotted fever last year I would have given my life for his. You have yet to know the pain, but you will find out, should God grant you children.'

'I lost my brother to fever and flux, I know what that pain is,' Joanna replied defensively.

'You know a vestige, not the whole,' Eleanor contradicted. 'For a child is born of your body and nurtured in your womb.' She gave Joanna a hard look. 'I shall speak plainly to you. My first husband was your uncle, and he too died of a flux. Had he lived, I would still be Countess of Pembroke, not of Leicester, and I would have the lands that have been vouched to you and your kin. You were not born with the expectation of prestige and now your lawyers fight mine to deny me my dower rights. You will understand why, unless you grant me those rights, we shall never be allies or even friends. You impoverish me, and you impoverish my husband and sons.'

Joanna's mouth was dry but she stood her ground. 'The law exists to negotiate such matters,' she replied with dignity. 'As you say, I was not born to the lands, but they have come to me – by the will of God, and the law of the land. We may have different views on this, my lady, but I am not your enemy, and I hope you are not mine.'

Eleanor shook her head and said with bitter scorn, 'You stand in my way and look at me like a wounded innocent, while you and that foolish boy-husband of yours take what should be mine.'

Joanna fought a scalding wave of anger. At least Eleanor was being candid. Now the antagonism had been voiced, she could see how deep it ran. 'I am truly sorry, my lady, that we should be in dispute over our inheritance, but this is not the time or place. The lord Edward is very unwell and the King and Queen are rightly worried for his wellbeing. Surely, even if we are on opposite sides of a dispute, we should make a truce and do our best to support them.'

Eleanor flushed, then nodded curtly. 'Indeed,' she said. 'The Queen is asleep and I am sure you have duties to attend to elsewhere for now, but we know where we stand.'

Joanna curtseyed formally to Eleanor. 'Perfectly,' she replied. She leaned over to touch Edward's damp cheek. 'I shall return later, sire, to see how you are faring. Remember what I said – be as strong as three lions.'

She left the Queen's apartments, and once she had closed the door she drew a deep breath and pressed her hand to her midriff. Dwelling at court, she was accustomed to the rivalries permeating and poisoning the air. The ones that led the men into intrigues, disputes and fights. The reasons why tourneys were banned and swords left at the door. Among women too there were rivalries of dynasty and more subtle struggles for power and control, the weapons those of words and bodily nuance. The exchange with Eleanor de Montfort had frightened Joanna but it had also made her more determined to seize her inheritance and hold on to it with tooth and claw. She too would be as strong as three lions.

William walked under the decorated archway of the Temple Church entrance and paused in the round nave, deep with night and shadows but illuminated by lamps and candle light enough for vision. Here, entombed under effigies, were various knights and worthies of the Templar order, among them two of Joanna's uncles and her grandsire, armed for battle, and reaching for their swords. William shivered and a feeling of unworthiness ran through him – that he should not be here in this sacred place, that he was a fraud.

Knights and chaplains of the order surrounded the prostrated Henry. William joined him before the altar and sank to his knees, signing his breast with the cross. Henry looked up in acknowledgement and directed William's attention to the embellished rock crystal vase standing on the altar surrounded by a blaze of candles. 'This,' he said, 'is a most precious relic, sent to me by the Patriarch of Jerusalem. It contains drops of Our Saviour's holy blood, for which I have the Patriarch's seal of authentication. I shall present it to the abbey on the Feast of St Edward, but for now I am praying that it will wing my prayers to God and that He will show his great mercy and spare my son.'

William gazed at the flask in awe, for here was a power greater than any earthly king's. The precious blood of Christ the Redeemer. Its presence took him to silence. He prostrated himself beside Henry and with arms outstretched prayed with all his might that Edward might live.

A mile away from the Temple, dawn light stole across the floor of Westminster Abbey, touching Joanna where she had been kneeling in prayer all day and night, enveloped inside a dream world of glitter and gold and building dust from the new alterations to the church. She had neither eaten nor drunk in that time and her lips felt flaky and dry as she tried to moisten them with her tongue. Others had been praying at her side, part of a large congregation from the royal household invested in beseeching God to spare Edward's life. And behind the prayers, the continuous chanting of the monks. The light and heat from the forest of candles had burned her supplications into her brain. Edward had to live because her brother had died; otherwise there was no balance in the world. Hour upon hour the words flowed together and became senseless.

A light touch on her shoulder jolted her out of her trance and she turned with a gasp to see William. His eyes were darkly smudged and he looked as exhausted as she felt. Fear flashed through her, but then she saw the relief in his expression.

'The lord Edward's fever has broken,' he said. 'He is sitting up and asking for food and drink. Our prayers have been answered.'

She uttered a small cry of joy and relief, and then swayed. 'I am all right,' she said, rallying as he exclaimed and caught her. Her throat was so dry she could barely speak. She managed to stay upright, but leaned against him, grateful for his strength. Together they lit more candles to thank God for His great mercy and then left the abbey side by side, touching shoulders.

To reach their lodgings at Westminster Palace they had to cross Henry's great painted chamber. In the breaking dawn, the first colours had begun to tint out of the grey light. The painted figures of Faith, Hope and Charity stood in three arched panels, each one wearing a jewelled crown. Faith carried a cross, Hope, clad in a lavender-blue gown, hinting at a gleam of silk, walked among the stars while trampling the serpent of Despair under her bare feet, and Charity stooped to bestow a cloak upon a beggar.

'That is what you are,' William said, standing before the middle figure of Hope. 'You look like her and you are my hope and my love.'

She gave him an exhausted smile and reached up to touch his face, feeling the prick of stubble under her fingertips. 'I do love you,' she said, and stood on tip-toe to kiss him. 'Even when we argue.' She turned to regard the figures. 'I remember the artist and his apprentice painting these. I often crept away to watch them.'

Diverted, he looked at her. 'How old were you?'

Joanna shrugged. 'A child, but an older one. Perhaps eleven. Sometimes I would give them food or drink from the King and Queen, and if I was walking Dame Willelma's dog, they always petted him.'

William looked between her and the figure, narrowing his eyes. 'I think the painter used your face for inspiration,' he said. 'Indeed, I am certain of it.'

Joanna blushed. The thought had never occurred to her before, but she suspected he was right. Hope had always been her favourite. Feeling shy, she looked down.

'What a discovery,' William said. 'You truly are Hope among the Stars.'

In their chamber, Weazel was curled on their bed fast asleep, his stomach full of fish trimmings fed to him by Jacomin. Bread, cheese and wine awaited Joanna and William. They wolfed the food in tired, hungry silence, occasionally looking at each other, taken beyond words by their ordeals and discoveries.

Eventually they retired to their bed, undressing to their under-garments. The church bells were ringing to celebrate Edward's recovery and Joanna remembered their joyous pealing on the night of his birth. The dance of life could end as suddenly as a single mis-step. She clung to William, seeking his lips, her fingers in the curling vigour of his hair. He kissed her in return and rolled over with her, and they made love, all dishevelled and exhausted and unwashed as they were, celebrating what they had in the moment – and hope for the future.

14

Palace of Westminster, October 1247

A sparkle of light on the cuff of his new mail shirt caught William's eye – a glint from God, he thought, and it seemed to him that everywhere was alive with His glory. His senses were heightened – every sound, every touch. The smell of incense and stone and sanctity. The feel of the cold flagstones beneath his knees as he knelt with John de Warenne and a group of other young men to receive the formal accolade of knighthood from the King before an enormous crowd of clergy and nobility present for the cele-bration feast of King Edward the Confessor. There had been a great procession and then a mass to accompany the presentation of the vial of Christ's holy blood to the abbey church. Sheltered under a magnificent silk palanquin, Henry had worn a plain brown robe to bear the precious object from Westminster Palace to the abbey. Now, back at the palace, he had changed into a tunic of cloth of gold, with a jewelled crown binding his hair.

William had spent the previous night in prayer before Westminster's high altar, kneeling in vigil, taking neither food nor drink and reflecting on what it meant to be a knight and serve God and the King. To strive to be just and fair and honourable in all his dealings. He was tired and very thirsty now, but exalted too. To receive a knighthood on such an auspicious day in front of so many of his peers was as far above his dreams as the stars. Although daunted, he felt grounded and solid too, for this day he had become a man.

Beside him, John de Warenne jutted a resolute jaw, forested by a newly grown, short dark beard – he said it made him feel older. He had married Aliza three days ago in the cathedral of St Paul and he and William had become brothers in marriage, as they were now about to become brothers in arms, knighted on the same day, kneeling shoulder to shoulder as friends and comrades.

Henry descended the steps from his throne solemnly. An attendant stood to one side, holding an enamelled blue and gold belt, scabbard and sheathed sword. Henry took the items and girded the sword around William's waist, exhorting him to be the chivalrous defender of the weak and the Church and to be honourable in all his dealings and duties. William made his pledge and Henry struck him on the shoulder with his clenched fist to remind him of his oath, before giving him the kiss of peace and hugging him fiercely. The same ritual followed for John de Warenne and the other young men as Henry moved along the line, conferring upon each young man the alchemic honour of knighthood. William was exalted and euphoric. He was a knight and a grown man, acknowledged in the sight of God, and honoured by the King before the entire court.

'I am so proud of you,' Joanna said with brimming eyes. Her blue and white gown matched his surcoat, making them two halves of one whole – William and Joanna de Valence, the lord and lady of Pembroke.

The celebration feast in the great main hall of Westminster

commenced with speeches and toasts. There were delicious meats and pastries, piquant sauces, Gascon wines bright as rubies, and effervescent golden ones from France. Musicians and singers performed on lute and harp and pipe. William's shield, made new for the ceremony, adorned the wall in pride of place beside the royal arms of England. William had his own board at the banquet and Henry presented him with a gift of silver tableware, embellished with the martel blazon William would carry into battle for the rest of his life.

Between the numerous courses there was time to socialise, and Joanna's red-haired cousin Richard de Clare, flushed and bright-eyed with an excess of wine, approached William to congratulate him. When in his cups, as now, de Clare rode the line between loud good humour and belligerence. Clapping William on the shoulder, he signalled across the table to Guy and Geoffrey. 'As we agreed yesterday, gentlemen, shall we approach the King?'

Joanna looked from one to the other with concern. 'William, what is this?'

'Don't worry.' He kissed her cheek and stood up. 'It is just something we wish to ask the King. I'll return in a moment.'

Joanna bit her lip, feeling anxious nonetheless as he turned from her.

Henry had been conversing with the Queen, her uncles and a couple of bishops, but stopped as the deputation approached.

'Sire,' William said, bowing deeply, 'I crave a boon of you for my day of knighting.'

Smiling, Henry spread his hands in a magnanimous gesture. 'Name it and it is yours.'

William cleared his throat and looked round at the others. 'I beg your permission to hold a tourney to celebrate prowess in arms and to prove valour.'

Henry's smile diminished. 'A tourney?' The second word fell like a stone.

'It would set the seal upon my knighting,' William said eagerly. 'It would be well received, I am sure.'

'Tourneying is a dangerous sport.' Henry shook his head. 'I would not have you risk yourself when I am only just coming to know you.'

'But it is a rite of passage,' William argued. 'It will be properly organised, I swear it. How else can we train for battle?' He looked round at his companions, who all made sounds of vigorous agreement.

'I hope you will not have to fight in battle at so tender an age.' By now Henry had ceased to smile.

'Hope will not keep me safe whereas practice will,' William persisted. 'Look at my wife's grandsire. He partook in the tourneys for more than ten years and lived to a ripe age and died in his bed. We shall all have an opportunity to demonstrate how well we are able to protect you.'

Sighing, Henry regarded William with troubled eyes. 'I have never understood why young men are so mad for the tourneys.' He shot a glance at Edward, who was leaning forward from his place further down the board, his expression avid. 'Even my own son has the passion and he is but eight years old!'

De Clare cleared his throat. 'I would captain the opposing team, sire, and I would see that the tourney was well ordered. The Marshal was my grandsire too.' He touched his chest for emphasis. 'It would be an honour and an opportunity for these young men you have knighted today to prove their worth. They will have much more to offer as they grow, but this is their contribution now and I say with all due respect, it should not be dismissed.'

Henry rubbed his chin, and finally exhaled and opened his

hands. 'What can I do against the persuasion of youth? Very well, I grant you permission to hold a tourney, but I want to see and approve the plans in detail beforehand.'

'Thank you, sire, thank you!' Kneeling, William kissed Henry's hand. The others knelt too, but Henry waved them away with an exasperated smile and a frown between his brows, decidedly less joyful than his supplicants, or his eldest son, who was squirming with glee.

William sat before the fire in his chamber. Heavy rain had forced the court to indoor pursuits. No hunting or hawking today, and the grooms had been handed the task of exercising the horses. William had eschewed the delights of socialising with his peers, and was deeply engrossed in the book John de Warenne had lent to him on the history of Joanna's grandsire the great William Marshal, regent of England during the King's minority.

William's mother had occasionally mentioned the Marshal, but without warmth since he was one of the reasons she had left England; there had been no room for a dowager queen in the power play following King John's death. However, William was much more interested in the Marshal's legendary career in the tourneys as a young man. The numerous enthralling details and anecdotes in the book made him want to rush out and perform great deeds.

Joanna entered the chamber and crossed the room to wrap her arms around his neck from behind. 'You haven't had your nose out of that book for two days,' she said. 'It is time for dinner.'

'Your grandsire was a great man.' Folding the book inside its protective cloth, he put it down. 'He took the ransoms of five hundred knights during his tourney career. And those are only the ones noted by a clerk. I wonder how many he took altogether.'

'My mother told me stories about him, but she was only a child when he died, so most of the tales came from her older brothers and sisters.' If she never heard another word about tourneys it would be too soon. If William wasn't reading about them, then he was training, planning tactics, and organising the event, set to be held in Northampton a fortnight hence at Martinmas. Her cousin John was no better. Neither she nor Aliza could talk sense into their besotted husbands, especially when they were being aided and abetted by William's brothers who were keen to display their military prowess. Joanna was hoping that, like a hot fever, it would run its course and then they might actually return to reason and proportion.

The King was quiet and preoccupied at dinner, and after everyone had eaten he took William and his brothers aside with John de Warenne, Richard de Clare and other young hopefuls involved in organising the tourney.

'I know this will disappoint you all,' he said, 'but I have been thinking about the tourney, and I believe it is unwise to hold it just now. I agreed on the spur of the moment when you pushed me into a corner, but I have had time to consider, and Martinmas is an inauspicious day to hold such an event since it marks the start of the slaughter month. You are young men full of hot blood and I do not want to see that blood spilled for sport.'

William stared at Henry in growing astonishment and furious disappointment, unable to believe his half-brother was snatching this from under their noses. He had all the equipment, and had paid a pretty penny for it. 'Sire, I pray you think again,' he said.

Henry shook his head. 'It was ill-judged to begin with. I should never have agreed.'

'But we need the practice,' Guy protested. 'And William needs to boost his military experience. He is untried, yet you have given him lands in Wales for which he might have to fight at any time. How will he win the respect of the other Marcher lords if he has no experience in combat? We all need to practise.'

'I would not forgive myself if any of you were injured. Tourneys all too easily turn to violence. The lances are shattered and then the swords come out.' Henry turned to William and opened one hand in appeal. 'You are young and impatient and ardent. I am only just coming to know you, and would never forgive myself if something happened. I need you, and I do not want to see you broken on the battlefield – nor any of my other good men.'

William wanted to spit with fury. All that training, all that time and energy and expense, for nothing.

'Your men need to practise for war so that we may have peace,' de Clare tried. 'We need tourneys to show the youngsters how to go about their business – surely you see that, sire? Even in times of quiet we must train – indeed especially then.'

'But this one has been organised in too much haste and on a day for blood-letting.'

'So, you agree we can have one if we organise it on a better day?'

Henry drew back, grimacing.

'How will I hold my head up in front of my peers?' William demanded, furious tears glittering in his eyes. 'You have made me a knight, but how am I to become one if I am not seen to become one? What is the point of having all this equipment if I cannot use it?'

Henry sighed with exasperation as if at the antics of a quer-ulous toddler. 'I shall consider the matter,' he said, 'but do not push me. The Martinmas tourney I forbid, and I will hear no more on the matter. I am the King and my word is final and you will heed what I say.'

He dismissed the others but bade William stay behind.

'I know you are deeply disappointed, my boy, and I am sorry,' he said, softening his tone.

'But you have said you will consider the matter,' William persisted. Although crestfallen, he had already decided to pursue the matter until Henry capitulated. Something worth having was often denied at the first hurdle, and giving up was a sign of weakness.

'And so I shall,' Henry said. 'Do not be too downhearted. I have a gift in mind for you – the castle and estate at Hertford is but a day's ride from Westminster. There is a fine hunting park attached and you shall have some of my deer to stock it. Hunting is also a good test of riding skill. My clerks are drawing up the details even now.'

'Thank you, sire, that is generous,' William replied with delight, although it also felt like distracting a thwarted child with sweetmeats. However, he did not want to appear ungracious or step over the line; such largesse might dry up, and he needed his half-brother's goodwill to flow positively towards him. Henry could probably be brought to allow the tourney on another occasion, especially since there were many more disheartened, keen young men to appease. Indeed, softening the disappointment with gifts of land and hunting preserves was almost worth the disappointment. 'Thank you, sire,' he said again, this time with increased gratitude, and when Henry embraced him, William embraced him warmly in return.

'Perhaps it is for the best,' Joanna said, secretly relieved when she heard about the cancelled tourney. 'I know how hard you have all worked, but Henry is the King and it is his right to decide.' Hertford was a generous gift and would hopefully divert William's focus.

177

'It is a waste,' William replied. 'All that preparation for nothing.' And then he shrugged as though shaking off a shower of rain. 'He has not refused outright. He says he will think on it.'

Joanna grimaced. It was typical of Henry. He would kick the matter down the road, hoping it would quietly go away, but it would only lurk in the grass, waiting to rear its head again. The men would be bored during the winter months. They would hunt, of course, but there would be no campaigns, no warfare. They might see to their estates and mend their kit and manage family business, but the lure of the tourney was like a lantern gleaming in the winter dark. She was coming to know her husband just as much as she knew the King. William possessed such stubborn tenacity that once a notion or challenge entered his head it was impossible to shift.

15

Winchester, Hampshire, February 1248

Joanna and Aliza sat over their embroidery in the Queen's apartments. The court had arrived in Winchester for the Feast of the Purification and for the annual discussion concerning the finances of the realm and intentions for the year ahead. Usually the King demanded money and the barons refused it except in return for promises and concessions and everything became very fraught. The women were excluded from the discussions, although there would be plenty of involvement afterwards in private.

Aliza sought among her silks for a new colour and said casually, 'I am not certain, but I think I may be with child. I have not bled in two months and this morning I was sick.'

Joanna hugged her. 'That is good news! I am so pleased for you and John.'

Aliza flushed. 'I am not telling him yet lest it be a false alarm, but I think it is true. You are the first person to know.'

Joanna hugged her again, genuinely glad for Aliza, but a small surge of worry and even envy lodged in her heart. Her own flux had been late at Christmas and she had begun to think she might have an announcement to make, but it had proved a false hope when a fortnight later she had bled, and another flux had followed since then. It was not for want of attention from William and she was becoming anxious. 'I promise to keep silent until you make an announcement,' she said.

Aliza made a face. 'My mother bore nine of us to my father, and before that five to King John. Year upon year upon year. It might be my duty and the will of God, but I have no desire to emulate her.'

Joanna shivered. She had no wish to emulate her mother either, who had died bearing her third child. Being fertile was an expectation, a duty and a reason for joy, but also a cause of fear and pain.

'There are ways and means of regulating one's family though,' Aliza said. 'The Queen has two sons and two daughters, but I have noticed the wool she keeps hidden in that pot at the bedside for when the King visits.'

Joanna stared at Aliza. 'You know about that?'

'Lady Sybil mentioned it in so many words when I was preparing to wed. Did she say the same to you? You soak the wool in wine or vinegar and put it inside yourself?'

Joanna glanced round, but no one was within earshot. 'Yes, among many other things,' she said quietly. 'It is not a lore that men need to know about though, and it doesn't always work.'

'I wonder if men would use it if they were the ones bearing babies. I think they would!' Aliza gave a throaty laugh, hastily suppressed as their husbands arrived from the council chamber.

Joanna was immediately alert, for William was flushed and tight-lipped and John was scowling. However, neither man would be drawn, and the women had to let the matter drop. But later, in their chamber, William made love to Joanna with possessive assertion. She enjoyed the vigour of his attentions, and met his need with her own, remembering Cecily's advice, but when they were regaining their breath, she leaned up on an elbow to look at him.

'What happened today?' she asked.

He sat up and folded his arms around his knees. 'Complaints to the King about how he constantly shows foreigners favour above loyal English subjects,' he said, scowling. 'Comments about how the King has disparaged good English heirs and heiresses by giving them to foreign parasites. Insinuations that my union with you has been against the interests of the country, and the same with John and Aliza. That the King should never have given our marriages. They demanded that Henry swear he would never do the like again.'

'That is outrageous! It is for the King to say and for the parties concerned to refuse if they so deem.'

'I said the same thing, that you could be summoned to say if you were dissatisfied with your marriage, but of course they would have none of that.' He looked at her, his hair tumbling over his brow. 'I came to make a life here and serve my brother, but many lords and prelates resent our connection. They had no right to speak as they did.'

'There are always those who will stir the pot out of envy for others,' she said, and kissed him. 'You must remain focused and make allies wherever possible – although it is easier said than done.'

'My wise Joanna.' His tone was mocking but tender. He let out a hard breath to release the least of his annoyance and took her hand. 'One piece of good news though: the King has finally agreed to let us hold a tourney, at Newbury on Ash Wednesday.'

Given what he had just told her about the council meeting, Joanna was dismayed, but knew she would more easily shift a mountain with a spoon than persuade William out of it. Perhaps better over and done with than always on the horizon as a lingering energy.

'It will be all right,' he said. 'I promise you.'

The morning of the tourney at Newbury dawned bright and cold. Barons and knights had assembled from every corner of England to take part.

Surrounding the tourney field, the pastures bloomed with brightly coloured pavilions. Pennants fluttered from the tops, and shields planted on staves outside the tents marked the devices of the lords taking part. Bigod and Clare; Ferrers, de Warenne, Lusignan and Valence.

Armed up and ready to go to his horse, William paused inside his blue and white pavilion with Geoffrey and Guy for a final moment. Anticipation churned inside him; he had been working towards this moment since childhood. To take part in a proper tournament. To couch his lance and face a real opponent across the field instead of his tutor. To not have to pull his blows but to strike hard and true.

'Watch de Clare and Bigod,' Guy warned. 'They are experienced, older and more powerful. They will be looking to take you and John.' He cast a glance towards their new brother-in-law. 'I know you think you can look after yourselves, but be on your guard. Even if this tourney is to celebrate your knighthood, make no mistake, there will be some heavy play. Many will seek to seize you for ransom and trample your pride.'

Geoffrey nodded in agreement, and their superiority irritated William. They themselves were hardly so accustomed to competing in tourneys as to be doling out advice. They were just throwing their weight around because they were older.

'Mayhap we will take theirs,' he said, jutting his jaw.

'I hope so, little brother.' From old habit Guy tousled William's hair despite William being taller than him these days. 'But it does no harm to take advice.'

William jerked away, and Guy laughed with good-natured scorn.

The young men trooped out to the horse lines where their mounts had been harnessed by the grooms. William had been schooling his new destrier Rous since October, and they had come to know each other well in the four months since then. He was a powerful ruby-chestnut with an arched neck and high-stepping gait. He wore a quilted coat for protection, covered by a surcoat of blue and white stripes embroidered with the red swifts of Valence. As he snorted and pawed, ready for the event, William's heart swelled with pride at his magnificence.

Wooden stands had been erected at the side of the main field for the spectators and William sought Joanna, and found her sitting with Aliza not far from the King's empty seat. The feeling in William's gut became a sunburst. He so wanted to acquit himself well and prove to Joanna that her worry was ill-founded.

John had mounted his destrier – a dark bay trapped out in the chequered blue and gold of de Warenne. On the opposing team, John's half-brother Roger Bigod rode not in his usual colours of the Earl of Norfolk, but in green and yellow, emblazoned with the scarlet lion that his grandsire the Marshal had made famous throughout England and Normandy as the greatest tourney champion of his age.

Refusing to be intimidated by such a visceral challenge, William checked his weapons and received his lance from Elias, determined to concentrate on his own business.

A fanfare sounded as the King arrived and took his seat on the cushioned great chair at the centre of the lodges. Wrapped in a thick fur cloak, Henry looked pinched and tight with cold – a man attending as a matter of duty, pushed into a corner and eager for the contest to end even before it started.

The tourney commenced with individual bouts between eager young knights burning with excitement. William rode against one of Roger Bigod's young protégés and performed well, breaking his lance on the other's shield and almost unseating him. Turning Rous, exhilaration coursed through him. He was born for this, and the truth of it glowed inside him like fire. He cheered on his companions as they took their turns to warm up against individual opponents while the older men looked on, leaning against their mounts, passing asides and comments. John de Warenne unseated his opponent, sending him backwards over the saddle, to loud applause from his Bigod half-brothers.

The next hour continued similarly. William rode again and shattered another lance and his confidence increased. He took part in sword fights and wrestling contests on the ground and won the prize for the latter – a bronze aquamanile and bowl in the shape of a swan, presented to him by the King, who was even smiling a little by now.

Once everyone had refreshed themselves and regrouped, the grand melee was announced.

William's breath shortened as he lined up with the rest of his team. Rous had caught his tension and sidled and pranced. William reined him in, forward and back, holding in the stallion's explosive power, waiting for the signal. Anticipation surged through his veins. He glanced at Guy, slightly to the right and in front of him. He held his stallion on a tight rein, the colourful plumes on top of his helm waving in the wind. William checked again to make sure he was in the right position. To his left he could hear Geoffrey humming softly under his breath.

William fretted Rous and levelled his lance. The shout went up and he gave the stallion his head. Rous lunged immediately into a ground-eating gallop. William felt the surge beneath him, the force and thrust of each stride. Elation washed over him as the lines clashed and his lance shattered on his opponent's shield. He drew his baton from his belt and attacked side on with a series of well-aimed blows that forced the other man to back off and yield.

Filled with triumph and fire, William pushed forward, but found himself facing a seasoned military campaigner in Joanna's cousin, Roger Bigod, Earl of Norfolk. The blow Bigod struck rocked William back in the saddle, and suddenly William was struggling. Roger Bigod was close to forty years old, vigorous and strong, and knew all the tricks. William had never come up against this level of opposition before; all the young knights against whom he had sparred in training had been within his range or just above it and he had been able to push himself while improving his technique and skill. But Bigod, his heraldry blazoned with the Marshal lion, was a different prospect. William had been fighting with the intensity of excitement and the confidence of youth, but Bigod had experience and mature skill. He pivoted his destrier into the killing zone at William's back, and although William managed to turn and meet him, the angle skewed his arm, and instead of delivering all the blows, he was receiving them, and having to work hard to stay out of trouble.

He took a blow across his knuckles, and although he was wearing stout gloves, tingles shot up his arm to his elbow and he almost dropped his baton. He tried to retreat but he was blocked in, unable to go forward or back, and no room to swing his weapon. He spurred Rous forward, but Bigod manoeuvred to foil his efforts and struck at him relentlessly. William fought to protect himself with his shield, but many of the blows still connected. His arms were burning with effort and his stamina started to fail. He looked round frantically but his brothers were on another part of the field and they too were taking a battering from the opposition.

Seeing a gap, William made a dash for safety, striking out on either side, attempting a defensive escape, his efforts fuelled by desperation. But everyone crowded in on him, beating him from all sides. The armour that had weighed so lightly at the outset, glittering with prospect, now seemed fashioned of molten lead. He could barely lift his shield to repel the blows and, unable to retort, curled over and endured the pummelling while praying to avoid the ultimate humiliation of being dragged from his horse.

Through the roaring in his ears, he heard Roger Bigod bellow with commanding authority, 'Come, come, enough! The lesson is well learned. Enough, I say, enough! Let him be!'

William was aware of his bridle being seized, and of being led out of the centre of the melee at a jerky trot. He swayed but gripped the reins and concentrated on staying in the saddle, determined that whatever happened he would not fall.

A knight of de Clare's rode to the centre of the field and waved William's helm plumes aloft as a sign of victory and the crowd roared their delight that the foreigner in their midst, the King's privileged younger brother, had been given the drubbing he so thoroughly deserved. As William was led away to his tent, he could hear the sound of the melee continuing. He desperately wanted to go back and fight, but while his mind was bright with determination, his abused body refused to answer the summons.

He slid from Rous, and his legs almost buckled. The stallion was led away, head down, steaming with sweat. Elias hastened to help him out of his armour and Jacomin gave him a goblet of wine laced with sugar. William could scarcely hold the cup because his hands were shaking so badly.

'This is not fear,' he snapped to Jacomin, feeling furious and ashamed.

'Indeed not, sire,' Jacomin replied. 'A fearful man would not act as you have done on the field. You are overset with the force of the fight, that is all. I could not have sustained such blows for as long as you did. I surely thought that they were going to kill you.'

William had surely thought it too. He managed to stand while Elias removed his armour and undertunic, and then, while Jacomin tipped pails of water into an oval bath tub, he slumped on a bench, because his legs truly had given out. He put his head in his hands and castigated himself for being outwitted, outflanked and outridden, and it had been over so soon he had not had the chance to regroup and seek revenge. Filled with shame, he dreaded facing Joanna when he had so desired to prove his valour to her. He had to face Henry too, after all the pressure he had put on him to hold the tourney in the first place.

He tried to straighten up but desisted with a gasp at the pain from the blows inflicted on him. His ribs were especially sore where he had taken a hard blow from Roger Bigod. Jacomin indicated the bath tub, fragrant with herbal steam. 'It is ready, sire. It will help with the bruises.' He held up a pot in his right hand. 'And this is my mother's marigold ointment – she swears by it. Always used it on us as nippers.'

William had not been expecting to bathe, but it would wash away the stink of battle and the ignominy of it all. Suppressing groans, he removed the rest of his garment with Elias's help and gingerly stepped into the tub. Red patches flowered on his body denoting the path of the hardest blows. At least he had not broken any bones or chipped any teeth.

Jacomin clucked his tongue in sympathy. 'My brother looked like that after a tavern brawl,' he said. 'Spent a week in bed he did. You did well, sire. It is not your fault they all piled on to you as a target.' The servant applied himself practically to tending his master's injuries, causing William to hiss with pain and clench his teeth. 'You'll defeat them next time round, sire,' Jacomin said cheerfully.

'Yes,' William said, looking at his swollen knuckles. 'I will indeed.'

Seeing William being led off the field by Roger Bigod, Joanna started to rise. The concentrated attack had filled her with fear and shock at so much antagonism. And those brothers of his, getting carried away with the fighting and not coming to his aid. At least the Bigods had been more watchful and protective of John.

Aliza caught her arm. 'Calm yourself. He is still in the saddle and he will not thank you for making a fuss.'

'What kind of wife would I be if I did not go to him?' Joanna shook Aliza off. 'You would go to John!'

'Of course I would, but I would give him a moment's respite. He will not want you to see him unmanned.'

Joanna swallowed and controlled herself, because if all the men were picking on William, then the ladies of the court must be feeding avidly off her distress. Aliza was right. She sat down and waited for a short while, watching and smiling, without seeing a thing. When she judged that enough time had passed, she turned again to Aliza. 'I need to go to him,' she said. 'Whatever it costs. Do not try and stop me.'

Aliza nodded this time. 'Shall I come with you?'

'No. I will talk to you later.'

Her maid Nicola in tow, Joanna made her way to William's pavilion, walking with dignity, wanting to run but aware that her every step was being watched and judged. Through the open tent flap, servants were carrying out pails of water followed by a bath tub. Joanna drew a deep breath and entered, dreading what she might find.

William was standing by his camp table dressed in a loose silk tunic, his curly hair damp and swept back. The beginnings of a black eye swelled like a ripening plum under his right eye. No longer able to maintain her façade, she ran to him and flung her arms around his neck. 'Are you all right? Dear God! I thought you would be killed!'

William stiffened as her body struck his, and then he gingerly folded his arms around her. The feel of them, vital and strong, filled her with relief because she had convinced herself he had been badly wounded.

'Let me see you. What have they done to you?'

He stepped back and spread his arms wide, managing not to grimace. 'Look, I am unharmed. You will have a husband for the next thirty years at least!'

Joanna swallowed tears. 'Not if you carry on like this!'

He glanced pointedly at the squires and servants still busy in the tent. 'It is nothing to complain about. It won't happen next time, I promise you.'

'Next time?'

'How else will I improve?' he asked, as though he was being perfectly reasonable.

Joanna shook her head, too full to speak. Aliza had been right: she should not have come.

At the banquet following the tourney, Joanna sat beside William and wore a forced smile. William played his role to the hilt, and no one would have guessed that his ribs were bandaged under his tunic and that he was in serious pain. He could not, however, conceal the swollen bruise that had almost shut his right eye, but most of the opposing team were sporting battle injuries too and his visible ones did not especially stand out above the others. He raised toasts and laughed and acted as if all was well, taking glory even in defeat, and Joanna smiled for all she was worth, and felt sick.

When they retired, he fell on the bed on his back and was

asleep within moments, still in his clothes. He had drunk far too much, although she supposed it might be a blessing if it rendered him insensible. She eyed him with exasperation. He had not even taken off his boots. She tried to pull off some of his clothes but he grunted and rolled over and finally she gave up and stalked off in disgust.

Going to the window seat, she sat down and picked up a cushion she had earlier been embroidering. Holding it against her body, she rocked back and forth for comfort. Why did men enjoy doing this? She had seen it in her brother and her male cousins the same, and her own grandfather had made a career of the sport.

King Henry was not obsessed with fighting, but men looked at him askance and thought less of him for lacking the warrior abilities. But perhaps he was the one in his right mind. What if she and William had sons who turned out to be like that? They would be regarded as fine, robust males by society and William would take great pride in them. She was starting to understand a little better the Queen's concerns about Edward.

She glanced at William's sprawled figure. She could not talk to him because he was heavily, drunkenly asleep. She was expected to tend his wounds, commiserate with him, and praise him for his endurance. But what was the benefit to her? After all the preparation, after all the energy expended and all the building of expectation, he had failed, and she had now to look others in the eye and take on his failure. What would Cecily say? The thought brought her to a standstill.

She ceased rocking and set the cushion aside. Whatever happened, she had to find her own strength and not depend on him or anyone else. William was what he was and at least he was true to himself. She had to be true to herself and make the best with him if they were to survive.

She left the window and undressed without summoning her maids. She washed her face and hands and climbed into bed beside him. She could have sought another place to sleep tonight, but doing so would be the first step away and it would lead to another and another until there was a gulf. However, she punched the pillow very hard before she set her head on it. William groaned in his sleep and then flopped over on his side, put his arm out and reached for her.

'Joanna,' he said, a catch in his voice. 'Joanna, never leave me. I could not bear it.' His hand slid over her hip and he nuzzled her neck. She gave a small shiver and turned towards him, and then he was over her, and despite all his injuries and the drink, he was ready, and so was she. She opened to him, still angry, but relieved too at the surge of his life force and that his injuries could not be that bad if he was this capable and interested.

In the morning, Joanna observed William closely as Jacomin helped him into his clothes. She took an inventory of the bandaged ribs, the cuts and scrapes. His black eye had flourished into a ripe purple cabochon, but he was trying to continue as normal, and there was no self-pity; despite his folly, she admired his fortitude.

They broke their fast together as they had done on their wedding morn. William took her hand and kissed it across the small trestle table. 'I know I am in a state, and I know you think me foolish, but I have learned from yesterday's drubbing and in a situation where I have survived. It would not have been the same on the battlefield, so the tourney has proved its worth. I have learned from my mistakes. Next time it will be different, you wait and see.'

'You are incorrigible!' Joanna shook her head. 'I love you, but do not ask me why, for our children may never have a father and I may not have a husband if you continue at such a pace, whatever you say about learning lessons.'

His ears grew red. 'I cannot live a coddled life. This is part of what and who I am.'

'I know, and I know it is your duty to be highly trained in military matters, but you must also understand the repercussions to me,' Joanna said firmly. 'You are playing for high stakes, and the things you say you hold dear may be broken along with your lance and never mended again.'

'It will not happen again. I promise. I will show you something to have faith in, and never let you down.' He leaned forward, intending to kiss her, but she drew back.

'Then do so,' she said. 'Sweet words and promises are nothing without deeds and true intent.' She rose from the table. 'And for my sake too, go and chew some liquorice before you try to kiss me again. Your breath smells like a wine cellar.' She tugged her cloak from its peg and swept it around her shoulders. 'I am going to see Aliza.'

When she had gone, William groaned and slumped. A dull headache invaded his skull. Weazel was watching him intently. 'Women,' he said to the cat in disgust, feeding him some scraps of smoked herring left on the side of the dish. 'It's the price you pay for being a man.' But eventually he sought a liquorice stick to clean his teeth, and for good measure chewed some cardamom pods too, because however exasperated Joanna made him, she was usually right and he still wanted to kiss her.

16

Palace of Westminster, August 1248

William stepped back from the baggage cart and wiped sweat from his brow. An August sun sweltered from a sky burned almost white by the fierce summer heat. Aliza was retiring to Lewes for her lying in and Joanna was accompanying her. Although the birth was still six weeks away, Aliza had judged it time to retire from the daily bustle of the court and the Queen had granted Joanna leave to attend the confinement. For his sins, William was supervising the loading of Joanna's baggage, including Weazel, who hunched in his wicker travelling cage, lashing his tail from side to side, growling ferociously and swiping a bad-tempered paw through the slats at anyone who came too close.

The court would be so empty without Joanna. Her presence soothed him, and helped him make sense of the world. He only had to look at her for his heart to fill with joy. Some of his companions had waggled their eyebrows and jested about just what he could get up to during her absence. William had smiled at the innuendo but said nothing, for that was not how it was between him and Joanna. Taking other women to his bed would be dishonourable and put him in bad favour with the King and Queen who were the most faithful of couples. Besides, why drink inferior wine when you already had the best in your cellar?

He would have more time for hunting and jousting, and for ordinary socialising with his friends, including the delights of dice and other gambling, but they were no substitute for lying with his head in Joanna's lap while she stroked his hair. Being parted also meant they had no opportunity to conceive an heir. They had been married for a year without a sign of a pregnancy and he sometimes worried that he and Joanna had displeased God; the pressure to perform was a weight upon both of them. Then again, not being together would alleviate the expectation.

More baggage arrived to be stowed, and he grimaced. At this rate they were going to need an extra horse to pull it all. Returning to the hall, to find out how much more there was, he noticed Aliza sitting in the window embrasure as her maids bustled around with last-minute tasks. The light outlined her full round belly. Catching his eye, she smiled and beckoned to him.

'I swear, I have never seen so much baggage in my life,' he said. 'Not even when the King moves palaces!'

'William, you do not understand the needs of a woman building a nest,' she replied with superior amusement, 'but your time will come.'

The sunlight shone on her bronze-gold braids, coiled over her ears and half concealed beneath a gauzy headdress. Pregnancy had lent extra plumpness and radiance to her face. He had the slightly blasphemous thought that his sister looked like a Madonna.

She glanced around the room, making sure no one was watching, and covertly handed him a small drawstring pouch. 'I want you to keep this for me.'

He looked down at the little bag, made from cloth of gold and expertly embroidered with the crests of Lusignan and de Warenne.

'You can open it,' she said.

He tipped a small object into his palm. Under a polished rock crystal cover shone a lock of bronze-gold hair twined with gold wire and secured with three pearl pins. He looked at her with a frown. 'What is this?'

Aliza put her hand on his wrist and lowered her voice. 'If anything happens to me when I bear this child – if I don't survive . . .' She gave him a direct, powerful look. 'I am entrusting you to give this to John as I give it to you now. I want you to tell him that my life will continue elsewhere through my eternal soul and although he is my husband and I love him dearly, he must not mourn for me but continue to live his life in joy. If he does that, I will be more than satisfied. Put it away carefully, and keep it for me against such a day.' She patted his sleeve and smiled.

Stunned, William wondered how she could contemplate such a thing in the midst of everyday matters. She was too deep for him and he experienced a moment of resentment because she was his big sister and supposed to comfort him. Confronting the possibility of losing her horrified him. And for her to tell him to exhort John to live his life in joy told William how little she knew about her husband's response to grief.

'If that is your wish, I shall keep it for you,' he said grudgingly, 'but I had better not have to use it.'

'God willing you won't.' She flashed him a perceptive look. 'You would set your house in order before you went into battle. It is the same thing.'

It wasn't at all, but he put the token away in his pouch with a curt nod.

'Thank you. I know it is a strange thing to ask, but I would not do so unless it was important for me and for John. It is settled now, and I do not need to worry.'

John arrived to escort Aliza to the travelling cart and she gave William a meaningful look as she rose to go with him.

William tried to imagine Joanna presenting John with such a token in similar circumstances and could not. Although they shared most things, he decided not to tell her about Aliza's gift.

Joanna rocked her little niece in her arms and smiled into the baby's cherub face. She had stood as godmother to little Alienor who had been born five weeks into Aliza's confinement at Lewes and named, diplomatically, after the Queen. At three months old the baby was delightful, with Aliza's bronze hair and John's dark eyes. John had not complained once about her being a girl rather than a son and heir. Indeed, he doted on her, and Joanna's affection for him had increased.

Cuddling her niece, Joanna's heart filled with a longing to hold her own child. Sometimes she was envious of Aliza for conceiving so quickly and giving birth so easily, but would instantly feel remorse for that envy. The will of God was the will of God. Now they had returned to Westminster, perhaps she might have good news in the spring. She had spent an hour this morning in the King's painted chamber, silently communing with the figure of Hope.

Sorting through the contents of a jewel coffer she had upended on the bed, Aliza picked up a smooth sapphire stone on a gold chain and dangled it before her daughter, who made a myopic grab for it. 'It belonged to John's mother,' Aliza said. 'She was a formidable lady and I was sorry not to know her well, and that she died before she could meet this little one.'

'She was indeed formidable – the last of my Marshal aunts

and uncles,' Joanna said. John's mother had been buried at Tintern Abbey in Wales beside her mother, her grandmother and her two youngest brothers. The passing of a generation like a breeze through a wheat field. Sad but inevitable.

After a pause, Joanna sighed. 'William is organising another tourney – on Ash Wednesday again. You did warn me.'

Aliza shook her head. 'Yes, I did. He has boundless energy and he has to expend it.'

'Yes, but I wish it could be in other ways.'

'He is talented too, despite what happened last time. Until he has proved himself, he will not let it go and you will not stop him.'

'I know.' Joanna chewed the inside of her lower lip.

'Men bond in battle practice. They get drunk together and spend their time talking about horses and harness and weapons,' Aliza said. 'They will commiserate with each other about their wives fussing over nothing even while their wives complain about their childish, rash husbands, but somewhere, eventually, we make compromises and we meet in the middle.'

'Yes,' Joanna said wryly, and Aliza gave her a swift hug.

'We are blessed to have each other, and we are blessed to have our husbands even if they drive us to distraction.'

'There is no doubt about that!' Joanna replied with an exasperated laugh.

Leaving little Alienor with her nurse, Joanna and Aliza went to attend on the Queen. Eleanor de Montfort was present among the ladies already surrounding the royal chair, while her husband, freshly returned from Gascony for the Christmas feast, held forth to a group of men on the far side of the room. Joanna noted William among them, hanging on the words as though they were jewels, and she tightened her lips.

Simon de Montfort had been blessedly absent from court

since her marriage, governing Gascony for the King, but had returned for the Christmas season to make his report. He had a powerful, carrying voice and the charisma to dominate a conversation. Nine-year-old Edward stood watching him with wide-eyed fascination. The King was looking too, and Joanna noticed his tension. Henry was always uncomfortable when de Montfort was at court. All they had in common was Eleanor, sister to one and wife to the other, and she was a source of conflict, not unity.

Eleanor de Montfort had been speaking to the Queen, but now approached Joanna and Aliza. 'I congratulate you and your lord on the birth of a daughter,' she said with a smile.

'Thank you, sister,' Aliza said. 'We have named her in memory and in recognition of the many illustrious ladies of that name and in our family.'

'Indeed,' Eleanor said graciously. 'I wish I had a daughter to my brood, but my lord is strong and vigorous and thus far has only planted sons in my womb.'

Aliza smiled. 'I am sure you will bear a daughter in the full-ness of time. Girls can be such comforts to a mother, and make fine marriages for the family.'

'You are wise, my sister,' Eleanor said, and turned to Joanna. 'No doubt your time will come even if it takes a little longer.' Her voice, sweet and light, managed nevertheless to hint that Joanna and William were deficient breeding material.

'As God wills it,' Joanna replied with dignity. 'After all, oak trees are slow to engender, but they are the strongest and most lasting of all the trees in the forest.'

Eleanor patted her arm. 'If that is the case then your sons will surely be mighty and surpass their father. I expect any of the ladies will be pleased to assist you with advice and nostrums if you ask.'

Joanna clenched her teeth and pressed her lips together. Thank God, the de Montforts would be returning to Gascony soon.

'Simon de Montfort is a fine soldier,' William enthused to Joanna later. 'We ought to get to know him better while he is here, since he is my brother-by-marriage.'

Preparing for bed, Joanna set her jaw and said nothing. Simon de Montfort stalked through the court like the lion on his shield and she well understood why William might strive to emulate such a strong personality.

'I thought we might invite him and my sister to dine with us before he returns to Gascony. I know we have a dispute with them over the Marshal estates, but why not leave that in the hands of our lawyers and strive for an amicable resolution?'

'You do not know what he is like,' she said. Weazel leaped into her lap and circled, preparatory to curling up. 'You do not know what he has done.' She stroked the cat, seeking comfort.

He looked at her askance.

'He and his wife consider that we have no right to anything,' she said bitterly. 'They want a bigger bite of my grandsire's estate than they have been legally apportioned and they want Pembroke. Simon de Montfort has contempt for the King even as he serves him. You were not there when he called Henry a simpleton to his face and wished him behind bars. You were not there when he intimidated me and my brother because we were heirs to what he saw as his wife's inheritance.'

William studied her with a perplexed frown.

'He is strong and powerful and he makes friends of the same ilk to further his own cause. You may be the King's brother but he will never treat you as an equal, and neither will his wife. I would not welcome them at my table even if I have to sit by them in the hall and be civil. It is a step too far.'

'I will not invite them if you do not wish it, but it is a missed opportunity.'

'In time you will see that it is not.' It would mend the atmosphere if she capitulated, but even for William, she could not do it. The notion of sitting at table with the Earl of Leicester and his wife not only made her skin crawl, it made her afraid. She had controlled her childhood fear, but it had never gone away.

William was still pondering Joanna's hostility towards the de Montforts the following day as the servants prepared the King's painted chamber for a banquet, decorating the walls with fresh greenery to match the embroidered bed covers. A fire blazed in the capacious hearth and de Montfort stood warming his back and gazing round the room with narrowed eyes.

William approached him and held his hands out to the heat. He wanted to know de Montfort better and to understand what drew people to this man, and also to get to the bottom of Joanna's antipathy. Clearly there was bad blood and a past of which he knew little. From what William had seen so far, de Montfort had a rod of iron in his spine. He was rigid, without flexibility, and possessed a forceful manner of speaking and a way of cutting men down to size with words in the same wise as he used his sword on the battlefield, but he had charisma, and military acumen. Henry appeared to avoid him, but nevertheless was paying him handsomely to deal with Gascony.

'This is going to be a magnificent banquet,' he said by way of an overture. 'The green and gold look particularly striking, do you not think? The King has a fine eye.'

De Montfort eyed him with raised brows, and a look of surprise. 'Indeed,' he said. His gaze swept over the lavish preparations almost impatiently. 'Perhaps it should be his sole calling in life.' He looked at William and shook his head. 'I wonder to myself what the King sees in you.'

'Sire?' William stared at him, taken aback by the scorn in de Montfort's eyes.

'You are barely a knight, you have never seen true battle or taken the decision of a statesman in your life, and yet he seeks your advice and you stand at his side every moment. Do I suppose that you prattle between you of colours and curtains and where next to spend the coin that he does not have?'

William could not believe his ears. 'I beg your pardon, sire. What do you mean?'

'I cannot speak more plainly,' de Montfort replied impatiently. 'To me you are an irrelevance. Do not boast to me that you are the King's brother. You only have this position at court because your wife has laid it open for you with her purloined wealth and because the King only has half his wits. I have better things to do than prate of frippery.' He turned on his heel and stalked off to join a group of other men, making it clear that William was not welcome to do the same.

For a moment, William was too astonished at the snub to be angry, and even when that emotion flooded through him he did not know what to do with it. As always, Joanna was far ahead of him. He had just been dismissed and insulted as a lightweight. He considered stalking over to de Montfort and having it out, but deemed it unwise to stir up antagonism in the face of de Montfort's amused and hostile cronies. He had been rebuffed and knew where he stood. De Montfort would soon be returning to Gascony while he would be at the King's side and making advantage. He suspected that was what really galled the Earl of Leicester.

Leaving the hall, he sought Joanna to tell her what happened. 'You were right,' he said. 'But even had I gone as far as asking him to dine, I believe he would have refused me.'

'You should avoid him,' she replied. 'You may have to stand in the same council chamber, but do not engage him unless you must, and leave the land dispute to the lawyers. His acquisitiveness knows no bounds.'

William nodded agreement. 'I was thinking once de Montfort has gone that we could ask the King's leave to visit Hertford. Perhaps in a couple more months when the spring grass has grown.'

'Yes,' Joanna said in a heartfelt voice. 'It will be good to escape the court for a while.'

17

Hertford Castle, Hertfordshire, April 1249

In the first week of April, William and Joanna came to Hertford on the banks of the River Lea. Their baggage train had set out the day before so that the servants could prepare for their arrival, leaving William and Joanna to enjoy the journey unencumbered. They had set out at first light from London and rode up shortly after noon. The sky was a delicate spring blue and they had heard the first cuckoo of the season calling throatily from a copse as they journeyed along the green-edged country lanes.

Hertford filled William with proprietorial joy, for it belonged to him alone, and was not tied to Joanna's Marshal inheritance. The King had given them gifts of deer to populate the park and building materials for repairs, alterations and improvements. Approaching the gatehouse with the keep beyond, a broad smile broke across his face.

Grooms hastened to take the horses and the steward escorted them within to the smaller of the two halls. A fire crackled in the hearth of the second one, and the walls were whitened with limewash. Daylight streamed into the chamber from several arched windows. William's shield had been hung on the wall above the lord's chair and a trestle table stood nearby spread with a white cloth and laid with utensils and dishes, the silver-gilt twinkling.

Robert, Joanna's cook, appeared in a waft of savoury vapours, an apron fastened over his tunic. He placed a bowl of golden-crusted bread on the table and bowed to William and Joanna, his cheeks fire-red. 'I have fine tender venison, from the park,' he said, 'and prime salmon and eels from the river with herb sauce, all ready for your delight.'

Joanna smiled and thanked him. Robert had been one of Joanna's first appointments after she had come into her inheritance, recommended by Cecily, who had helped her to select her core household employees. 'You have surpassed yourself,' she said.

He puffed out his chest with pride, flourished a bow and retired to his task.

Joanna looked at William who was gazing around, wide-eyed and smiling. 'Are you hungry?'

'Ravenous.' He squeezed her hand. 'This is a feast for the eyes as well as the belly.'

The dishes arrived, succulent and well seasoned. William, Joanna and their household ate until they were almost too full to move. The afternoon sunshine slanted through the windows, and William raised his first toast as master of Hertford, his eyes alight with pride.

To work off their meal, they set out to explore the rest of the keep. A well-appointed room lay beyond the hall and their bed had been set up at its far end with an adjoining private chapel, and there were two latrines with new wooden seats behind red-painted doors. Joanna went to look out of the window at the sun-polished river. 'What excellent light for sewing. I shall have my frame set up here tomorrow.'

They investigated the rest of their kingdom – the upper rooms and battlements, the spacious courtyard, and the intimate garden with a small orchard and a water course running through it. Beyond that lay the majestic spread of the hunting park waiting to be stocked with game at the King's pleasure.

Eventually they separated, William to have a word with his knights and Joanna to their chamber to oversee the unpacking of the rest of their goods.

She hummed softly, liberated to be away from court. It might be the vibrant hub of power but she had to be constantly on her guard for both herself and William. He had learned to be a little more circumspect these days, but remained vulnerable to becoming involved in trouble, and the King's affection made him a target. William tended to play on Henry's love for him and basked in his favour, partaking of all that the court had to offer. He drank and gambled and went out riding with the other young men and Joanna worried, for in her eyes he needed to be more responsible and sober.

He had organised another tourney for February. Henry had refused permission, but William had decided to hold it anyway, promising the competitors he would go surety for any difficulties that arose. She had had a massive argument with him about defying the King's will, but William had stood his ground, determined to prove his manhood and skill. How else, he demanded, could he gain the necessary experience? One day it might mean the difference between life and death. All Joanna could think of were Cecily's words about a husband's behaviour reflecting on his wife and that she might be considered a party to his defiance. Trying to tell him he should be protecting the King and that going against his word might be construed as rebellion had met with a stony refusal to compromise.

At her wits' end, she had prayed desperately for the event not to happen, and God had heard her plea. On the eve of the tourney a heavy blizzard had put paid to the arrangement and all the grandiose plans had come to nothing. In her mind's eye she could still see the snow whirling around her as she left the chapel, and feel that white, muffling silence. William had flung about cursing, marching up and down, throwing things and shouting. He had sent out letters postponing the tourney until a later date, as yet unspecified. For the moment all was in abeyance, but she knew he had not forgotten and his determination to hold another tourney remained as strong as ever. He was still practising his manoeuvres at every opportunity and acquiring new equipment.

They had mended their disagreement. He had brought her thoughtful little gifts and been charming, amusing and attentive, but it had not changed things. She recognised his need to vent his vigorous physical energy. Without that, he became grumpy and sharp, but when that side of his nature was fulfilled and content it opened up a calm space within him, and then he was hers, and she lived for those moments.

Removing her shoes and stockings, Joanna lay down on the bed to rest for a moment, but no sooner had she stretched out her legs than she noticed a cobweb ghosting the canopy and had to be rid of it. Standing on tip-toe, she batted it away and drew the curtains to check for others, and for chrysalises hiding in the folds. She would chivvy the maids later, but doing this herself gave her great satisfaction.

She heard William arrive and say something over his shoulder to Jacomin in the antechamber, and then he came fully into the room.

'Joanna?'

She tensed as she heard him walk over to the bed, and then she leaped out on him with a cry of 'I'm here!' He had to move swiftly to catch her and she laughed aloud. He thought her too staid and sensible and she was determined to show him she could be joyous and playful too when not having to be on her guard.

He spun her around in his arms until they were both dizzy before dropping her on the bed and pulling her on top of him. 'Ah, Joanna!' he said with a laugh. 'I adore you!' He rolled her over and moved down the bed. 'I love you from the finest hair on your head right down to your littlest toe!' He kissed her feet, small, nibbling kisses, and pushed her gown above her ankles. 'I love your feet,' he said, rubbing them. 'Your ankles, your legs . . .'

Joanna arched and gasped. He moved over her, speaking softly, kissing, caressing and stroking as he named each part, and then he rose above her and she drew him into her with triumph and joy that he wanted her with just as much hunger as she wanted him. She clasped her legs around him and let the pleasure come. In their own bed in their own castle on their first day here. It was very right.

When it was over, they slowly drew apart. William rolled on to his back and Joanna kissed his cheek.

'What you do to me,' he said with a soft chuckle. 'I swear I lose all sense but one.'

'Do not blame me!' she retorted, and tugged his hair.

'What else do you expect when you are hiding behind the bed-curtains, barefoot! What else is a husband to do when thus accosted!'

Joanna shot him a coy look. 'I have no idea what you are talking about.'

'You know perfectly well. Put on your shoes before I lose my senses again. De Bussy has arrived to make a report on the dower claims of your cousins. Oh, and the Abbot of Dene is here seeking hospitality for the night.'

Joanna's face grew hot. 'Why didn't you tell me?'

'I just have done,' he said smugly.

She hit him with a pillow, and then bounced off the bed and hurried to the garderobe. 'You had better send in Nicola,' she said. 'I need to make myself presentable.'

Grinning, William cast the pillow aside and stood up. 'You look very presentable just as you are,' he said as he adjusted his garments. 'All wild-haired and wanton.'

She looked at him over her shoulder. 'It might be appropriate for my husband in our bedchamber but hardly the attire for greeting lawyers and abbots!'

'It might be interesting though,' he said, and sauntered out, sinuous as Weazel on a hunting expedition.

Nicola arrived to coil and tidy Joanna's hair and pin on her wimple, all without comment. Joanna pushed her feet into her shoes and smiled in a way that would certainly have raised the brows of the Abbot of Dene could he have seen it.

William and Joanna spent the remainder of spring and early summer at Hertford, making occasional forays to nearby manors but never staying more than a day. They studied the accounts with their stewards and lawyers, and embarked upon building and decorating projects, aided by gifts of wood and building materials and more money from the King. They went hunting together with the hawks and dogs, and explored every inch of their domain.

Sometimes William returned to court and spent a few days with the King and occasionally Joanna accompanied him, but then they would eagerly return to Hertford and their delayed honeymoon.

One morning in early June, Joanna woke to sunshine streaming on to the bed clothes through the open shutters. She had slept longer than usual and still felt tired even though the dawn had long gone. William's side of the bed was empty, but he was an early riser and had left her to slumber. Sitting up, a wave of nausea assailed her and her breasts felt sore and full. She would have to tell him today. For several mornings she had been thinking about it, but holding back because she had been wrong before, hoping and not daring to hope. Leaving the bed, she began unplaiting her hair and counted again the weeks since her last bleed. Before they came to Hertford. The end of March or early April. And it was now the second week of June.

William breezed into the chamber smelling of outdoors and hot horse. He had a small loaf in a cloth and a large piece of cheese. Joanna inhaled the various smells and her stomach wallowed. She pressed her lips together and clenched her fists until the sensation diminished.

'Everyone will be calling you "slugabed",' he teased. 'Never mind breaking your fast, this will be your dinner!'

Joanna shook her head. 'I am not hungry.'

Immediately his face filled with concern.

'Well, perhaps just a little dry bread – not the cheese.' Even saying the word made her feel sick.

'Are you ill? Shall I fetch a physician?'

She saw the fear in his eyes – there was summer pestilence in London less than a day's ride away. 'No, but I will do better if you take that cheese away . . . leave the bread.'

He did as she asked and brought her a drink of wine. She took a sip, washed it around her mouth, and nibbled on the bread. Her stomach still roiled, but with anxiety.

'What would you say if I told you that you were going to be a father?'

He stared at her. And then slowly he smiled, wider and wider, a big smile full of hope. He took her by the shoulders. 'Truly?'

She looked down demurely. 'I believe there is a very good chance, and that with God's help, come midwinter, we may have an heir.'

'This is the best news you could have given me!' His voice caught. 'This is proof that . . .' He shook his head, unable to continue.

'That neither of us is barren?' she said tremulously.

'Well, that, yes . . . but it is validation too. Of us. Of our marriage, whatever the detractors say. I am so proud.' He wrapped his arms around her and they hugged. She leaned against his chest and felt his heart beating in solid, steady strokes and thought that there was a child growing inside her womb with a beating heart too, and that they had at last been favoured by God. It was indeed validation against all comers.

18

Palace of Westminster, November 1249

Sitting with the women in the Queen's chamber, Joanna felt as dull and heavy as the low grey clouds of the November afternoon. Her pregnancy, now into its seventh month, had been difficult and she had been sick for much of the time. The growing baby was vigorous and busy, just like his father – she was certain it was a boy. Sybil Giffard had been feeding her mashed liver and dosing her with all manner of strengthening tisanes and potions, and William fussed over her with a combination of anxiety and pride that she appreciated even while it almost drove her mad.

Aliza was accompanying her to Hertford for the lying in. Her daughter, little Alienor, was just over a year old, a beautiful little moppet, already toddling, providing she had a hand to grasp. Joanna wondered what it would be like to have a small person, part her and part William and all God's creation, holding her own hand in complete and vulnerable trust.

She looked up at a flurry of motion at the door as the Queen's uncle, Boniface, Archbishop of Canterbury, arrived. He had been absent in Rome during the year of Joanna's marriage. Tall, florid-faced and authoritative, he had a mind like a trap and was highly protective of his own power and the boundaries of affinity. An enamelled gold cross flashed on his breast, and he punctuated his stride with thumps from an intricate ivory-headed crosier.

Everyone dropped to their knees in obeisance. Hampered by her size, Joanna was the last to do so, swallowing bile. Boniface greeted the Queen warmly and she knelt to kiss his ring of office. The rest of the ladies were presented, and the Queen gestured for Joanna to rise. 'You will excuse my sister,' she said. 'She is soon to retire from court to her confinement.'

'Sister?' Boniface eyed Joanna speculatively.

'Wife to my lord King's brother, William de Valence.'

The shrewd eyes narrowed. 'I bless you, my dear, for your fortitude and courage,' he said. 'I am sorry I was not present to celebrate your marriage.'

Joanna sensed a nuance of distaste in his manner, as though he was regarding something soiled and debased. The Queen looked between them with raised brows. The tension was subtle, like a cloud crossing the sun when previously Joanna had been unaware of any clouds in the sky.

Boniface stayed to drink a cup of wine with the Queen and talk about his various projects, and Joanna retreated to her sewing. Edward arrived to visit his mother, his fair hair a dishevelled mop and his freckled face scarlet with exertion. One of his knees poked through a large tear in his hose.

'What have you been doing?' Alienor asked, horrified. 'Come and greet the Archbishop even if you are in no state to do so.'

'Uncle William let me ride Talent,' Edward said, beaming, even as he knelt to his great uncle, exposing the rip even more.

Joanna lifted her head. The Queen's gaze widened. Talent was William's newest destrier, a powerful, bronze-bay Spanish stallion, young and skittish.

'What?'

Edward grinned cheerfully. 'He's faster than the wind. He outstripped all the others.'

'And he let you ride him – race him?' Alienor's voice rose a notch.

'Yes.' Edward's gaze slipped, and Joanna suspected an adjustment of truth.

'Is that wise, niece?' Boniface turned to Alienor. 'It seems rather irresponsible to me.'

'Uncle William is the best tourneyer in the world!' Edward enthused. 'He's going to teach me to joust just like him – and then I will be the best instead. And we're going hunting tomorrow.'

'We shall see about that,' Alienor said, tight-lipped. 'Go and change your hose and then come and sit with the Archbishop in a proper, civilised manner.'

Edward puffed out his cheeks in irritation, but bowed and departed.

Boniface looked sternly at Alienor. 'It is not good to be encouraging your son in folly. He is intelligent and forward but not at the stage to be riding a spirited stallion.'

Alienor sent an accusing look towards Joanna, who was the scapegoat in William's absence.

Joanna said, 'My husband loves the lord Edward dearly and would do nothing to cause him harm I am sure.'

'Not intentionally perhaps,' Boniface replied, 'but encouraging a headstrong boy to take risks is foolish. From my observations thus far, certain exuberances must be curbed. Edward is the heir to the throne. Encouraging him to ride a dangerous warhorse is the height of recklessness.' He looked at Joanna as if it was her fault too for failing to mediate between her husband's rash impulses and his reason.

The Queen said, 'My husband's brother is heedless at times, sometimes to excess. Be assured that I will deal with the matter.'

Edward returned in clean garments, his face washed, his hair combed, and this time made the proper obeisance, before perching on a stool at his mother's feet, the picture of angelic innocence. Worried, Joanna excused herself. Since their return from Hertford, William had taken part in another tourney, permitted this time, but a young knight had been seriously injured and William had taken the blame. Now this. It was almost as though he was deliberately trying to ruin their standing at court.

'What on earth were you thinking with Edward and Talent?' she demanded of William in their chamber later.

He laughed and shook his head. 'The little monkey came across him saddled up and was on his back and away before I could stop him. He'd been waiting his opportunity; I cannot fault his patience and cunning.' William's eyes shone with admiration. 'He sits a horse really well, Joanna, no fear whatsoever, and his skill is excellent.'

'Well, you are now in Boniface of Canterbury's bad graces because of it,' Joanna snapped. 'William, you must think of these things.'

He snorted. 'Hah, everyone who is not a Savoyard is the Archbishop's enemy. He's already made it clear he considers me and my brothers as rivals for influence. I've seen him whispering to the Queen. I'm not entirely wet behind the ears.'

'Well then, don't give him reasons to make a complaint.'

William grimaced. 'It was pure mischance this afternoon. It won't happen again. Boniface is just making a meal of it.'

'You must be careful,' she persisted. Soon she would not be here to curb William's excesses and mishaps.

William shrugged. 'You have nothing to worry about, and you should not – it is not good for you or the child.'

'Well, do not give me cause to worry then.'

He sighed impatiently but kissed her. 'I swear I won't.'

'And be careful with the lord Edward. If he keeps coming into his mother with ripped clothes and wild tales of escapades with you, it will not aid our cause.'

'Joanna Worry-wort,' he teased, pressing his forefinger to the tip of her nose.

'Worry-wort?'

He grinned at her. 'It means you worry too much.'

'Do you blame me? It's not a game, William!'

'I know, and I hear you,' he said, and kissed her again, but Joanna suspected he was mollifying her without paying full heed.

Boniface set down his goblet and wiped his lips. 'The King's Lusignan brothers have made a big difference at court since last I was here,' he said to Alienor. 'They seem to me to have had a detrimental influence on the King and the lord Edward.'

'You know what the King is like,' Alienor replied. 'These young men are his womb-brothers. I do sometimes think he loves them beyond reason.'

Boniface raised his brows. 'That to me is folly.'

'I am fond of William,' Alienor said, trying to be fair in the midst of newly kindled resentment. 'I love Joanna dearly. I thought she might curb some of her husband's excesses, but you are right, he is a rash and headstrong young man. I agree that my husband gives him too much privilege, and certainly he was irresponsible with Edward today. He has no heed for consequences.'

Boniface pressed his fingertips together. 'I would hate to think of him usurping your place in the King's counsels. It is not good to exchange rashness for service, and if your husband is giving him money, estates and favour then who is he pushing aside to do so?'

Alienor studied the rings on her fingers and nodded at the point.

'You do not want him gaining influence over the lord Edward. Today it is just a horse, but what of the future? My dear, you would do well to look to the situation and do something about it. You need people around you with your interests at heart, not their own. All of the King's brothers need reining in. I have heard that Aymer's studies involve more wine, women and gambling than they do serious learning.'

'But you can do something about it?' she said. 'He is clergy.'

Boniface said tautly, 'If he does gain a bishopric he will be under my supervision and I shall keep him within my sight and under my boot. The King may have control of secular interests, but the wellbeing of the Church is my jurisdiction.'

'Thank you for your support and advice, Uncle,' Alienor said. 'You have given me much to think upon. I fear I have been lax and you have made me realise I must deal with this before it grows worse. I shall be on my guard from now on.'

He patted her knee and spoke with a benevolent smile, but his eyes were hard and calculating. 'I am here to help you and our family, and to guide the lord Edward so that he may be worthy of kingship and not be subject to undesirable influences.'

William looked out of the window on to a cold January morning. Snow had been threatening since dawn and now desultory flakes had started to fall, harbingers of a heavier burden. He had arrived at Hertford from court two days ago, for Joanna's lying in. Sybil Giffard was coming from Windsor, a day's ride away, to look after Joanna's labour, but had yet to arrive, and now the snow might hamper her journey.

'I think I'll go and check the roads,' William said. 'It is not snowing too hard yet and the horse needs the exercise.'

'You mean you do,' Joanna said with a rueful smile.

William grimaced at her. 'You have found me out,' he said, but anxiety glimmered beneath his jesting. Aliza had borne a child but was no midwife. Sybil, however, was an expert in these matters, and Joanna had not had an easy pregnancy. She had been troubled by pains in her back and squeezing sensations for several days and had spent much of yesterday evening in the garderobe voiding her bowels. If he was riding out, it was because he felt so helpless sitting here twiddling his thumbs.

With William gone, Joanna sat with her feet up and drank a warm tisane. Aliza read to her from a romance of Alexander borrowed from the Queen, and Joanna smiled at the irony because it was full of tournaments, jousting and heroic deeds – all the kinds of sport banned at court.

The back pain was steadily intensifying and Joanna could not find a comfortable position. Outside, the snow continued to fall lightly but steadily. Aliza arranged a warm blanket over Joanna's legs and had the maids light more candles. The flames danced on a little statue of St Margaret, patron saint of women in travail, emerging from the belly of the dragon that had swallowed her. Joanna had been praying to her every day since realising she was with child.

A sharper, stronger pain squeezed her belly and released. Then a short while later, another one.

'I do not think that the baby is waiting for Sybil,' Joanna said.

Aliza's gaze widened, but she set the book aside and set out to be practical. Helping Joanna to bed, she instructed the other ladies to heat water over the fire and have clothes and napkins made ready.

'I expect you still have a while to go. When I was having Alienor, it took almost a day.'

Joanna grimaced. She wanted the labour to be quicker than that, but she would also rather that Sybil was here.

Several hours later the pain had increased and the contractions were coming at close and regular intervals, strong and hard. Joanna prayed with all her might to St Margaret. William should be back by now. What if he had taken a fall in the snow? She gasped her way through another contraction, telling herself not to be foolish. He had his men with him and they would look after each other.

The gripping pain released her, and as she fell back, panting, the door opened and Sybil Giffard entered. 'My horse cast a shoe and went lame,' she said breathlessly as she bustled forward. 'Your husband found us and put me up on his squire's palfrey.' She threw off her cloak, which glittered with melting snow.

Joanna bit her lip and could only manage a wordless nod as another contraction tightened her belly.

Sybil curtseyed to honour the statue of St Margaret and then pushed up her sleeves. 'Come,' she said to Joanna, 'we have work to do.'

Just after dusk, Joanna pushed her son into the world, and a querulous wail filled the chamber as he released his first-drawn breath.

'A fine boy!' Sybil declared triumphantly. 'Well done, my dear, well done indeed. You have given your lord a son and heir.'

Joanna heard the words from what seemed like a long distance. Her womb contracted strongly to expel the afterbirth and she clenched her teeth against the pain for she hated crying out and losing control. Aliza smoothed her brow and soothed her while Sybil gave the baby to an attendant and dealt with the placenta. 'It is almost finished now. You have been very brave.' Satisfied there was no excess bleeding or damage, Sybil gave Joanna a warm tisane while a maid washed the baby at the fireside in a bowl of warm water. Joanna revived enough to sip the drink but she was shivering, and immediately Sybil wrapped warm furs around her. 'All is well,' she said. 'Come, see – your beautiful son.'

The maid brought the baby from his bath, enfolded in a soft blanket. His little hands were furled into fists and his eyes were open – calm and unsurprised, as if he already knew the world he had entered. A son and heir for Pembroke and Goodrich. A child to rear, to be proud of and to cherish. Joanna put the tisane aside and took him in her arms. 'Tell William,' she said. 'Give him the good news.' She kissed the baby's crumpled brow.

'I will do it,' Aliza said. 'You rest now.'

Joanna closed her eyes, feeling exhausted. Sybil checked the soft rags between her thighs again and then removed the hot stone wrapped in cloth from under the bed clothes and replaced it with a new one.

Feeling sleepy, the pain easing, Joanna gave the baby to Aliza so that she could present him to William.

Aliza kissed his cheek. 'Welcome,' she said, 'firstborn son of my little brother.'

William had been praying at his small, personal altar in his chamber. The room was dark, lit only by a couple of guttering candles, and the fire was dying, but he had not noticed for he had wanted to be alone to concentrate on his prayers and had dismissed all the servants. His mother had borne fourteen children without any difficulty, but he knew the risk. God had been generous to him, but he had not always been a good man for his part of the bargain.

The soft knock at the door jerked him out of his reverie and to his feet. He heard Jacomin speak and Aliza answer, and his whole centre lurched. He stumbled to the door and opened it to find his sister on the threshold holding a bundle in her arms.

'You have a son, William,' she said. 'A beautiful little boy.'

William swallowed. 'A son,' he repeated.

Smiling, she placed the child in his arms. William parted the blanket and marvelled at the perfection of the little miniature human within. His son, his child, and proof of his virility. 'He has Joanna's chin,' he said, 'and her nose. I wonder if his hair will grow like hers or mine, and what colour his eyes will be.' He couldn't stop talking; he was babbling but couldn't help himself.

Aliza put her hand lightly on his arm to steady him.

He wiped his eyes with his free hand. 'Joanna . . . how is Joanna?'

'Do not worry, she is being well looked after by Lady Giffard, but she needs to rest. You will see her in the morning I expect. Now, I need to take this little one back to the chamber, or I shall be in trouble with Lady Giffard, and so will you!'

'Of course.' He was still dazed and a little reluctant to hand over his son. He imagined a time stretching forward when an older child would stay with him to play chess or go out riding.

'You must write to the King,' Aliza said, finally reacquiring the baby, 'and send a messenger as soon as the snow has cleared.'

'I will do it now,' he said eagerly, 'without delay.'

In the morning William visited Joanna, and the sight of her, looking pale and exhausted against the bed covers, shocked him. Her braided hair in a neat plait falling over her shoulder made her appear child-like and vulnerable rather than a mother in her own right.

He touched her face. 'They told me you were well,' he said, 'but truly, how are you?'

She reached for his hand. 'They were right, I am well,' she answered with a smile. 'Do not worry on my account.'

'I will try not to, but I shall miss you. I want you to recover as soon as you can – faster indeed!'

'As best I can, but you cannot expect me to rally on the instant. It is hard work, pushing a child into the world. You need to have patience – although I know that is not your strong suit,' she added with a wry smile.

He rolled his eyes in self-deprecation, then said, 'I have something for you, before I leave you in peace.' He gave her a small rock crystal vase with a pouring lip, and a matching phial containing oil of roses. 'For when you want to perfume your hair or yourself,' he said.

Joanna looked at the exquisite little objects and experienced a powerful wave of love and appreciation for him that he had thought of her personally. 'Oh William,' she said. 'This is perfect.'

'And so are you. I am a very fortunate man.'

The baby started to snuffle and fuss in his crib, and William went to look at him. 'He shall be baptised later today,' he said. 'Aliza shall stand as his godmother, and he will be named Iohan after your brother to remember him.'

Joanna gave him a look bright with tears. 'It is fitting.' Without her brother's death she and William would never have married. A fierce, protective surge towards her husband and helpless new-born son swept over her. She would stand like a lioness in front of both to defend them, as William would do for her and their child. It was for ever.

19

Swanscombe, Kent, Spring 1250

Fastening her cloak, Joanna inhaled the smell of the estuary through the open window – the enduring scent of her childhood at Swanscombe. She remembered walking along the river bank as a little girl, tightly gripping her mother's hand, smelling the tang of salt and reeds in the brackish water and watching the swans that gave the place its name, floating in white majesty on the current.

She had arrived on a barge sailing downriver from Westminster leaving William occupied with the King's business, and had come to show her father his baby grandson. Joanna had thought long and hard about returning to Swanscombe but had eventually decided it must be done. She was a great lady in her own right, and nominal Countess of Pembroke. Her husband was the King's half-brother and their son his nephew. What greater prestige could there be? She had left Swanscombe as a little girl without prospects, pushed from the nest, and was returning in triumph, gowned in silk, a jewelled circlet on her head and a collar of gems at her throat. The plain little cygnet had become a swan.

Her father had leaned over his paunch to embrace her with an awkward kiss of welcome. He had always been overweight but vigorous, now time had made his jowls pendulous and his hair was retreating from his brow faster than an ebbing spring tide. After the court and Hertford, the chambers at Swanscombe seemed small and dingy. The plain hangings and the lack of embellishment were a contrast to the colour and opulence of the court, and she realised how different her life had become. Her childhood home was now an outgrown shell.

Her stepmother, Dionysia, had curtseyed to her when she arrived and had pushed her half-brother Guillaume forward to make his greeting – thirteen years old and wearing a thunderous scowl. Last time Joanna had seen him he had been a blond toddler. Now, on the cusp of manhood, he was Swanscombe's heir. Joanna had tried to swallow her antipathy with little success, for its cause was rooted in her childhood and her resentment of the woman who had taken her mother's place.

Leaving Iohan with his nurse, Joanna made her way to the church to visit her mother's tomb, and as she knelt, she remembered praying beside the slab on the day she left for the court – a miserable, unhappy little girl, sent away so that Dionysia could make way for her own cuckoo. She had travelled a long way since then. Her heart still hurt, but she could detach a little now and see from a greater distance. Her father had been trying to do his best by her, and her life at court had changed her world. What a different path she would have trodden had her mother not died.

Her thoughts were interrupted by the arrival of her father, who joined her and struggled to kneel down beside her.

'We have not been close, have we, daughter, and I am sorry for it,' he said, his voice breathless and a wheeze in his chest. 'I would mend it if I could but I fear it is too late for that. I want to tell you I am proud of you. I could never have imagined you becoming sister-by-marriage to the King and Queen. You were such a quiet, plain little thing. When I look at my grandson, I know his future will be far greater than I could have mapped for any son of mine.'

She wanted desperately to be left alone, but she made herself answer him. 'Caused by accidents of birth and death,' she said. 'I too wish that the past had been different, but I am here to leave it behind and move forward.'

'You are a good girl. I am sorry your husband could not come too.'

'He has business with the King,' she replied. 'I am sure William will visit on another occasion.' Another platitude. William did not think her quiet and plain. And these days she knew her own value – Cecily had taught her that.

Her father cleared his throat. 'There is something I want to ask you.'

'Of course,' she said stiffly.

He hesitated, then said, 'Now you have the King's ear at court through your husband . . . and I know the King is fond of you . . .'

'You want me to ask for favours?' she finished for him.

His complexion reddened. 'I would not have put it as bluntly as that, daughter. What I would say is that you are in a position to enhance your family's standing.'

'You may take it as a given that I will always do my best for my family, as will my husband,' she said primly.

'Then thank you.' He rubbed the back of his neck. 'There is another thing though . . . I am not getting any younger.

If anything happens to me before your half-brother reaches maturity, I ask you to take care of his welfare. You are well positioned to see to his wardship until he comes of age.'

Joanna suppressed a grimace, but it was a matter of duty and family, as he said. Besides, should her father die before Guillaume attained his majority then she and William would have the right to administer the estates, not Dionysia, and that was a satisfying thought. 'Of course,' she said, 'but you must make it very clear in your will that it is your wish, lest others object.'

'There will be none,' he said curtly. 'I am head of the house-hold. But you are right, the intention needs to be mooted beforehand, and I trust you to speak to the King.'

'Then I will do so.'

He gave a forced laugh. 'I have no intention of dying before my son comes to manhood, but it is better to be safe, and I trust you. Swanscombe may not approach the value of your inher-itance, but it is still a wealthy estate and I do not want it picked over by carrion crows.'

Joanna looked down at her clenched fists, feeling ill.

'Well then, I shall leave you in peace with your prayers,' he said gruffly. 'I know what your mother meant to you, and I am proud of you as I was proud of Iohan.'

Joanna pressed her lips together.

'I did love her,' he said quietly. 'No matter that you think I did not. But she was the river and I was the land.'

He left, but she heard him pause and speak at the chapel door. Glancing round, she saw him talking to her half-brother, who had clearly followed him, and had probably overheard their discussion. He sent her a narrow scowl before their father turned him by the shoulder and took him away. Joanna bowed her head and tried to focus on prayers for her mother's soul. It took a long time, but eventually she found the necessary calm. When

225

she had finished, all she wanted to do was go home to William and be a family with him.

Joanna watched William playing with their son, dandling him in his lap. The baby laughed and danced his sturdy legs on William's thighs, and her heart swelled with love.

At nine months old, little Iohan had four teeth and two more coming through. He had William's hazel-mica eyes, and her smooth brown hair – a confident child with a happy chirrup. Now crawling, he had to be constantly watched for Weazel's tail fascinated him, although the cat usually stayed well out of the baby's reach and slept on the sideboard.

William had recently taken an oath to go on crusade, horrifying Joanna. It had been a general vow taken by many courtiers including the King, but she did not want to lose him for years on end, if not for ever. Simon de Montfort might have taken his wife and children halfway to Egypt with him when he had gone on crusade, but Joanna had no intention of traipsing across Christendom, through hostile lands, living in camps, even for love of her husband. She was keeping silent and hoping that the idea would lose its shine.

The King arrived and William started to hand Iohan to his nurse but Joanna took him instead. Holding their son in her arms and portraying an idyllic family moment was not an opportunity to miss when it came to the King.

Henry embraced William before turning to kiss Joanna and his nephew. 'He's a handsome chap,' he said warmly. 'I can see our mother in him.'

'He has her eyes,' William said. 'Not the same colour, I grant you, but they look out at the world in the same way.'

'They do, don't they?' Henry chucked Iohan under the chin. 'I want you to be among the first to know that the monks of

Winchester have accepted Aymer as their bishop when he comes of age and completes his training. I am going there tomorrow to consolidate their decision.'

'That is wonderful news, sire,' William said.

'Indeed, it is.' Henry gave him a candid look. 'I will always support you. My kin are my greatest treasure on earth and your love and loyalty are the coins I value most.'

'And we shall always serve you with that love and loyalty, sire, not only for your gifts, but for yourself.'

Henry's eyes moistened with pleasure. 'I just wanted to tell you,' he said. 'I will see you later at dinner.'

'Well, Aymer as a bishop,' William said when Henry had gone. 'I knew he would have a position eventually, but the mitre of Winchester is a powerful one with some fine estates.' Including part of Southwark across the river from London, where the Bishop was the landlord of the cookshops, bathhouses and brothels that serviced the city. It was a lucrative source of income, and knowing Aymer, he would make full use of it.

'But he will be acting bishop for a little while yet,' Joanna said with reservation. 'He is not yet old enough for consecration even if he takes up some of the duties.'

'True, but he will grow into the position and learn by experience. It is excellent news for him, and for us.'

In Westminster's great hall, Joanna stood at Cecily's side behind two huge cauldrons. Feeding the poor was an obligation of their position in society and their humble duty to Christ. They were down to the last of the beef pottage they had been serving and one basket of loaves. The hundreds of paupers for whom the King had provided the Christmas feast sat at rough wooden trestles wolfing their food, drinking their ale, and staring wide-eyed at a different world of painted walls, colour and warmth.

227

I remember how afraid I was the first time I helped you to do this,' Joanna said as she ladled pottage into the bowl of a stooped old man. He lifted his eyes briefly to hers, nodded his gratitude and shuffled off. 'I thought that they might do me harm, that they might pull at my hands or my clothes, but you steadied me and made it calm and ordinary. You said that if we give goodness, then we shall receive it in return.'

'Ah, that memory of yours,' Cecily said with a smile. 'Nothing ever escapes it once taken in. Did I truly say that?'

'You did, and as you say, I have always remembered.'

Cecily added stew to the dish of a young woman, her body heavily swollen with child. Her clothes were rags and lice crawled in her hair. A little girl of about three years old clung to her skirts, hollow-cheeked, nose streaming. Joanna stooped to hand the child a crust of bread and gave the mother two silver pennies. The woman looked at the coins in astonishment, then closed her reddened knuckles over them, her eyes full of dignity and despair. Her expression tugged at Joanna's heartstrings. But then they all did. She could not give her more because it would be robbed from her or ill-spent. The woman bobbed her head and moved on, and there stood the next one in the line to receive the last scraping of stew.

In her own womb, Joanna felt a stir and a kick and put her hand there. The child had been moving for a week now.

Cecily asked quietly if she was well, and Joanna nodded. 'Very well. I have barely been sick. Were it not for my growing belly I would hardly know I carried another child. I am thinking this one must be a well-behaved little girl,' she added with a smile.

Cecily patted her arm. 'It is always good to have balance. You took a little time at the outset, but that is no bad thing. You have a beautiful son and now a brother or sister to join him in the spring.' She gestured for a servant to take the last of the bread to the gate for any latecomers, together with the table scraps. Everyone dining at the high tables had an alms bowl in which to put aside offerings for the poor who had not gained a place to dine.

As Joanna and Cecily were removing their aprons, Cecily swayed and almost fell, but a quick-thinking servant came to her rescue and supported her. 'I am all right,' Cecily said, brushing off everyone's concern, but Joanna thought she looked terribly pale. She had her taken to the Queen's chamber, where she helped her to a cushioned bench and propped her feet on a stool.

'Tush, my dear.' Cecily waved her hand, trying to make light of the incident. 'You should not be fussing over me in your condition. You should have your own feet up.'

'Being with child does not render me incapable,' Joanna answered firmly. 'You are the one who needs care.' She removed Cecily's shoes and began rubbing her feet, noticing how swollen her ankles were.

'You are a good girl.'

Cecily's eyelids drooped, and within moments she was fast asleep.

The Queen arrived, having been informed of the incident, and frowned. 'She has not been well recently,' she said, 'but she does as she wills, as she has always done, and she would not thank us for coddling her. All we can do is watch her and be there at need.'

Returning to her own chamber, Joanna found William entertaining his older brother Guy, newly returned from crusade.

She stared at him in shock and surprise. His robust build had been whittled away to a gaunt wiriness. His skin resembled brown leather, and a beard of sun-streaked gold fringed his jawline.

'Look who's here!' William said.

'Sister! You are blooming like a rose!' Guy greeted Joanna with a sound kiss on the cheek and looked her up and down.

'Indeed, I am!' She fetched Iohan from his nurse. 'Have you met your nephew?'

Guy tickled the infant under his chin. 'Indeed, I have. Let us hope he has William's prowess married to your good sense.'

'I pray so, and perhaps his uncle's ability to weather storms?'

Guy snorted with dark amusement as she returned Iohan to his nurse.

'How is Cecily?' William asked.

'Recovering,' Joanna said, not wanting to make an issue of the matter while they had a guest. 'She takes too much on herself.'

She drew Guy to their fireside. He sat down, stretched out his legs and sighed as he accepted a cup of wine.

'You do not know how many times I thought of this when we were in the stinking hell hole of Damietta,' he said. 'No man in his right mind would go there.' He looked at William. 'I hear you and Henry have taken the cross.'

'Yes,' William said, 'but I do not know when it will happen – there is money to raise and matters to be settled at home. What about you? What will you do now?'

Guy gave a laconic shrug. 'Return to the Limousin and deal with business for Henry there and in Gascony. I find myself embarrassed for funds and equipment, so it will depend what our brother can spare from his coffers. I expect there will be the usual complaints – that the King is enriching foreigners at the expense of true English men and doling out money he does not have.'

'It is no jesting matter.' William sent him a warning look. 'There is always animosity from certain quarters.'

Guy drank his wine and looked at William across the goblet rim. 'Are you still tourneying?'

'When they are not being banned.' William looked at Joanna, whose lips were pursed. 'It is where a great deal of that animosity is put on display, but it won't stop me.'

'I do not know how anyone would stop you,' Guy said. 'You were the youngest and always dogged our heels no matter what obstacles we put in your way. You would confront us with bloodied knees and a tear-stained face but your fists would be up with fire in your soul.' He turned on the bench towards Joanna. 'He never gives up.'

'So I have noticed,' she said ruefully.

'Aymer is to become Bishop of Winchester – when he completes his studies,' William said.

'Hah! Landlord of the Southwark stews.' Guy chuckled. 'Do you think he will give special prices in the bathhouses to friends and relatives?'

'You will have to ask him.' William decided it was best if he stopped looking at Joanna for her reactions.

'I shall do so at the earliest opportunity.' Guy stroked his beard. 'I hear Boniface of Canterbury has been stirring up trouble. Nothing like his name. "Sour-face" suits him better.'

'He's been visiting monasteries and demanding money with menaces mainly,' William said. 'Reform is necessary, but the Archbishop is keen to see that all dues are paid and everyone bows to his authority. I suspect he and Aymer will disagree on how far it should go.'

Guy shrugged, and finished his wine. 'Well, it is all to play for. My own path is to gather funds and return to affairs in the Limousin. I need to speak with Geoffrey too.' He rose to take his leave. 'Do not be so swift to ride to Outremer, little brother. The climate, the landscape, the people will take their toll and

suck you dry. Stay home for now and mind domestic business.'
He winked at Joanna. 'Your wife will love you much better if
you do.'

Joanna carried little Agnes to the window and looked out on a
beautiful summer's day. Heavy dark-green leaves clothed the
trees, and the sky was the same blue as the stripes on William's
shield.

She had just returned from her churching ceremony, forty
days after her daughter's birth. This time the carrying and the
labour had been smooth and easy, the pain nothing like the
excruciating twists when Iohan was born. Soon she would hand
Agnes to her nurse and go to preside over the celebratory feast,
but she had wanted a moment's breathing space alone with her
daughter.

'There you are.'

William entered the room and came to slip his arm around
her waist, now slender again. Tonight, they would share a bed
for the first time since Agnes's birth and she was melting with
need for him – and from his looks and touches, that desire was
mutual.

He kissed the side of her neck under her wimple. 'I wish it
was already tonight,' he whispered, 'but we should join our
guests before they come looking for us – and before I yield to
temptation.' He gently adjusted the enamelled gold neck pendant
he had given her as a churching gift to go with her new blue
silk gown.

'I suppose we should,' she said, giving him a coy look, then
drew back to give Agnes to her wet nurse.

They joined their guests in Hertford's great hall. Joanna sat
in the place of honour at the dais table under a silk canopy
painted with the arms of Valence and Munchensy. William's

brother Aymer had ridden over from Oxford and John de Warenne was here too with Aliza.

Aymer, although busy with his theological studies in Oxford, was finding time for more secular pursuits. Joanna had heard rumours about his fondness for wine and gambling, not to mention composing scurrilous verses about the Archbishop of Canterbury and some of the Queen's uncles. As Bishop Elect of Winchester he was landlord of the brothels on the Southwark side of the Thames, and she knew that Elias, Jacomin and several of William's knights had availed themselves of the services, charging their pleasure to the Bishop's account.

Despite her exasperation, Joanna was fond of Aymer. A few moments earlier, before Iohan's nurse had carried him off to bed, Aymer had been jogging his little nephew on his knee, totally absorbed in the moment, playful and good-natured. However, now he was lasciviously eyeing several of the younger women at the feast and had just winked at one in particular while smoothing his forefinger either side of his mouth, before catching Joanna's outraged eye.

'Aymer, I trust to your good manners,' she said.

'Mea culpa.' He gave her one of his devastating smiles. 'I swear I am the soul of discretion.'

'I hope you are,' she said reprovingly, and then looked towards the messenger being escorted up the hall to the dais. He bore a letter for Joanna, and as she read it, her heart filled with dismay. 'It's Cecily,' she said, giving William a stricken look. 'I must go to her.'

Cecily lay near the window in her sickroom, the summer light falling on the plain blanket that covered her frail body. Her sallow skin was stretched taut across her cheekbones and her lips were blue. Joanna knelt at her side and touched her stick-thin arm, and Cecily raised her lids and turned her head on the pillow.

'You came,' she whispered. 'I did not know if you would be in time.'

'Of course I came! I am so sorry to hear you are not well.'

'I shall be better by and by.' Cecily's tone gave Joanna the clear meaning of the words. 'The wait is wearisome, but I am glad you are here. I have something for you.' She pointed to the chest at the side of the bed. 'I want you to have my prayer beads. Take them, and use them well.'

Joanna swallowed the lump in her throat. Cecily had few possessions; in many ways she was a secular nun, and these well-used, ordinary-looking wooden beads were precious to her and imbued with years of devotion to God. 'Thank you,' she said. 'I am not worthy, but I shall treasure them and do my best to honour your trust. I shall think with gratitude of all your care and diligence, and how you were a mother to me when I had no mother.'

'Just so.' Cecily smiled and closed her eyes.

Joanna kissed her brow and sat with her, holding her hand and praying.

Cecily died a short while later as the sunset burned the horizon with fiery gold, and Joanna did not weep. Cecily would have had no patience with tears and her end was a rightful and natural thing.

Joanna stayed in St Alban's for the funeral, held in the chapel of St Andrew, where Cecily's shrouded body was laid to rest in a stone vault before the altar. Eleanor de Montfort had travelled to the deathbed but not arrived until the morning after Cecily had passed away, and now stood amid the mourners, her lips tight and her eyes shadowed with grief. A look of distaste crossed her face as she saw Joanna, and when she noticed the rosary beads, her cheeks flushed with anger.

'It is a great grief, but also a great happiness that our tutor and mentor has gone to be with God,' Joanna said courteously to Eleanor.

'And you were there as I was not,' Eleanor said stiffly.

'I know you would have been there if you could.' Joanna tried to be solicitous.

'Do not presume to know anything about me,' Eleanor snapped. 'You would be wrong, and you know nothing.'

'I know what I learned from Cecily and I will always thank her for it in my life and in my prayers and try to follow her example.'

Eleanor gave her a disparaging glare and stalked off. Joanna remained quietly in prayer until she had recovered her equilibrium. By the time she left the church she was at peace, and Eleanor had gone.

20

York, late December 1251

Joanna gave Henry's daughter Margaret a warm hug. 'You look very beautiful,' she said. 'A perfect bride.' It seemed barely possible that Margaret, whom she had seen born in Bordeaux eleven years ago, was about to marry the nine-year-old Alexander of Scotland to whom she had been betrothed since she was four years old. Alexander's father had died in July, and Henry was moving to secure the match even though the young couple were under age and would not come into their rule for many years to come.

Striving to conceal her sadness, Joanna smiled at Margaret, who was excited to be the centre of attention and loving her beautiful gold dress and embroidered slippers. Joanna hoped the child would be treated with kindness and affection away from her family and that she would bond with her young bridegroom. With good fortune they would grow up together and be friends first and more intimate companions later, but there was no certainty of such an outcome. The forthcoming marriage of such young heirs had unsettled Joanna, even though she knew that Henry and Alienor were concerned parents. The imminent parting had churned up the silt from her past, reminding her of all the painful partings in her life. Her mother, her brother, her uncles, and Cecily. And with each farewell, everything changed.

'Don't be sad, Aunt Joanna,' Margaret said, patting her shoulder.

'I am sorry to leave you, that is all,' Joanna said. Dear God, the child was comforting her when it should be the other way round. 'You will be a great queen, just like your mama.'

The royal company processed to the chapel, a small, elite gathering of close relatives and interested parties surrounding the young royal couple. Margaret and Alexander performed their parts flawlessly and were seen to smile at each other, which everyone took as a good sign for the future.

That night, when everyone had retired and the newly-weds were settled in their separate households, Joanna folded clothes to keep her hands busy, feeling irritable and out of sorts. There had been much talk at the marriage feast of wardships and alliances and plenty of covert match-making had been taking place.

'I would never consider marrying our daughter at eleven years old,' she said, the words emerging forcefully like steam bursting out from under a cauldron lid. 'I hope you would never consider it either.'

William looked up from pouring a last cup of wine. 'What has brought that on?' he asked warily.

'Listening to the talk, hearing all the bargaining. Wardships are bought and sold for the land and the profits and the right to marry the heirs that come with them. I was a ward myself, but I was seventeen years old when I married you. Our sons and daughters shall not be children when they wed, for it is not a good thing.'

William poured a second cup of wine and brought it to her. 'It is different for the King and Queen. They do not have the leisure to wait because of the necessity to the kingdom.'

'Then I am very glad we are not high royalty.'

'There is a clause that the marriage is not to be consummated for four years, and in that time they will come to know each other,' William said in a reasonable voice. 'The King and Queen will keep a close eye on both of them. They are doting parents.'

Joanna shook her head. Doting parents or not, it did not sit well with her. 'Promise me you will make no bargains involving our sons or daughters.' She gave him a hard look.

He drank, and said nothing.

'Promise me,' she repeated fiercely. 'And that you will make no agreements, even casual ones, without my yeasay.'

He lowered his cup and sighed heavily. 'Very well, I promise, for I know if I do not, you will fight me tooth and nail, and I would rather have you by my side than sticking a dagger in it – but you have to accept that it is how many do business.'

'But I do not have to like it,' she said, 'and I do not have to follow their example.'

Simon de Montfort had returned from Gascony to attend Margaret's wedding. William had managed to avoid him during the nuptial celebrations but was standing at Henry's side the next day when Simon approached to speak to the King.

William's stomach clenched, his fists too, although he remained expressionless. Before they had travelled north for the wedding, a deputation of Gascon lords had arrived at court to complain about de Montfort's heavy-handed rule, and had laid out details of the injustices, beatings and torture the people had been suffering at the hands of his harsh regime. Henry had been shocked and horrified by the reports and had promised to deal with the situation and ascertain the truth.

The atmosphere sparked with tension, and William sensed Henry's trepidation. His half-brother detested facing de Montfort, who made a point of putting him at a disadvantage.

De Montfort knelt, performing his obeisance, but making William think of a lion with a lashing tail.

'Sire,' de Montfort said, 'I wish to make my report on Gascony. The people are in rebellion. They constantly burn my camps and stir up insurrection. I have had to expend far more than expected to control the situation. If there is to be a peaceful and smooth changeover when the lord Edward comes of age to inherit these lands, I must have more funds from you to control these people.'

Henry frowned. 'So you say, but I have received reports from my loyal liegemen that they are suffering wrongfully from your enthusiasm to quell insurrection. I need to know you are targeting the rebels and not the general population.'

A look of angry astonishment crossed de Montfort's face. 'Sire, I root out your enemies where I find them. I know their many petty treacheries and they cannot be treated with lenience. The sword has the greatest value in the region. You do not understand the situation.'

Henry's hands twitched on the arms of his chair. 'I understand that if this continues, my son will have nothing but scorched earth and corpses to inherit. You must be discriminating in who you choose to censure and make proper accord with those who are not involved. I will not have you engaging in broad destruction. Many of these people are friends and allies. You will desist from your harsh policy forthwith and be more discerning.'

De Montfort fixed Henry with a contemptuous glare. 'Sire,

you have no knowledge of military matters, as so often has been proved. That is why you employed me to do this work.'

'I did not employ you to destroy everything in your path,' Henry snapped. 'You will remain at court for the moment while I decide what is to be done.'

De Montfort's lip curled and he abandoned all pretence of diplomacy. 'You are a parody of what a king should be. You have no more idea of governance than that beetle running across the floor.'

Henry stared at him in furious astonishment. 'You speak the words of a traitor. You are free to break our agreement any time you desire, and take the consequences. You will not insult me. We shall see who rules here. I think you will find it is me. You are dismissed!'

De Montfort flourished a sarcastic bow and strode from the room, his footfalls like hammer blows.

William watched his departure with an open mouth. He had been ready to draw his sword to protect Henry. De Montfort had surely burned his bridges now, and with this insult had given the King a reason to act.

'You have done the right thing, sire,' he said.

'This is not the first time he has disrespected me,' Henry said, trembling. 'He may be my sister's husband, but the ties of kinship can only go so far before they snap.'

'You cannot let him return to Gascony and continue to wreak havoc there, or the lord Edward will have no territory to govern.'

'I know that,' Henry said tersely. 'Do not you treat me as a fool as well.'

'Sire, I would never do that.'

William brought Henry a cup of wine, pouring it himself rather than summoning a servant.

'Perhaps you should send a group of trusted advisers to discover what has truly been happening in Gascony and ask the

Archbishop of Bordeaux to oversee. Our brother Guy might have a notion too since he is close by in the Limousin.'

Henry drank, lowered the cup and sighed. 'This must be investigated thoroughly. I wanted the Earl of Leicester to govern Gascony, not slaughter it.'

'From the tales I heard growing up, his father was of that ilk,' William said. 'It is as though he has been born with sword steel in his spine and knows no other way but war. His father had no love for the Gascons. He died in Toulouse, trying to bring the barons of the south to heel. Perhaps for the Earl of Leicester this is unfinished business.'

Henry lifted his cup again. 'There is merit in what you say, but am I like my father? Are you like yours?' He shook his head pensively. 'Your wife's grandsire warned me on his deathbed that should I grow up to become like my sire, he wished me an early death before it came to that.'

William had no wisdom to answer, and a platitude would be wrong. It was a question for a chaplain. 'Sire, it has clearly not come to that.'

Henry grimaced. 'This commission . . . I shall need to speak to the Queen and others and send the chosen men as soon as it may be arranged. I shall write to your brother too. He is not directly involved, but a neighbour all the same.'

'I could go,' William offered. 'I know Gascony well.'

'No. I want you here with me. You are staunch family and I trust you above anyone. There are others who can fulfil the task of finding the truth.' His face wore a haunted look. 'All I want is peace, and all I receive is war and strife and discord.'

The commission's findings against Simon de Montfort were damning, but in the three months that de Montfort had spent in England he had grown a fine crop of supporters among both the clergy and the barons who considered the King weak and who viewed the Gascon deputation as foreign troublemakers – sly, underhand liars who deserved what they received. De Montfort, in their eyes, was a man doing his best in trying circumstances. The findings and testimony of his accusers were hearsay, and who could trust a Gascon to speak the truth? Besides, there were two sides to every story. Each tale of atrocity had a counter-claim of insurrection and rebellion. De Montfort's oratory, his powerful standing and exemplary military reputation gave him the advantage. The claims of the Gascons were viewed as cunning trumpery. Many believed the King was playing out a grudge against de Montfort and was treating him shabbily.

'Why should I not act as I have done?' de Montfort demanded, standing again before Henry, now at Westminster. 'The King gave me a contract to govern Gascony for six years. He ordered me to put down uprisings and crush rebellious vassals. He was supposed to give me aid and guidance, but not one iota have I received.' He looked disdainfully at Henry. 'Keep your promise to me and your agreement, or repay me all the money I have expended in your service to the impoverishment of my estates.'

'I make no bargains with traitors,' Henry replied furiously. 'I know well that you would supplant my authority. It is fully permitted for a man to break his contract with a false partner who deals in shame.'

De Montfort took a step towards him. 'Were it not for your kingship I would crush you for what you have said to me.'

'And I will see you in the Tower for this!'

Henry looked round to command his guards. William prepared to step forward again, but the King's brother Richard intervened, gripping Henry's shoulder. 'Brother, if you do this, there is no going back. I counsel caution. Let us all be calm.' He sent a warning look to William, who eased back.

Henry glared at de Montfort. 'You speak of the perfidy of foreigners at court, but I should never have permitted you to enter England all those years ago or have given you land and honour and my sister to wife. I will hear no more!' Henry stormed out of the gathering, his face white with rage.

'I swear I shall have him in the Tower, I swear!' Henry shouted to Richard and William as he strode around his chamber, picking things up, putting them down.

'It would avail you nothing and bring war to the kingdom,' Richard said with exasperation. 'De Montfort has too many supporters for you to do such a thing with impunity.' He held up his hand as William started to protest. 'The judgement will find in his favour, I can tell you that now, and you will have to agree to it. You asked him to govern Gascony. He has done so after his own fashion. It may not be your fashion and he may have overstepped his bounds, but he has not been as faithless as you say he has. It is because he browbeats you. It is because you are two very different men. And yet, you are brothers by marriage.'

'Would that such a thing had never come about,' Henry said bitterly.

'You agreed to it,' Richard said pointedly.

'Only because he had seduced and bedded our sister, and because my heart was moved by the love she had for him. I admit I was a fool.'

'And now you are saddled,'

Henry paced the room and chewed his thumb. 'What options do I have?'

'Well, you cannot throw him in the Tower of London, that much is for certain. You could pay him off.'

'Money,' Henry said with exasperation, lifting his hands. 'It is always about money, especially with the Earl of Leicester. My treasury is not a bottomless pit. Indeed, it is an empty purse half the time.'

'Men might say it is because you spend it on luxuries and beautifying cathedrals.'

'Better than spending it on war and strife,' Henry snapped.

Richard shrugged. 'You asked what options you had. You can pay him and send him back to Gascony or you can terminate his contract, but you will have to pay him to do that too. What you cannot do is throw him in the Tower.'

Henry grunted and paced. 'I shall go to Gascony myself.' He looked meaningfully at William. 'I have loyal men who will do my bidding gladly. Edward is swiftly growing to adulthood. It will only be until he is ready to take on the role.'

'But again, you will need money if you choose that route, and it may be difficult to get the lords to pay for it.'

Henry continued to walk back and forth. Usually he did his thinking at prayer and in stillness; this agitation was a different beast, forced out of him by the intensity of the circumstances. 'Nevertheless,' he said stubbornly, 'something must be done.'

Joanna stood beside William on the wall of the Tower of London and looked out over the river. The tide washed brackish green water up the estuary. Their two-year-old son perched on William's shoulders and bounced with excitement. A crowd had gathered to watch the King's white bear fishing for salmon in the river. The keeper had attached a harness to the creature to prevent it from escaping as it swam in the choppy water, refreshing itself and, in sudden flashes of silver, catching fish.

'Look, Papa, look!' Iohan shouted as the bear swam into the shingle shore with its latest catch and proceeded to devour it.

Water streamed from its fur, melting its outline, before the bear shook itself, flinging a spray of droplets.

Joanna smiled, watching her son's vivid excitement. The bear had been a gift to Henry from the King of Norway. She marvelled at its massive paws and its great head. John and Aliza had accompanied them to see the spectacle with their daughter, Alienor. Joanna had left baby Agnes with her nurse.

'What a creature,' Aliza said. 'Henry is very proud of it, but it is more a spectacle for the people than for him. He has seen it once or twice, that is all.'

'I suppose he has had other matters to concern him,' Joanna replied.

Aliza nodded. 'I do not know whether to be delighted or worried that Simon de Montfort is returning to Gascony.'

The bear plunged back into the river, firmly attached to his harness.

'Who knows what he will do there – or perhaps we know very well, and there will be no stopping him.'

Joanna grimaced. Only death would put a stop to Simon de Montfort. The man was born of the sword and relentless in both the defence and pursuit of his own ambition. Thank God he was returning to Gascony; at least she would not have to endure his intimidating presence at court.

'What does William say about it?'

'He is all for Henry visiting Gascony in person rather than debating it in court.' Henry had voiced his intention of calling a truce to all military activity in the province and of appointing an overseer and visiting as soon as he could, but Joanna did not think it would be easy even if William was keen.

'John said the same. He thinks the King will eventually buy de Montfort out. It is what de Montfort is hoping for – unless he gets killed of course.'

The women exchanged glances, neither voicing the hope behind the statement.

De Montfort had demanded leave to return to Gascony to consolidate his affairs while an overseer was sought. Henry had replied coldly that he should return to do as he would, and hoped he would receive the same just rewards as his father for his efforts. Since de Montfort's father had died while besieging Toulouse, his skull crushed by a stone flung from a trebuchet, it was a damning farewell. De Montfort had declared that he would bring the King's enemies to heel and have them grovel at his feet, and had departed forthwith. He had left his family behind, including his pregnant wife, so Joanna still had Eleanor de Montfort's influence to counter, and the continued pressure of her lawyers for compensation from the Marshal estates. But Joanna was as determined as Eleanor. She would rather perish than see her inheritance go to the sons of Simon de Montfort.

They watched the bear catch several more fish and then returned to Westminster. With de Montfort gone, the atmosphere in the King's great painted chamber had lightened. Henry himself was tetchy and out of sorts, but Joanna believed it would pass – like a heavy meal that had been inadvisably consumed, and now had to be evacuated.

As always when she visited the chamber she made a point of visiting the murals and touching Hope's gilded shoe. Gazing into her far-seeing brown eyes, Joanna wished that her mortal self had such distant vision, and wisdom.

21

Hertford Castle, August 1252

Joanna drew rein, and patted her mare's sweating neck. Griselle snorted and tossed her head, ears flickering. They had set out to hunt soon after dawn with their guests in a boisterous group of men and ladies, the affair as much a social occasion as a serious hunt. By early afternoon they had ridden far across the estate and were several miles from home. The men had galloped off in pursuit of a hart but it had escaped across a breached deer leap on to the property of their neighbour, the Bishop of Ely. The dogs had lost the scent and the men were gradually returning to where the women waited on the boundary between the lands.

The sky had been a dazzling blue when they set out but had darkened steadily to become ominous and bruised. Wind raced through the grass and trees like swift unseen cats while thunder rumbled too close for comfort.

'We're going to get wet,' Aliza said.

Joanna grimaced, having no desire to be caught in a thunderstorm miles from home.

'We will not reach Hertford in time,' she told William as he circled his courser. 'If we are not under shelter when those clouds break, we shall all be drenched. Some of the horses will bolt I am sure.'

He squinted at the angry sky. 'I agree. Hatfield's nearby – we'll ride over and seek shelter there.' He reined aside to announce their destination to the rest of the party, who were eager to detour to the Bishop of Ely's manor.

Scattered drops of rain started to fall, fat and heavy, and the thunder drew nearer, riding in on dazzles of lightning. The group set out at a brisk pace towards Hatfield as the rain turned from single drops to a silver-grey curtain. The brisk trot became a canter, then a head-on gallop, with the men vying with each other to take the lead, especially William and his brothers Aymer and Geoffrey. Even Joanna flung caution to the wind and urged on Griselle, leaning over her neck to take Aliza's bay as they hurtled through the gateway and into the Bishop's courtyard, the elderly porter looking on in open-mouthed astonishment mingled with dismay.

Clouds of steam rose from the horses amid good-humoured jostling as everyone strove to get under the cover of eaves and overhangs. The manor was much smaller than the castle at Hertford and there was not enough room. The Bishop's servants had come running out to investigate the commotion and stood overwhelmed by the sudden shock of their visitors' arrival. William set about trying to organise them but they resembled a flock of disturbed poultry. Eventually he ordered his disgruntled squires to help out with the horses, and entered the hall. A couple of the Bishop's serjeants, who had been left in charge of the manor, came forward, hitching their belts, expressions belligerent and officious. Joanna knew the type. Lacking the rank to have manors of their own, and seldom required for regular soldiery, they kept guard and performed mundane duties and grew slack and dull if not strictly supervised.

'The Bishop is not in residence, sire,' growled the foremost serjeant, folding his fists over his belt.

William raised his brows. 'Your lord would take in his neighbours knowing they had been caught in a thunderstorm,' he said. 'If he was here, he would make us welcome without question, as would my own household to any stranger who came to my door in a rain storm.'

The men looked at each other and shuffled. 'We're not expecting guests,' said the first one again.

Aymer shouldered forward to stand at William's side. 'I am the Bishop Elect of Winchester,' he said curtly, stripping off his gloves. 'We expect your hospitality – now. Surely, even without the Bishop's presence you have food and drink in this place while we wait out the storm?'

The sound of the rain increased, drumming and rebounding on the oak roof shingles.

'There is very little here in the Bishop's absence,' the serjeant said, eyes darting, but he stepped aside. 'The servants will bring you what we have.' He stabbed a forefinger at an elderly man and a spotty youth. 'Bring refreshment, and quick about it.'

The old man and the boy shuffled off and the hunting party gathered around the meagre hearth, shaking out their wet garments while the thunderstorm rumbled and growled like a wild beast. The servants eventually returned bearing jugs and a motley collection of earthenware cups.

Geoffrey took one of the cups, tasted the liquid, spluttered, and sprayed it out on the floor. 'God in heaven, what cat's piss is this?'

Joanna could smell the sourness of the drink from where she stood. Others were spitting it out too. Aliza coughed and pressed the back of her hand to her mouth.

Aymer flushed with anger and chagrin. 'It might have been once, but I wouldn't even put this in the swill trough. Is there no wine?'

'No, sire, there is not.' The servant licked his lips.

Aymer shook his head. 'I don't believe that of a bishop. What's in the cellars?'

The old man began to wring his hands. 'Sire, we are not permitted to open the cellars, not in the Bishop's absence.'

Intensely aware of his duty to his guests for he had suggested they take shelter here, William was hot with humiliation at the way they were being received. 'If the Bishop sought shelter at my home, even in my absence, my servants would give him the warmest hospitality and see to his needs without cavil,' he said curtly. 'I would be ashamed if any man of mine did not, and I am certain that the Bishop would have no time for your behaviour.'

Geoffrey hitched his belt. 'I will go and see what is in the cellars myself,' he said. 'Leave it to me.' He stamped off with Aymer and a couple of squires.

A huge clap of thunder shattered overhead, shaking the building, and rain began dripping through the roof. People ducked out of the way, exclaiming.

'We should not be doing this,' Joanna said, shaking her head at William. 'The storm will pass over soon enough and we can just leave.'

William set his jaw. 'I will make it right with the Bishop afterwards.'

'You do not need to make anything right with the Bishop if you go no further,' she said in exasperation.

From under their feet came a tremendous crash and the sound of splintering. Joanna gasped and looked at Aliza, who caught her underlip in her teeth.

Aymer, Geoffrey and the squires returned from the cellars bearing two casks of wine between them. Geoffrey proceeded to knock out the bungs and fill the now empty ale jugs, and everyone set out to share the bounty, toasting each other with the earthenware mugs and setting to with a will, partly in revenge for being denied a proper welcome.

The noise of conversation increased in volume and the laughter grew boisterous. Someone did a turn juggling bread rolls. Someone else had stolen the steward's hat and began tossing it between his companions. Aymer had cornered an attractive red-haired servant girl and was telling her what wonderful opportunities there were for work in his diocese of Southwark.

Joanna grasped William's arm. 'Do something,' she said furiously. 'How will you explain this to the Bishop? This is not right. Indeed, it is dishonourable!'

The rain had started to ease as the storm rumbled off into the distance. William set her to one side and turned to the carousing company. The Bishop's serjeants and servants had made themselves scarce. Indeed, they had probably ridden off to report on the proceedings. William clapped his hands loudly. 'The storm is passing over. We should return to Hertford. Jacomin, Elias, go and see that the horses are made ready.'

'There is no hurry, little brother,' Geoffrey said loudly, and tried to hand William a fresh cup of wine. 'Have another drink. There's plenty more where this came from!'

'No,' William snapped, 'there is not, and it is time we left.'

He left the room, and going to the cellar he gazed at the doors hanging at drunken angles on their hinges. A dark stain trickled from the nearest barrel like blood. He stooped and turned off the tap.

Joanna had followed him, and she gasped in horror. 'Dear

God, this is terrible. You should not have let them do this. Why didn't you stop them?'

'How could I have stopped them?' he said in exasperation, and then palmed his face.

'They are your brothers and the ringleaders. Just because they are older than you and Aymer thinks he can throw his weight around as clergy does not mean you should let them get away with it!'

'It got out of hand too quickly. I will write to the Bishop and make reparations – and I will speak with my brothers.'

'Make sure you do; this has gone too far. Your opponents will make a meal of this. You must indeed write to the Bishop, and the King, immediately, before anyone else does, or we shall never live this down. Our reputation will be in tatters at court.'

'Yes, yes,' he snapped. 'I will see to it, stop fussing. You are building matters out of all proportion. I shall apologise to the Bishop and tell Henry what has happened and all will be well.'

'You do not understand, William. You say I worry too much, but it is like a fire. It begins with one twig and before you know it the whole forest is ablaze. Do you really want to live with the sort of behaviour that happened this afternoon? Do you? William, it has to stop!'

He puffed out his cheeks. 'Done is done, but I take your point. You do not have to labour it so fiercely. We will deal with it and move on.' He turned on his heel and marched back to the hall.

Joanna swallowed and closed her eyes, her stomach churning with the awfulness of the situation. She could clearly hear Cecily saying that a husband's actions reflected back on his wife. Not that she could entirely blame William, but his brothers had taken full advantage and it could not continue. Her own servants would never turn away guests and treat them in such a fashion, but neither would she expect those guests to behave like mannerless boors.

A band of sharp sunlight edged out the storm, glistening on wet roof shingles and courtyard puddles. John de Warenne was helping William to usher people out, his own expression slightly hang-dog. Aymer had to be dragged away from the red-haired girl, but not before he had pressed a ring into her hand and curled her fingers over it. The old servant snatched his trampled hat from the floor and dusted it off, his face set and his jaw working.

Jacomin helped Joanna to mount Griselle. Despite everyone else's laughing high spirits, Joanna felt close to tears.

Aliza leaned across her horse to touch her arm. 'It will be all right,' she said consolingly.

Joanna shook her head. 'It won't. This is my reputation as well as William's.' Not only would the King get to hear of the matter, but the Queen too, and Alienor was becoming increasingly purse-lipped and disapproving of William and his brothers.

The company returned to Hertford in the sparkling, rain-washed afternoon. William's servants were swift to take the horses to good stabling, and everyone was efficiently attended to. Joanna retired to her chamber to change her gown, but then plumped down on the bed and folded over herself. Weazel leaped up and rubbed against her, purring, and she buried her face in his warm golden fur and tried not to cry.

22

Hertford Castle, November 1252

Iohan sat on the back of the pony William had purchased for him at Smithfield horse fair – a barrel-shaped little animal, pale chestnut in colour, with stumpy legs and a white snip on its nose. William had been putting Iohan on a horse since he could sit up, his sister too, but the time had come to progress – to hold the reins and control his own mount, even if closely observed.

'Can I gallop?' Iohan demanded.

Joanna rolled her eyes. 'Oh, he is exactly like you!'

'He is nothing like me. If he was, he'd be asking when he could learn to tourney!' Grinning, William attached the pony to a lungeing rein. 'Very soon,' he said. 'Just a few lessons for you and Ginger to get used to each other.'

He instructed Iohan to ride in slow circles to develop his balance and soon the little boy was letting go of the reins and fearlessly stretching out arms, while William called encouragement.

Observing father and son, pride warmed Joanna's heart. Iohan was so good-natured, so fearless, and yet earnest and eager to do the right thing – already the man in waiting, even though he would not be three until after the Christmas feast.

Life at court, however, was uncomfortable. The incident at the Bishop of Ely's manor had cooled relations considerably. As Joanna had feared, William and Aymer's reputation had been badly damaged – Geoffrey's too. The story ran that William and his party had wantonly broken into the Bishop's house having trespassed on his land to hunt his deer. No mention was made of sheltering from the storm or of hospitality being shunned. Instead the tale had concentrated upon the boorish behaviour of the hunting party, the smashed cellar doors and the stolen wine. She suspected that the Bishop's retainers had increased the devastation once the hunting party had left, and probably helped themselves to a jug or two before making a report. To add to the opprobrium, one of the dairy maids had run off and her mother seemed to think she had departed for a life of debauchery in London, encouraged by the Bishop Elect of Winchester.

William had profusely apologised to the Bishop of Ely and offered to replace the wine. The elderly clergyman had replied with the gentle reproach that he was sorry William and his guests had deemed it necessary to break into his cellars and create mayhem. He would have willingly given them access if only they had asked. His mild, understated rebuke had only worsened the situation. Henry had taken William, Aymer and Geoffrey to task, but the courtiers hostile to the Lusignans had viewed the rebuke as insufficient punishment and a sign of favouritism and weakness rather than saintly forbearance. The Queen was being decidedly chilly and Joanna had lost her place as one of her favoured ladies, although Alienor remained icily civil.

Then there was Simon de Montfort. He had returned to Gascony after his exoneration in the spring and had proceeded to hound and harass the Gascons, who had retaliated with bitter determination. Last month, Henry had finally paid Simon off with a severance agreement of seven thousand marks, which William said was utterly extortionate. Edward was to receive Gascony and Henry intended going there next summer to try and settle matters, with a truce in place until then. Henry's relationship with de Montfort remained prickly, but the Queen had renewed her bond with Eleanor de Montfort and was treating her as her bosom friend. Joanna suspected that private discussions were going on between the women, aimed at bringing Henry and Simon closer, while detaching William and his brothers from royal influence.

The riding lesson over, William lifted Iohan up on to his shoulders. Iohan bounced up and down and clutched his hair.

'Hah, if you ride like that you will exhaust your horse before you have set out!' William declared.

They sat down before the fire to spiced wine and sweet wafers, with buttermilk for Iohan. William gave him the smallest sip from his cup and laughed as the child screwed up his face. 'That will change, believe me,' he said, and then glanced up as a messenger arrived with a parchment bearing Aymer's seal.

Joanna's heart plummeted, for she had had quite enough of Aymer for the time being. His letters usually meant trouble of some kind, as borne out by the messenger who was dusty, mud-spattered and stinking of hot horse.

'I have ridden hard from London, sire, but darkness comes early. I've been two days on the road.'

William read what Aymer had written. 'Tell him I will come as swiftly as possible.' He tossed the messenger a coin. 'Take a fresh horse from the stables and make sure to eat and drink before you turn around. You have a couple of hours of daylight left.'

'What's wrong now?' Joanna demanded.

'Boniface,' William replied, grimacing as if the word itself was a slug. 'I have to go to Aymer.' He handed her the letter.

Joanna read swiftly. The prior of St Thomas's hospital in Southwark had died and the right to elect a new prior belonged to Aymer because St Thomas's was within the Bishop of Winchester's jurisdiction. Aymer had carefully selected the priest he wanted for the office, but Boniface's representative, Eustace de Lenn, had opposed Aymer's choice, excommunicated Aymer's man on the spot, and had him flung into Boniface's gaol in Maidstone.

'That is outrageous!' Joanna gasped.

'Indeed, it is,' William said grimly as he picked up his cloak. 'Aymer wants to discuss it with me and decide how to reply. I have to go to him. Boniface has overstepped the mark by a long way.'

'Be careful. Boniface is a dangerous man to cross.'

'That is part of the problem. He throws his power about and expects people to back down, but this is a step too far.'

William called for his palfrey and pack horse to be saddled.

Joanna folded her arms. 'I hate you being involved in all this.'

'Aymer is my brother. I would never abandon family.' He gave her a sombre look. 'I watched my father do it, and I swore I would never be like him. My word is my faith, and I will protect Aymer even as he would protect me. Do not worry, I will return as soon as I may.'

'Of course, I am bound to worry. Do not get yourself excommunicated!'

'Well, if that happens there will be hell to pay,' William said darkly.

'Do not jest!' Joanna was appalled.

'I'm not jesting, and it is Boniface who will be doing the paying.' He gave her a hard kiss and swept from the room.

*

Biting his thumbnail, Aymer looked at William. 'What am I to do? I have the right to appoint my own priest for St Thomas's. Boniface and his man think they can get away with what they have done because they have the protection of the Queen, but I cannot ignore this.'

William grimaced. He knew what he would do, but Joanna would be horrified and it would make their position precarious when they were already in dubious favour. Aymer's man had been wrongfully imprisoned, and they had to retaliate in no uncertain terms. 'You are in the right,' he said. 'Take some knights, go to Maidstone and free your man. Then find Boniface's official and deal with him tit for tat.'

Aymer stared at William, and William looked back steadily, acknowledging they had crossed a boundary.

'Do it,' Aymer said.

'I need men,' William said. Attacking an ecclesiastical building was no light matter, but Aymer's man could not be left at the mercy of the Archbishop's soldiers. 'Reliable, fast, loyal. But I dare not accompany them. When it comes to standing before the King, I have to be as innocent as a lily.'

'I have a couple of trustworthy knights.'

William nodded. 'I will send Roger d'Aguillon and his men, but none must wear badges or identifying marks. Let plain surcoats and livery be the order of the day.' He swiftly set about organising a band of knights and serjeants to go to the rescue of Aymer's priest, with instructions then to seize Boniface's man, Eustace of Lenn. He knew there were would be repercussions, especially when the Queen got to hear of the matter, for she would defend the Archbishop to the bone, but he would speak to the King and do his best.

*

The following evening, William and Aymer were sitting at the fire in the Bishop's palace at Southwark when the knights returned from their mission. Roger d'Aguillon reported to the chamber, ushering before him a filth-stained cleric. The priest sported bruises and a black eye. Raw weal marks encircled his wrists where he had been manacled. He rushed over to Aymer and prostrated himself. 'Thank you, my lord, thank you!' he sobbed. 'You have saved my life!' A strong smell of excrement wafted from his garments.

'All right, all right.' Aymer patted his shoulder then quickly removed his hand, his nostrils flaring. 'Pull yourself together, man, and sit down.' He directed a servant to bring wine.

'We found him at Maidstone,' d'Aguillon said, 'trussed like a chicken, as you can see from his wrists. No cloak, no food or water, and he had had to piss and shit on the floor. His robes are foul because they'd kicked him around the courtyard.' D'Aguillon curled his lip. 'We considered setting fire to the place but decided it would be a step too far, but we did borrow a good horse to bring your man away with us.'

'Did you find Eustace de Lenn?' Aymer demanded, his eyes bright with fury.

D'Aguillon grinned. 'Yes. Skulking at the Archbishop's palace in Lambeth. We paid a visit on our way back and found him dining in his quarters, but we persuaded him to leave his meal and accompany us.' He jerked his head. 'He's in yonder garde-robe, blindfolded and tied up.' He looked at William. 'I thought you might not want to be seen, sire.'

William pursed his lips. He had not wanted to be involved at all, but now it had happened a sense of adventure and dark amusement was rising inside him, not to say a desire for justice. 'He is blindfolded, you say?'

'Yes, sire – thick dark cloth; he can't see a thing. And we put a sack over the top for good measure and tied it around his throat – although he can still breathe.'

William and Aymer went to the garderobe where d'Aguillon had thrown Eustace de Lenn. From within came the sound of furious grunts and bumping about. As Aymer opened the door, Eustace scrabbled backwards.

'When my master learns of this you will be excommunicated and flung into the furthest pit of hell!' he screeched through the sacking. 'You will be eaten by devils and all your line will be cursed for eternity! Sons of fornicators and whores! You will—'

His voice cut off in a strangled squawk as William lunged and grabbed him by the throat. 'You might want to mend your words lest they be your last on earth.'

'His words have no power,' Aymer said with a shrug. 'No more than the hissing of a cat.'

They dragged a cursing, struggling Eustace into the courtyard and pushed him on to a horse, tying his wrists to the pommel. William clipped on a lead rein.

'Do your worst!' Eustace spat. 'I will be avenged. Kill me and hack my corpse into a thousand pieces!'

'I am sure you would love to become a martyr like Thomas Becket,' Aymer replied, 'but I am disinclined to oblige your tendencies.'

They set out in the small hours of the morning, their first intention to house Eustace in the dungeon of the Bishop of Winchester's keep at Farnham. However, after a while, William called a halt. Eustace was making loud, inarticulate noises of protest behind them.

'We have gone far enough with this sorry excuse for a cleric,' he said to Aymer. 'I don't want to waste any more time on him. We should let him go, although I see no reason to lose a good horse into the bargain.'

Aymer pondered briefly, and then nodded. He dismounted, and going to Eustace, hauled him from the saddle, threw him on the ground and, leaning over him, cut his wrist bindings. 'I'm sure you can find your way to your master from here,' he said. 'But if ever you trespass above your authority again, you will not live, and that is a promise.'

William and Aymer rode away, leaving Eustace in the middle of the road, wrestling to unfasten the sack from around his neck.

Joanna had been waiting for two days without news – no messengers, no stories from passing folk, nothing. Now, suddenly, she heard the dogs barking a furious warning and welcome.

'Papa's home!' Iohan yelled, dashing to meet him.

William crouched to pick up his son and swung him round in his arms.

Joanna studied William anxiously, checking for signs that he had been fighting. 'Are you all right?' Kissing him, she surreptitiously felt him, waiting for him to wince.

'Yes, yes,' he said impatiently. 'It is all sorted out.'

'What happened?' She led him inside and summoned servants to take his hat and cloak and bring wine.

Sighing, he threw himself down on the bench near the fire. 'I told you, it's dealt with, don't worry.'

Joanna scowled at him. William's 'dealt with' could mean any manner of things, mostly disastrous. 'Tell me what happened,' she said again, her tone brooking no prevarication, and gestured for the children's nurse to remove their offspring from the room. She knelt to remove his boots. 'This is bound to turn into a matter for the King.'

'Yes, it will, and rightly so. I had to go to Aymer's rescue. I had no choice – you agreed with me. The less you know the better. I am home and I did not fight, nor did I go to Maidstone. All of that is the honest truth.'

With glaring sins of omission. She pressed her lips together. At least he was safe.

'I have to make sure the King takes our part,' he continued, 'because the Archbishop will seek the Queen's support and make a mountain out of a molehill.'

'You have to tell me what happened! Not knowing is dangerous too!'

He rubbed his palms over his face, and after a moment told her.

She looked at him, horrified.

'He cannot prove anything and we were totally justified. Boniface of Savoy is responsible – or his representative is, but Boniface will back him. As will the Queen, since Boniface is her uncle.'

'You must tell the King the truth and speak to the Queen without making a confrontation of it,' Joanna said, thinking rapidly. 'Blame Eustace for what has happened. We all have servants who can be liabilities. Give a gift to the Church. I have a silver cup we can present where it will have the most influence. It cannot continue like this, William, truly it cannot.'

'This was hardly Aymer's fault!' he protested.

'He may not have started it, but each time something happens, the situation escalates, and Aymer is usually involved somewhere.'

She fetched his indoor shoes.

Jacomin arrived bearing platters of hot roast chicken and bread.

'I promise I will do my best,' William said. 'It will be all right.'

He set about the food with a will. Joanna had no appetite. It would take a miracle for it to be all right.

*

'Treating a man of God that way!' Henry cried with shock and righteous anger when he heard the story of what had happened to Aymer's man. 'Disrespecting my brother! Matters have indeed gone too far!' He glared at the Queen. Friction was already rife between them over a recent ecclesiastical appointment where their opinions had clashed.

Aymer expanded his chest self-righteously. 'I felt it necessary to rescue my priest immediately, as you can imagine. I had no time to seek permission because of the threat to his life, but I know I have done the right thing.'

'I thought you would approve by proxy, sire,' William said. 'I advised Aymer that you would, and I apologise if I was presumptuous or wrong.'

Henry tutted with irritation. 'You should have told me first. This is a clerical matter. You had no cause to become involved, although I understand your desire to support your brother.'

'Indeed, sire, and I am sorry we have had to bring the matter to your attention. I hope it will not happen again.'

'So do I,' Henry said darkly. 'For all our sakes.'

Two days later a messenger arrived at court bearing the story according to Eustace de Lenn, by which time Aymer had returned to Oxford, leaving William to bear the brunt as Henry heard of how Eustace had been abducted, roughed up and dumped on the road in the dead of night, gagged and bound. Archbishop Boniface was demanding that every bishop pass a sentence of excommunication upon those responsible.

As Henry listened, he became so rigid that his head started to shake. Hectic spots of rage burned on the Queen's cheeks.

'Now we have the truth of the matter!' she said, rounding on her husband. 'How many times have you been warned about your troublesome family? Taking over and doing all manner of badness as they please and lying to their back teeth. How dare that jumped up brother of yours take the law into his own hands and defy the Archbishop of Canterbury!' She turned to William. 'I know you are involved in this. You and your kin are as thick as thieves. Where one goes, all go! It is time that order and decorum were restored to this court and certain people were put in their place.'

'I entirely agree, madam,' William said, bowing. He turned to a bewildered, agitated Henry. 'My brother exercised his right to appoint his own man in his own diocese and the Archbishop's representative refused him that right. He seized and imprisoned Aymer's man, beat him and humiliated him. Aymer had no choice but to act. I do not know what happened in full, but I am sure the details have been blown out of proportion, as these things so often are.'

Alienor drew breath to do battle. 'Do not believe all you are told, sire,' she snapped. 'Aymer is not yet old enough to be a bishop and is still under tuition. The Archbishop's servant was beaten and abused too and made to walk down the road, gagged and bound like a common beggar. That is unconscionable. You are condoning a great wrong. The head of the Church of England is your appointed prelate, and all clergy must accept his authority. It is his prerogative to say, not that of some half-trained rake who happens to be your brother.'

Henry stared at her open-mouthed.

Flushed with rage, Alienor ploughed on. 'If your brother had sought agreement for this appointment in the first place, none of this disgraceful quarrel would have happened. I will tell you what the trouble is, sire. It is too many fingers stirring up once clear water and polluting it. Those fingers should be cut off at their source before any more damage is done!'

Making an immense effort, William swallowed his anger and

replied in a voice of reasoned neutrality, 'I beg your leave, sire, to say that my brother has recognised jurisdiction over the living of St Thomas's, and it is within his gift to appoint his own representative at that level without prior consultation. He had the right to do so, and that right was violated.'

'But not to the detriment of the Church and the authority of the head of the Church!' the Queen retorted.

'You do not know the man my brother appointed, madam, so I fail to see how you could know such a thing.'

'I will not be spoken to in such a wise!' Alienor spluttered.

Henry leaned towards her. 'Calm yourself, madam. This is indeed a sorry situation and I am hearing two different stories and being pressed in the middle. My judgement is that Aymer's appointee should keep his place, but reparations should be made to the Archbishop and the damage done to his property and his man. Let amicable agreement be reached and let this be an end to unseemliness.'

Alienor was not mollified. 'This goes against your own Archbishop of Canterbury!' she hissed. 'Your head is so turned by these brothers of yours that all sense has dribbled out of your ears. You side with them and let them get away with murder while they laugh behind their hands! Your authority is being slipped out from under you as if they have stolen your very cloak. The sooner you return to your senses the better, and to your true queen and partner whose opinions you have been neglecting in their favour!'

'What do you think I do for you, madam?' Henry demanded, shaking with rage and distress. 'I could not do more! I am sick of it all. As I have said, let Eustace of Lenn be reprimanded and let Aymer make reparations, and that will be an end to it.'

Alienor struck the arm of her chair. 'Why should Eustace of Lenn be reprimanded for loyalty to his lord the Archbishop?

Why should Aymer go unpunished? You are a pawn in the hands of your Lusignan kin! I am starting to think that they are like lice on the back of a dog!'

William stiffened at Alienor's vitriol.

Henry jerked to his feet, and looked at the Queen, his jaw wobbling with grief and rage. 'Enough, madam! If you will not accept my authority then I have no recourse but to order you to leave. You shall depart the court and go to Winchester, to the seat of my brother's bishopric, there to contemplate your loyalties.' Then he rounded on William. 'And you! You protest your innocence and defend what has happened, but this is part of a long string of events that always appear never to be your fault; yet somehow, at the bottom of it, you are always involved. I am cutting your funds and reining you in, because clearly I cannot trust you either! When I give you money, I do not expect you to spend it in fighting the Church and abetting quarrels with the Queen's kin! What I give you, I give from my heart, and if you misuse it, then I might as well keep it. If you cannot respect a precious gift, then it is a vile disrespect to me.'

Alienor gave a satisfied sniff, but Henry whirled again. 'And you, madam, will not meddle in my affairs! Send me your purse before you leave. We shall speak when you have had time to consider your actions. That is all I have to say, for you have both cut me to the bone and should be ashamed!'

Henry rose from his chair and stalked out. The Queen gave William a terrible glare before she too stormed from the room.

Horrified, Joanna stared at William as he sat on a bench in their chamber, his face in his hands, having just told her what had happened during his audience with Henry and the Queen. She wanted to scream and throw things at him but controlled her vexation by pretending they were in a public place. He was not entirely to blame, and on his own terms he had valiantly fought his corner, but in ways that backed him further up against the wall – and in consequence herself too, for she owed allegiance to all the parties concerned.

'You must conciliate,' she said, sitting beside him.

'I do not see why.' He raised his head. A muscle twitched in his cheek. 'Aymer was not the one at fault, and the Queen has already defied the King recently in the choice of priests for a particular decision.'

'Perhaps so, but we cannot afford to make enemies of either the King or the Queen. They are our family and our livelihood. Nor is it for you to speak for Aymer. Let him speak for himself. He has his own voice. Why should you take this upon your shoulders?'

William shook his head. 'I had to defend our honour and Aymer wasn't there . . . if you had heard . . .' He cut himself off. 'It is done,' he said, 'and even if I know I must conciliate, I cannot do it today.'

Joanna sighed heavily. 'Words have been spoken by all that cannot be unsaid, but at least they are out in the open now instead of continuing to fester,' she said, trying to think her way through the morass. 'The King has not banished you from court so you will be able to show him you have taken his words to heart. I have to go to Aliza for her lying in but I will bid a respectful farewell to the King first and also the Queen, for I want neither of them as enemies.'

'You are right of course,' he said with reluctance. 'In the meantime, we will need to find some things to sell that will not be missed, for I do not know how long the King intends to keep me without money. I have never seen him so angry.'

'He has deprived the Queen too,' Joanna said practically. 'I do not believe it will be for too long.'

He gave her a contrite look. 'I do not know what I could have done that would not have dishonoured me in one way or another. I am sorry.'

Joanna leaned her head against his arm. 'It is what it is, and we will manage.' She would stand with him against the world and the Queen if she had to, but she desperately prayed it would not come to that.

Joanna found the Queen packing to leave. Attendants were flinging items into baggage chests and sacks and removing jewels and silks from the wardrobe, while Alienor sat on the bed, angry tears streaming down her face.

'Madam, I am sorry for all this,' Joanna said, curtseying.

Many of the other chamber ladies ignored her. Some even turned their backs.

'I am sorry too,' Alienor snapped. 'Sorry that I ever approved of my husband's notion to marry you to William de Valence.'

Tears pricked Joanna's eyes at the rejection and unfairness. 'If I could mend this, I would,' she said.

'Oh, don't start sniffling.'

'I'm not, madam.'

Alienor sighed and held her hand. 'Oh, in God's name, it is not really your fault, save that you should have worked harder to bring your husband into the fold as I exhorted you when you married him. I had better expectations from you than this. Never mind. I want you to be very careful what you say to him from now on. I don't want every conversation held in my chamber to be carried back to him. Do you understand?'

The Queen's words stunned Joanna, but they also dried her tears. 'Yes, madam,' she said with rigid dignity. 'I understand, but I want you to know I have never carried your conversations back to my husband, nor ever would. May I have your leave to depart to my sister-in-law's confinement?'

'You may,' Alienor said frostily. 'There is nothing for you in my household after all. I think it for the best.'

Joanna curtseyed and left. She had done all she could, but her stomach was knotted with grief and she was heartsick.

The Queen departed the court within the hour with her baggage train and the King remained shut in his chamber and did not bid her farewell. Joanna set out for Lewes with a heavy spirit.

'Be very careful,' she said to William. 'It is not good to have the Queen against you. Do not antagonise her further, for it is not just your head at stake, but mine.' .

'Of course,' he said, far too nonchalantly for her liking.

'I mean it, William.'

'I will do what is right for all of us,' he replied with laboured patience. 'I will not say "do not worry" because it is futile, but I will not let you down . . . I promise, Joanna.'

He always promised, but she had learned that his promises were not rock solid when faced with a wall of circumstance even if he meant them at the time. She held her tongue on bitter words that would only worsen the situation.

He kissed the children and handed them into the cart. 'Be good for your mother,' he told Iohan. 'I will see you soon when you return at Christmas.'

The cart lurched forward and Joanna waved farewell to William before leaning back against the travelling cushions and closing her eyes. She pressed her hand to her belly. Her flux had not come this month and she suspected that her underlying queasiness and lethargy were more than just a reaction to recent upheaval.

In late December, Joanna returned to court. Aliza had borne a second daughter, baptised Isabelle after Aliza's mother and other ladies of that name in John's family. Cocooned in the birthing chamber, the women had received snippets of news from the world outside as a December frost settled over the land and hardened the muddy ruts in the road. The Queen, exiled from the court, had been forced to ask Henry for money because she had exhausted her emergency supply. Archbishop Boniface had read out a sermon of anathema at Oxford where Aymer was studying, and the dispute had continued to rumble for several weeks. However, as Christmas approached a cautious thaw had begun and it seemed that conciliation might be possible.

William helped Joanna down from the travelling cart, swung her round and kissed her. 'I have missed you! Let me look at you! Hah, you are a better feast for the eyes than all the gold in every shrine in England.'

'Flatterer!' she said, laughing, for absence had made her heart grow fonder. 'You look very fine too.' He was wearing his marriage robes which still fitted him well, even if a little tight across the shoulders where he had broadened out, but the effect emphasised his height and strength. A single sapphire ring glinted on the index finger of his left hand where usually there would have been many. His eyes were wary with new knowledge and hollows shadowed his cheekbones.

'I do not feel quite so fine,' he said, lifting their son into his arms. 'I swear you have grown again, little man! And you too, young mistress.' He leaned over to kiss Agnes in her nurse's arms.

'How are matters progressing?' Joanna asked as they entered their lodging.

He shrugged. 'I have not had to pawn all the jewels yet and the King and Queen are at least talking to each other. We shall come to peace soon enough.' He noted the way she was looking around. 'I had to sell the Limoges candlesticks to pay a debt, and a few jewels, but we can buy better ones as soon as everything returns to normal.' He took her hand. 'I have been doing my utmost to mend fences with the King and Queen and so has Aymer. Whatever you think, I learn by my mistakes and try not to repeat them.'

'But you always rush to defend your brothers,' she pointed out.

'As they rush to my defence, or why else have a family. Henry is my family too and I know he is in a difficult position. The Queen resents our influence over him and especially over the lord Edward. I am not blind.' He looked at her sombrely. 'The Queen is formidable and her power is not only a grindstone, it is the mill that turns the stone. She is a woman to fear.'

Joanna wanted to say that in the past the Queen had always been kind to her, but the Queen had not been a grown woman then, and Joanna had been a little girl with limited prospects. Alienor had given her brooches and ribbons and been fond of her like a pet. When Joanna had unexpectedly become an heiress and married the King's brother, Alienor had been happy for her and had approved the match. But things were different now. Alienor had matured and begun to wear the crown for herself, and for Edward's future as much as for Henry. William and his brothers were a danger to her construct of power. At least William had recognised the peril now.

'Yes, indeed,' she said. 'You should not antagonise her.'

'Even if she is formidable, she cannot rule without the King and he is the source from which she draws her power,' William replied. 'She must keep within his favour. She will conciliate because she must. Aymer is going to present her with a gift of silver plate on the Feast of the Circumcision and she will recip-rocate with gifts to us.'

'At least it is a sign of resolution,' she said, but thought it was smoothing mud over the cracks rather than repairing them. The battle for power would still exist, with plenty of potential to escalate again.

William shrugged pragmatically. 'The King has to deal with Gascony next and he cannot leave a divided court behind; he and the Queen must be united. She will be responsible for ruling England during his absence, and she knows my brothers and I are essential to any campaign in Gascony, especially now de Montfort is no longer the governor.'

Joanna gave a judicious nod. William had clearly thought about the way forward and what would happen.

'I told you all would be well.'

'Perhaps, but it is a warning to tread carefully and not to cross the Queen, or Boniface. They could still do much damage.'

'I know, and I will have a care.'

Joanna took his hand and placed it on her belly. 'As you must, for you will have yet more responsibility as a father in the early summer.'

He looked her up and down and began to smile. 'That is wonderful news!'

'And God willing, let the new little one be born into a life of peace and stability,' she said firmly.

Joanna knelt before the Queen's chair and bowed her head. 'I have returned from attending the confinement of the Countess de Warenne,' she said, 'and I hope to serve you while I am at court.'

Alienor rose and gave Joanna the kiss of peace. 'And I am pleased to see you returned,' she said, her manner reserved, but at least with some warmth in her eyes, 'and glad to have your service. Let us put what has happened behind us.'

'Yes, madam, I would be glad of it.'

'Good, then it is settled. Come and rub my feet as you used to do.'

Joanna obeyed, fetching a footstool, and kneeling at the Queen's feet with a small pot of oil of roses.

Three days ago, on the feast of the Epiphany, the Queen had presented two jewelled belts to William and Aymer and they had reciprocated with a fine set of silver plate and candlesticks for her chamber. For now, an uneasy peace reigned. The royal couple themselves had mended their quarrel and were like two turtle doves. Resolving their differences had rekindled their romantic interest in each other.

The landscape, however, had changed for Joanna. She was wary of Alienor, for she had seen how easily they could become enemies, and the root cause was William and his brothers. William and Aymer had been charming youths when they arrived at court and no threat to the Queen's power. Now they were virile, experienced men. Edward looked up to William in a way he did not look up to his father, and as he grew, he was turning away from his parents and gravitating towards his dashing Lusignan uncles. The rapprochement following the quarrel was supposed to be a new start, but it seemed thin to Joanna and lacking in trust. She might rub the Queen's feet and perform other duties with a smile, but the whole-heartedness had gone from her service.

23

Portsmouth, Hampshire, August 1253

Henry's fleet rode at anchor, waiting the morning tide to set sail for Gascony. Tonight, the stars pinpointed the gloaming and a cool breeze shivered the surface of the sea lapping against the strakes of the assembled cogs and galleys.

Sitting over a meal in their lodging, Joanna gazed intently at William and tried to fix his features in her mind, knowing they would be apart for several months. Beyond that awareness lay a darker knowledge that he was going to war in Gascony. Henry had plans for a lasting peace and was arranging a marriage between Edward and the half-sister of their rival for the province, Alphonso, King of Castile, but the details were still being brokered. There was a rebellion to quell and groundwork to be laid.

Joanna was staying behind, having recently been churched following the birth of their second daughter, Margaret. Queen Alienor was remaining too as acting regent with the aid and counsel of the King's brother, Richard of Cornwall. She expected a child in the late autumn, the result of the reconciliation between her and Henry, but was not going to let such a detail prevent her from governing.

Joanna intended visiting her lands in the Marches centred around Goodrich for the remainder of the summer and autumn. She had building works to oversee, and she wanted to spend time away from the court for a while.

Having finished their meal, Joanna and William retired to bed. Tomorrow they would make a public farewell, but tonight was for private goodbyes.

'I am going to miss you,' William said, unfastening the laces on her gown.

'As I will miss you too.' Saying the words brought Joanna's emotions to the surface and she had to blink back tears.

'I will write to you, I promise.'

She ran her hands over his chest. 'And I will write also, but it will not be the same. It will be like sailing in a ship that is tilted and I will always be looking over the side for you. Come back to me, whole, you promise?'

'I promise, God willing.' He pushed her chemise off her shoulders. 'You and the children give me an overwhelming reason.'

She curled her arms around his neck and they took each other to bed and made love with tender abandon. Afterwards, while William slept, Joanna quietly left him and went to pray at the small portable altar set up in her chamber, beseeching God to keep him safe and protect him from harm.

Joanna and the children arrived at Goodrich Castle on a warm day in mid-August. Joanna inhaled deeply of the fresh air and her sense of constriction started to fall away. Guards saluted her arrival as the covered cart rolled through the great gates into the courtyard. The servants had travelled ahead to make everything ready for her arrival.

Stepping from the cart, she faced the great rectangular keep, flanked by timber service buildings, and smiled as she gazed at the solid stone tower and the highest window arches decorated with chevron zig-zags. 'See,' she said to Iohan, taking his hand. 'Your great-grandmother lived here. Her name was Aoife and she came from far away in Ireland. We shall sleep up there tonight, safe and secure.'

The nursemaids in tow, Joanna climbed the great tower with the children, up and up, pausing on the wedge stairs, peering into the chambers with their swept floorboards and empty hearths. They came to the room where Joanna's great-grandmother, the Countess Aoife, had dwelt in her widowhood.

A fire had been kindled with a small cauldron set ready at the side to cook pottage. Joanna's brass washing bowl stood on a chest by the bedside and the floor had been covered with woven rush matting and sheepskin rugs. A jug stood in one of the window embrasures, filled with roses and marigolds from the small castle garden. The beds had been prepared with fresh linen sheets. Joanna looked round, drawing a deep breath tasting of musty air and flower petals. Much needed to be done, but the prospect filled her with relish rather than dismay. This place was a home, a refuge, a project. The connection had sparked within her the moment the cart rumbled through the gateway.

A latrine stood at the far end of the chamber and another doorway, partly open, blew a cool draught into the room. Iohan ran to it and peered upwards, then started to climb, lithe as a monkey. Joanna hurried after him and in moments emerged on to the battlements where a wide vista of woods and gently sloping fields greeted her through the crenel gaps. A strange sensation filled her – of knowing, of coming home. Raising her face to the cool wind, she felt it sweep around her like an embrace, flowing energy into her body.

Joanna spent three months at Goodrich with the children, taking stock and recovering from life at court. However, she did not dwell in isolation, and often entertained guests on their travels through the Marches. Even so the pace was much gentler and she was relieved not to be constantly on her guard. She visited Dene Abbey, a Cistercian foundation eight miles away that had rents and farms from Goodrich, and she became friendly with Osmund, the Abbot. She would eat with him once a week while they discussed business matters and items in common with the estates. Elderly but spry, Osmund had an especial interest in astronomy and he delighted in teaching Joanna about the constellations.

On clear evenings she would climb to the top of the keep and pick out the shapes in the heavens – Capricorn, Pisces, Taurus the bull, Orion the hunter. Knowing William would be looking at the same stars in Gascony brought both comfort and longing. She would envisage his face and imagine running her fingers through his thick curls, and would feel the bite of loneliness. While she delighted in having the bed to herself in the summer heat and being able to curl her toes in the coolest corners, she missed the reassuring security of his body, and the pleasure he took in her and she in him. However, on a parallel course, she set such longing aside, knowing she must become both lord and lady in his absence.

After a few weeks the letters had begun arriving from Gascony, often worn and curled at the corners from their long journey, sometimes salt-stained and smelling of wood smoke, but at least William had remembered his promise to write. He told her he had been involved in several skirmishes and seen fighting, sometimes leading as the battle commander, but he had played a part in diplomacy too, and was busy advising the King and witnessing documents. He expected to be gone for some time yet, but hoped to see her in the spring – in Bordeaux, if she would come.

She returned his letters, telling him of her life at Goodrich and the daily running of the estates, and how well the children were progressing with their lessons. She wrote a little about her star-gazing, but not in great detail, for she wanted to share it with him in full once they were reunited.

Summer turned to autumn with golden harvests of wheat. The castle's flock of geese roamed the fields, fattening on the grain that had dropped through the stubble. Apples were pressed for cider and the hogs sent into the forest to feast on beech mast and acorns. The days shortened and morning mists floated in veiled layers above the grass. Fires were lit earlier and the smell of wood smoke permeated the air. Still Joanna lingered, eking out and savouring the last days while watching the weather.

Receiving news that Queen Alienor had been safely delivered of a baby girl, christened Katharine, was the catalyst that set Joanna to packing carts with her household goods and closing up the castle, leaving it to the care of a small garrison and necessary servants. Glancing over her shoulder, as the cart rumbled away from the castle, she vowed to return and make it magnificent.

At Westminster, the Queen welcomed Joanna back to court with cordial but formal courtesy. The earlier quarrel, although mended, had left its scars. Joanna was no longer part of the Queen's inner circle, even while afforded the respect due to her as a family member by marriage. She was given a place of honour at the feast held to celebrate Alienor's churching, but the conversation lacked the old warmth and intimacy, which saddened Joanna, even while she realised that time had changed and moved on.

Edward had grown again and his voice had broken, becoming strong and rich. He towered above many of the mature male courtiers and reminded Joanna of a virile young lion prowling his domain.

'Aunt Joanna!' He kissed her cheek before lifting her in his arms and swinging her round. 'Hah! You used to do this to me when I was little, but now I can do it to you.'

'That does not mean you should, Edward,' she remonstrated, but she was laughing. 'Just remember that when you are King.'

He set her down with a flourish. 'Uncle William always says how wise you are.'

'I am glad to hear it. A sensible husband should always listen to his wife, because she knows best.'

'Not to his mother then?' he asked with an expressive grin and a glance in Alienor's direction.

'You should always respect your mother, and she has raised you to do so,' Joanna answered diplomatically. 'But the final responsibility lies with you. We all hope for great things from you, nephew.'

His smile was disarming. 'Is that so?'

She gave him a level look. 'Yes, indeed.'

He returned her stare. 'I am to be wed in order to make peace in Gascony – to the half-sister of Alphonso of Castile if all goes to plan. Her name is Leonora.'

Joanna touched his arm. 'Be good to her and you will do well together.'

'I shall be as chivalrous as Uncle William is to you,' he said gallantly. 'When my bride comes to England, I shall bring her to see you, for she will need someone to give her advice and friendship. My mother will love her as a daughter, but she will still be my mother.' Joanna understood his meaningful gaze. Alienor would always consider herself the most important woman in Edward's life and the new bride would be a daughter-in-law, not a daughter.

Edward went off to join his companions, a spring in his step, and Joanna went to look at the new baby, Katharine, cradled in her wet nurse's arms. She had rosy cheeks and dark-blue, myopic eyes. Joanna had brought her a gift of an ivory rattle, but when she shook it in front of Katharine, the infant paid no attention, although she had a beautiful smile for her nurse.

'What a fair child,' Joanna said. She shook the rattle again, but the baby still did not look towards the sound. Joanna put the toy on a cushion at the nurse's side. 'Perhaps she will like it later,' she said, and departed to work on some correspondence dealing with her estates, although first she went to the King's painted chamber, to visit the figure of Hope, and touch her gold-painted shoe.

24

Bordeaux, France, June 1254

Hot sun burned down on Joanna's head as she arrived in the courtyard of the Queen's residence in Bordeaux. Alienor had travelled from her regency in England, bringing Edward so that he could go forward to his marriage in Castile. After greeting Henry, there had been a grand entrance parade, and together the royal family had presented gifts of gold cloths to the three great churches in the city.

Last time Joanna had visited Bordeaux she had been a child, a chamber damsel of minor prospects. Now, she returned as the lady of great estates, married to the King's brother, and the mother of three children.

She had glimpsed William several times amid the ceremonial throng, but the formality meant they had yet to speak. He looked different. Lean and hard, his skin deeply tanned from time spent under a hotter sun than England's. Watching him, her stomach fluttered with desire, mingled with a little fear, for it was like gazing at a stranger, and it might be like embracing one too.

Joli, her groom, helped her to dismount and she smoothed her gown.

'Joanna?'

Drawing a short breath, she faced him, holding herself so stiffly that it had the opposite effect and she began to tremble. He pulled her against him and relief surged through her, for instead of standing alone she had a partner, and he was real, solid flesh and blood not just a scribe's salt-stained letter. Her knees almost buckled, but she rallied and straightened again.

'What's wrong?' He looked at her in concern.

She shook her head. 'Nothing. I am so pleased to see you, but it has been too long a time.'

'Yes, it has, and I have so missed you!'

She had been in a separate flow while they were apart, and becoming part of the greater river again and entering a merged relationship was like negotiating rapids. She felt his body against hers – the body that had given her the children she had borne through hers in pain and travail. They were each half of a whole and that was how they were perceived by the people smiling at their tender embrace. She turned within William's arms to face the external things and do everything expected of her formal position, deciding she would leave the rest until later and deal with what lay on the surface first.

Following a banquet and entertainment hosted by the King, Edward retired to his lodging. In a few days he would ride to Las Huelgas to marry the thirteen-year-old Leonora of Castile. The King and Queen were spending the night together, freeing Joanna to go to the house William had hired close to the Ombrière Palace – a fine merchant's dwelling with cool, tiled floors, a courtyard and a fountain. Upstairs, the windows were open to a moonlit summer night, the sky as deep as indigo silk.

Joanna dismissed her maids, and as they closed the door it was as if they had taken the air with them, for suddenly she could barely breathe. William sat in the embrasure, foot up on the sill, slowly unlacing his boot. As a good wife, she ought to go and assist him, but she felt as unsure and tense as on their wedding night. He was being studiously attentive to his task, his focus on his fingers. She slowly removed her veil and untwined her plaits, watching him covertly. They were two strangers, and the strain between them was the greatest thing in the room. All that she wanted to say to him filled her up, but she could not speak.

Dallying, she slowly took off her shoes and her gown. He removed his tunic and stood in his loose linen shirt and hose. Bracing his arm on the window ledge, he leaned forward to look out on the darkness.

Joanna dredged up all her courage and joined him, tentatively touching his shoulder, and that was all it took to snap the tension.

Turning, he took her round the waist. 'I have missed you so much,' he said, and buried his face in the juncture of her neck and shoulder. 'You do not know how deep, how wide, how far. It is almost too much to cross the divide.'

'I do know,' she said breathlessly. 'Ah God, William!'

And then they were kissing and tearing at their remaining garments, frantic, all earlier caution and hesitation thrown to the wind as the rivers melded and became an overwhelming spate.

In the aftermath they lazed together, and Joanna reacquainted herself with his face, his body, the feel of his skin. His hair had lightened under the southern sun and gold twists glinted in the candle light. She ran her fingers through his curls with a joy so keen that it was almost pain.

'I have missed you beside me,' he said. 'Not just your body, but you are my comfort. I can tell you things that I would never tell anyone else, not even John, for he would not understand. I find myself asking "What would Joanna do?" or "What would Joanna think?" and I imagine your face and your voice, and I have my answer.'

She laughed, and tugged on his chest hair. 'You always sighed at my advice and called me a "worry-wort", as I recall.'

'Yes, but that doesn't mean I stoppered my ears entirely. It is reassuring to have you in the chamber and I know I can trust you with my life and our children's lives and you will never let me down.'

Her eyes stung with emotion. She had had to stand on her own feet during their time apart. She had followed Cecily's advice and trusted herself foremost, but William would love, protect and defend her for all he was worth. He saw her as she was.

She left the bed to bring wine and a platter of cheese pastries to share while they caught up with each other's lives. Tension had robbed her of her appetite at the banquet, but now she was ravenous and set to with a will.

'We have seen some fighting,' he said between mouthfuls, 'but I took no unnecessary risks and we were successful.' His eyes sparkled. 'Henry entrusted me with the military detail of the campaigns and all has worked to our advantage. I have also been involved with diplomacy and administration. The people trust me.'

She recognised his need for praise, and his desire for her to believe in his abilities. And indeed, she did believe him. He had matured and learned some hard lessons since his quarrel with the Queen. She had seen from the way Henry favoured him at the banquet, and how others had treated him with deference, that he had won respect during the campaign.

'I am proud of you,' she said. 'You have done so well.'

They kissed again, tenderly, before continuing with their meal.

'I wish I could have brought the children to you,' she said, 'but we did not know what we would find here, and it was better to leave them at Windsor with their cousins. I wish you could see how much they have grown. Margaret has your curls, Agnes can recite the full creed now, and Iohan is learning to read.'

'I am looking forward to seeing them,' he said, 'although they will have grown even more by the time that happens. But I am glad at least to have my wife.'

He raised his cup in toast, and she raised hers in reply.

'What do you think of the lord Edward's marriage to Alphonso of Castile's sister?' she asked.

'It seems a fine solution.' He reached for another pastry. 'It avoids the dispute over Gascony, and secures our borders. The princess has been raised among men of military standing and she is well educated and of a compatible age with Edward. Like us, if God is good, they have the opportunity to grow old together and raise their children.'

'Edward certainly seems amenable – indeed keen.'

'Well, he is going to be free from his mother, isn't he?'

She gave him a sharp look. 'You need to remain on cordial terms with the Queen.'

He shrugged. 'We shall never be bosom friends even if we have mended our relationship for now, but I meant no insult to her. Edward has always wanted to be his own man. His marriage is going to let him off the leash, with a new young wife at his side. His mother may be there in the background for support, but she is part of his past – even if she does not think so.' He finished the pastry and poured a second cup of wine.

Joanna left her seat and went to the window. The summer breeze gently billowed her chemise. 'What about the Pope's proposal to make Edward's brother King of Sicily? The Queen and her uncles are keen, and I think Henry will be interested.'

285

William rose and joined her. 'It will be glorious if it can be achieved, but it will be expensive on top of all other expenses – and that includes payments to Simon de Montfort for releasing him from his Gascony contract. It might be worth pursuing, but it is mostly a matter of advantage to the Queen's uncles. It is their influence at work on this.'

Joanna shivered. She didn't want to become involved in any more arguments surrounding the Queen and her faction.

'What of de Montfort?'

William curled his lip. 'We have managed very well without him. Naturally he is still demanding money with threats but he can wait a better time.' He put his arm around her waist and changed the subject. 'Now, what did you write to me about Goodrich, and studying the stars?'

At Fontevraud Abbey a richness of sun imprinted the turning autumn leaves with an additional patina of gold and the clear October air was kind enough for cloaks to remain open. Joanna had never before visited the abbey, housing the royal tombs of Henry's dynasty. Of William's too. Henry had arranged for their mother's body to be removed from its original burial place outside the abbey and transferred to a more exalted tomb in the choir.

In the nuns' cemetery, two lay brothers had opened the grave and piled a mound of soil to one side like a gigantic molehill. On the other side stood the sealed lead coffin of Isabel of Angoulême, erstwhile Queen of England, and Countess of La Marche.

Joanna could see from William's taut expression how affected he was as the priest brushed away the soil and draped the coffin with a rich pall of purple silk and another of cloth of gold.

The coffin was placed on a bier, and each of Isabel's sons took a pole. William and Henry at the front, Geoffrey and Guy at the rear, they bore their mother's remains into the abbey church for a funeral mass followed by reinterment before the altar. Henry had commissioned a wooden figure, designed to match the other effigies already present, and the carver had excelled himself, depicting an elegant woman robed in a blue gown, her cloak swirled stylishly across her body. Her hands were crossed at her breast and a jewelled crown secured her white veil. The effigy's eyes were closed, as though she was resting for a moment rather than for eternity. Moved by the grace and beauty of the image and the evocative, holy chant of the requiem mass, Joanna began to cry, and taking the music into her heart, she allowed it to be sung for her mother too, and found healing comfort.

In the clear night, the stars were scattered like salt crystals across the sky as Joanna and William walked hand in hand back to their pavilion from the guest house where they had dined with the King at the requiem feast.

'I think your mother is at peace,' Joanna said.

'I hope more than she was in life.'

'It is a tranquil and holy place.' She slowed down. 'I have some news for you. I believe I am with child again.'

He slipped his arm around her waist. 'So soon?'

She laughed ruefully. 'I thought I might be barren when I wed you, but these days you only need to look at me and I quicken.'

'I would not make of you a brood mare,' he said sombrely, 'even though it is good news.'

She shook her head. 'You do not, and we both know there are ways of being careful. We need another son – one to name for his father.' She touched his face and smiled. 'I wanted to tell you now, at Fontevraud. If it is a girl, we shall name her Isabelle, and if a boy, he will bear your name.'

*

From Fontevraud the court travelled to Chartres where Henry and Alienor were greeted by Louis of France and his queen Marguerite, Alienor's sister. Also arriving at Chartres were Alienor's younger sisters Sancha, who was married to Henry's brother Richard, and Beatrice, wife to the King of Navarre. The four sisters, all wed to royalty, had come together for a reunion. Joanna thought she had seen all the glory possible at the English royal court, but this gathering surpassed all her previous experience.

Riding into Paris they were greeted by the citizens, cheering and waving. The students from the university serenaded the royal procession with music played upon lute, viol and gittern and escorted them into the city, to the pinnacle of Christian worship at the exquisite church of St Chapelle, glowing with jewelled colours like a reliquary. The gold and silver and filigree light graced the relic of the holy crown of thorns that had pierced Christ's brow. On his knees, Henry wept over the arte-fact, overwhelmed almost to the point of drowning in passion.

The English court spent its first night in Paris among the labyrinthine buildings and passages of the Old Temple, but moved next day to lodgings in the royal palace. From his own purse Henry fed copious numbers of the Parisian poor and presented lavish gifts to all who dined at his tables, determined to have his largesse witnessed and exalted, even if it was not officially a contest to decide which monarch expressed the highest generosity.

It was a family gathering too, and even if the hosts and guests were often rivals and sometimes enemies, they still had much in common. Henry and Louis respected and acknowledged the bond of marital ties and shared experiences, opinions and senti-ments. Like the fires that burned in the great hearths for everyone's comfort in the deep winter season, warmth and friend-ship glowed beyond the spectacle.

One frosty morning, as Henry prepared to depart for England, King Louis took them on an excursion to a hunting lodge outside the city. With sparkling eyes and in high good humour, he led them to a large, closed barn. Joanna could hear something huge lumbering about inside and grasped William's arm for reassurance.

At a gesture from Louis, two of his knights pulled out the great wooden bars securing the doors and swung them open. The winter daylight poured into the barn to reveal the strangest creature Joanna had ever seen. It was twice the height of a horse with wrinkled grey skin, huge, flapping ears and a long, snake-like nose. Its feet were the size of giant drums, and two enormous ivory tusks thrust upwards from either side of its pouting mouth. Heavy chains hobbled the animal's feet and it had a keeper, bearing a stout, knobbled club. Joanna had read about elephants in bestiaries and had heard tall tales from merchants who had seen them on their travels, but the reality took her breath.

Louis presented Henry with a basket of apples and gestured him towards the beast. Henry looked positively aghast.

'It is a harmless creature, I promise you,' Louis said, smiling broadly.

Henry, stiff with tension, approached the elephant and extended the basket. The trunk came questing, delicately lifted an apple, and conveyed it into a pursed mouth. Then again and again. Emboldened, Henry held one in his hand, and the elephant took it with courteous dexterity. Henry laughed aloud, captivated. The elephant raised its trunk and trumpeted so loudly that everyone clapped their hands to their ears.

'I knew you would like it,' Louis said. 'And who in our lands has ever seen such an animal before? You have many marvels at your Tower in London. Lions, I am told, and a great white bear that fishes in the river.'

'Yes indeed,' Henry said, smiling but dubious.

'It is only fitting, then, that I should present this beast to you as a parting gift, so that it may further enhance your collection.'

A look of startlement crossed Henry's face, swiftly concealed. 'That is very gracious and generous of you, my brother.'

Louis inclined his head. 'I can think of no worthier recipient.'

Henry rubbed his chin. 'I was thinking of Hannibal, and how he crossed the Alps with a multitude of such creatures armed for battle. Truly it must have been a wondrous sight.'

The elephant polished off the basket of apples and looked for more.

'Edward and Edmund will love it,' William remarked to John de Warenne, who shook his head.

'How is he going to get a behemoth like that across the Narrow Sea?'

'Calm weather and a large ship?'

John folded his arms. 'It is well thought of by Louis to present the creature as a gift. It is so magnificent and unique that nothing will exceed it save a unicorn, but at the same time he passes the responsibility for housing and feeding it to Henry.'

'Yes, but think of all that ivory when it dies.'

'Trust you.' John rolled his eyes.

'The King will be thinking of it too. His mind will already be working on how to carve the tusks, mark me. I wouldn't mind riding it. I wonder what it's like.'

Joanna shook his arm. 'No, I forbid it, I absolutely forbid it!'

John and William exchanged amused glances.

'I have always found it better to do as my wife tells me,' John said nonchalantly. 'It saves a lot of trouble in the end.'

25

Windsor Castle, April 1255

Aliza and Joanna sat together in the nursery chamber at Windsor, sewing, talking and keeping an eye on the menagerie of playing children, confined indoors by heavy rain. Joanna smiled as she watched them, all busy with their games and mostly innocent of the world's machinations. Cousins and brothers and sisters. The garrison children too, romping with royalty.

Iohan and his sister Agnes were playing with a wooden elephant that Jacomin had carved, complete with a miniature stable to house it. They had a bear and three lions too and played with them endlessly. The elephant had fired their imaginations when they had gone to watch it arrive from France in February, brought up the Thames on a purpose-built ship to its new house at the Tower of London. Iohan was constantly demanding to go and visit the beast.

Joanna's youngest, Margaret, eighteen months old, had been taken away for a nap by her nurse and Joanna decided she would retire soon to do the same. Well into her seventh month of pregnancy she was cumbersome and constantly weary.

The Queen's youngest daughter, Katharine, lay on a small bed in one corner, tended by her nursemaid. She smiled at people and always beamed at her father and held her hands up to be picked up, but something was very wrong. She never turned to the sound of voices and even the loudest of claps or ringing of bells had no effect. She was a beautiful child with fair curls, delicate features and wide blue eyes, but she was not of the world. Henry and Alienor were extremely protective and no one dared speak of the child's strangeness. Henry said little Katharine was a precious gift from God precisely because she was flawed. They were all God's children and a reminder that everyone should be humble before Him, from peasant to king.

Aliza said, 'I wonder when we are going to see the lord Edward and his new wife.'

'William says in the early autumn,' Joanna replied. 'Edward is supposed to be going to Ireland and Leonora is coming to Westminster.' Joanna cast a swift glance at Aliza. 'William told me they had consummated the marriage.'

Aliza frowned. 'That is dangerous. Boys of fifteen are led by their lusts, and even girls of thirteen, but it is not wise. I would not want that for any daughter of mine.'

Joanna leaned closer to Aliza so they would not be overheard. 'William says she is with child and that is another reason they are not here yet. She is resting and awaiting the birth in Bordeaux while Edward administers Gascony.'

Aliza shook her head. 'Oh, that is not good at all.'

Joanna nodded. 'It is perilously young to be bearing a baby.'

'Poor girl,' Aliza said. 'It is difficult enough to come early to marriage without having to contend with that as well.'

'Indeed, and none of my daughters shall wed until they are

of a safe age to bear offspring. I will light candles for Edward's wife, and Edward,' Joanna said. 'And their baby.' She placed her hand on her own womb, seeking reassurance from the flicker of life within.

Joanna cradled her six-week-old son in her arms and stroked his soft cheek. Conceived on a hot August night, he was strong and healthy, suckling vigorously at the wet nurse's breast. He had been christened William, and Joanna was pleased to have everything in balance – two boys and two girls. They had heard that Edward's young Castilian wife had miscarried of a baby girl in May, born three months too early. While tragic for the young couple, Joanna thought it a disguised blessing, for had Leonora carried the baby to term she could have died or been damaged for life.

Joanna placed little Will in his cradle and tapped the rocker gently with her foot, watching as his eyes grew heavy and then closed. Smiling, she turned away to her needlework, but stopped as a messenger wearing the Swanscombe livery was ushered across the room to her by her chaplain, Father Guydo.

'Madam,' Guydo said. 'There is grave news from Swanscombe.' He stood aside so that the messenger could kneel to Joanna and present his letter.

'Madam, I am sorry to tell you that your lord father passed away two days ago at Swanscombe of a seizure,' the messenger announced, head bowed.

Joanna took the sealed letter, the words ringing in her ears. She had been prepared for this, given her father's state of health, but expecting the news was not the reality. Stiffly, she thanked the man and instructed him to be ready to ride with a reply.

'It is God's will,' Guydo said as the messenger departed.

'Yes,' she replied with outward composure and looked at the

piece of parchment. 'I shall have masses said for him.' All the unresolved issues churned inside her like threads waiting to be stitched into a tapestry, but now she lacked a needle and the threads were drifting in the wind. 'One day' had become 'never'.

William arrived, walking swiftly. 'Ah, Joanna, I am so sorry!' He took her in his arms. She leaned into his embrace and gripped his sleeves tightly.

He called for a reviving drink, and Mabel brought her some hot wine with a grating of sugar.

'I will come with you to Swanscombe,' he said.

Joanna swallowed, and nodded gratefully. 'My half-brother is not of age to inherit and that means a warden must be appointed. I do not want the estates falling into my stepmother's hands.' She shuddered with visceral revulsion. Her eyes were wet, but she did not know where the tears had come from.

'We shall speak to the King and make all arrangements,' William soothed, stroking her spine.

Joanna bit her lip. Whenever she had to deal with matters concerning her parents she always returned to the memories of her mother in her tomb, her father's swift remarriage and the end of childhood. 'No, I shall do it myself,' she said, pushing away. 'It is my duty while my half-brother is in his minority. I am the eldest child and he is my responsibility, as my father wished.'

'Your half-brother is of squiring age. I will do what I can to help – take him into my household if you wish.'

'Yes,' she said, glad of his strength and practicality. 'It would be a good idea I think.'

By the time Joanna arrived at Swanscombe, her father had already been buried because of the sultry summer weather. The grave slab, lying beside her mother's, was carved with a foliate cross that had come from the mason's general stock rather than being personal to her father, but which could be replaced later with something more ornate. Joanna knelt on the cool stone floor to pay her duty if not her respects with William and their two oldest children at her side. Margaret and the baby were at the manor with their nurses. Joanna's stepmother, thank God, had already departed for one of her dower properties and would not return.

Her half-brother was present with the knights and servants of the household. Guillaume at eighteen was a sullen youth with a blemished, oily complexion, lank, fair hair and hostile grey eyes.

Later, when Joanna showed him the writ with the King's authority to put him in wardship to her and William, until he was twenty-one, he recoiled in fury. 'I am old enough to rule Swanscombe! If the King's son can rule Gascony, then I can be responsible for my own estates!'

'That is a different thing entirely,' Joanna said curtly.

'Hah, it is not. My father has raised me to care for these lands since my birth. I know you have always wanted them – you cannot accept that I am the heir, not you!'

Joanna recoiled as if he had slapped her, but part of that recoil came from knowing that a poisonous splinter of that accusation was true, and she was ashamed.

'That is enough!' William warned. 'Your sister has your welfare at heart, and so do I. If not us, then someone else would have been put in charge of your interests.'

'Then I would rather someone else!'

'Who would milk the land without care,' William said. 'You share the same father, and your sister's mother is buried here. She will administer for the best and with the King's goodwill, and we will see to finishing your education and given affinity at court.'

'You think I should be grateful to snakes?' Guillaume shouted, beside himself. 'You want this for yourself. Everyone knows you are a greedy, grasping Poitevan thief!'

William seized a fistful of the youth's tunic and almost lifted him off the floor. He thrust his face into Guillaume's. 'If my wife or I wanted this, we would take it and there would be nothing you could do, believe me. Perhaps everything you "know" from what "everyone" says is true. Perhaps we shall do away with you and make it very simple indeed!' He released the boy with a shove of contempt. 'You are under age for three years yet, and a guardian must be appointed. Better your family and close to the King than anyone else. You have a choice. Use your time productively, or spend it in scowling belligerence. It matters not to me or your sister. Now, go and prepare your things.'

White-faced, Guillaume glared at him and then stormed off, yanking the door curtain off its rings.

William breathed out hard and dug his hands through his hair. 'I should not have lost my temper. If he riles me now, how much more difficult is he going to be when he is my ward?'

Joanna looked down. 'He is right in a way. I do feel as if this should be mine. It is hard to know it belongs to him, but I ask myself what Cecily would say, and she guides me. Perhaps he will change. Boys of his age are often sullen and unruly.'

William raised a sceptical eyebrow. 'Perhaps, but I doubt it. I shall do my best with him.'

They departed Swanscombe with Guillaume in their entourage, still scowling like a thundercloud. At least she could administer Swanscombe for the time being, Joanna thought, and keep an eye on her half-brother, although she suspected William was right in doubting that they could turn him around.

26

Tower of London, Autumn 1255

As an autumn dusk fell over London, mist rising in curls of vapour from the river, Joanna entered the chamber the King had prepared for Edward's new young wife. Candles and lamps imbued the room with a soft golden light and a hearty fire burned in the hearth. The white mantle canopy sported the image of winter portrayed as an old man in a heavy cloak who bore a certain resemblance to Henry, which Joanna suspected was a deliberate whimsy on the King's behalf.

Red and gold fabric rugs in geometric patterns overlaid the rush matting covering the floor. Joanna had seen such rugs in Bordeaux, usually draped over furniture or on the dais under the King's chair, but never to walk upon, because they were too rare and costly. However, Henry had spared no expense in preparing this chamber to honour his son's wife.

To a trumpet fanfare of announcement, Joanna advanced to the royal chairs set on the dais and bent the knee. Henry sat in the middle, with the Queen on one side and his new daughter-in-law on the other. Henry rose and stooped to give her the kiss of peace, before taking her hand, and presenting her to Leonora of Castile.

Joanna curtseyed again, and Leonora bade her rise in fluent French, with a slightly exotic accent. A gown of olive-bronze silk, subtly embroidered, clung to her narrow figure. Leonora's eyes were brown with a glint of amber surrounding the pupil and Joanna received an impression of intelligence and maturity; but then, if the rumours were true, the girl, at fourteen, had already been through a mill of experience.

'Madam, I bid you welcome to England,' Joanna said. 'If I can be of assistance in any way, I shall gladly honour and serve you.' She presented Leonora with a little carved ivory box filled with small nuggets of frankincense.

Leonora's gaze brightened with pleasure. 'You are thoughtful, my lady. My husband has spoken to me of you and his uncle, and expressed his fondness for both of you. I am pleased to meet you and I am sure we shall have much to talk about later.'

Joanna curtseyed and moved aside while others came forward to greet Edward's young bride. Feeling Alienor's gaze on her, Joanna determined to be discreet when cultivating this new, future Queen of England. Alienor was the dominant lioness for now and Leonora the kitten, even though it would change in time.

Over the next two months Joanna came to know Leonora, discovering her to be an interesting and delightful young woman. She was indeed kittenish and playful, but she had a serious side and possessed the intellect and understanding to absorb copious amounts of detail along several strands at once. She loved being outside and Joanna often walked with her around the palace and its environs, or accompanied her on horseback or in the royal barge. They strolled in the winter garden between beds of dark earth with everything dormant and the trees almost bare except for evergreens.

'I love gardens,' Leonora said wistfully. 'In Castile we have many beautiful ones with fountains and flowers. I would spend my days in them if I could – they lift up my soul.'

Joanna nodded in agreement. 'There is great pleasure in nurturing and watching things grow to fruition.' She touched Leonora's arm. 'England must seem dank and colourless now in the winter, but wait until you see how green it is in spring.'

'Edward has told me of this,' Leonora said. 'He has been delayed with other business in Gascony, but he will be here very soon. His father wants him to go to Ireland next, but he is coming to England instead – he is coming for me.'

Not wishing to be indiscreet, Joanna said nothing. If Henry was expecting Edward to go to Ireland and Edward was defying him in coming here, then the young lion was indeed flexing his muscles and taking matters into his own hands.

Leonora paused in front of a bare flower bed and gave Joanna a sidelong look from her lovely brown eyes. 'When we were wed, we consummated the marriage,' she said.

'Yes,' Joanna said gently, 'I know.'

'He did not force me, I want you to know that. We made the decision together, for once we consummated the marriage, it could not be dissolved. There is trouble between my brother and Edward's father even now, but whatever happens, the marriage cannot now be annulled.' A pink flush stained her cheeks. 'When I first set eyes on Edward, I knew I was looking at the rest of my life, and Edward saw me the same. People say we are too young to understand, but we have been raised since birth to know who we are.'

Joanna's heart went out to the girl. 'I do understand. I was a little older than you, but I felt that way about my husband. A match where duty and compatibility mesh is a rare gift indeed.'

Leonora's flush deepened. 'We lay together in order to seal the bond, but also because we wanted to. My fluxes had been coming for half a year before the marriage, but we did not think I would get with child so quickly.' She began walking again. 'When it happened, we were shocked – but pleased. I bore our daughter in my sixth month, but she entered the world too soon. People said I would have died if I had carried her for nine months for my hips were not wide enough, but I grieve all the same. She was my flesh and Edward's united.'

'I am sorry,' Joanna said. 'It must have been terrible for you.'

Leonora wiped away a tear on the side of her hand and drew a steadying breath. 'It was, but I must go forward. Edward and I know we must wait. When he returns, we shall not lie together in that way again until the time is ripe. We do not need chaperones and constant watching.' She set her jaw. 'If we are old enough to be wed, and to cope with the loss of a child, then we are old enough to deal in the world.'

Admiration filled Joanna for this fourteen-year-old young woman, barely beyond childhood, but a queen in the making, facing the world with courage. 'If you need a friend and confidante, I am your aunt-by-marriage and I swear that whatever you say to me will go no further.'

Leonora gave her a sweet, genuine smile and touched her sleeve. 'Thank you, and I shall think on it well and kindly, my aunt.'

'Although I am afraid I shall be leaving court for a little while soon,' Joanna said as they resumed their walk. 'My sister-by-marriage, the Countess de Warenne, expects her third child soon and I am going to her for the birth.'

'Then I wish her well,' Leonora said, 'and I shall hope to meet her after her churching.'

*

'How is that half-brother of yours progressing?' Aliza enquired.

Joanna looked up from the letter William had sent her from court which she was reading in the embrasure by candle light in Aliza's confinement chamber at Lewes. Yesterday, Aliza had given birth to a healthy baby boy with a bellow on him like a young bull. This morning his proud, joyful father had borne him to the chapel where he had been baptised William to acknowledge all the Williams in his bloodline. Joanna had stood as his godmother. He had recently suckled heartily at the wet nurse's breast, and now slept in his cradle at the bedside.

Joanna grimaced. 'He has a quick mind, but he doesn't use it except to be sullen and do all he can to thwart William's efforts to train him. As far as he is concerned, this has been forced on him and he thinks he is perfectly capable of ruling his estates without being anyone's ward.' She sighed and shook her head. 'He speaks to me when he must. At the Christmas court he spent all of his time with Simon de Montfort and his sons.'

'Is it deliberate – because he knows you have no love for Simon de Montfort and that you are in dispute with him over his wife's dower lands?' Aliza asked shrewdly.

'It is likely. He plays dice with Leicester's squires and socialises with them and they encourage him. I am sure he spreads rumours and gossip about me and William, but he covers his tracks well. The more we take him to task, the more he rebels. William tries with him – you know how he hates giving up on anything – but I suspect that my half-brother will win this particular battle.'

'William was difficult at that age too,' Aliza said. 'If my brothers thrashed him, it only increased his resentment and taught him to be more cunning. He was always better led with love, but I do not think from what I have heard that such a ploy will work with your half-brother.'

'No,' Joanna said. She could find no love for him, and it only added to her resentment and guilt.

Aliza grimaced and rubbed her stomach, and Joanna was immediately attentive. 'It is nothing,' Aliza said, 'just after-cramps.'

'I will get the midwife to make you a tisane,' Joanna said with sympathy. 'I know how painful they can be.'

The next day Aliza's cramps were worse. The discharge from her womb was red and copious; she had a fierce headache and a fever. She vomited up the potions the worried midwife gave her to drink, and as the day progressed, her condition deteriorated.

Joanna bathed Aliza's face and hands with rose water, while the baby suckled from the wet nurse with gusto.

John came to the lying-in chamber and looked at his wife with anxious fear. 'You must get well,' he told her. 'For me, for our children.'

Aliza turned to him, her hair soaked with sweat. 'I am doing my best,' she said, her voice weak and hoarse. 'God will do as He decides . . .'

'Then I will defy God!'

Joanna gasped at the blasphemy and bit her lip.

'Hush,' Aliza whispered. 'None of that, John. Know that I love you and will always love you.'

He turned away, pinching tears from his eyes. Joanna reached to him, but he pushed her off and went around the bed to sit at Aliza's other side.

Silently, Joanna wiped Aliza's body and tidied and plaited her hair.

John took his wife's hand, and Aliza fell into a restless slumber. Her eyes moved rapidly under her lids, now and then fluttering open, but they were rolling and white. When the chaplain arrived to administer the sacrament, she barely roused from her increasing delirium. John jerked to his feet and strode from the room, and Joanna hurried after him.

'I will send a messenger to William and bid him come immediately,' she said. 'He is less than a day's ride away.'

John nodded tersely. 'Do that,' he said, and swallowed. 'Joanna, I cannot bear it.'

'I know . . . I know.'

'I won't let her die.' He flashed her a look filled with anguish, and Joanna returned it steadily.

'I will write to William now,' she said, touched his arm, and hurried away to see to it.

Sitting at a lectern by the window, she penned the letter without a scribe, wiping her eyes so that her tears would not blot the ink, and it was the most difficult thing she had ever had to do – to summon her husband to his sister's deathbed.

The messenger had been gone a little over two hours and evening had taken the light when Aliza shuddered and ceased to breathe.

'No.' John stared at Aliza in disbelief, her folded hands clutching a cross, chrism oil glistening on her brow. 'No!'

Joanna gazed on the body of her sister and her friend. Just two days ago they had been laughing together as they joyed in the triumph of the birth of a healthy baby boy, and now her life had blown out like a snuffed candle.

'I will never find anything so beautiful in my life again!' John sobbed, leaning over her body. 'You have taken my life with you; there is nothing left for me!'

Joanna attempted to speak to him but grief was a wall of thorns for both of them, and when she tried to put her arms around him, he threw her off so violently that she staggered and almost fell, but he did not apologise, for he was wild and beyond reach.

Leaving him in the care of the priest and his senior knights, she pushed down her own anguish and set about organising the household. Other letters had now to be sent, and instructions given. The King and Queen had to be told. Someone had to do these things, and applying herself to practical matters was a way of coping. She had to put her faith in God, even as John was denying Him. As mortals they could not see the patterns of His infinite wisdom. William would know what to do when he arrived. Of anyone, he would have the words and perhaps the comfort as John's closest friend and brother-by-marriage.

William cantered into Lewes on a sweating, hard-ridden palfrey. He had received the news from outriders looking for him and could not believe Aliza was dead. Had she experienced a premonition all those years ago when heavy with her first child? The token she had given him had taken some finding at the bottom of his coffer and he was sick with sorrow and with dread at finding the words to say to John.

He dismounted, threw his reins to a groom and hurried into the keep. Joanna ran to greet him and flung herself into his arms, sobbing. He drew her against him, full of gratitude that he still had a wife, and grief that he no longer had his beautiful sister.

'I am so sorry,' Joanna said in a breaking voice. 'The childbed fever took her and we were powerless. She was overjoyed to have a son, and by God's mercy he thrives, but John refuses to look at the child. You have to know what to say to him. For he will not listen to me.'

William brushed away her tears on his thumb and kissed her wet cheeks. 'I will go to him,' he said. 'Where is he?'

'In her chamber.'

He kissed her again and then drew away, heading to the stairs and pausing briefly to draw a deep breath before climbing to the solar.

The bed was made up neatly with the silk embroidered curtains Aliza had ordered last year. A scent of beeswax polish rose from the oak bench and light sparkled on the gold in the cushion covers. A beautiful room, but already a shell. John sat on a stool at the empty bedside, his head bowed, black hair flopping on his forehead, his clothes stained and dishevelled. Filled with pity, William went to him and touched his shoulder.

'John, I am here. I have heard the news . . . dear God.' He drew up a stool and sat so he could look into his friend's haggard, beard-stubbled face. 'There will never be another like Aliza. She was my dear sister. I shall know the loss of her as part of my firmament. I grieve, but God needed her for Himself, and God's will is not an easy task.'

John curled his lip and his dark eyes flashed with rage. 'Do not prate to me of God's will,' he snarled. 'How can it be God's will she should die? I say that God does not exist!'

It was blasphemy, but William understood the depths of John's despair. 'I need to give you something,' he said, and placed the crystal-encased lock of hair in John's hand. 'Aliza gave this to me many years ago when she was with child for the first time, and asked me to pass it on to you in the event of her death. I did not want to take it, but she would not let me refuse – you know how determined she was. She said I must tell you that her life would continue elsewhere through her eternal soul and you must not mourn for her but continue to live your life in joy. She said if you could do that to honour her memory, she would be content.'

John made a choking sound and closed his fist over the token. 'She asks the one thing I cannot do!'

'Even then she was thinking of you and what might happen. I did not understand at the time, I thought she was being macabre and fanciful, but she had true wisdom.'

John rocked back and forth with the token clutched to his breast, and William wrapped his arms around him tightly as if swaddling an infant.

Joanna arrived with a jug of wine and some venison pasties. She cast a wordless look at William, poured a drink for both men, and quietly departed.

'Aliza would not want you to grieve like this, but I know you will.' William disengaged to bring the cups of wine. 'Drink,' he said.

'I will never love again,' John said bleakly. 'My heart is dust. Nothing is worth this pain – nothing! I would rather never have had my son than lose Aliza. I would rather have remained celibate all my life than this.' He snatched the cup, drained it to the lees and held it out to be refilled.

The words jolted William, but he knew they came from grief and John was not in his right mind. For now, he needed someone to sit with him while he found oblivion. William refilled his cup and sipped slowly, while allowing John to drink for both of them and fall into a stupor, Aliza's token still clutched tightly in his hand. Eventually, when he slumped, William carried him to bed, covered him with a blanket and sat by him, listening to his ragged breathing, tears sliding down his own face.

At last, he left John in the care of his chaplain and sought Joanna. He found her kneeling in vigil at a small portable altar in a chamber off the great hall. Gazing at her neat, bowed head he tried to imagine how it would be to live without her. Would he wish their four beautiful children unborn if it vouchsafed her life?

He knelt beside her and clasped his hands together. 'It is a terrible thing how quickly the wheel can turn and bring a man to nothing,' he said. 'We are powerless before the will of God. Aliza prepared as best she could. She was always wise . . . and now she is gone. I hope and pray that she is with our mother in heaven. Surely, she could not be anywhere else, my dear, sweet sister.'

'William . . .' Joanna looked at him with eyes full of grief and tears.

He took her in his arms. 'I do not know what tomorrow holds for us, but I swear I shall cherish every moment with you. Even if we must be apart, I will be mindful of what I have and what I could so easily lose.' He kissed her, and the kiss became passionate with grief and desire born of that grief. They went to bed and they loved each other with desperation, but at the last moment William withdrew, for even if they did have more children in the fullness of time, now was not the moment to be conceiving them. Lying beside her, stroking her hair, he felt guilty and sad that John would never have this solace again – and that Aliza would never know anything.

27

Palace of Westminster, May 1257

Joanna swallowed tears as she carried a bundle of fabric from the wall cupboard and placed it in an open chest in the Queen's chamber, trying to maintain a neutral expression so no one would realise her distress. The women kept casting her looks, some quick and sympathetic, others speculative, and one or two filled with malicious satisfaction.

Alienor had just publicly asked Joanna for the return of the keys she held to the coffers where the royal belts and jewels were kept and had given them instead to a lady who was a protégée of Eleanor de Montfort. Alienor had set Joanna to emptying the cupboards of the ordinary fabrics and scrap lengths – a task Joanna had performed as a junior lady at court.

'I can trust you with this,' Alienor had said. 'You should remember where you started in my household, when you had nothing.'

'Madam, I am always your loyal servant,' Joanna had replied, bowing her head.

'So you say. Well, let your deeds prove your words,' Alienor said before turning away to deal with other business.

The Queen's ladies were packing the royal baggage for a journey from Westminster to Windsor. Alienor was eager to visit her daughters and escape from the city and the recent outbreak of sweating sickness. Several folk opined that the malaise had been caused by the unseasonal cold weather and the rain that had not stopped falling since late February, around the time that the King's elephant had sickened and died. Iohan had been utterly distraught, but the King had given him one of its teeth as a keepsake and it now occupied a wall niche in their chamber at Westminster.

The sky was an overcast swirl of grey with droplets spitting in the wind. Joanna hoped it would improve for their journey upriver in the Queen's barge. She had considered leaving the court and going to one of her manors but that would mean losing even more face and influence. Besides, she suspected that the Queen would not allow her to go. Alienor was keeping her dangling in order to make a point about who held the power.

With her back to the Queen, Leonora gave her a sympathetic look; she had to keep the peace with Edward's mother and choose her battles wisely.

Joanna knelt by the chest and folded the fabric neatly into it while pretending not to notice the new woman bringing a belt to the Queen. She knew exactly why she was being ostracised. William was riding high in favour with Henry and the bullish young Edward, and Alienor feared she was losing her influence and her power in matters of patronage and policy.

The Welsh had recently been raiding with great success in Edward's territories and when Edward tried to take them on, he had swiftly discovered that fighting the determined and war-hardened Welsh was a new and difficult experience.

Embarrassed for funds, he had been forced to borrow money. Alienor had lent him some, but not enough, and Edward had approached William and Joanna for a loan, offering to mortgage several properties in return – properties that were part of Leonora's dower, submitted with her willing consent. They had agreed, and so had Aymer when similarly approached. The contract was amicable, with full understanding on both sides. However, it incensed Alienor that her eldest son was running up debts and obligations to his Lusignan uncles. Henry had seen no harm in it and, since he was dealing with other difficulties, had dismissed the complaints with an impatient wave of his hand.

Seeking elsewhere for allies, Alienor had turned to the de Montforts, who had their own grievances with the house of Lusignan, not least the continuing dispute over the Marshal dower lands. As the King continued to favour William and the latter's relationship with Edward grew ever closer, so the Queen's treatment of Joanna had become increasingly stilted and glacial.

Joanna had once loved Alienor, and still owed her gratitude from their early years, and for that debt, she remained loyal. She would not be the one to break the bond, but she was near the end of her tether. Leaving the chest, she went to fetch another pile of cloths from the cupboard. The top pieces, of slippery silk, started to slide. Leonora hurried to help and surreptitiously squeezed her hand. Joanna's eyes stung with tears at the kindness.

'Thank you, madam.'

'You are very welcome, Aunt,' Leonora replied. 'We must all help each other after all.' She went on her way, eyes downcast and manner modest.

Bolstered by the quiet support, Joanna continued to the chest to stow the fabric.

The Queen's uncle, Peter of Savoy, arrived, returning from a morning in council. Passing Joanna, he flicked her a sharp, less than friendly glance and joined the Queen.

'I have never seen such unseemliness in court before,' he said with distaste. 'The Earl of Leicester and William de Valence coming to blows, but I suppose it was only a matter of time. I thought the Earl of Leicester would do murder and the King had to intervene.'

Joanna's hands stilled on the cloth and her heart began to pound. Standing at the Queen's side, Eleanor de Montfort had frozen, eyes widening.

'I am sure the King will tell you himself,' Peter continued, 'although he may not give you the full tale.'

'I do not expect so,' Alienor said tautly, 'but I know you will. What happened?'

'It was over the raids in Wales,' Peter said, shaking his head. 'De Valence had some preposterous complaint about the Earl of Leicester stealing property from one of his manors and turning a blind eye while the Welsh raided and plundered as they desired. Earl Simon claimed the opposite was true, whereon de Valence called him a traitor to the throne, out for his own gain, and they came to blows. The King had to intervene to prevent a full-blown brawl. It is a good thing that no man comes armed into the King's presence, or one of them would be dead – de Valence, I suspect.' He stroked his moustache, as if the notion did not displease him.

Joanna put her hand to her mouth, feeling sick. Dear God, William.

'How unseemly,' Alienor said with distaste. 'This kind of trouble always involves the same people.' She cast a reassuring look at Eleanor to show that her anger was not directed at her husband. 'Go on.'

'The King and the ushers had to pull them apart. I doubt any apologies will be forthcoming. To be frank, madam, there is a fire under the cauldron and the pot is likely to boil over again.'

'I shall speak to the King on the matter before I leave,' Alienor said. 'Thank you for bringing this to my attention, Uncle.'

Joanna rose to her feet and curtseyed. 'Madam, I crave your leave to go to my husband. If women are the peacemakers, then it behoves me to do what I can.'

Alienor lifted her eyebrows. 'I commend your optimism, but you do not seem to have had much success thus far.'

Joanna flushed, and Alienor gave an impatient wave of her hand. 'Yes, go. Someone else can finish your task.' She turned to Eleanor de Montfort. 'You should go to your husband too. Tell him I would have words with him.'

'Yes, madam.'

Joanna was left in no doubt that Eleanor was being sent with the Queen's blessing, while she was being dismissed under a cloud.

She sought William and found him at the stables, white with anger as he waited impatiently for his groom to saddle his courser. He compressed his lips when he saw her.

'Peter of Savoy has just visited the Queen,' she said. 'You and Simon de Montfort came to blows in the council chamber? You called him a traitor?' She noticed a red graze along his jawline.

He pulled his hat out of his belt and jammed it over his curls. 'And so he is,' he snapped. 'He does not serve the King, or Edward, he serves himself. What am I supposed to do when he raids my lands and runs off with our cattle?' His eyes were bright and flinty.

'He says they were his cattle.'

'Am I going to believe my steward or his?' he demanded. 'He

is making trouble because he has growing sons and he needs to feed their bellies with land and money – but it won't be at our expense, I promise you that.'

Joanna bit her lip. 'The mood of the court is ugly; you should be calming the waters not stirring them up.'

'I didn't start it,' he said tersely, and gestured to the groom to make haste. 'I have to stand my ground if I do not want to see it taken from me by vultures.'

His hurt and rage were coming straight from his heart – both his advantage and his downfall.

'Be very careful facing up to de Montfort and his faction,' she said.

He grunted, and moved to take the courser's reins.

She caught his hand. 'For my sake.'

He briefly squeezed her fingers. 'I will do what I must. You go and do what you must.' He gathered the reins.

Joanna watched him ride out into the windy May afternoon. Wild drifts of pear blossoms were carpeting the ground and snowing into the steel-grey river. She rubbed her arms and shivered. She had never experienced a May-time like this before.

Returning to the Queen, she encountered Simon de Montfort, striding briskly towards her, his expression grim. Several knights of his entourage followed on his heels. Her cousins Richard de Clare and Roger and Hugh Bigod were with him too. Joanna stepped aside to let them pass, her heart pounding and her mouth dry. De Montfort paused and pierced her with his stare.

'A reckoning is coming,' he said. 'We have tolerated injustice for far too long. Tell your husband that no one calls me a traitor with impunity, whatever protection he thinks he has from the King.'

Joanna's legs were shaky but she met de Montfort's stare. 'Sire, that is between you and my husband. I hardly think that intimidating a woman before all these noble lords is an act of glory. And surely the King is our sovereign lord and you owe him your allegiance.'

De Montfort narrowed his eyes. 'Madam, you and your husband are two of a kind.' He continued on his way. Roger Bigod followed him, head down and dogged. His brother Hugh, gentler of nature, gave her a sidelong glance and a warning shake of his head.

Joanna leaned against the wall when they had gone, feeling sick and afraid, but furious too. She clenched her fists, determined not to be intimidated.

Following in de Montfort's wake came a group of squires and younger men, including two of de Montfort's sons, youths of a similar age to Edward. Swaggering along, they ignored her as though she was of no more consequence than a serving woman. Her half-brother was among them, and smirking. She called out to him sharply.

'Guillaume, why are you not with the lord William's household?'

He faced her while waving the others to go on. 'My horse cast a shoe and I could not ride out.' His tone was insolent.

His horse was always casting shoes – Joanna suspected he loosened them deliberately in order to be a nuisance. 'Well then, you can come and help load my baggage, and I have a few other jobs for you.'

He stiffened, and jutted his jaw. 'I am your brother and your ward, not your lackey.'

'You are also a squire training in our household and these are tasks I would ask any noble youth to perform.'

'My lord said I was to go and get my horse shod,' he said sullenly.

'Well, it did not look as if you were doing so just now,' Joanna retorted. 'Go and do as you were bidden, and then, if your lord has not returned, report to me.'

He flourished a sarcastic bow and sauntered off. Joanna glared after him, fulminating.

'He is a bothersome youth,' John de Warenne said, strolling up to her, his gaze on Guillaume's retreating back.

'Would you believe his horse has cast a shoe yet again?'

John snorted. 'Really? William told me he was of a mind to give him a different mount – one that won't let him near its hooves to do whatever mischief he intends.'

'Were you in the court earlier?'

'Yes.' He gave her a pained look. 'There is brewing discontent, some of it justified, I admit. There needs to be reform and the King has not always acted with discretion and good sense. William is a bulwark between him and the barons, so the King favours him and the situation escalates again. But today it was a matter of personal territory and tit for tat. De Montfort should not have driven forward as he did, and William . . .' John grimaced.

'William what?'

'Should not have taken the bait.' He shook his head. 'He called de Montfort a traitor.'

'I heard,' Joanna said stonily.

'It was because of Gascony – because of what de Montfort did there, and his father before him. Many of the victims are de Lusignan allies and neighbours.'

'It is also because de Montfort wants our lands,' Joanna replied. 'William suspects that not all the raids on Pembroke have been Welsh.'

John folded his arms. 'Perhaps, but he needs to be more cautious.'

Joanna touched his arm. 'Look out for him, John. There are

so few I can trust at court, and you are William's closest friend . . . and our brother.'

'You know that is a given!' He looked almost indignant. 'I have no intention of being drawn into de Montfort's affinity. He pestered my mother about the Marshal inheritance too and if she had not been so determined he might have intimidated her. He will never do that to me or my children, on that I am sworn.'

'I shall stand my own ground too,' she said proudly. 'Even if I am terrified, I shall not back down before such a man. Cecily taught me well on the matter of worth.'

He gave a wry smile. 'I am sure she did, knowing Dame Cecily.'

'You are often in my thoughts, John,' she said after a moment. 'Do you continue to fare well?'

He shrugged. 'I manage in daylight but I have no shield against my dreams, nor from waking from them. I shall never be whole, but I manage, and I have my children to protect and safeguard.' He adjusted his cloak. 'I shall go and ensure that young Guillaume de Munchensy sees to the proper shoeing of his horse and then I shall wait for William.' He kissed her cheek and was gone.

Heaving a sigh, Joanna returned to the Queen's chambers to continue packing.

On arriving at Windsor, Joanna hugged her children whom she had not seen in several weeks. Iohan had grown again and at seven years old was very much the man in waiting in his own eyes. Agnes had her usual sweet smile and hug for her mother. Margaret's brown-gold hair, exactly like her father's and wild with life, had been bound away from her rosy face by a garland of blue silk flowers. Little William was walking.

'Oh, I have missed all of you so much!' Joanna cried, and vowed fiercely to spend more time with them. All the wealth and influence in the world was not as precious as this. She hugged and kissed her cousin John's daughters: Alienor bronze-haired like her mother, Isabelle dark like John, and baby William, a chubby red-cheeked infant in his nurse's arms.

The Queen went straight to see little Katharine, who was giving her nurse cause for concern. She had been sick with fever the previous month and had not properly recovered, remaining listless and quiet. Although she had been weaned, a wet nurse had been re-employed to feed her to sustain her thin little body and at least she could be persuaded to take suck for comfort. Gazing at the little girl, comparing her with the other boisterous children in the royal nursery, Joanna was moved to tears. Well might the King have had a silver image made of Katharine to invoke God's help. She had always been a fey ghost-child, never properly of the world, and now her presence in it was further diminished.

The morning after their arrival, Katharine developed a raging fever and a choking cough, and by the following evening, despite all the prayers and entreaties and nostrums, she died in the Queen's arms, with the household praying in a semi-circle surrounding her bed. Grief squeezed Joanna's chest, and fear too, because a child's fragile life could be taken like a puff of wind disintegrating a dandelion ball.

That night Joanna knelt in vigil with the Queen in Windsor's chapel where Katharine rested before the altar, surrounded by hundreds of candles, shining so brightly that the child's body could barely be seen through the waxen forest of light. Alienor prayed, hands clenched upon her rosary beads, her voice a grief-drenched whisper.

Kneeling behind Alienor, Joanna felt the heat from the candles on her face and the cold spring evening at her back. By now a messenger would have reached Henry at Westminster with the calamitous news.

The dawn sent soft fingers through the church windows, smoky with incense and dull because it was raining again – a long, steady downpour that reminded Joanna of never-ending tears. The Queen refused to leave her daughter's bier, but she had neither eaten nor drunk since keeping vigil at Katharine's bedside, and although refusing to abandon her place, she could not sustain it and collapsed, and had to be borne back to her chamber half insensible. Her physician brought a tisane but she refused to drink it and turned her face to the wall.

At noon a barge arrived from London and the clergy came to take Katharine's body away to Westminster for burial. Joanna had left the Queen fitfully sleeping and arrived in the hall to find William there, cloaked and booted, talking with the Queen's steward.

Since they were in the public domain, she approached him formally. He took her hands and bowed over them. 'The King has sent me as a secular escort to see that all is done fittingly for the lady Katharine,' he said, and then touched Joanna's face. 'You look tired.'

'I have not slept, and the Queen is ill,' she replied.

He wearily palmed his face. 'I was there when he heard the news – it was like the end of the world. He has taken it badly indeed, grief-stricken and weeping, but I think it is a vent for many other things.'

'The Queen is the same,' Joanna said. 'She blames herself, but there was nothing anyone could do and the poor child had been ailing for some time.' Her voice wobbled. 'I need to go and hold our children and kiss them and tell them how much

I love them, but not until I have washed death from my body.' She shuddered.

Abandoning formality, William pulled her to him, and rubbed her back. 'Hush now, it's all right.'

There was a sudden commotion as the Queen stumbled into the hall, dishevelled and distraught. She still wore her chemise with only a cloak over the top and her hair straggled loose down her back. 'You!' she cried, as though William was her deadliest enemy. 'What are you doing here?'

Joanna gasped at the venom in the Queen's voice.

William took refuge in icy courtesy. 'Madam, I am but obeying the King's command. He has sent me to bring the lady Katharine back to Westminster for burial – or at least to escort the procession. He is grieving deeply, as we all are. I am sorry you do not think it fitting for me to be here, but my service is loyal and the lady Katharine is my kin.'

She swayed where she stood. 'Why did it have to be you? Why couldn't he have sent someone else?'

'Because the King trusts me,' William replied. 'I have done exactly as he requested and I shall honour that trust. He was in no fit state to come here, for which I am sorry.'

Alienor's whole body shook. She let out a long, grieving wail and collapsed to the floor, tearing at her hair.

William stepped back, wide-eyed. Joanna hurried to Alienor's side. The physician came running and she was carried back to her chamber. Joanna shot a frightened look at William, before accompanying the Queen. As the ladies changed Alienor into a clean chemise, they realised she was burning with fever. The physician immediately bled her to try and balance her humours and shook his head over her condition.

Joanna returned to William and found him surrounded by various children, including their own. Little Margaret perched

on his shoulders, her curls bobbing. He was feeding the youngsters sweetmeats from his pouch, like a falconer taming hungry
young hawks.

'The Queen is too unwell to travel,' Joanna told him. 'She
has a fever and the physician is worried for her health.'

William lifted Margaret from his shoulders and set her down.
'It is probably for the best,' he said. 'I should go. The King is
waiting at Westminster, and like the Queen, he is not himself.' He
looked at her and the children. 'When the Queen has recovered,
I suggest you leave court for a while. I will be better for knowing
you and the children are safe. I trust you to do what is necessary,
and I will continue to stay with the King while he needs me.'

Joanna nodded. 'Yes,' she said. 'I understand, but be careful.'

Joanna watched the funeral cortege escorting Katharine's bier
set out from Windsor on the royal barge down the Thames.
The little body had been wrapped in silk cloths and lay on a
raised platform in the centre of the barge, covered by a canvas
awning to protect it from the rain dimpling the river. Wrapped
in furs and borne on a litter, Alienor insisted on coming to the
wharf to see the barge depart. As the vessel cast off she made
a sound like a wounded animal and reached her hand towards
the craft. The rain increased as the barge sailed downstream
and vanished from sight. With the physician walking beside her
litter, Alienor was taken back to her chamber, weeping in harsh,
gut-wrenching sobs.

Joanna turned away from the river, the hem of her skirts
heavy with water wicking up from the grass, her last sight of
William a misty figure through the rain. She gathered Iohan
and Agnes under her cloak to bring them back inside.

Iohan looked up at her. 'My throat hurts, Mama,' he said.

*

The weeks passed in a blur as pestilence struck Windsor's occupants. Some attributed the malaise to the constant rain for scarcely a day passed without a downpour and spotting the tiniest patch of blue became cause for pointing and wonder. The sun, the moon, the stars, all vanished behind heavy clouds for days on end, and a bitter wind blew. The crops failed to germinate and a murrain and foot rot struck the sheep and cattle.

All of the children succumbed, and Joanna spent one sleepless night after another tending Iohan then Agnes and Margaret, and little William. The smell of sickness and nostrums pervaded the nursery. Fires remained lit when usually the hearths would have been swept for summer, and anyone well enough to be out of bed huddled around the hearth coughing and sneezing. An elderly maid died, and so did the son of a garrison soldier.

As others made a slow recovery the Queen remained perilously ill, refusing sustenance and sleeping propped up against a bank of pillows, her ribs creaking with each breath, and eventually arrived at a plateau where she grew no better but no worse, day upon day the same.

Joanna nursed her children out of danger, but as they started to recover, she succumbed, and spent a fortnight in bed, exhausted, wheezing and snuffling.

At last the weather cleared for a few days and the Queen left her bed and sat by the window, wrapped in furs. Her frame was skeletal, deep hollows shadowed her cheekbones, and her eyes were dull with misery.

Clutching her ribs, sore from coughing, Joanna craved leave of Alienor to take the children to Hertford.

Alienor waved her hand. 'Do as you will,' she said indifferently and stared out of the window, gripping her prayer beads like a drowning sailor clinging to a rope from the shoreline.

Joanna hesitated in the doorway, but without looking round the Queen said flatly, 'What are you waiting for? I said you could go.'

Joanna curtseyed and left, feeling hollowed out. All the nurturing warmth of loyalty and trust between them had become a barren wasteland.

28

Bishop's Palace, Southwark, London, Autumn 1257

William leaned back from the gaming board and handed a pouch of coins to Jacomin. 'Go and bring three pies from Albricht's shop,' he said. 'The beef and marrow ones.'

'Sir.' Jacomin pouched the money and reached for his cloak.

'And no loitering in the bathhouse.'

'No, sire.' Jacomin looked thoroughly offended, as if such a notion had never crossed his mind.

Aymer leaned back in his chair as the door closed behind Jacomin. 'I could have sent for pies earlier if you'd said.'

William shrugged. 'No matter, Jacomin will bring them. Albricht's are the best. No gristle or umbles under the crust. You should employ him.'

'I'll think on it,' Aymer replied. 'How is Joanna?'

'She is well,' William said. 'I'm riding over to Hertford to join her for a few days. She will be at court for Christmas, so you will see her then.'

Aymer nodded, and his eyes strayed to the red-haired young

woman replenishing the wine jug. An ornate gold and gemstone brooch closed the neck opening of her gown. William's gaze followed Aymer's but he said nothing until she had moved away to serve John de Warenne.

'Isn't that the brooch the Queen gave you last year?'

Aymer shrugged. 'It suits Emma more than it does me and I like to give her pleasure since she pleasures me.' One side of his mouth quirked upwards.

William shook his head and stifled a laugh. Aymer was utterly incorrigible. Emma in her furs and jewels was no longer recognisable as the serving girl from the Bishop's manor at Hatfield. She was a swift learner and working hard to retain her position as the mistress of a well-connected bishop in waiting. Aymer, who remained greatly at odds with Archbishop Boniface, declared that unlike certain men of the clergy he was not a hypocrite to kick his sins under the rug and pretend they did not exist.

'Do not worry, I won't bring Emma to court. I know that the higher our star climbs, the further our reputations sink into the mire.'

'And the more we garner enemies and rivals. The Queen is furious that we are assisting Edward with his finances and that the King continues to favour us.'

'We are rivals for patronage and power,' Aymer said. 'And we have every right to it too.'

John sauntered over from the window, cup in hand. 'You ought to tread carefully though. I received a warning from my brothers today – a friendly one, but a warning nevertheless.'

William eyed him sharply. 'What about?'

'They advised me to spend less time in your company. Roger said I should drink with honest men instead of lounging around with "that Poitevan rabble".'

William raised his brows. 'I do not always see eye to eye with your eldest half-brother, but I do not understand why he should so take against us.'

'It riles him to see you and your brothers being given privileges when others receive no such preferment. He has always dwelt outside the golden court circle. Perhaps he is jealous of me because of my closeness to you. I call you brother and am more filial with you than I am with my own flesh and blood. He thinks you have too much power and influence. Roger is not easily led, but he is susceptible to a sustained campaign.'

'Hah, by the Queen and de Montfort,' Aymer said contemptuously. 'They both hate us.'

William shot him a warning look. 'The Queen has been very unwell and in deep mourning. She almost died after losing her daughter. Grief does strange things to people. We should take that into account.'

'Perhaps,' Aymer said, 'but I do not think it strange that she is cultivating an alliance with the de Montforts. To me, it smacks of political manoeuvring.'

Knuckles rapped on the door and Emma went to answer, humming a tune. William anticipated Jacomin's return with the pies, and his stomach rumbled. Then Emma screamed. William launched to his feet and shot downstairs. She stood at the door, her fists to her mouth. Albricht the pie shop owner and his son stood outside, with Jacomin's lifeless, bloody body on a hurdle.

William stared, taking in the scene but not believing his eyes.

Blood smeared Albricht's working apron and his hands, the fingernails dark-rimmed. 'A mob set upon him in the street, sire. He put up a hard fight, but there were too many of them. I could not leave him lying there like a dog – I had only served him a moment since.'

William stepped aside and gestured for them to bear Jacomin up to the chamber. Emma continued to sob.

'Who did this?' William demanded in kindling fury. 'Tell me what happened!'

Albricht spread his red hands. 'They came out of the Mermaid bathhouse, sire, and started picking on him, accusing him of working for Poitevan scum – beg your pardon, sire. When Jaco replied he was as English as they were, they said it was even worse in that case and set on him. And then the knives came out and there was nothing we could do.'

'How many?' John asked, grimly.

'About seven or eight. They recognised the badge on his sleeve and started taunting him about you, and when he answered in your defence, they set on him.'

William stared at the body of his manservant. Faithful, loyal Jacomin. Hostility had been increasing as the harvests failed and people sought to place the blame, especially given the costs incurred by the Welsh war, and Henry's foreign policies. Even if William made a point of employing English knights and servants, they still perceived him as a foreigner when others chose to whip up hatred for their own ends. And now Jacomin had paid the price.

He knelt and set his hands over Jacomin's, which were slashed to the bone where he had tried to defend himself. 'I will find out who did this,' he vowed. 'I will find out and they will pay.'

John quietly thanked the pie seller and his man for bringing Jacomin to them, handed them silver for their trouble, and sent them home with an armed escort.

Aymer had Jacomin brought to his personal chapel. Emma, who had rallied, fetched a bowl of rose water and a cloth to wash the body and prepare it for a shroud. As the vigil candles were lit, William battled his grief, desolation and fury. He wanted to take his sword, find the culprits and kill them, but they were long gone by now. An investigation would be useless, for no one would cooperate, although he would insist. They would close ranks and claim to know nothing.

'He deserved better than this,' he said, and swallowed. 'He was a faithful, loyal servant.'

Watching the people dining on watery pottage and salt fish at the far end of the great hall, Joanna worried about how much longer she could keep them fed. Even though it was almost April, snow remained on the ground and the bitter wind owed more to January than spring. Crops should have been planted by now but the soil was too hard to sow the seeds and it had snowed again this morning. At least they had supplies of stock-fish, even if it tasted vile, but the grain had almost gone and providing bread and ale was a constant worry. The famine had started to bite hard following last year's ruined harvests, and this year's weather was as bad. She could not remember another time like this and she feared that God had turned his face away from mankind.

She had attended court at Christmas and the King had welcomed her warmly, although fresh lines of care had engraved his features and there had been little evidence of the vibrant, benign sovereign of her early years at court. She could see the shadows in him now, although he had done his utmost to celebrate the season and the feast of his beloved St Edward.

The Queen too had changed. All the weeping, hysteria and grieving over the death of her daughter had scoured her being, and only bare, sharp steel remained. Her hostility towards William had not abated and Joanna would have found life at court unbearable had it not been for the subtle support of Edward's young wife Leonora. Joanna often sat in her company and they spoke together of literature, music, hawking and estate management. Leonora was keen to nurture and increase her acquisitions, and often sought Joanna's advice on the subject.

William, for his part, had an excellent rapport with Edward. Many nobles strove to enter Edward's golden circle, but William was woven into it as an integral part, although Edward, these days, was completely his own man. William might be his uncle but the young prince did not regard him as senior in any way. He listened to William's advice, and filtered it through his own desires, but he tended to pay more attention to William than he did to his mother and her kin. Less pleasingly, he took interest in what Simon de Montfort had to say, and Joanna was well aware of the push for influence emanating from that area. Edward shared none of William's antipathy towards de Montfort.

She was chewing her way through a hard sliver of cod when a messenger arrived – one of William's harbingers with the news that his lord and retinue would be here before compline.

Joanna thanked him calmly while silently panicking. How was she to feed so many more mouths? It would take for ever to boil up more stockfish and she had intended the evening meal to be a simple collation of bread and cheese with some wizened apples and nuts from the store. 'How many?' she asked.

'My lord with his knights and household,' he said.

Joanna's heart sank further. Fifteen knights, their attendants and squires. Two chaplains, a groom, various valets and scullions. What in God's name was William doing in Hertford when he could be warm and fed at court? It was hardly the weather for travelling, with snow still covering the ground and the potholes and ruts filled with mud and slush. What if there had been another contretemps in the royal household? Then she felt guilty for her exasperation. The court was more volatile than usual just now, and William was still brooding over Jacomin's terrible demise. No one had been apprehended for his murder even though Henry had summoned a full investigation involving the civic officials, but there had been little interest in Jacomin's death; indeed, there had even been a nuance of gloating satisfaction in some quarters.

Joanna finished her meal and made the excited children do the same. She sent an alert to Robert her cook, who cast his gaze heavenwards, and then she put the servants to preparing bedchambers and stuffing pallets with clean straw. For the rest, they would have to make do.

Hertford's gates opened to admit William's troop and several baggage carts covered in heavy sacking. As William dismounted from his palfrey, Agnes dashed up to him, her brown plaits flying. He picked her up and swung her round, and kissed her, doing the same to Margaret. For Iohan there was a back slap and a hair tousle.

Joanna stood at the door holding baby William in her arms, and looked at him askance. 'What is all this?'

'Wheat.' He kissed her and then the infant. 'The King's brother has sent several grain ships to London and this is part of our share to feed us and our people until harvest time. I have escorted the carts myself because the roads are unsafe and grain is more precious than gold just now – sixteen shillings a bushel.'

'I fear many will starve,' Joanna gave little William to his nurse. 'The hall is full every day and more come to the gates.'

'It is the same at Westminster. There is nothing to eat lest it be fish from the river. All the wild birds have been netted and eaten and even dogs, cats and rats. I can only stay a day. I have to be back at court for Parliament but I wanted to make sure you and the children were safe and well.'

'We are.' She organised the grain to be taken to a barn under guard. 'I can only offer you hard bread and cheese,' she said as she led him into the keep, 'and little enough of that, but we have some wine.'

'That will do. You will find other supplies on the cart – a few eggs and some barrels of herring.'

They went to the private chamber, and William sat down before the hearth to remove his boots and inner socks. His feet were white and clenched with cold, apart from red, swollen chilblains. Joanna brought a bowl of warm, scented water to soak his feet, and gave him a cup of wine heated with spices. He folded his hands around the cup and blew on the surface. Weazel rubbed around his stool and chirruped a greeting. He stroked the cat and pulled his hand gently up his fluffy banner of a tail.

'I am beginning to wonder if spring will ever arrive. It is nearly April now and still we shiver as if it is January. They are saying it is God's punishment on the kingdom and the King.'

'Who is saying?'

William shrugged. 'The rumours originate all around. It's always someone's servant who hears it from another servant. There is discontent among the barons though. It will come to a head when Parliament convenes because the King will ask for money and no one will accommodate him. Everyone will be summoned to military service against the Welsh, and then of course we have the matter of the French truce. It's a vipers' nest, and so many tangled up that you don't know where to begin cutting off the heads and you know you will be bitten before you have completed the task – but still you have to try.'

'I could return to court,' Joanna volunteered.

William shook his head. 'Later perhaps. First I want you to move some of our assets – both goods and coins.'

Joanna stared at him, suddenly alert.

'It is just a precaution,' he said quickly. 'It is prudent in these times to keep some resources well concealed. I am going to lodge some funds with the monks at Waltham Abbey and some at the Temple, and then Winchester and Southwark. Better to keep it separate and have funds that only we know about. I have been thinking about it for a while now – ever since . . . well, for a while now.'

Ever since Jacomin died. She did not have to think hard to follow his reasoning. Although perturbed, she could see the sense in what he said. 'There's the abbey at Dene,' she said. 'It is no distance from Goodrich and the abbot is a good neighbour. He will help, and no one will think of looking there.'

'That is a good idea,' William said with an approving nod. 'And some of the manors – Bampton and Sutton perhaps.'

'Do not worry, I will see to it.'

She dried his feet and rubbed them with some aromatic unguent, her touch deft. William groaned. 'Ah, that is good. Joanna, you are a woman without equal.'

'I know,' she said, with amusement. Glancing up along his body she saw clear evidence of just how good he thought it was.

He unfastened her veil, drawing out the golden pins, then stroked her hair. 'So smooth,' he murmured, 'and it always smells of roses. I dream of your hair, and when I do, I wake up wanting you so much that I ache.'

Heat settled in Joanna's pelvis, heavy and melting. She continued rubbing his feet, admiring their shape, the fine, pale arch. She stroked the hair on his shins. 'I wonder why your hair here is not as curly as it is on your head,' she murmured.

'I do not know, for it is curly elsewhere.' Taking her hand, he drew it to his groin. 'Why is your own hair straight on your head and not elsewhere?'

They moved to the bed and made love with urgency, lust and joy. She felt him full and hard, moving within her, and she became a part of him, as he became a part of her. He gasped her name in crisis and she gripped his shoulders and hung on for dear life. And then she was falling back into Joanna and returning to the world with his sweat and hers cooling on her skin. He pulled the coverlet over their shoulders and spoke soft love words, and she snuggled into him. There were times when she enjoyed having the bed to herself – usually when they had been together for a long time and space increased its value – but for now she craved the closeness.

A sudden soft weight landed in the space between them, accompanied by a low rumbling sound, and then a rhythmic kneading motion on the coverlet. 'I suppose you let that animal sleep on the bed when I am not here,' William said wryly.

Joanna made a shrugging motion. 'There are already furs on the bed, what is another one? He has the advantage of being warm.'

'You don't need him when I am here to do that.' He scooped up the cat and deposited him on the floor. 'Shoo, go and catch mice.'

Weazel stalked off in high dudgeon to sit on William's discarded shirt and groom his fur, while William folded himself against Joanna's body and closed his eyes.

By morning the rain had stopped, although the threat of another deluge still hung in the low grey clouds. Some of the grain had been ground in the mill and Joanna and William sat in their chamber to break their fast on fresh warm bread and honey. Joanna had plaited her hair, but wore no veil, and William kept sending her admiring looks.

'I will start work this morning on what we discussed,' she said as he eventually rose and dusted crumbs from his tunic. Elias appeared to help him don a thicker tunic for travel and then brought his cloak and hat.

'Good, I will have my stewards write to you.'

'I will also see to the distribution of grain,' she said, 'and see that the most depleted manors are supplied.'

He latched his belt and pulled her close for a kiss. 'I wish I could stay. I will think of you every day and send messages often.'

'And I of you,' she said, 'and write to you the same.'

William was setting his foot in the stirrup when a messenger arrived at a hard canter and drew rein, dismounting almost before his horse had halted. 'Sire,' he said, and handed a letter to William. William looked at the wax figure imprinted on the seal and grimaced.

'What is it?' Joanna demanded.

'I don't know, it's from Aymer.'

Joanna rolled her eyes.

William's lips tightened as he read the letter. 'There has been a brawl and a steward in the Bigod affinity has been killed. Aymer borrowed some of the men I left in London to help him out in the fighting.'

Joanna stared at him, her exasperation turning to horror as she took in the full implications. The last thing they needed was to become embroiled in a squabble that had led to a death that wasn't their fight. Silently she cursed Aymer and his penchant for dragging William into scrapes.

'I have to ride for London now.' William stuffed the letter in his saddlebag and mounted his palfrey.

Joanna bit her lip. 'Perhaps you should stay.'

He shook his head. 'No, I have to go to Henry. This is going to be difficult to contain. I will write when I know more.' He kicked the palfrey's flank and departed at a rapid trot, splashing through the icy puddles.

*

William stood behind Henry's chair in the great painted chamber in the Westminster complex. The sun had finally broken through the clouds, but the day was still chilly, and a fire blazed in the hearth. Bundled up in a fur-lined cloak, a clear drip hanging from the end of his nose, Henry had a cold, and his temper was foul.

Parliament had gathered to discuss the finances of the realm, but the day's session had yet to begin and William felt decidedly uneasy. Learning of the murder of Geoffrey FitzRobert's steward he had been furious with William and Aymer, demanding to know why they could not keep better control of their men. Why did it always come to violence? They had to take a share of the blame. In public court, he had dismissed the incident, saying he had bigger fish to fry and no time to deal with petty disputes that were always six of one and half a dozen of the other, which had not been well received – and it was not the only troublesome matter.

Three days ago, Henry had asked his barons for money that they had been reluctant to give. They had eventually promised to deliver him an answer today by the third hour after sunrise. It was that third hour now and thus far there had been an ominous silence.

Henry clucked his tongue impatiently, wiped the drip from his nose and ordered a servant to pour him a fresh cup of wine. But before the youth had reached the flagon they heard a series of loud crashes outside the doors, like the clash of weapons. William's hand shot to the eating knife at his belt.

The hall doors slammed open on a group of barons and knights. They had deposited their swords in the anteroom, hence the cacophony, but all were wearing mail shirts with their heraldry emblazoned on their surcoats and the sound as they approached Henry on his dais chair was that of the battlefield.

The ushers and doorkeepers were conspicuously missing, but then they were in the Marshal's remit and the current Marshal was Roger Bigod, Earl of Norfolk, who was the leading mailed figure striding up the hall with his brother Hugh at his side.

William gazed rapidly around the hall, seeking a means of escape should it become necessary, and prepared to defend Henry with his life. He hoped to God Edward was safe. John de Warenne, who was standing nearby, moved closer to Henry's chair. Among the nobles confronting them, William saw Joanna's half-brother wearing a sneer of enjoyment.

'What is this?' Henry demanded, a quaver in his voice.

Roger Bigod halted the men behind him, stepped forward and went down on one knee. His right fist clutched a sheet of vellum with numerous seals dangling on long tags. 'Sire, my lord King, we have come as your humble and faithful servants,' he said.

Henry's eyes rounded in astonishment. 'If that is the case then why are you armed in my presence? Am I your prisoner?'

'Sire, of course you are not!' Bigod looked thoroughly indignant at the notion. 'We come to you in our armour to show that we are your loyal barons willing to serve on your behalf – we have left our swords in the vestibule.'

'Well then.' Henry leaned back in his chair. 'Do you have an answer for me to the business we conducted at our last meeting? If you come in loyal service, what is it you would say to me?'

Roger Bigod fixed William with a steely look. 'We have come to ask you to rid yourself of these wretched and intolerable Poitevans and other alien parasites that suck the life blood from this court. We have endured slights and insults from them for far too long. They have seized lands belonging to good English men and appropriated goods, wardships and heiresses to which they have no right. They are violent troublemakers and disturbers of the peace as they have recently yet again demonstrated, and we ask you to dismiss them from your presence on the instant.'

Rage boiled in William's chest. 'Alien parasites?' He almost choked on the words. 'Do I not see men older than me, aliens themselves, who have received great bounty from the King, and then been unfaithful to him? Hah! You would never find me marching to confront my sovereign clad in armour and making vile demands.' His gaze fixed on Simon de Montfort, who stood close to the forefront of the gathered barons, but content to let Roger Bigod hold forth.

'It is for the King to speak, not you, my lord,' Bigod retorted. 'You are too full and fond of giving answers for him when you have no right.'

'I have as much right as any of you, indeed more, for I am not standing before my king in armour threatening him like a traitor.' William shot a glance to the others and saw the avid gleam of hunters scenting a kill. While the sight of Simon de Montfort came as no surprise, de Clare was a worry, because he had considered him an ally, and his son was wed to William's niece. But then de Clare had always pursued his personal interests with vigour and had several axes to grind – including, like de Montfort, disputes over Welsh Marcher lands.

'I know why you are here.' William directed his focus to de Montfort. 'You, my lord of Leicester, want my lands in Wales and you collude with the Welsh themselves and let them raid to their heart's content and let me stand the cost. You are a traitor and the son of a traitor.'

'I am neither of what you say!' de Montfort spluttered in fury. 'In that, our fathers were nothing alike!' He lunged at William, fist raised to strike, and Henry shot to his feet as though released from a spring and put himself between them.

'Enough!' His voice cracked with panic. 'You forget yourselves in the presence of your king!'

'No, I remember everything, sire,' de Montfort snarled, but he took a step back, shoulders heaving. 'I remember every moment, every insult, every missed payment on my wife's dowry and her entitlement, both of which were promised by you in good faith. I remember every failed campaign, every sneer and posture and lie! This is how you are being served and this is how you are serving us and we are sick of it. There shall be reform!'

Roger Bigod proffered the document to Henry, heavy with its burden of seals. 'These are our demands for the common wealth of the realm. We ask you to appoint twenty-four prudent men to your counsel table who will discuss policy and advise you. Twelve chosen by your barons, and twelve by yourself. Men of equal measure to represent the issues of the country, issues which are being crushed by the encroachment of foreigners. For ten years we have sustained their tyranny. We ask you to put a halt to their depredations and dismiss them to their own lands so that all may praise your name and your rule. We beg you to accept this document and do as we request so that we may move forward and discuss the matter of money for Wales and Sicily.'

William clenched his fists until his knuckles ached. He wanted to seize the document and cast it into the fire. Henry received it with trembling fingers and looked at him, and shock jolted through William as he realised that Henry was afraid of him too.

'I cannot reply to this here and now,' Henry said hoarsely. 'You will appreciate that being approached by my barons armed as for battle and making demands is not conducive to rational thought. I will peruse this document and report to you in due course.'

'It should take no more than a day,' Roger Bigod said tightly.

Henry stood erect. His detractors often accused him of weakness, but he possessed a rod of steel at his core. 'It shall take as long as it takes,' he replied, 'and you shall not tell me the length of it. I recognise that this is a weighty matter but I shall not keep you more than three days for my answer. You have clearly talked among yourselves and arrived at your own decision, and I am sure it took you much longer than a single meal-time to agree this piece of work. Therefore, you will grant me the same courtesy. Go by all means and find yourselves food and drink. My cooks will accommodate you. You may remove your armour now you have made your point. We know where we stand. Gentlemen, I require you to depart while I consider.'

The lords exchanged glances. 'Three days then, sire,' said Roger Bigod, and bowed curtly. The group departed as one. The clashing sounds ensued again outside as they collected their swords.

Henry put his head in his hands and slumped.

'You should not bow down to them,' William said fiercely. 'They have no right and they are out for their own gain. If they wish to rid themselves of foreigners, then the Earl of Leicester is one just as much as I am, and so is Peter of Savoy and the Archbishop of Canterbury.'

Henry said flatly, 'It would be for the best if you and your brothers withdrew from court for a few weeks until this blows over.'

Shock jolted through William that Henry would even think of dismissing him. 'If we do that, it will be impossible for us to come back, and then what will you do? It is a plot to be rid of us because of our loyalty to you. It would be like cutting off your arm. What would happen to you without us?'

Henry shook his head. 'Then what am I to do?'

William held out his hand. 'May I?'

Henry gave him the document and William took it to the window to peruse in the light, passing the figure of Hope walking among her stars trampling upon Despair. He looked at the numerous seals hanging from the base of the parchment; this threat was real and grave. Remembering the smirk on Guillaume de Munchensy's face, his stomach curdled. 'It is an attempt to limit the power of the reigning King,' he said with disgust. 'And to force through their own agendas and desires.' He wanted to rip the document to pieces. 'Since you are invited to appoint twelve advisers, I suggest you appoint me and my brothers. Also, my lord de Warenne, because the Bigods are his kin and it will offset their influence. Perhaps the Archbishop of Canterbury – better in our corner than theirs, and he is an experienced negotiator, even if we have quarrelled with him in the past. Choose men who can deal with these protesting lords.'

Henry tugged his beard in a repetitive motion. 'They will not be overjoyed at the list you propose.'

'What is the alternative? Who else will serve you well?' William studied the list again. 'De Montfort wants money, land and power. De Clare is just sizing up what he can gain as usual. Peter of Savoy does not want to lose influence. I am in dispute with Roger Bigod over several wardships and the matter of the dead steward, even though I'm not involved. They say they want rid of foreigners but what they want is nothing short of treason.'

'I think we should agree to look at their terms and consider them while we decide what to do,' John said, frowning heavily. 'This is not going to blow away like mere chaff in the wind. At least give the semblance of listening.'

'And what of their demand to be rid of all foreigners?' William demanded.

'Listening does not mean acting,' John said. 'You concede a

few points and hold firm on the rest. They are united in their grievances, but they will not remain united for long. Tell them you need more time to consider what has been said, and arrange a meeting for later in the year, preferably with the lord Edward in attendance. We don't have to decide anything in three days' time at all, except to extend the time required.'

Henry nodded. 'You have the right of it,' he said. 'That is good advice.' He looked at William. 'What do you say?'

'It seems a way out of the situation for now,' William agreed.

He doubted that Henry was robust enough for a protracted battle. Edward was, but Edward was complex, and his relationship with William, although friendly, was a step removed. He was a nephew not a brother, and he was also a king in waiting. A cold sensation filled his stomach, for he realised that this challenge might well become a fight to the death.

29

Manor of Bampton, Oxfordshire, June 1258

Joanna stooped to William's travelling baggage, waiting to be loaded on to the sumpter horses, and checked that his new valet, James, had packed his new shirt rather than the old, favourite threadbare one. They were lodging at their manor of Bampton, as William prepared to go to Oxford for a court gathering before Henry sent an army marching on Wales to put down its troublesome princes.

William had been short-tempered and preoccupied ever since the confrontation with the barons in April. Simon de Montfort and several of the twelve barons selected by the reforming side had been absent in France as part of a delegation negotiating a truce with King Louis. Now, everyone had returned and the matters of Wales and baronial reform were to be discussed. De Montfort was pushing hard to have his wife's dower lands reassessed to his benefit. He had to provide patrimonies for his four sons – hungry eaglets with wide open beaks. There was so much hostility directed towards William that Joanna feared for his life.

He joined her, putting on his favourite hat with the peacock feathers in the band.

'Have a care,' she said, 'and God keep you.'

'And you,' he replied with a quick smile. 'I will send you word.' He kissed her cheek warmly, but she knew his mind was already on the road.

She watched him ride out and, sighing, returned to her accounts. Although the last year's shortages had eased a little, food remained scarce, and eking out supplies to feed a household was a constant worry.

Weazel came and curled up beside her for a sleep and then seven-year-old Agnes arrived bringing the pair of red silk tassels she was making to dangle from her cloak ties.

'How quick and neat you are,' Joanna praised, as Agnes finished the first one and fluffed it out. Noticing her daughter's frown, she put an arm around her shoulders. 'What's wrong, moppet?'

Agnes looked up at her from light hazel eyes. 'When I grow up, shall I be like you?'

Joanna stroked Agnes's smooth honey-brown plait. 'Perhaps you shall, for you are very like me when I was a child.'

'Were you good?'

Joanna laughed. 'Well, I tried hard to be, for the King would have sent me away otherwise, and I did not want that to happen.' A frisson ran through her body, as she remembered the fear of not measuring up, or of being ostracised and punished. None of that had occurred. She had had to wait until she was older to realise such nightmares.

Agnes hugged herself. 'I would not want that to happen to me.'

'And it will not, my love. The King is your uncle and he loves you dearly. Besides, you are mine, not his, and I would never send you away. You will always belong to me, even when you are married with children of your own.' She gave her a cuddle.

Agnes played with the tassel for a moment. 'Mama, I am frightened,' she said in a small voice.

Joanna's stomach twisted, for she was frightened too. 'Come now, what of?'

Agnes shook her head. 'I hear you and Papa talking but then you stop if you think I am listening, and then I know something is wrong, or I think that it is something I have done.'

'Oh, hush child, never that!' Joanna cried, mortified that Agnes should harbour such fears, and kissed her cheek. 'We love you dearly and if we needed to scold you, we would do it openly, not in whispers. Do not be afraid. Your father and I will deal with whatever problems arise, and do our best to protect you, for you are our first consideration. Whatever is happening is caused by the quarrels of grown-up people. It has nothing to do with you or your sister and brothers.'

'If you were not here, I do not know what I would do,' Agnes said with a little sniff.

'But I am here,' Joanna said fiercely, 'and I always will be here for you – now and when you are a grown woman. Wherever I go, I promise you shall come with me. Now, dry your tears.' She wiped Agnes's face with a scrap of linen and hoped she could keep that promise. All her children were precious, but she had a special, tender spot for her eldest daughter who was swiftly coming to understand things beyond the nursery. Iohan, over a year older, was more resilient. 'Come,' she said, 'bring your cloak and we shall sew on this lovely tassel.'

In Oxford, the sun had finally pierced the clouds and for once it was not raining, although still cool for June. William sat on an oak bench in the recently constructed Dominican Priory where the barons had gathered to continue discussions arising from the confrontation in April. They were also using the gathering as a muster to march on Wales to deal with the threat from Prince Llewelyn, although William knew the latter was a ruse for men to bring retinues and weapons to the meeting.

The atmosphere in the city overflowed with tension like the air before a thunderstorm. William had taken to wearing a light mail shirt under his tunic. There was widespread discontent over Henry's rule – with his inability to control the finances and govern with a firm hand; with his spendthrift ways and his favouritism towards his friends and relatives. Some even blamed him for the bad harvests, as if he was a conduit for the very failure of the land.

The reforming barons were determined to curtail Henry's powers and were like stampeding horses in their eagerness, but William knew the ringleaders were out for their own profit, however much they dressed it up in the language of a campaign for justice. A new document had been drafted for the perusal of the King's twenty-four counsellors filled with grievances and demands. Hugh Bigod had been appointed to the role of justiciar and was to go on a judicial circuit to hear and deal with pleas and complaints. The twenty-four had been whittled down to fifteen with an authorisation to govern in Henry's name. William, his brothers and John de Warenne had been omitted from those fifteen. No chancery writs of any importance were to be ratified without the agreement of the fifteen and all castles and royal possessions were to be returned to the Crown. Any major grants to be made would have to go under the scrutiny of the fifteen too. Already the constables of more than twenty of Henry's castles had been replaced with men favourable to Simon de Montfort. Effectively, Henry was being robbed of his power.

The demand for the return of the castles was a direct attack on William. Hertford, Pembroke and Goodrich were all on the list. Now the fifteen were demanding that every baron present at this parliament swear an oath to uphold the provisions and return their castles to the Crown. Anyone who refused would be considered a 'mortal foe' and treated as such.

William unclenched his fists. He breathed out slowly but his tension remained at the same level. Henry had asked him to take the oath in order to keep the peace and preserve his skin, but he could not bring himself to do it. Even Henry's promise that he would restore the castles after William had taken the oath had not been enough, because he did not believe him.

He looked up as John de Warenne arrived. 'I cannot swear to this, John,' he said. 'For my own sake, for Henry's and for Edward's. They are taking away our very manhood.'

'I cannot agree to it either,' John said. His mouth twisted as though he had taken a gulp of vinegar. 'My brothers are all for it of course, although Hugh sees it in terms of reforming the law. Roger wants to punish you for disputing with him over estates, and he is angry with the King. Indeed, many are angry with the King, and I understand why, but much of this is an exercise to seize power and wealth. Edward says he is going to refuse to take the oath because it weakens the monarchy, and what will be left for him when it comes his turn to rule?'

William exhaled hard. 'We are looking at King Simon de Montfort. His ambition is boundless.'

He pushed to his feet, and together they entered the friary where a crowd had already gathered. Henry sat on a dais, raised above his barons, his complexion so pale it was almost waxen. He wore one of his many crowns, and a robe edged with cloth of gold. In his right hand he clutched a jewelled rod of state.

Needing to feel the solidarity of kinship, William crossed the room and joined his three brothers Guy, Aymer and Geoffrey.

Edward and his cousin Henry of Almain walked over to the Lusignans.

'They are going to demand that we agree to the conditions of the provisions,' Edward said.

William nodded grimly. 'I know, sire.'

'It is your choice whether or not you do.' Edward gave him a calculating look.

'I have no intention whatsoever of swearing to the terms,' William replied with revulsion. 'My estates were given to me from the hand of your father as my sovereign lord, my own brother. I serve him, not Simon de Montfort, Roger Bigod or Richard de Clare.'

'My father may have no choice but to agree to the provisions,' Edward said quietly. 'For now, at least.'

'That may be so, but I shall not let the likes of Simon de Montfort coerce me into anything.'

'I have told him I shall not, and neither will my cousin.' Edward indicated Henry of Almain, who nodded agreement.

One by one the gathered barons swore an oath before Henry to abide by the provisions set out in the reform document. Some gave their fiat with firmness, others with less aplomb, but still with compliance. The ruling fifteen, including de Montfort, the Bigod brothers and Richard de Clare, all willingly attached their seals and vowed in clear, carrying voices to abide by the terms. Young Guillaume de Munchensy, who had not long come into his patrimony, smiled broadly as he took the oath and shot a look of triumphant challenge at William.

When it came William's turn to stand before Henry, he paused and stared around at the gathered nobles. Some men met his gaze, but many looked away. 'I refuse to put my name to a document that is treason to the King and takes away all that he has given me in clear and fair honesty,' he declared in ringing tones. 'I will never concede to these pernicious terms and yield the castles, wardships and lands that are mine and my family's.'

'My lord, you are bound to do so, or be called a traitor and pay the traitor's price,' de Montfort said, indicating the document, a curl of satisfaction to his lips.

'I am not the traitor here,' William replied with scorn, 'but I can see plenty of others in this chamber who would see their king in fetters.'

De Montfort lowered his brows. 'You have a clear choice before you. Either yield your castles or lose your head. We are ready to accommodate you either way.'

A brief, taut pause hung between them like an arrow on the bowstring before the loose, and then the moment exploded, and the air filled with the sound of shouting, men roaring for William's head and shaking their fists. Henry shrank back, white-faced, horrified – powerless. William turned on his heel and stalked from the chamber, his heart hammering, for at any moment he expected the verbal attack to become physical. His fine mail shirt might protect him from a single stab wound but not a multitude. His brothers hastened out with him, and John de Warenne, who shoved several people aside and shouldered his way through.

Arriving in his chamber, William stared down at his hands which had started trembling like Henry's. He was sick with frustration, fury and fear, because Simon de Montfort had meant every word and he would carry it through given the chance.

'We cannot stay here,' Aymer said, breathing swiftly. 'It is too dangerous and it is their territory. It will be impossible to negotiate anything but our downfall.'

'Then what do you suggest we do? I have no strongholds close, only manor houses, and if we go to one we will only incite them.'

'My Bishop's palace at Wolvesey is only half a day's ride and they will think twice about attacking an ecclesiastical building. We can be there tonight. If we stay here, we will either have to swear to give up everything, or be killed.'

'I will accompany you,' John said. 'They will not dare to attack me and I certainly have no intention of agreeing to their outrageous demands.'

'I will come too,' Edward announced from the doorway. 'They shall not dictate to me; I am not their lackey.' He entered the chamber, his expression fiercely determined but holding, too, a glint of relish. 'My father has no choice for he has been backed into a corner and he does not have the force to stand up to them, but they shall not say that the monarchy is toothless and nor shall I throw my uncles to the wolves.'

'I am grateful, sire,' William replied, 'but this will not end well whatever happens. What if they besiege us at Wolvesey? Where will we go from there?'

Edward gave him a calculating look. 'You will have to leave England for a while – the opposition is too strong. But you cannot negotiate here for you will die. Leave now with your heads intact and regroup at Wolvesey. With me, de Warenne and my cousin of Almain as escort, you will be able to negotiate a safe outcome.'

'An outcome that involves my castles and lands being taken from me,' William said, starkly.

'Bide your time,' Edward replied. 'When the wind is set against you, wait for it to change, and in the meantime, use the time to prepare.'

Looking into his nephew's eyes, William did not see a nineteen-year-old youth staring back, but a king. Ruthless and hardened to practicality. The unspoken energy in the reply convinced him, and he gave a wordless nod.

'Muster what baggage you can without calling attention to yourself. The summons to dinner will come soon. Put it abroad that you are coming to the table and are considering your answer. I shall order the horses saddled; there is no time for baggage carts. We will need to ride fast, but if you have sprightly sumpter horses, bring them. You can send messages and everything else you need once we are away from here.'

William nodded curtly. 'The grey sumpter and the chestnut palfrey. Both have good legs. I'll ride my destrier and bring my spare.'

'I will see you down there,' Edward said, and took his leave.

William covered his face with his hands. What would happen to Joanna and the children without him here to protect them? He stood between the fire and the cliff edge. The imperative was to leave Oxford and escape the clutches of the hostile barons.

He changed into his finest robes – a red silk undergown and magnificent blue and white tunic. He could sell the jewels and gold thread from the garments later if he had to. He ordered his knights to go to the stables a few at a time and sent his new manservant James to the hall to place his cup on the table and announce that his lord would shortly be coming to dinner. Then he turned to Iohan, who had recently entered John de Warenne's household as a page, and who had been watching the proceedings with wide eyes. They needed to ride hard, and if they were pursued, who knew what might happen. Better to send the boy to Joanna, and pray that Henry still had enough influence to protect them.

'Iohan, you must go to your mother with Elias.' He turned to his grim-faced serjeant. 'See my son safely to my lady at Bampton and report to her what has happened. I will write later. I need you to do this and do it well.'

'You can rely on me, sire,' Elias said stoutly. 'I swear on my life to keep them safe.'

William put his hand on Iohan's narrow shoulder. 'You are my heir. You are the man of the house. Look after your mother and sisters and brother but do as your mother tells you. I am proud of you and I am trusting you until I return.'

'Yes, sire.' Iohan puffed out his chest, acting bravely but with a glisten of fear in his eyes. 'When . . .' He swallowed. 'When will that be?'

William gave him a man-to-man look, although his heart lurched. 'I do not know, but it will all be sorted very soon. I just have to leave for a while.'

'I hate Simon de Montfort,' Iohan said, clenching his fists.

'You are not alone,' William answered wryly. 'But be very careful what you say and do because others are always listening and your life and the life of your family might depend on your discretion. Think before you speak. Knowing your heart is not always the same as speaking your heart. Quickly now, go with Elias and fetch your things.' He embraced Iohan, kissing the soft cheek of the child he was exhorting to be a man, and watched him leave the room with Elias. Then he turned, his body stiff with suppressed emotion, and nodded briskly at the men remaining in the room.

In the stable yard, William's warhorses Talent and Rous had been made ready, with his palfrey and a sumpter horse put on lead reins. Most people were at dinner in the hall, but there were still servants around to bear the message that the Lusignan party was leaving. William mounted Talent and reined him around towards the priory gates. Edward, astride his grey, was smiling. William had seen the king in him earlier, but the youth with a love of wild adventure was still vying for position.

'I warrant we'll outrun them,' Edward said. 'I had my grooms hide all their tack and cut the reins and girths. It is going to be a while before they can set out in pursuit.'

William's jaw dropped.

Edward grinned. 'I have found that God tends to help those who help themselves, Uncle.'

They settled down to cover the miles, constantly looking over their shoulders for signs of pursuit, but it appeared that Edward's ruse had worked. William had girded on his sword, but if they were caught it would be useless, for they would be massively outnumbered. Their best protection was Edward's presence – not even de Montfort would dare to harm him – but they were still in a bind, and William knew he might indeed lose everything. The thought of facing Joanna and the children and telling them they would have to live as penniless exiles made him feel sick with shame and he immediately pushed it aside. He and his brothers had to have a strategy, and that strategy depended on Edward and the King. De Montfort and his associates might have the upper hand now, but they would not have it for ever.

On arriving at Wolvesey, the gates were immediately barricaded behind them while guards ran to the battlements. William made sure that all the windows were shuttered and secure. Pausing in the hall as the lamps were lit, he drew a shuddering breath and wished he could awake from this nightmare.

John de Warenne gripped his shoulder. 'Steady.'

William shook his head. 'I am all right,' he said, 'but we are in no place or position from which to make a counter-attack or resist them if they throw their all against us.'

'No,' John said quietly, 'but we can negotiate.'

'And I have you and the lord Edward to thank for that. But what of the King and my family? How do I protect them?'

'I will take care of Joanna and the children,' John said. 'Never fear, I will make sure they are safe. You are my dearest family and you have stood by me in my time of need. I will guard them with my life, although I do not believe it will come to that.'

'Don't you? I am not so sure,' William said bleakly.

That night, rolled in his cloak for a blanket, William tried to sleep but without success. He left his pallet and prowled the room, checking entrances and exits, restless with tension. He hated being impotent and trapped. They had only bought themselves time by coming to Wolvesey, and the space to negotiate terms so that he and his brothers might survive, but he would be robbed of his wealth and influence – and his home. The only option was to go into exile and regroup. Henry, he suspected, would be unable to do anything, and the Queen was hand in glove with de Montfort and his followers. He dared not think about Joanna and the children.

Eventually he lay down and dozed fitfully, but every sound jolted him awake and at last he conceded defeat and rose to use the piss pot. A fair summer morning was breaking, tingeing the sky with pink and gold. He loved English dawns and dusks. Indeed, he loved England, and had become attuned to its changing seasons and its climate, cooler and greener than the place of his birth. And now he was being forced into exile.

As the light brightened, he went in search of food, but a guard forestalled him, reporting short-breathed that Simon de Montfort and his sons, the Bigods and other nobles from the Oxford gathering had arrived at Wolvesey's gates, demanding that William and his brothers come out. Clearly it had not taken them too long to find new tack for their horses.

Edward arrived, fastening his hose to his braies and batting away the servant who was trying to dress him. His hair was sleep-tousled, but his eyes were alert and sharp. 'Tell them we shall parley,' he said, 'but they must come inside to us and we shall hear what they have to say. And when they decide on their spokesmen, they will yield their weapons before they enter my presence.' He turned to William. 'I will do what I can, but do not expect miracles. Be prepared to leave England. It will only be for a short while, but it is like playing chess. In order to win, sometimes you have to bide your time and make sacrifices.'

William nodded stiffly. 'I have come to that conclusion too, sire. I ask that you do what you can for your aunt Joanna and your cousins. Protect them if it be within your power, and do not forget them.'

'It shall be done, I promise you,' Edward said, sombre now. 'And I promise you also that you shall return.'

Joanna was sewing with Agnes when Elias was ushered into her chamber, sheltering Iohan under his becloaked arm. Her son was pale with exhaustion, his eyes wide open as though they had seen the horrors of the world, but he stood manfully.

Her heart lurching, she rose to face them. 'What has happened?' she demanded. 'Where is your lord?'

Elias came forward and, kneeling, presented her with a sealed parchment. 'Madam, he has gone to the Bishop of Winchester's castle at Wolvesey. He entreats you to remain calm and do what you can.'

Joanna opened the letter and read the brief words penned in haste and smudged because the message had been sealed before the ink was dry. Elias's words did nothing to reassure her.

'Simon de Montfort said he was going to cut off Papa's head if he did not agree to his terms,' Iohan piped up.

Agnes started to cry.

'Be quiet,' Joanna snapped at Iohan. 'You are scaring your sister.' She turned to Agnes. 'And no need for tears. Your father is alive and well. Go with Mabel now and I will talk to you later.' She gestured to the maid, who took Agnes by the hand and led her from the room. Iohan stiffened to resist, but Joanna indicated that he should stay. 'Tell me what you know,' she said to Elias.

Swiftly and succinctly he summarised what had happened. As Joanna listened, her alarm grew, for de Montfort would now be coming for her and her lands. Thank God they had possessed the foresight to hide their valuables.

'What of the King?'

'He is under the rule of the fifteen barons for now,' Elias said. 'I believe he is very shocked by what has happened. The lord Edward is with my lord, and so is the Earl of Surrey.'

'I would like you to leave me to think,' Joanna said. Her stomach was clenched to her spine. She needed time unobserved to digest this terrible news; she needed William, but he wasn't here, and she only had herself to call upon.

When Elias had gone, taking Iohan with him, she sat down and read the letter again. The terse, smudged words were like stones crushing her and she crumpled the parchment and allowed herself to weep – harsh, racking sobs. If she cried all her tears now, there would be none left to betray her in front of the household when she had to be strong.

Eventually, she wiped her eyes and raised her chin. Her grand-sire, the great William Marshal, had faced worse dilemmas when made the regent of England in the middle of a civil war with a nine-year-old king to protect. She had that heritage to carry her through – blood and bone and will.

William adjusted his sword belt and tugged his surcoat straight. He was wearing an alternative blazon, featuring the lions of England instead of his usual red swifts. He had eschewed full armour to go into exile, although he had considered it, for in order to leave he had to ride past a gathering of hostile barons, including the Earl of Leicester. Edward had negotiated a truce and safe conduct with their opponents, and they would not dare to attack him in the former's presence, but he remained wary.

The baronial party had declared that Guy and Geoffrey must leave the country for ever, but William and Aymer could remain in England under house arrest while the barons considered their position. Since house arrest could swiftly become imprisonment and even execution, they had chosen to depart. The outcome was never going to be in their favour with the fifteen set up as judge and jury. Edward had awarded Guy and Geoffrey lands and money on which to live, but whether they received it remained to be seen, since Edward himself had little to spare.

William fastened his cloak and joined his brothers, who had been making similar preparations. 'Are you ready?'

Guy and Geoffrey nodded as one. Aymer picked up his crosier and adjusted the garnet cross on his breast. 'The sooner the better.'

In the courtyard, Edward and John were already mounted. Under a light drizzle, a groom removed the rug covering the saddle as William came to his horse. Edward turned his mount side on and briefly addressed him and his brothers. 'I wish you Godspeed and a fair wind to Normandy,' he said. 'I hope we shall all be reunited soon and in better circumstances.'

The palace gates opened and, with Edward's heralds going before, bearing banners of truce and others flying the lions of England, the troop rode out from the safety of Wolvesey's walls. William looked at the barons waiting beyond the moat and felt as though a cold sword blade was pressed to his spine.

Edward drew rein and addressed them in a voice that rang full and clearly, without any sign of an adolescent crack. 'My lords,' he said, 'shall we return to Oxford now that we are agreed on our course, and let my uncles depart under a banner of truce?'

The animosity boring into William from the gathered nobles made the threat horribly real, even though agreement had been reached that he and his brothers would be escorted into exile. De Montfort's two eldest sons glowered at him and his brothers, their hands hovering at their sword hilts. Their father glanced their way but did not castigate them. Joanna's brother was mounted among de Montfort's entourage and openly smirking. William flashed him a look of utter contempt. If the young fool thought that by hanging on to the tail of de Montfort's horse he would gain favour and prestige, he was sadly mistaken. He was far more likely in that position to receive a face full of droppings.

William saluted the barons and bowed in the saddle to Edward. 'Until we meet again,' he said, and turned his rein.

'I cannot believe you are letting them ride away!' William heard de Montfort's eldest son protest. 'It is too dangerous! They will be plotting all manner of mischief behind our backs.'

'Peace,' his father growled. 'We shall discuss it later. Now is not the time. I have given my word.'

'Hah, we have not given ours!'

'I said peace!'

William rode out of earshot. The rain spun down, cobweb-fine, from lowering clouds. 'We should pick up the pace,' he said. By increments he was being tied up in a sack; constricted into a dark, claustrophobic place with no escape.

It took two days to reach Pevensey. William constantly looked back for signs of pursuit, but the road stayed empty. He had chosen Pevensey rather than one of the other south coast ports because its lord was ally and kin to John de Warenne. Had they selected Dover, they would have been searched and stripped of what wealth they carried. Aymer had emptied Wolvesey of its plate and silver to pay their way and they had several pouches of coins including gold. Edward might have promised money to Guy and Geoffrey but William only had what he had brought with him from Oxford, although as part of the negotiations he had been promised the sum of cash belonging to him that he had stored at Waltham Abbey. He hoped Joanna had been thorough in concealing their other funds, because de Montfort would not hesitate to sequester whatever he could find.

William stared at the sea, cold green and crested with spray. A strong breeze flapped the sails of the two ships they had commissioned to bear them, their goods and horses across the sea.

John gripped his hand. 'Godspeed. I will pray for your swift return.' He handed William a large leather pouch, heavy with coins. 'Twenty marks to cover your immediate needs. It is all I could lay hands on at short notice. I will send more when I can.'

'You are a good friend.'

'You are my brother,' John answered, reddening. 'Indeed, you are closer than my own blood kin.'

William blinked hard against the gusting wind, and a deeper emotion. 'Take care of Joanna and the children for me,' he said. 'They will need help.'

'I promise I shall,' John replied. 'And I will send news when I am able.'

'Thank you.' William had to swallow.

'Don't let me lose you too,' John said. 'Aliza would never forgive me and I would never forgive myself.'

'You will not lose me,' William said fiercely. 'I have suffered a setback, but it is not an ending and there will not be one while I draw breath. De Montfort and his followers might be at the top of Fortune's wheel, but there is only one way to go from there, as I well know, and it is their turn next.'

*

Joanna looked around her bare, swept chamber at Bampton, ready to leave. She had stripped everything of value, the hangings, the textiles, the coffers and their contents. Money and jewels were stitched into cloaks, gowns and belts. Bolts of precious fabrics and the document chests had been loaded on to the baggage cart and were being closely guarded. She had hidden more coins and gems in the cavities of her children's toy boxes. Little Will's hobby horse had a hollow staff filled with silver coins, and she had stuffed the carved head with gems. Even Weazel's new collar was woven from gold thread and studded with pearls and sapphires. The Abbot of Dene had agreed to store some items for her, and she had also buried a few hoards in places known only to her and Elias.

She had received news that William and his brothers had been forced into exile for the foreseeable future unless they agreed to abide by the Provisions of Oxford, which meant having their land and wealth removed anyway. They had included her inheritance in the order, deeming it part of William's power base. All her assets were to be frozen and eked out to her in grudging increments for fear that if she had access to resources she would send them across the sea to William to help him buy mercenaries.

Iohan entered the room wearing his cloak and hood. 'Everyone's ready, Mama.' He gazed at her with William's eyes, grey-hazel and keen.

'Yes, I am coming.' She returned his look. 'Be very careful what you say when we get to court. Think before you speak and do not believe what anyone tells you, but bring it to me first.'

He gave her a responsible nod. 'Yes, Mama.'

'I do not wish to set this burden on your shoulders but I must. And you must help Agnes to understand too. You are the man of the house either until your father returns or until we can go to him.'

'I will not let you down, Mama,' he said stoutly.

He looked so young, so vulnerable, so determined that she had to swallow tears. Stooping, she hugged him swiftly. 'Come then, let us go.' She glanced around the room a final time before she closed the door.

To have all this taken when it was hers by right made her burn with anger. In the week since she had wept she had grown steely and determined to prevail over her foes. Whatever it took, she would do it, and they would not prevail.

30

Palace of Westminster, Summer 1258

Joanna smoothed her hands over the blue silk skirts of her court gown and tried to assume a calm frame of mind. She and her household had been allocated living space at Westminster – not in her usual chambers but in smaller, shabbier quarters on the other side of the King's hall. The room smelled of musty stone and had a poorly ventilated central hearth for heating and cooking. All the beds were rowed together, although Joanna had drapes around hers for a modicum of privacy.

Her requests for an audience with the King had gone unanswered, although she had been here more than a week. Officious messengers brought her various excuses. The King was not well, or too busy to see her, or he was absent for the day. She would have to wait. Finally, the Queen had summoned her, which filled Joanna with trepidation, for these days the Queen was not her ally.

Accompanied by Nicola, she made her way to the Queen's hall. Passing a shadowed entry, she heard her name spoken and, turning, saw John de Warenne beckoning to her, his cloak powdered with dust from the road. Joanna gasped his name in relief and sped to him. She wanted to throw her arms around him and sob, but once she started she knew she would not stop. Her chin wobbled with the effort of not bursting into tears.

'I am so glad to see you – to see any friendly face! They have been denying me an audience with the King but now the Queen has summoned me.'

'I will not keep you long,' John said. 'William is safe. I saw him on to the ship myself, and either he will return or I will arrange for you and the children to join him.'

Tears filled her eyes despite her best efforts and she wiped them away fiercely on her cuff. 'I am so relieved to see you, and to have at least one ally at court. Everyone is avoiding me as though I am cursed.'

John took her hands. 'Never that. I must warn you. Simon de Montfort has the rule here now. Do not show anger or malice towards him or his supporters, and do not complain of him to the King. Speak softly and lower your eyes. Tell Iohan to do the same, for your lives and liberty may depend on it.'

Joanna swallowed. 'Yes, I know,' she said, 'but the King—'

'You have to understand that the King is not as he was and you cannot expect him to rise up on your behalf for it would be too dangerous for him,' John said, his voice soft but vehement. 'He is deeply distressed about William's situation but he can do nothing for you openly. Do not approach him yourself. It will cause even more suspicion and hostility than there is now. We have to play a subtle game. I am here for you even if I have to be circumspect. I shall do what I can. You will need money. Take my pouch for now.' He unfastened his purse and pressed it into her hands. 'I managed to give William twenty marks before he sailed.'

She gave him a swift, fierce hug. 'Bless you, John, from the bottom of my heart. What would I do without you?'

'You stood by me when I needed succour,' he said as they disengaged. 'You are my sister in marriage, and I will do all in my power to keep you safe, and visit when I can.' He bowed, and walked off down the entry.

Joanna dropped the pouch down the front of her gown so that it came to rest against her belt where the fabric bloused out and no one would guess.

The Queen's hall was bustling and full of people Joanna either did not know or with whom she had no affinity. An usher led her to the dais to make her obeisance to the seated Queen.

Alienor regarded Joanna neutrally, and spoke courteously enough. 'Joanna, my sister. It is good to see you at court again, and we shall accommodate you for the duration of your stay, however long it happens to be.'

'Thank you, madam,' Joanna replied, her voice subdued. 'You are kind.'

'It is not within my heart or my charity to turn you away,' Alienor said. 'You may join my ladies if you will.'

Feeling deeply uncomfortable, her cheeks burning, Joanna curtseyed and withdrew from the Queen's chair. The women were gathered in a sewing group by the window, and the avid looks they cast her as she joined them reminded her of Weazel stalking a mouse. One lady smiled and made room at her side. Joanna was initially grateful for the kindness, but the woman swiftly exposed her motive.

'How is your husband?' she enquired. Her voice was sweet, but icy too, like a sharp knife.

'I am told he fares well,' Joanna replied warily.

The knowing little smirk on the woman's face told Joanna that rather than wishing her well, the lady had only made space in order to bait her.

'Oh,' she said, her eyes widening. 'I did wonder because I

had heard that he and his brothers were in Boulogne being besieged by the Earl of Leicester's sons.'

Cold prickles ran down Joanna's spine, but she refused to give this woman and her little gossip group the pleasure of seeing her react. 'I do not know anything about that, my lady,' she replied. 'You may be right, but if so, I am sure the situation will be resolved very swiftly. The Earl of Leicester will not want to endanger his sons.'

'Oh, I do not think the Earl of Leicester's sons are in any danger,' the woman said, smiling.

Joanna lifted her chin and did not reply. Thinking of William under attack in France was horrible.

The ladies spoke among themselves and mostly ignored her, and if they did address her their conversation was clipped and minimal, leaving Joanna feeling ostracised and close to tears.

Leonora arrived to visit her mother-by-marriage, and spend a little time over wine and wafers. Her gaze wandered to the group of chamber ladies. On taking her leave, she paused to speak with them, asking after their families, admiring the needle-work. Then she lightly touched Joanna's shoulder and said with a smile, 'I am pleased to see you back at court, Aunt.'

'I think you are the only one,' Joanna replied ruefully.

Leonora's touch became a squeeze. 'You must come and share sweetmeats with me and my ladies tomorrow. Bring the children too. I would love to see them.' She continued on her way.

Joanna wanted to weep with gratitude at Leonora's kindness, but sat quietly with downcast eyes. The women continued to ignore her, but the atmosphere changed and the claws were sheathed because no one wanted to put a foot wrong with the wife of the heir to the throne.

The following day, Joanna went to pay her respects in Leonora's household and was immediately welcomed with wine and sticky

Spanish sweetmeats. Leonora's coterie of young ladies made a fuss of the children, especially little William with his curly hair and angelic features.

After the first warm greeting they found her a place to sit and join the sewing. The ladies conversed quietly among themselves while Leonora's musicians played in the background on lute and harp. The women included Joanna in the conversation. She could listen and even relax a little, although she was aware of being on trial – like a stray dog being observed to decide whether it should have a permanent place at the hearth. Leonora was kind but cautious, and Joanna understood the boundary. She was only sixteen, and reports would be made to the Queen of her conduct and associations. She had to protect herself.

When Joanna rose to leave, she thanked Leonora for her hospitality.

'You are welcome whenever you choose to come,' Leonora answered graciously. 'I know you have business of your own to conduct and I shall not expect to see you tomorrow, but come again in two days. Whatever has happened, you are still my husband's dear aunt, and my friend. Nothing changes that.'

'Thank you.' Joanna had to swallow a choke of tears. 'There is one boon I would ask if it is at all possible.'

Leonora glanced at her chattering women and then beyond at her clerks, busy with their parchments and quills. 'If I can,' she said warily.

'I have gifts for the King and the lord Edward. I would like to present them myself and I wonder if you could intercede on my behalf. I am the King's sister-by-marriage after all. I am not going to do anything untoward, but I want very much to see them . . . I also need to ask for money to keep my household and my horses.'

'I shall see what I can do,' Leonora said, 'but you must be

prepared for disappointment. The barons know your loyalty to your husband and they believe any funds they give you will be sent straight to him.'

Joanna flushed, because she would indeed do that, and more. She had to play a subtle game, even with people who were sympathetic to her. 'I just need enough to tide us over.' She bit her lip. 'One of the Queen's ladies told me that the sons of Simon de Montfort were besieging William and his brothers in Boulogne. Surely that cannot be allowed when they had a safe conduct to leave the country.'

Leonora shook her head. 'I think it is just a petty intimidation on the Earl of Leicester's part, like setting your small dog to snap at someone's heels. His sons will return soon enough. Do not worry on that score. Concentrate on what you must do, and I will help you as much as I can within my limits.'

Leonora's petition succeeded, and a week later Joanna presented herself to the King and Edward. She had dressed with great care for the occasion. Nothing too fine and ostentatious lest they think she had wealth to spare. She had chosen a gown of soft brown wool with a few fine lines of embroidery and her veil of plain white linen severely framed her face. Cecily's prayer beads hung at her belt and her fingers were unadorned save for her wedding ring. She had pinned the little silver brooch Henry had given to her as a child on the breast of her gown. She stood quietly at the back of Leonora's women with Iohan, Agnes and Margaret, and they too were sombrely dressed, and on their best behaviour. William had been left with the nurse.

Simon de Montfort stood close to the King, broad-chested, lips pursed, alert to all that was happening. Her Bigod cousins were there too, and Richard de Clare. John de Warenne was also present, but in the background, not attracting attention.

An usher called Joanna and the children forward to kneel before Henry's chair. She was shocked at how much he had aged in so short a time. The fine lines between nose and mouth had deepened and one eyelid drooped heavily.

'A sight for sore eyes, my sister,' he said, giving her a tremulous smile. 'And my nephew and nieces so grown up too. I hope you are all in good health.'

'Yes, sire,' Joanna replied. 'We are indeed, and very pleased to be at court.' *Because we have nowhere else to go.* She tried to keep smiling. 'I have come to present my loyalty to you, my liege lord and King. I ask you to accept my faith, and I wish to bestow this gift as a token of my esteem.' She turned to Iohan and, with a very correct bow, her son presented Henry with a box containing a small jewelled orb to fit on top of a staff.

Henry laughed with delight like a child as he held the orb to the light to admire the intricate work. He shot a look at de Montfort, almost as if asking his permission to keep it, and then put it down at his side, away from the Earl of Leicester's scrutiny. 'A very fine gift indeed, sister, I shall treasure it.'

Joanna then turned to Edward. 'And I have this for you, sire.' Once again Iohan performed the honours and gave Edward a slim wooden box holding a pair of hunting arrows with tiny lions carved into the shafts. Edward's face lit up and he leaned forward to kiss Joanna's cheeks. 'My thanks, Aunt, these are very fine. I shall think of you when I am hunting. You are indeed thoughtful.'

Joanna curtseyed to him and Henry, and to de Montfort, because she must.

'I know your loyalty is not in doubt, Aunt,' Edward added, thereby extending her his protection.

With a churning stomach, Joanna withdrew to safety among Leonora's ladies, but she was triumphant because she had succeeded in making Henry and Edward acknowledge her presence and their duty to her. They were hemmed in; she understood now. She had to make her own plans and obtain a safe conduct to go to William – but not yet. He needed financial resources first.

William and Aymer were busy in their lodging in Boulogne dictating letters to a scribe when Guy and Geoffrey returned from the tavern.

'You should have come with us!' Geoffrey slapped his taut belly. 'Best mussel broth I've ever tasted, good wine and a serving wench with breasts like pillows.' He turned to Aymer, grinning. 'When you get Southwark back, she'd earn you some money.'

Aymer shook his head at them.

William said curtly, 'While you have been out entertaining yourselves, Aymer and I have been working on a request for letters of safe conduct from the King of France.'

Guy flopped on to the padded bench before the hearth and belched. 'You could still come with us. Safe conducts will be simple enough to obtain. I don't know why you are fussing.'

'Because the Queen of France is Queen Alienor's sister,' William snapped. 'It cannot have escaped even your notice that Alienor has been delighted to see us sent into exile with our lands confiscated. We are the enemy, and she will whisper in her sister's ear. This letter must be worded with diplomatic skill, not scrawled in assumption. If we set off now for the Limousin without a safe conduct, we would get no further than fifteen miles from Boulogne before we were picked off.' William rubbed his hands over his face, feeling tired and irritated. 'We have to have a plan and we have to have money. Aymer is writing to the French clergy to intercede and hopefully we can be out of here by the end of the week.'

'Ah,' said Geoffrey, 'well, that's why going to a tavern has its merits. I have arranged with a merchant who travels between here and Dover to bring us in a consignment of silver.'

William raised his eyebrows. 'Through Dover?' he said. 'How much?'

'Five hundred marks.' Geoffrey went to the flagon on the trestle and poured the dregs into a cup.

'Then that is five hundred marks we will never see again. They will seize and search every entourage and every cargo entering the port or crossing the sea.'

'Do you have a better idea?'

'Joanna has matters in hand.'

'She's a woman!' Geoffrey snorted. 'I know you think the sun shines from every part of her, but how will she manage it? Pretend that she's with child and stuff a money sack up her gown?'

William shot him a glare. 'I have every faith in Joanna for good reason,' he snapped. 'If she says she will accomplish a thing then she does.' He rose to his feet. 'Our first need is to reach our own lands safely, and that means not taking risks. We have to be brothers in more than name.'

Geoffrey puffed out his cheeks, but nodded and came to put his arms around William in an embrace, pungent with aromas of wine and garlic. 'Aye,' he said. 'Brothers to the end. Very well, let us get these requests written. The sooner done, the sooner we can leave this Godforsaken place.'

'There's a fresh jug of wine on the sill,' William said to be conciliatory. 'You should have brought some of that mussel broth back with you.'

One of Aymer's clerks arrived, bringing some fresh rolls of parchment and candles. He too had been out in the town and he was breathing hard, for he had run all the way back to their lodging. 'Sires,' he said, 'there are soldiers in the town, fresh off an English ship. Mercenaries bearing the badge of de Montfort and de Montfort's two eldest sons at their head. They were enquiring after your whereabouts.'

'Now you see why we should not be in the town drinking,' William said. 'I knew this would happen. They let us leave, and then they come after us intent on assassination. Now we see what the word of Simon de Montfort is worth.' His belly curdled with fear even while he kept a face of fury. If they were willing to pursue him to this end, then what might they do to his wife and children? Involuntarily, he put his hand to his sword hilt.

Aymer laid a calming hand on William's wrist. 'We do not know the full story yet. Simon de Montfort's sons are not de Montfort himself. This may just be a crowd of callow youths out to prove some kind of manhood to themselves. Indeed, this may have done us a favour. It will be easier to obtain our safe conduct now these lamentables have pursued us to Boulogne. The King of France will not want English warring factions borrowing his turf for their disputes.'

Geoffrey fetched his sheathed sword from where he had propped it against the wall. 'I will send them home,' he growled, 'but not with their tails between their legs. Those they shall leave behind, nailed to these tower doors.'

'No,' Aymer cautioned. 'If we answer their provocation, it will lessen our chances of receiving a safe conduct.'

'And not doing so will make us seem weak,' Geoffrey retorted. 'Since when has caution stayed your hand, brother?'

'Aymer's right.' William sat down again and pushed his hands through his hair. 'I am as keen as you are to put a blade through Henry de Montfort and his brother but if we spill blood here in Boulogne, where do you think it will end? For our lives we must stay within the law. King Louis will be displeased with de Montfort's sons, not us.'

'Hah, so we sit here like poultry in a chicken coop watching a pair of foxes slavering at the latch?' Geoffrey tossed his sword on to the table.

'I will write to Henry and to Edward,' William said.

'Well, I am sure that will have a great impact,' Geoffrey scoffed.

'More than you think. Some at court will not respond well to the news that de Montfort's sons have violated the safe conduct. I will ask Henry to intercede with King Louis on our behalf, and I will write to John and his Bigod brothers.'

'Letters.' Geoffrey waved his hand dismissively.

'There is nothing to stop us from defending ourselves, but we should not go on the attack,' William insisted.

Guy stood up and flexed his broad shoulders. 'Time was when we couldn't keep you out of a brawl, little brother,' he said with a sour smile.

'Perhaps I have grown up,' William replied. 'I am no coward, you know I am not, but we will only make this worse by fighting, and the stakes are already too high.'

Guy fetched his own sword but left it sheathed. 'We are going to face some great provocation,' he said, rubbing his chin, 'but I am inclined to agree with you.' He looked at Geoffrey. 'Cool your heels for now, except in the matter of making sure we are well supplied to resist them, and meanwhile write the letters. De Montfort's sons are unproven puppies. We should not be complacent but I doubt they will have arrived armed with money and siege machines and certainly no one in Boulogne will help them.'

The clerk cleared his throat. 'Sire,' he said to William, 'you should know that your wife's brother is with them.'

William snorted contemptuously. 'Hah, that does not surprise me. He's been dogging their heels like a stray whelp for months, chasing scraps.'

*

An hour later Simon de Montfort's sons and a small entourage of soldiers arrived at the fortified tower house where William and his brothers were lodging.

'Come out if you dare and face us!' roared Henry de Montfort, pounding on the barricaded door, his face scarlet with self-righteous rage. 'Come and face us for the crimes you have committed and the inheritances you have stolen! Cowards and thieves! Come out now!'

Geoffrey muttered under his breath and gripped his sword.

Several letters had already been sent and the scribes were furiously writing more, one ear cocked on the noise outside. Climbing to the top of the lodging, Aymer opened the window to bellow down at them to go home and cease disturbing the peace of the King of France. His reward was jeers and a barrage of stones from slingshots.

'The de Montfort boys don't have sufficient men to make a serious assault,' Geoffrey said. 'But we might be in difficulties if they manage to rally others to their banner or bribe the porter.'

'I doubt anyone else will be foolish enough to join them,' William replied, 'but to be safe let us make it worth the while of the servants to remain loyal. We might not have money to spare beyond the essentials, but I would call that essential.' He silently vowed that de Montfort and his sons would pay. He would never permit a son of his to behave with such dishonour, disrespect and lack of discipline. The same for Joanna's brother. Young Guillaume de Munchensy had to be taught a lesson.

Joanna too was busy with her clerk writing letters and evaluating her resources. She had sold three silk gowns and her second-best cloak, but was being careful. The line was narrow between being frugal and looking shabby. She had dismissed some of her attendants and retained a loyal core. Anything she spent beyond necessities detracted from the resources she intended taking to William when she joined him. The King's administration, overseen by the hostile barons, made acquiring new income difficult, and running a household without making inroads into the funds she had brought to London challenged her resourcefulness. She dined among the King's retainers at court whenever she could, and tried not to let it look too much like receiving charity. Rather than becoming demoralised, she channelled her frustration and fear into seeking ways around her conundrum.

Her chaplain, Nicolas, quietly entered her chamber and stooped to murmur in her ear. 'Madam, the King requires you to attend him in his private chapel for prayer.'

Nicolas often spent time with Henry's chaplains and he kept his ears open around the court. Joanna immediately understood the message as a summons to a meeting for purposes beyond prayer, even though the latter would be involved.

'I shall come at once,' she said, and left the clerk to continue with the accounts.

Henry was waiting for her in his chapel, adjoining his great painted chamber. Joanna quietly approached the altar where he was kneeling with his eyes closed, and folding herself beside him, bent her head. The smell of incense filled each breath she drew and the candles twinkled in their gilded holders. It was like being enclosed inside a darkly glowing jewel.

For a while they prayed in silence. Joanna begged God, the Virgin and every saint she knew to keep William safe, counting their names on each prayer bead, imploring their help and their mercy.

Eventually, Henry breathed a soft 'Amen' and raised his head. He looked at Joanna with mournful eyes and took her hands. 'Oh, my dear girl. I am so sorry about what has come upon you and William. If I could change all of this, I would.'

Joanna swallowed emotion. 'Sire, I am very sorry too. I am deeply worried about what will happen to William, and to me and the children. My husband has been forced into exile. Hostile strangers occupy my manors and castles and who knows where the revenues are going – certainly not into my coffers.' She raised her eyes to his beseechingly. 'How am I to live and feed my household and my children when I have nothing?'

'But money is being kept for you at the Temple Church,' Henry said, looking distressed. 'You have an allowance.'

'Money may indeed be stored for my use at the Temple, sire, but I have received none of it. Before long you will be feeding me and my children at the paupers' table in your hall.'

'Never!' Henry's eyes widened in horror. 'I would never allow that. Something will be done, I promise.'

'Thank you,' Joanna said, without confidence. 'It was also agreed by all that William would go into exile for the time being. Now I hear that the sons of Simon de Montfort have pursued him and his brothers – your brothers – to Boulogne to harass them.'

'I know of this, for I received a letter from William,' he said, 'and I have written to King Louis asking him to intervene.' His face twisted with anxiety. 'I have also spoken to my sister and the Earl of Leicester, and the young men concerned have been recalled. A messenger left before dusk with the order. That is partly why I summoned you tonight – to tell you.' He lowered his voice. 'We will prevail and in time William will return, I promise.'

Joanna's relief at Henry's intervention was tempered by the knowledge that until the messenger delivered the letters, William was not safe. She was dubious too about what Henry's notion of prevailing actually meant when facing a charismatic and dominant opponent like Simon de Montfort.

'Thank you, sire.' Despite her misgivings, she was grateful, for at least something had been set in motion. 'I hope to join my husband once he is in the Limousin. I may be under your protection at court, but it is still a difficult situation for me.'

Henry gently kissed her forehead. 'I know, my dear, and I will do my utmost to obtain you a safe conduct to join my brother. I had no choice but to send him away – it was never my wish to do so.'

Joanna nodded, chewing the inside of her lip.

'This might help both of you.' Taking her hand, he turned it palm upwards, and placed a key in it. 'This is for the coffer I keep in the chapel on the altar shelf. I am entrusting it to you, and giving you permission to take from it what you need. The items are personal to me and it is my business and no one else's how I allocate them. You may take and dispose of a few items to help keep you and the children, and to assist William. I am counting on your utter discretion. My chaplain knows you have the key, and I trust him to stay silent, but tell no one – certainly not the Queen, for she would not understand. Take what you wish, my dear, and use it wisely.'

Joanna felt the cool, solid brass in her hand as Henry took her behind the altar and showed her the long, decorated chest, securely padlocked.

'Everyone shall be told that I have given you special permission to use my chapel for peace and prayer whenever you choose.'

'Thank you, sire,' Joanna said, her voice tight with emotion. 'I have no words for what is in my heart.'

'Neither do I,' Henry replied, wiping his eyes. 'I am helping you in the only way I can at the moment and I expect you to take full advantage.'

He took the key from her, unlocked the chest and pushed back the lid. Joanna gazed upon the gleam of gold and silver-gilt, of colourful Limousin enamels and the sparkle of gems. The peacock dishes that the King of France had given him as a parting gift. He removed a small leather pouch containing four heavy gold rings set with precious stones. 'Tie this to your belt,' he said, before delving again, like a child riffling through a toy box. Although he had given Joanna permission, the consent was as much for himself. She noticed how his hand lingered upon certain items before moving on, and she resolved to leave those items alone for they were clearly precious.

'Whatever I use, I will replace,' she said. 'I know what this means to you.'

He glanced at her and smiled. 'Does it not say above the door in the great chamber that he who has and does not give will not receive? And indeed, I willingly give.' He closed the chest and straightened up. 'We shall weather this. We just have to endure the mud at the bottom of the pond for a while.'

Joanna left the chapel with the bag of rings at her belt, two silver-gilt candlesticks and a little reliquary with a fragment of Mary Magdalene's finger bone. It seemed strange and almost wrong to be taking treasure from the King's private collection, even with sanction, but she was grateful to Henry and a little tearful to know he had not abandoned her or William.

Slipping through the great chamber, she paused before the figure of Hope, trampling Despair, and renewed her acquaintance with a part of her own likeness. In silent communication she asked the boon of her company in the days to come, for to travel without hope was a terrible thing and there were times when she was perilously close to despair instead. Tonight, though, she held the stars in her hands.

31

Boulogne, France, Summer 1258

'They're leaving,' Guy announced, hurrying into the room.

William abandoned the piece of harness he had been mending and went to look out of the window. The de Montfort sons and their hangers-on including Joanna's brother had packed up their equipment and were showing signs of quitting their flamboyant but ineffectual siege of the lodging tower.

'I told you,' Aymer said. 'It would seem our letters have had an effect.'

While the de Montfort contingent were still busy with their baggage, an envoy from the French royal court arrived, and on being admitted he presented William and his brothers with their safe conducts in the form of parchments bearing the royal seal. William was also requested to attend on King Louis before he departed south, to apprise him in person of what had been happening.

'I spoke to your guests as they were leaving,' the envoy said, eyeing them curiously. 'You have some bad enemies in England.'

'There are always those who quarrel with others because of their own lack,' William answered grimly. 'I am glad the King of France has been gracious to us and risen above petty sordidness.'

'He is a lover of peace as much as any man,' the messenger replied with bland diplomacy.

William and his brothers swiftly packed their belongings and an hour after noon emerged from their refuge into the hot, sea-scented air. William almost expected a last-minute ambush from their tormentors, but they had gone, leaving wind-blown ashes and a broken ladder. It was almost a disappointment to release that tension, like air farting from a pig bladder.

William squared his shoulders and approached his saddled horse. Now that they had their safe conducts, they could begin the fightback.

John de Warenne sat before the brazier in Joanna's small room and took the cup of spiced wine she gave him. It was raining heavily and the sound of water gurgling along the gutters filled the chamber. The wall by the ill-fitting shutter gleamed with damp.

'That is the last of the nutmeg,' she said with regret, 'but at least the wine is decent. The King sent me a keg yesterday, and a haunch of venison.'

'It's very good,' he replied after an appreciative sip, and then looked at her over the rim of the cup. 'How are you faring?'

She sighed. 'I am doing my best to keep the household on what I have. The King does what he can and the lady Leonora is very kind to me. But when I make approaches to have what is mine by right, I become invisible. I know why, but it is not the justice of which those around the King speak so loftily. My lands have been taken from me – stolen.'

'I am sorry.' John looked embarrassed and cleared his throat.

'I have brought you something that might help a little.' He handed her a small leather pouch. 'It is only five marks, but it will keep your household in food and firewood for a little while.'

'Thank you.' She took it because she could literally not afford to be proud.

'If there is anything else I can do, you need but name it – I mean it.'

'There are a couple of things. I do not know if you will be able to accomplish them but—'

'Tell me and we shall see.'

She gave him a steady look. 'The first concerns my missing funds. You could speak to your brothers since they are part of the King's advisory group, Hugh in particular. He might lend a sympathetic ear and have some influence. I have received nothing even though I was promised I would have money to provide for my household. There is more than sufficient coin stored in the Temple Church.'

Weazel twined around John's legs, and he gently scratched between his ears. 'I will have to choose the right moment, but I can try. Hugh is indeed the person to approach, not Roger.' He grimaced.

'I am grateful,' she said.

'And the other matter?'

Joanna lowered her voice. 'The King has given me the key to his personal treasure and bidden me to take and sell whatever I need.'

John's eyes widened and he stopped petting Weazel.

Joanna fetched the little jewelled reliquary to show him. 'I need to obtain the best price for this I can get,' she said, putting it in his hand. 'I cannot sell it myself, too many questions would be asked. I need to convert it into coin and I wonder if you could do it for me?'

John looked down at the intricate, beautiful object and then closed his hand over it. 'Yes, of course I will, but it may take a few days to arrange a buyer. I will come back to you as soon as I can.' He looked at her with eyes full of wonder and a dawning wariness – as if a cat had suddenly become a lion.

'Bless you, John. There is more than this, but we must be very careful. I would not want either of us to be caught.'

'Of course not.' He tucked the reliquary in his purse. 'I know certain members of the clergy who will be very keen to have this in their collections and who will not ask too many questions.'

She nodded. 'I intend leaving England with the children and joining William, but not in penury. It will be very difficult to gain access to our treasure at Waltham and the Temple Church, but I have other sources and not all the funds from my lands are reaching the Temple anyway.'

John blinked at her. 'So where is it going?'

Joanna took her cloak from the back of her chair. 'Come with me.'

He eyed her askance but stood up and put on his cloak and his hat.

'I am worried about my mare, and I would value your opinion. I am not sure but I think she may be going lame on her offside hind leg.'

'I trust this has a bearing?'

'Oh indeed, yes. I would be so much happier if you would tell me what you think.'

'Then by all means lead on.' He gestured.

She took him to the palace stables where she was paying for the upkeep of several horses – her grey mare, her children's mounts, and four good-quality palfreys. 'Their care is a drain on my finances,' she said, 'but I do not want to sell them unless I must.'

Joanna entered the mare's stall which was on the end, and of sufficient size to contain some barrels of feed with several horse blankets and empty wool sacks folded on top. She indicated the barrels. 'If you were to delve under the oats by a foot, you would find silver and gold. Under the floor too. I have several cartloads of wool from the clips on some of my manors waiting for my ladies to spin into yarn to sell. The wool sacks shall be sorted and each one will eventually have wool on the outside and a heart of value at its centre. When all is in place, I shall leave and go to my husband.'

John stared at her, open-mouthed, and then he shook his head. 'This is a very dangerous game you are playing.'

'It is not a game,' Joanna replied with cold fire. 'I have never been more serious in my life. They want to take everything from me and I refuse to let that happen.'

'But what if you are discovered?'

'I will take the risk. William would have taken it if he were here, you know he would.'

John gestured in concession. 'You are a brave and determined woman,' he said with a mingling of admiration and misgiving.

'I have no choice.' She shivered. 'I am desperately afraid, John – not only for myself, but for the children and William. If anything happens to him, I know I will be married off for nefarious purposes and my children taken into wardships God knows where – I know exactly how these things are manipulated for gain. I was lucky the first time, but now I am at the bottom of Fortune's wheel and barely keeping my gown above the mud.'

'I will not let that happen to you or my nieces and nephews,' John said fiercely, 'and neither will my brothers. Blood is still thicker than water.' He kissed her cheek and then pretended for appearances' sake to look at the mare's leg. 'You certainly need to keep an eye on it. I am glad you came to me. I have several remedies that might help the situation.'

'I am glad to hear it,' Joanna said. 'I have been so worried about her.'

'Leave it with me. I will come to you in a couple of days when I have dealt with the matter in hand, and in the meanwhile I will see what I can do about obtaining you some household funds through less clandestine ways.'

Over the following weeks, as autumn encroached, Joanna continued to make her preparations to leave England and go into exile with William. She set her ladies to spinning some of the wool from the sacks of fleeces that had arrived from her manors and arranged to sell the spun wool to go towards her living expenses. Quietly, steadily, some of the wool sacks were packed in the middle with bags of money, tightly wadded so that they would not move or jingle. John sold the reliquary, the candlesticks and the rings. She used a small portion of the proceeds to live on and hid the rest in the wool bales.

Still no money had been forthcoming from the allowance she was supposed to have, and once again Joanna prepared to face the court and seek her just dues. She had chosen her day carefully – one when Simon de Montfort was absent but her Bigod cousins present. John had already paved the way with them for this meeting.

Once again Joanna came to the hall as a petitioner and knelt before the King. He gestured her to her feet and welcomed her with a neutral expression, but knowing eyes.

Joanna straightened her shoulders. 'Sire, you have known me since I came to court as a child, and I have always been true and obeyed your will. Now, I find through no fault of my own that I have been denied access to funds of any kind to run my household. I am reduced to running up debts and to asking friends to lend me money out of compassion and kindness. My women are spinning wool for pennies, but this should not have to be. I have a right and entitlement to the revenues from my estates during my husband's absence.'

She paused to collect herself and calm her pounding heart.

'I have heard it whispered that I am not to be trusted and that I shall send whatever I am given to my husband, but how would I do that? I would not know where to begin. All I ask of this council are the necessary funds to pay my way and give alms to the poor as I have always done. You know my loyalty is to you, sire.'

'Indeed, I do know that loyalty,' Henry said, and glanced at the impassive Hugh Bigod.

'What threat am I to anyone?' Joanna continued. 'I wish only to support you. I ask for the full restoration of my lands and revenues which came to me through my mother's hands and through my ancestors whose lineage has served you well and without blemish. Would they wish to see me begging in your court for justice?' Her voice strengthened. 'I have the documents and charters that prove my right in law to have my lands. I ask that these rights be properly implemented and put forward as an urgent task so that I may secure food for my children tomorrow. I ask in the name of God for this injustice to be put right through your command, my lord King.'

Joanna had not realised how much she had stored up inside her until she unravelled it before Henry, but while emotional, she had no tears. Drawing a deep breath, she knelt again at his feet. His skin was dry and cold under her lips as she kissed his hand, and his rings were loose.

Henry gently touched her shoulder. 'If you were a man I would have you as one of my ministers for that speech, my dearest sister,' he said, blinking moisture from his eyes. 'We shall see what can be done to remedy this state of affairs immediately.' He turned to Hugh Bigod. 'What say you, my lord?'

Joanna looked at her cousin, but could not divine his thoughts. She hoped John had been right in saying that Hugh would help her and that family came first.

'Indeed, I would hate to see you destitute, cousin,' Hugh said, frowning. 'Perhaps there has been an oversight. I shall check most carefully to see if this is the case, and in the meantime, here are some funds for your immediate needs.'

He presented her with a pouch of silver, satisfyingly large and heavy. She knew from its weight that she could keep her household for a couple of weeks on the contents; but it still fell short of the sum to which she was entitled. She thanked him, feeling relieved, but cynical. At least this purse meant she did not have to delve into her other sources.

Henry said, 'If you are troubled again, then ask and we shall see what may be done.'

'Thank you, sire, I am grateful.' She curtseyed again and withdrew with the pouch, feeling sick and besmirched at having to do this; she would be glad to leave when the time was ripe.

On her way to her chamber, she encountered her half-brother, swaggering towards her. He deliberately crossed her path, forcing her to stop, and gave her a thin smile, filled with mockery. She had heard he had been with Simon de Montfort's sons in Boulogne in the summer, baiting William.

'Sister, how are you faring?' he asked. 'I have barely seen you since we both returned to court.'

'Well enough,' she answered curtly and tried to continue on her way, but he moved with her, blocking her path, and indicated the pouch of money in her hand. 'I am glad to see you have some allies to keep you from destitution. Know that I will look out for your welfare should anything befall your husband.'

Joanna set her jaw.

His smile deepened as he opened the pouch at his belt and removed five silver pennies. 'This is all I have, but it might buy you some kindling and soup.'

Her first instinct was to dash it from his hand and slap his face, but she controlled herself. The coins would indeed buy what he said. She took them from him and looked him in the eye. 'I will repay you,' she said with quiet intensity. 'Be certain of that.'

She stepped around him, and this time he let her go on her way. Joanna reached her chamber and cast the pennies into a small wooden box at her bedside. And then she washed her hands.

A fortnight later, Joanna was in the stables ostensibly checking her horses but in reality making sure that a delivery from one of her secret stores had been safely concealed. She was almost ready to seek permission to go to France and join William with her wool carts, and this was the last consignment. Satisfied, she was leaving the stables when a troop of horsemen arrived. Watching Simon de Montfort dismount, she became a little girl again, seeing him ride into the courtyard at Woodstock. Her gut lurched as she imagined him searching the stables and finding the several hundred silver marks stowed in sacks under the floor.

'My lady de Valence,' he said as he noticed her. 'Skulking in the stables again?'

'I was not skulking, sire,' she replied, her icy dignity shielding her fear. 'I have come to see my horses and talk to my grooms, or is that not permitted to me either these days?'

'The King's little pet mouse,' he said with amused contempt. He cast a glance at the barrels of oats and piles of hay at the back of the mare's stall. 'It seems to me that in the reduced circumstances of your household you do not need to go to the expense of feeding all these animals. Your resources could be more profitably engaged.'

'Horses are as much a part of my household as anything else,' Joanna answered coldly. 'None of them are warhorses so you cannot accuse me of keeping them for my husband's use. There is my mare, and four horses for my attendants. There are my children's mounts, two cart horses and two sumpters. I do not think the number excessive when measured against those of certain other ladies.' Irritation filled her, because Simon de Montfort, for all his accusations of profligacy, had a much greater entourage than William's.

De Montfort looked round, hands on hips. 'It still seems extravagant to me. You could easily hire them at need. To diminish the amount of fodder you must pay for this winter you should sell two of those palfreys and the sumpters. The servants can ride in the cart anyway. What do servants need to ride for? You could sell the tack too. I will take the black and the bay palfrey and you will thank me not to have to feed them. I will pay you a fair price to help your strained circumstances.'

It would be foolish to refuse and she did not want to keep him longer in the stables than necessary. He watched her with a gleam in his eyes to see how she would respond – pushing her.

'You are right, sire,' she said. 'I am hoping for permission to take my children and join my husband by Christmas. Do you think that might be possible? I have nowhere else to go.'

He gave her a calculating look. 'I will talk to the King on the matter and in the meanwhile I will send my groom for the horses and have one of my clerks bring the payment to your chamber.' He inclined his head and walked off.

Joanna's groom, Joli, cleared his throat. 'Forgive me, but did he just help himself to two of your horses, madam?'

'Yes,' she said. 'He knows I cannot argue. He does not want me around the court, giving people consciences and being a nuisance, and he will make it difficult for me to remain. It matters not. Rather the horses than . . .' She inclined her head towards the rear of the stable and Joli touched his forelock. He was one of the few who knew what was concealed.

Returning to her chamber, Joanna resolved to do her utmost to avoid Simon de Montfort. She would not visit the stables again unless necessary, and the sooner they left, the better.

John leaned back from the table and wiped his lips on a napkin. 'For an impoverished woman, you keep a magnificent table,' he said. 'I need to loosen my belt.' He slipped the leather a couple of notches.

Joanna smiled. 'The King's poultryman brought me the hen. It had stopped laying and my cook has the perfect recipe for simmering in wine with onions and mushrooms.'

'Well, compliments to him,' John said as she refilled his cup. 'Have you brought . . . ?'

'Yes,' he said, and put a pouch of money on the table with a heavy clink. 'That's for the belt with the pearls and sapphires. You are taking all of this out in carts of wool?'

'It is the wool clip from various of my manors,' she said. 'Hugh Bigod gave his permission for me to take the fleeces with me when I go. It is woman's work and spun or unspun it does not amount to the kind of money with which William could mount an invasion.'

'And if you are stopped at Dover?'

'If the cart is searched, they will find nothing.' She dabbed up the breadcrumbs on her platter with her fingertip. 'I intend to travel as a noble lady of frugal means, without silk or trimmings – perhaps a little embroidery and a good brooch, but nothing that will shine in the light.' She warmed to her theme. 'My equipment will be of good quality but with a few scuff marks. My personal baggage shall go in a single plain cart and no silver bells on the harnesses.' She gave John a serious look. 'If I leave in a proud and haughty manner it will encourage them to search. Let them see a dignified, modest matron going to join her husband out of duty. If they question the wool – well then, I must make a living. I am a woman who has been taught her place in the world.'

John gazed at her. 'I think both William and I have underestimated you. My mother would greatly approve.'

Joanna gave him an almost superior smile.

'I also think Simon de Montfort has greatly underestimated you,' he added quietly.

She shuddered at the mention of his name. 'Let us hope so.'

'De Montfort is going to take a step too far at some point. He cannot hold the rebel barons to his cause. They have their own interests at heart, particularly Richard de Clare. He will not allow de Montfort to dictate to him. My brothers have been carried along by de Montfort, but not for much longer. The Queen will find she has climbed into the wrong bed.'

Joanna looked away, tight-lipped. Her own bond with the Queen was damaged beyond repair. She no longer trusted her and had lost that duty of service. Her loyalty had transferred to Leonora who had grown in her affections as her love for Alienor had corroded. She would serve her without reserve. 'Yes,' she said. 'She will come to realise when it is too late.'

'Edward is a force to be reckoned with,' John continued. 'For now, he is playing a subtle game and appeasing the rebels with smiles and words of conciliation, but his claws are sheathed. He will help William, mark me.' He finished the wine and rose to leave. 'I should go.'

Joanna rose with him. 'Thank you for all you have done. You are a true friend. We owe you a debt we can never repay.'

'Do not speak of debts.' John kissed her cheek. 'If you did, I would have too many owing to you and William. The sooner you are restored to your rightful place, the sooner all will be well with the world.'

Joanna knelt before the Queen to take her leave, feeling as though she was standing before a pile of cold ashes that had once been a warm fire.

Alienor bade her rise and then, with a heavy sigh, drew a ring from her finger set with a cabochon ruby. 'You think I am against you, but I am truly not, my dear. If you ever need my help, then send this to me, and I shall answer. Who knows what the future holds in such uncertain times?'

Joanna easily read the meaning behind the words. If William should die, or should she want to impart useful information, then the Queen would welcome her – at a price. 'Thank you, madam, I am grateful for your support.' She spoke with stiff courtesy, but she was too shrewd to knock the pieces from the board. There might come a time when she could use the ring to advantage.

She turned to bid farewell to Leonora, who gave her a piece of silk so fine it could be drawn through the gold ring around which it was wrapped. 'This is my parting gift to you,' Leonora said. 'You must write to me if you have need. I have valued your advice and company, my dear aunt.' She kissed Joanna gently on the cheek.

Joanna curtseyed and maintained a formal attitude; it would be unwise to show too much affection towards Leonora in the presence of the Queen. Leonora had already gone out on a limb by taking Joanna into her bower over the past weeks. 'Thank you,' she said gracefully. 'You have been very kind to me.'

The children and Joanna's diminished household waited in the courtyard with the single baggage wain and the wool carts. John de Warenne was present too, with a small entourage of knights to escort her as far as Dover.

Joanna was gathering her reins when Hugh Bigod arrived. Her stomach clenched, but he greeted her courteously.

'I wanted to bid you Godspeed, cousin,' he said. 'I wish you no ill, although I know you might think otherwise.'

Joanna shook her head. 'I harbour no grudge, Hugh. Whatever has happened is for your conscience, not mine, but I would hope never to call you my enemy.'

'Never that,' he replied, red-faced, and gave her a piece of parchment. 'This is an extra safe conduct bearing my seal as justiciar. I know you have one from the King, but this is a further endorsement.'

It was indeed valuable to have, and not something she had expected. 'Thank you,' she said, with more warmth in her tone.

Hugh touched the brim of his hat in salute. 'I hope to see you in better circumstances, cousin.' His gaze flicked over the wool carts. 'You are enterprising.'

'I have to be,' she replied. 'This is wool clipped from my own sheep and my ladies will spin it into yarn to be sold. It will keep the wolf from my door a while longer.'

Hugh gave her a shrewd look. 'You do know the carts may be searched in Dover.'

'Let them,' she replied with a shrug. 'I have nothing to hide. I have no money as you know.'

'Indeed, cousin, and my safe conduct may well assist you to a smooth passage.' He bowed to them and departed.

Joanna looked at John. 'How much does he know?' she asked in a low voice.

'I have no idea,' John answered, 'but I would never underestimate Hugh. He may be quiet but he's as sharp as a knife.

He also has his own set of principles and loyalty to kin. I would say he is trying to help you, and he knows how to be silent.'

Reassured but still tense, Joanna tucked the safe conduct into her satchel and they set out for Dover.

They arrived the following day with a short space of time before the tide turned. John had procured a merchant ship bound for Royan to transport them and it rode at anchor, awaiting Joanna's arrival. Joanna presented her letters of safe conduct to Dover's constable and stood calmly while the documents were examined.

Some of the constable's serjeants poked the wool sacks with their spears but she had wrapped the money with great care and they soon tired of their inspection, especially being under the hard gaze of the Earl of Surrey and Warenne, who might favour the de Lusignans but whose brothers were of the de Montfort faction. The ship's master was keen to sail with the tide, and after a cursory show of officialdom, the carts were permitted on to the ship with the horses and passengers.

Joanna ushered the children aboard. 'Soon we shall see your father,' she said, and looked out across the choppy green waves. The biting wind brought tears to her eyes. At least it would be a little warmer where they were going.

She turned to bid farewell to John and embraced him with a full heart. The one person she had fully trusted over the last few terrible months, and the only one willing to become embroiled on her behalf.

'You saved my life,' she said.

'Oh, come now.' He rubbed her back with the flat of his hand. 'We help each other and that is all there is.' He embraced her a final time and then stepped to shore. 'Tell William I look forward to sharing wine with him very soon.'

The ship cast off, and the waves hissed beneath her keel. As the land diminished behind a wall of sea, Joanna's heart swelled with joy at having outwitted Simon de Montfort, and because she was bringing a full complement of treasure to her husband. His money, his children – herself. The latter two were anticipatory, emotional joys, but the first was so glorious and visceral she could almost taste it. What had been a defeat was now framed as victory. And if they had triumphed once, they could do so again.

32

Royan, Gascony, December 1258

The earlier rain storm had rolled away to the north and as Joanna's ship sailed into the harbour at Royan, the sun sparkled through the clouds, gilding the houses in a wash of pale gold winter light.

The journey had been brisk but no one had been ill beyond mild nausea. The main difficulty had been controlling the children who were brimming with excitement at the prospect of seeing their father, and filled with the sheer joy of the adventure. She had reprimanded them several times for clambering around on the deck like monkeys, but she understood their exuberance. She too had the impulse to leap and scream to release her tension but she was not a child. She was the hub at the centre of the wheel, holding everything together.

Joanna searched the harbour side for William but could not see him and her stomach lurched as it had not done while they were at sea. She had sent messages ahead to announce their arrival, but did not know if he would receive them given the vagaries of travel.

The mooring ropes were cast and the walkway run out. Joanna took a deep, steadying breath, collected her dignity and ushered the children before her on to the dock. The solid feel of the land of exile under her feet sent an unexpected surge of emotion through her like a bow-wave. She stumbled, and Robert, her cook, quickly took her arm and helped her to a net mender's stool. Joanna waved his concern aside. 'I am but changing my sea legs for land ones,' she said with a brave smile. 'I will be all right in a moment.' She took a sip from the wine flask he offered her, and looking up, saw William pushing his way along the busy dockside towards her.

She returned the flask to Robert and stood up. 'William, thank God, thank God!' She flung herself into his arms, uncaring of dignity, for in an instant it no longer mattered. He was alive and vital, and she could touch him. 'I thought never to see you again!'

'Oh tush!' He hugged her. 'I am still in one piece as you see for yourself – but missing you and the children sorely. My greatest fear was being unable to protect you and them.'

Breaking their embrace, he turned to their offspring. 'Well done.' He gripped Iohan's shoulder. 'You have brought everyone here safely, and how you have grown! I am looking at a man!'

Iohan flushed with pride and puffed out his chest.

'And you, my little mistresses, what ladies you are!' He stooped to kiss Agnes and Margaret.

Finally, he picked up curly-haired William and perched him on his shoulders. 'And you are biggest of all!' he said with a laugh, then turned back to a tearful Joanna. 'I have a lodging outside the town for tonight – it's only a short ride. We shall set out for Cognac in the morning.' He returned William to his nurse and had the horses brought forward.

Joanna insisted firmly that the wool carts come with them under escort.

William eyed her askance. 'Surely they can wait and go directly to one of the barns at Cognac?'

Joanna had no intention of letting them out of her sight, nor of revealing her secret here on the dockside. She wanted a full accolade for the achievement she had sweated blood to accomplish. 'It is the finest English wool, and very valuable. Indulge me for now, husband.'

He raised his eyebrows, but smiled. 'If that is your wish, of course – you know I will never gainsay your wishes.'

The lodging on the outskirts of Royan belonged to one of William's childhood friends – a fortified house of warm, creamy stone. Its lord was absent elsewhere, but the servants took Joanna to a well-appointed chamber with a good fire and a comfortable bed. An adjoining room had been prepared for the nurses and children. Joanna, after a cursory glance around, insisted on going to make sure the wool carts were safely stored under cover in the stables, and that a guard remained with them.

William wondered at the privation she had suffered to make her so anxious. He could tell from her clothes, and those of the children, that she had been economising and a pang of guilt ran through him that his proud and beautiful wife, whom he would have given the world, should have been driven to worrying over something so mundane as a cargo of wool.

Joanna returned from her mission and said nothing more about the carts. She opened her baggage and changed into a much less dowdy gown of rose-coloured silk with thread of gold embroidery. While they dined on venison in pepper sauce, she told him all the news from England and he in his turn told her about being under siege in Boulogne. He also told her that besides renewing his contacts in Gascony and keeping diplomatic channels open in Paris he had been in touch with Edward.

'Henry may be in a tight corner,' he said, 'but he and the

King of France are well acquainted and understand each other diplomatically even in times of dispute. And they are kin. Sometimes the proper gesture at the right moment is worth a thousand swords.' He shrugged. 'Sometimes it is the other way round too, but the future belongs to Edward, not to de Montfort and his allies, not to the Queen, and not even to Henry, and we should remember that.'

That night they lay together, the curtains drawn around the bed as they loved each other urgently at first, and then again, with tender slowness. Joanna wrapped her arms around him, a little tearful to have the security of his warm body at her side. To talk with him and despite everything to still be facing a future together. Hope trampling Despair.

He lay against her, heavy with satiation and sleepiness. 'You are what has kept me strong,' he said. 'You have given me hope. I have often disappointed you I know, but I shall love you until I take my last breath – may God give me the grace of a lifetime with you.'

Joanna swallowed tears. 'And the same for me.' She pushed her fingers through his curls and kissed his warm mouth, and against her body she felt him laugh.

'Ah, I need to sleep,' he said. 'I fear the sun will rise before I do again.'

She lay down and cuddled at his side. 'I confess that I too need a rest from the journey. Until sunrise, then, my dear, fair husband.'

While they were breaking their fast the next morning on bread and cheese, Joanna looked at him. 'You have not asked yet what monies I have brought to you from England, although we have discussed everything else.'

He shook his head. 'I would not press such a thing – I know how difficult matters have been for you. I can see very well the straits to which you have been reduced – worrying over carts of spinning wool.' He grimaced.

She eyed him with amusement. 'It is from my wool clips in the Marches. Why should I not bring it?'

'Of course,' he said slowly, his expression doubtful. 'But even so . . .'

'However, I have still managed to make a small contribution to our finances.'

'Yes, indeed.' He reached to his cup and drank.

He was humouring her, and she smiled inside with anticipation and glee. 'I will show you once we are dressed.'

Joanna summoned Nicola to assist her and selected a gown of rich blue wool. No longer did she have to look like a frugal widow and it was so satisfying to put on her rings and a decorated belt.

When she returned to the hall, William was playing with the children, chasing the girls who were shrieking dramatically. Joanna laughed to see their antics, but bade them go to their nurses for a while. She received some pouts and stamping, especially from Margaret, but she was adamant. 'I have some business with your father for the moment; he will return soon enough.' Shaking her head in exasperation, she took his arm and led him towards the door.

'You make them wild!' she said.

He grinned at her. 'And if I do?'

'They need no encouragement!'

'Where are we going?'

'To the wool carts in the barn, but when you see them, you must not make a show.'

'You are being very mysterious about all this.'

'I have had to be so careful. You are going to be surprised, but I don't want you to react.'

'Very well. Whatever it is, I promise not to cry out or flinch.' He made the sign of the cross on his breast, and she could tell he was still humouring her.

'Hah, what do you think I am going to show you?'

He slanted her a smile. 'I have no idea, but I am preparing myself. It could be the King's great bear for all I know, or the bones of his poor elephant.'

She gave him a withering look.

Arriving at the barn, she dismissed the guards and looked round to check that there were no lurking stable boys or servants. Reassured that the coast was clear, she went to the first cart and began unhooking the canvas cover, gesturing for William to help her. He eyed her askance but did so with willing dexterity, before standing back, hands on hips, to gaze at the piled wool sacks.

'Is this it?'

'Give me your knife.'

'What?'

'Your knife, give it to me.'

Mystified, a little reluctant, he unsheathed the dagger, and she took it with a smile.

'You think I am mad, don't you?'

'I am beginning to wonder,' he said wryly, 'but I suspect there is more here than meets the eye – and that you are enjoying yourself and leading me on.'

'Well then, let me satisfy your curiosity and set your mind to rest.' She cut open the side of a bale and returned the knife to him. Then she plunged her arm into woolly froth. 'It's the finest fleece,' she told him. 'From the flocks at Goodrich.' She groped more deeply and eventually brought out a tight package of felted wool from the middle of the bundle. 'Silver,' she said. 'There are ten packets in there, each holding ten marks.'

His eyes widened in astonishment.

She pushed the package back into the fleece. 'I will bring needle and thread and sew this up in a moment.'

William indicated another sack. 'How many?'

'All of them, every single bale.'

Quiet triumph flooded through her as, flabbergasted, he puffed out his cheeks and with one hand to the back of his neck walked around the cart, mentally totalling the amount.

He looked at her. 'Dear God, Joanna, there is enough here not just to keep us solvent but to make a huge difference to our situation. How did you manage it?'

'A woman's guile,' she said smugly. 'I led them to believe I was a sad little mouse under their hand, and I beat them at their own game.'

He laughed, then grabbed her, picked her up and whirled her round. 'Joanna, Joanna, my clever, resourceful wife! It is a king's ransom in truth. We can be players again with this sum.'

'Yes indeed, but put me down! Remember what I said about not shouting it to the world.'

He immediately set her on her feet and stood back, straightening his tunic, but his eyes were sparkling and his smile was a sunbeam. Together they tugged the cover back over the bales of fleece.

'Who else knows about this?'

'Joli and Robert, because they helped to fetch and carry, and Mabel and Nicola. Iohan has half a notion but does not know the full story, but he is not foolish. Agnes too, I hazard, but they know it is more than the family honour is worth to say anything. John de Warenne knows, of course, and a couple of his trusted men. Indeed, I could not have done this without his help. I will tell you the story as we ride. Hugh Bigod was willing to look the other way. He is still in the de Montfort camp but not unsympathetic, and may change allegiance. He supports the reforms but he is not a natural ally of de Montfort's.'

'I suppose others will learn in the fullness of time. I have to tell James and Elias about the wool cart but they are trustworthy.'

'I agree, and I leave you to tell whom you see fit, but I have more to show you first.'

He gazed at her in utter astonishment. 'More?'

She took his hand and led him back to their chamber where she handed him her fur-lined cloak. 'Feel the hem.'

He did so, and looked at her.

'Gold coins,' she said. 'The children have silver stitched in theirs. There are jewels in my feather quilt and more coins sewn into the hems of my gowns.' From there she showed him the silver cups hidden in the false bottom of the children's toy chest and the coins and jewels concealed inside little William's hobby horse. A toy carved knight and warhorse, the cavity filled with silver, and hollowed-out distaff rods full of rings and gold chains.

William stared, open-mouthed. 'Now I am truly lost for words, save to say that before me is a massive debt I can never repay.'

'And I would never ask you, for it is not your debt. This is my inheritance. It belongs to me, to you, to our children. Simon de Montfort shall not have it as long as there is breath in my body.' She took his arm. 'Come, we should be on our way.' Her eyes shone. 'You have business to conduct – and I have some wool to spin.'

33

Cognac, the Limousin, November 1259

Joanna gazed at the letter in William's hand. 'You are summoned to Paris?'

He nodded. 'Henry wants to see me and my brothers.'

She bit her lip. They had spent the last eleven months dwelling on William's holdings in the Limousin, being frugal in their daily lives and industrious in diplomacy, writing letters to allies and potential allies. They had corresponded with friends in England using trusted spies and messengers and John de Warenne had been keeping them reliably informed.

Reforms had been going forward, but de Montfort had delegated much of the work and was often absent from gatherings. Impatience and disillusionment had set in. A peace treaty between the kings of France and England was being arranged. Henry had agreed to renounce his claims to Normandy, Anjou, Maine and Touraine, as had his heirs. Eleanor de Montfort had at first refused, before finally, and begrudgingly, consenting.

'Will this mean a return to England?'

William pursed his lips. 'I do not know yet. Henry wants to see us because we are his kin and de Montfort cannot prevent it because we are not on English soil. It will be a good opportunity to observe the lie of the land and see what can be done. Even if it is not a way back, it might well be a way forward.'

In Paris, Henry greeted William with a warm embrace and joy in his eyes, but after they had hugged and kissed, by mutual agreement, they stood apart, alert to Simon de Montfort's hard scrutiny.

'You look well, my brother,' Henry said.

'Yes, sire,' William replied, thinking he could not say the same for Henry who was haggard, his drooping eyelid sagging more than usual, and a tremor in his hands. 'I have not been idle on my homelands and there has been a fine harvest. I had forgotten how excellent the chestnuts are when fresh from the region, and the ears of grain have been full too. I have enjoyed renewing bonds with my neighbours – although I miss England.'

'Yes indeed,' Henry said, flushing. 'How are your beautiful wife and children?'

'Joanna is incomparable. I bless the day you vouched her to me. Perhaps you can arrange to meet her during your visit. I know she would value it greatly.'

'Yes, I would like to see her.' He raised a knowing eyebrow. 'As you say, incomparable. I hope there will soon be peace, for I deeply miss you and your brothers.' He moved on.

De Montfort gave William a cutting look and stalked past, making it clear that William would have to approach him, and thus seem like a supplicant. William had no intention of being caught in that particular trap, and stayed at the gathering just long enough to speak to people in a modest and mature way, without rancour. As dusk fell over the city, he prepared to return to Joanna and the children at their lodging.

He was fastening his cloak when de Montfort's senior squire approached him. 'My lord asks you to meet him at the Temple,' he said, lowering his voice. 'He is keen to settle any differences and misunderstandings that lie between you and him.'

William looked at the young man askance. 'And why could he not do so here and ask me himself?' he demanded. 'He has had plenty of opportunity at this gathering.'

'It is not the court; it is neutral territory,' the squire replied.

Settling their differences could mean anything, perhaps even an assassination attempt. He would put nothing beyond Simon de Montfort. 'And if I choose to decline his offer?'

'That is your choice, sire, but I am sure it will be in your interest.'

'Then you are more certain than I am,' William said.

Something was afoot, and he knew it would not be of any benefit to him unless it also benefited de Montfort.

William entered the great tower of the Parisian Templars and looked around, feeling wary. Elias had accompanied him, armed with a sword and a stout cudgel, and he had his knight Geoffrey Gascelin too. He was wearing his fine mail shirt under his tunic and had a slim dagger up his sleeve and another in his boot. The Templar compound might be neutral ground, but he was taking no chances.

De Montfort's squire led him to a room that bore the function of a waiting chamber for guests who had business at the Temple. Simon de Montfort was already present, sitting in a curve-backed chair, leaning back with his legs crossed, his top leg swinging in a pose that was dominant, casual and nonchalant.

'My dear brother-by-marriage, I am glad you chose to come,' he said. 'I do not think we need the presence of these men.'

William gestured, and Elias and Geoffrey withdrew with de Montfort's squire.

'Please, sit.' De Montfort indicated a second chair, smaller than his own.

'I would rather stand,' William replied stiffly and, planting his legs wide, folded his arms. 'What is it you wish to say to me, my lord?' He glanced around the shadows, half expecting figures to dart out and assault him.

'Do not worry,' de Montfort said witheringly. 'Had I wanted to do away with you, it would not be here. I have asked you to come for a purpose other than assassination. Will you have a cup of wine?' He left his chair and went to a table where a flagon and cups had been set out.

'I am not thirsty – I had sufficient with the King at his gathering,' William replied. He had no intention of drinking in this man's company. Certainly, murder was in his own thoughts. One quick thrust in the right place from his concealed dagger. It would not be that difficult and might even be worth it.

De Montfort poured wine for himself and drank it down in several swallows. 'As you please.'

'What are you going to say to me here that could not be said at my brother's court?' William asked, to the point. 'Let us stop this nonsense and come to business.'

De Montfort lowered his cup. 'As I instructed my squire to say to you, the Temple is neutral ground and no one to overhear and carry tales. I have asked you here for one reason only and that is to make peace for England. You know what I am talking about.'

William regarded him blankly. 'No,' he said. He was not sure he did know, and had no intention of giving Simon de Montfort help with what he had to say.

'It is like this,' de Montfort said impatiently. 'The barons must unite in protecting the King from others and himself, and you must play your part. I am willing to give you the opportunity to return if we can settle our differences.'

William inclined his head to show he was listening, but remained cynical. It was not about 'protecting' the King; it was about incarcerating him and removing his power.

'If you will honour me with the same respect that you grant the King as his confidant in his affairs, then I will welcome you back to England and not stand in your way, if you will not stand in mine.'

William said flatly, 'I honour you only insofar as I honour the King and his choice of minister, and no further than that.'

De Montfort eyed him narrowly. 'Would you, for example, be prepared to welcome the accession of the lord Edward in the event of the King's ill health?'

William knitted his brows, for he suspected trickery, although it was a sensible question. 'If the King becomes unwell, then of course Edward is the rightful successor. I would not disagree with you.' He hazarded that de Montfort was exploring how William would react if Henry was deposed and replaced by Edward, perhaps as a puppet ruler controlled by de Montfort. If so, the latter was underestimating Edward. William could taste the danger, and not only to himself. It was a case of either drinking the poison or being stabbed in the back, and the whole scenario sickened him. Whatever the circumstances, he would not go against Henry, but he had to play the game.

'Well, we are agreed on that then,' de Montfort said. 'Would you support Edward's aunt and myself as his protectors?'

'I would see you as part of the wider family who would support their nephew in his role of successor to my brother, and I would not veer from this.'

De Montfort gave him a hard look. 'Then you will serve the King, and England, best if you take such an oath now.'

William felt such intense revulsion that he wanted to vomit. 'What do you wish me to say?'

'That you will serve the King, whoever he is, and that you are loyal to the trust the King puts in me.'

William turned away for a moment. The oath itself was innocuous, but what it might mean in practice was entirely different. They were in a church, and he sent up a silent prayer asking God to send him the wisdom to come through this morass.

'You know I am loyal to the King,' he said. 'I have never once been disloyal to the Crown and I would never stoop to that dishonour. If you yourself keep your faith to the King, then we have no quarrel on that score, but I will not give my oath to disloyalty of any kind either to my brother or to my nephew. I will die first.'

'Then we are agreed and we can make our peace,' de Montfort said smoothly. 'In the fullness of time you can return to England, providing you swear to the provisions laid down at Oxford.'

William set his jaw. 'We are agreed in principle, but I refuse to give up what the King has given to me without the strongest of guarantees. I am prepared to move my stance but there is a line that I will never cross. In Oxford, I spoke unwise words in the heat of the moment and I should have curbed my temper, but I have not forgotten your threat to take my head, my lord.'

De Montfort bared his teeth in a humourless smile. 'We all say things that are better left unspoken. We have no love for each other, but fortunately it is not a requirement of our mutual business. Let us call a truce for the moment and I hope I can count upon your support in future negotiations.'

William was disgusted by de Montfort's efforts to manipulate and bribe him. He could have his lands restored, but at a price that would beggar his honour. He inclined his head without saying anything and, keen to escape, walked towards the door.

'Wait, I have another matter to discuss.' De Montfort went to refill his cup.

William turned. He could smell the wine; he badly needed a drink, but refused to raise a cup in de Montfort's company. 'You should be quick, my lord,' he said. 'I have little stomach for any more of this tonight.'

De Montfort gave him a hard look. 'Then swallow your gorge,' he said. 'I have interests not that far from you in Bigorre. It is necessary for me to arrange a truce between myself and other factions in the region, but I have little time to deal with the matter. I am asking you to act as my go-between in the interests of that truce.'

William's throat burned with bile. 'I am not your dog, to do your bidding in the hope of being tossed a bone, but I shall certainly give your request some thought.' He had been expecting de Montfort to bring up the subject of the Pembroke lands, and the Bigorre request had thrown him. However, agreeing to it would increase his bargaining power when it did come to that matter. He suspected de Montfort was calling on him because his own rapport and reputation with the people of Bigorre were unsullied by atrocities.

De Montfort nodded curtly. 'I would have you say nothing of this meeting to anyone else.'

'My wife shall know,' William said. 'I am sure yours does.'

De Montfort's mouth twisted as if he had taken a drink of sour wine. 'We have a truce?'

'Yes,' William said. 'Because it suits both of us for now, but nothing is forgotten.'

'As you said earlier, there are times when a man speaks words that he should have kept to himself,' de Montfort said. 'We need to discuss the matter of Bigorre in detail, but it can await another moment. It is sufficient for now that we have an under-standing.'

*

406

Joanna leaped to her feet when William returned and hurried to take his cloak. 'I was beginning to worry; you were gone so long.'

'He wants a truce,' William said in bemusement. 'For his own reasons of course.'

She brought him wine and he told her what had happened. 'I swore to honour the King and his rightful successor,' he said, 'but I sidestepped the issue of swearing to de Montfort in person. The only binding oath of loyalty I will ever swear is to my brother the King.'

'But you are still in a dangerous position.'

'Not as dangerous as before. My agreement to a truce has given us room for manoeuvre. I shall go to Bigorre and sort out this matter for him.'

'But no sign of a return to England yet?'

He shook his head. 'Not unless we become de Montfort's allies. That is his price. I suspect he has some scheme to depose Henry and set up Edward in his place and then rule as Edward's chief adviser. I only hope Edward's head is not turned by dreams of wearing a crown before his time. If he usurps his father there is no going back.'

Joanna looked at him in shock. 'Surely Edward would not.'

'I think it hangs in the balance. Edward is headstrong and ready for rule, but on the other hand, he is his own man and he is learning swiftly. He is ruthless, and I say this even though he is my nephew. He knows how to wind a thread around men and he is fast developing military skill and diplomacy. However, he lacks experience, and de Montfort will play it to his own advantage.'

'What about the King?' Joanna said anxiously.

'Henry may seem weak, and he has made some bad decisions, but whatever de Montfort says of him, he is not stupid. He can be clever in ways so subtle that men who go straight in for the kill do not see the delicacy of the webs he weaves.'

Joanna gnawed her lip, unconvinced.

'He may be in danger, but he is not helpless. He is here to make peace with the King of France, and Louis wants this treaty ratified too. He will do all he can to make sure Henry is secure on the throne. Moreover, Henry is his brother-by-marriage and a fellow king, and anyone who threatens that position will not be tolerated.'

'But Queen Alienor backed de Montfort when we were forced to leave,' Joanna pointed out.

'Because we were a threat to her influence over Edward. Now de Montfort has taken our place as that threat and the wind has changed direction. She will not allow anyone to come between her and Edward – although Edward himself will battle her for the right to make his own choices.'

Joanna said shrewdly, 'Do not dismiss Edward's wife in this. She is like him – very young, but very astute. If he listens to anyone, it will be Leonora. While we bide our time, I think I should write her another letter.'

William nodded. 'Yes, I think you should do so. For now, I shall go to Bigorre, but because it is to my future advantage, not because I am de Montfort's puppet.'

34

The Limousin, France, November 1260

Banners flew from the pavilions in magnificent array and it seemed as if the Limousin had grown fields of flowers even though the trees were bare and the harvests all gathered in. Having returned from the final effort of his arduous task of truce-brokering for Simon de Montfort in Bigorre, William was directing the erection of his own pavilion of blue and white silk, ensuring enough space remained for Joanna's entourage which had still to arrive. A feeling like a sunburst filled William's belly, part tension, part glowing excitement. His life of exile might be ending, and the longed-for return to England was almost within his grasp.

The last pegs were driven into the soft winter soil and Elias and another attendant began carrying William's bed and travelling chests into the tent and hooking up an internal screen to make a public space and a private partition.

'William!'

He turned at the shout from a familiar voice and the sunburst expanded. With an answering shout of delight, he opened his arms to embrace John de Warenne and they fell on each other, slapping backs, laughing.

'It is so good to see you!' John cried.

'And thanks to you I still have my head and my wife and my fortune. I owe you everything!'

'You owe your wife most of it. I protected her as best I could, but all the ideas were Joanna's. I admit I had difficulty at times selling the items she gave me, but we succeeded.'

'Well, I am grateful, and hope you have not suffered for doing so.'

John laughed darkly. 'No, I was glad to do it. No one guessed for a moment how valuable that cargo of wool Joanna brought to you really was.'

'Do they know now?'

'My brother Hugh suspects, but he is very good at looking the other way. Our conversations are often filled with interesting gaps and silences. I rather think Hugh and Roger will not object to your return to England. They are not as convinced as they were that reform under Simon de Montfort's bludgeon is what they want.'

'And the Queen?'

John shrugged. 'I think she realises she overplayed her hand and is now suffering the consequences. She is also starting to realise with Edward that she must let him go in order to have any influence at all.'

William smiled bleakly. 'I was thinking of the saying above the door in the King's great chamber – about giving everything away in order to receive. How very true it has proved to be. Here, do you want some wine?'

John shook his head. 'I have come to bring you to the lord Edward's tent. He is asking for you.'

William's gaze sharpened.

'It's nothing bad. I suspect you and Joanna will be in England by the spring.'

Leaving Elias and James with further instructions for the setup, William followed John through the camp. The sunburst was now full of tension. He had last seen Edward at Wolvesey while being besieged by Simon de Montfort and on the eve of being sent into exile. It seemed a lifetime ago, and perhaps it was.

Edward was in his tent dining on bread and cold venison. A fluffy white dog occupied his lap, delicately taking meat scraps from his fingers. On seeing William, Edward leaped to his feet and thrust the dog into the arms of a surprised attendant. 'It's for Leonora,' he said. 'You know women and their pets.' He engulfed William in a hug. 'Uncle, well met!'

They were of a height now and Edward had broadened out. His beard stubble was harsh, no longer the fluff of a youth. He resembled neither parent, but William suspected from the tales he had heard he must be a throwback to his celebrated warrior great uncle, Richard Coeur de Lion.

'Help yourself to food and drink,' Edward said, gesturing. 'The wine is excellent.'

'I understand you are here to tourney.' William sat down.

'In part.' Edward resumed his seat. 'How is my dear aunt Joanna?'

'On her way with the rest of the baggage train. She will be here shortly, but I came ahead to greet you, sire.'

'I appreciate it. I have missed your advice and your company.' Edward gave him a shrewd look. 'I had not realised how much of a buffer you were between me and my father. You have the skill to reach out to both of us.'

'I hope you have settled your differences with him since the spring, sire. I heard rumours you had joined the Earl of Leicester's camp.' It was more than rumour, but William erred on the side of diplomacy, glad that he had been busy in Bigorre during the time that Edward had come close to rejecting his father, even though he had drawn back from crossing that line.

Edward slanted him a look from under his golden brows. 'You should know how that particular mill grinds by now, Uncle. I would never harm my father or our royal position. I am his son, born of his seed, and I am his heir. We have differences, but the good of the family is all. No harm shall ever come to my father through me, and I know we are united in this desire.'

'Assuredly, sire,' William said. 'Does your father know you are here now?'

'Of course he does. Supposedly he has sent me to stay out of trouble and sow some wild oats on the tourney circuit, but he wanted me to liaise with you. Come the spring, I hope you will be back at court in England, although there are still those who would rather you did not return.' His brows drew together. 'You will have to take the oath to the provisions made at Oxford, there is no getting around it for now, but I promise you will not have to give anything up – you have my word, and my father's, on that.' Edward lowered his voice. 'My father hopes that a papal dispensation to cancel out the provisions made at Oxford will be ready in a few months.'

'I had heard. Your uncle Aymer has been at the papal court during most of our exile and has kept us informed.'

Edward smiled. 'I would have expected no less from Uncle Aymer.'

They finished eating and left the pavilion. A messenger was waiting with the news that Joanna had arrived with the rest of William's baggage. Edward accompanied William to greet her, and Joanna swept him a curtsey. She was red-cheeked and wind-blown from her journey, and a little flustered still to be in her travelling clothes.

'Dearest aunt.' Edward embraced her warmly. 'It is so good to see you!'

'You tower above me now, sire!'

'Hah, I do, don't I, Little Aunt,' Edward teased.

'How is Leonora?'

'Well, and hoping to see you soon.' He glanced at William. 'Perhaps in the spring.'

Joanna looked between them, but Edward did not elaborate, and moved off to attend to business. Joanna handed William a linen food cloth containing a small ball of marchpane wrapped around a date. 'I brought this for you,' she said. 'There is more when we unpack.'

'That is very "sweet" of you,' William jested. Knowing that she had remembered him was even better than the taste of the confection. Happily chewing, he turned to supervise the raising of the other tents she had brought in the baggage train.

'You do not have to do that,' she said with amused exasperation. 'They have done this so often that they know very well to place the entrance away from the smoke and the smell from the latrine pits.'

'But if I see it done right, I know it will be right,' he said. 'It's like you supervising the maids when they are sweeping.' He finished the delicacy and took her hands. 'I have spoken to Edward and it is likely that we can go home in the spring.'

'Home?' She gave him a slightly quizzical look.

'England is my home,' he said. 'It might not be my place of birth, but it is the place of my heart. My life is there and my service is there.'

He watched a serjeant hammering in a tent peg and had to

step forward and make an adjustment, although it was not really needed. The action made him feel more settled.

Joanna said quietly, 'Just be careful. Do not wear your heart on your sleeve for all to see. It takes a head as well as a heart to play the game. Not everyone in the lord Edward's group is an ally. Some will be watching your every move and waiting to make advantage from it. Do not be over-friendly with Edward in front of others, but judge it carefully.'

He shook his head at her but forbore from calling her Joanna Worry-wort. 'I hear you,' he said, 'but the lord Edward is ahead of all of us and he made all the overtures. I suspect he wants people to report back because it will worry the Earl of Leicester and make his authority less secure, but you are right, I shall be on my guard.'

Joanna and William travelled to Paris in Edward's entourage and there, with the city silvered in a sharp December frost, attended a court gathering at the royal palace at the invitation of the King and Queen of France.

Joanna was looking forward to the imminent banquet, but felt anxious too, for gaining permission to return to England would either happen or be postponed, depending on diplomacy and negotiation. She and William had been playing an understated and subtle game for a long time and she was eager for a resolution, and to go home.

Aymer had travelled to Paris from Rome where the papal court had officially recognised him as Bishop of Winchester, and he too was eager to return to England and begin administering his diocese even if some clerics still opposed his appointment. He was here to renew his acquaintance with Edward, and secure his support.

Joanna thought Aymer looked unwell. Despite the cold weather, he was sweating and clammy.

'You will be the first of us to return and set foot on English soil,' William said to him. 'Home by Christmas.'

'I shall tread a path for you to follow,' Aymer answered with a strained smile.

'Or find a way round,' Joanna said. 'That might be wiser.'

'Yes,' he said, looking wry.

Edward entered the room to a fanfare of trumpets. He had changed his travelling robes for a tunic of scarlet wool embroidered with the golden lions of England, and wore a golden circlet on his head. The King and Queen of France were announced, resplendent in gowns of blue and gold heraldry, trimmed with luxuriant furs. Queen Marguerite had the look of her sister Alienor in the set of her mouth and her determined chin. William made a deep obeisance to both her and Louis, and withdrew to the background. The Queen acknowledged him with a dip of her head. For Joanna she had a smile and a glint of warmth in her eyes.

'I hear certain rumours that you have the ability to spin wool into gold,' she said mischievously. 'Would that we all possessed such talent.'

Joanna's cheeks grew warm as she rose from her curtsey. 'Only at necessity, madam,' she said. 'I am a loyal subject of King Henry and Queen Alienor.'

Marguerite smiled at her again, and moved on. Aymer she ignored.

The company sat down to dine. Close-woven white cloths covered the tables, and the silver-gilt serving dishes gleamed in the candle light. Rare, expensive glass goblets twirled with drizzles of sapphire-blue glass stood at each place.

Edward set out to be charming and dynamic and paid particular attention to his aunt Marguerite, who swiftly fell under his spell. He steered the conversation away from political and fiscal matters, keeping the tone light and pleasant. Between courses jugglers, tumblers and musicians entertained the diners. Joanna cautiously relaxed and began to enjoy the gathering. William was drinking in moderation and behaving with punctilious decorum. She kept a side eye on Aymer, who had been very quiet and eaten virtually nothing, which gave her cause for concern.

John de Warenne leaned across to him. 'Will you bring Emma back to England?' he enquired.

Aymer shook his head and pressed his napkin to his lips. 'She's not with me any more. She took a fancy to a visiting legate from Florence and she is with him now. Always had an eye to the highest roll of the dice that girl.' He spoke without rancour. 'There are always more fish in the sea. What about you?'

'Me?' John blinked at him.

'Have you considered marrying again? You only have the one boy. You need more than that to secure your heritage.'

John shook his head. 'I shall never remarry,' he said with quiet vehemence. 'Nor take a mistress. I could never replace pure gold with anything less.'

Joanna's eyes smarted with tears. Aymer clumsily reached across to pat John's back. And then he withdrew and gasped in pain.

Joanna touched his arm. 'Aymer?'

'Just wind,' he said, trying to shrug. 'Had it a few days. It stopped but then returned and it will not shift. I'm sure a sea crossing will get rid of it one way or another!' He tried to smile at her, but it became a contortion, and he suddenly hunched over and retched into his napkin.

'Forgive me, my brother is unwell,' William said, and swiftly helped Aymer away from the table. Guy and John hurried to assist, and between them they half carried Aymer to a bench in the adjoining chamber. He folded over, groaning in agony, struggling to draw breath. In consternation, Edward summoned his physician. Aymer's pain had taken him beyond the ability to speak, and he could only gasp like a fish. The physician arrived at the run, black robes flapping, and crouched beside him. He examined him with swift competence and his lips tightened. Aymer would not straighten up, and when William tried to make him, he screamed like a snared rabbit. The physician managed to make him swallow a dose of syrup of poppy and arranged for him to be borne to his lodging at the nearby Priory of St Genevieve.

As a litter arrived to carry him, William took the physician to one side.

'What is wrong with him?' he demanded.

'I cannot say for sure, my lord,' the physician replied, 'but from the symptoms I have had occasion to view in others, it is a serious affliction of the stomach that comes on suddenly. It flares up and desists. Sometimes, with rest, it will go of its own accord, but when it is severe like this over several days . . .' He hesitated, but the look in his eyes said everything his words did not.

'We should stay with him,' William said, 'and keep vigil.'

'I think that would be wise, sire.'

William turned to Joanna, who had been listening and squeezed his hand in sympathy. 'Go with him. I will have the servants escort me to our lodging, and I will set everyone to praying for him.'

He returned the squeeze and fetched Aymer's bishop's cloak, the one especially made for his full appointment to the See of Winchester, its edges shimmering with gold braid. William laid it gently over Aymer's body. His brother was quieter now as the poppy began to work on his pain, but he was still grey and clammy and groaning through parted lips, and William knew he was looking at a dying man.

When William returned to Joanna at dawn, she hurried to his side.

He looked at her and shook his head. 'He is gone,' he said. 'At the hour of first matins. They had to give him more poppy for the pain . . .' He sat down heavily on the bench near the fire and pinched the top of his nose between forefinger and thumb. 'I cannot believe it.'

'I am so sorry,' she said, putting her arms around him. 'What a terrible thing.'

'There was nothing we could do except try and ease his suffering . . . nothing.' William bowed his head. 'He has been a part of my life since I was born . . . I have loved him unconditionally all my days.'

Joanna rubbed his back and murmured soothing words. 'I know, I know.' After a moment she brought him a cup of hot wine, and he drank it slowly and stared into the fire. He had Aymer's cloak with him, and he smoothed it under his hands. 'He asked while he could still speak for his heart to be removed, taken to Winchester and laid to rest in the cathedral that was his by right. I shall see to it; that is my duty, and the least I can do for him.'

'I can think of nothing more fitting,' she said. 'He was a good man despite what many have said about him, and God has a fine servant beside him. Let that be your comfort now. You should go to bed and sleep for a little, if you can, and when you wake, we can begin organising all that must be done.'

'Ah, Joanna,' he said, pulling her close, 'the world was a fine place when I had a cloak of innocence to cover me, but now I am threadbare.'

'No,' she said softly, 'now you have a different cloak, that is all – one of experience, and it better protects you in the world you inhabit now. Everything changes. Water weathers stone, and stone grinds the ear of corn into flour, and flour becomes bread.' She stroked his hair, and thought of the brother she had lost suddenly to sickness when he was little more than a boy. 'Truly, I understand.'

'Sensible Joanna,' he said, and kissed her. 'But you are wrong, for you never change – not for me. I will go to bed, but come with me. I need to hold you close.'

35

Rochester Castle, Kent, April 1261

Kneeling at Queen Alienor's feet, Joanna made her obeisance.

'Welcome home.' Alienor kissed Joanna's cheek, displaying more warmth than during their previous encounter over two years ago. 'I am delighted that your husband has made his peace and returned to us.' She gestured for Joanna to sit on a stool at her side.

'I too, madam,' Joanna said. 'I have missed England and the court.' She was not so sure about the peace. William had sworn at Dover to agree to the terms of the Provisions of Oxford, and to answer those who had claims against him, but it was mere lip service. Henry had succeeded in overturning the provisions in February by means of a papal decree, which Aymer, in the months before his death, had helped to obtain. William now had to navigate a careful path through the murky gutters of court politics. They also had their lands to repair following the depredations of their enemies.

Alienor indicated Joanna's right hand. 'I see you still have the ring I gave you.'

'Yes, madam.' Joanna stretched out her fingers and the ruby gleamed like a dot of blood. 'I remembered what you said to me on the day I left and I have always borne your words in mind – and I am glad to wear it now, returning to you.'

Alienor's expression softened. 'We may have had our differences, but I have regretted our estrangement. Still, I do not expect you will be staying at court?'

'Not unless you command it of me, madam,' Joanna replied, thinking that the rapprochement was still tepid, otherwise the Queen would have insisted on her attendance. 'I have my estates to put in order.'

Alienor graciously inclined her head. 'I was sorry to hear about the death of your brother-by-marriage, and so sudden.'

'Yes, madam, it was a shock to us all.' Joanna kept her tone neutral, and lowered her gaze. 'We are going to Winchester when we have completed our obligations here, to pray for Aymer's soul and bury his heart in the cathedral, as was his wish.'

'Indeed,' the Queen murmured, her tone making it clear that she had no desire to take the matter further than platitudes. 'But I hope you will return to us for the Feast of St Edward.'

'Of course, madam.'

They would never regain their earlier rapport, but at least they had weathered the storm. Perhaps the Queen believed she had broken the bond between William, Henry and Edward, and that William had been suitably warned and punished by his time in exile. Besides, too, she needed William back in England as a counterbalance to Simon de Montfort and the baronial reform party.

'Good. I admire your resourcefulness. Your husband has a treasure in you second to none.'

Joanna did lift her gaze to the Queen's then, for the word

'treasure' had been spoken with deliberate emphasis. Alienor's expression held knowing and grudging respect.

'You have my leave to go,' she said, 'and my blessing.'

Joanna made her escape, relieved, almost euphoric, but still tense. It was like a chess game where she had made all the right moves so far, but one slip would mean her destruction. She had time to take a breath, but she dared not drop her guard.

Joanna was packing for Winchester next day when Leonora came to see her. 'I hope all goes well for you,' Leonora said, 'and that your estates have not suffered too greatly in your absence.'

'The King has promised his aid, and we are to be reimbursed from the treasure at the Temple for what went missing while we were gone,' Joanna said. 'He is also giving us some oaks from his forest so we can continue building at Goodrich and Sutton.'

'Edward and I are returning to Gascony for a few months.'

'So I have heard.' Joanna folded a shirt. She could have left it to her maids, but the task gave her a sense of orderly satisfaction and it soothed her, especially when the linen was freshly laundered.

'I think I may be with child,' Leonora said after a moment, and blushed. 'I am not certain yet, but each day makes it more likely.'

'That is very good news!' Joanna smiled at her. 'I am pleased for you.'

'I have not told Edward yet, or the King and Queen. I want to be sure, but I am telling you because I may not see you again before the child is born, and you were a friend to me when I was grieving our lost daughter.'

'I shall keep you in my prayers every day, I promise,' Joanna said. 'And ask that you write and tell me your news.'

'Of course I shall!'

Leonora gave her a swift, spontaneous hug, and departed. Joanna resumed her folding, and her smile remained.

At Winchester Cathedral, William presented the monks with a casket made of the famous copper-gilt enamel ware of Limoges, patterned with the de Lusignan colours. Inside, a smaller, second sealed lead box held Aymer's embalmed heart. William had carried it with him from Paris and it had been both a comfort and a burden. A part of him, a part of his brother.

Henry had not attended the ceremony, but he had wept and prayed over the little box when shown it at Rochester. William had distributed Aymer's clothes to the poor and had given the magnificent cloak to be sold for alms. Every part of his brother's material life was disappearing, and at the end of the obsequies, the hardest thing for William was leaving the little casket with the monks. Aymer's heart had been a heavy one in several ways. Now was the time to begin afresh and not look back.

John de Warenne had accompanied William and Joanna to Winchester for the ceremony, and as they emerged from the cathedral, he wiped his eyes and cleared his throat. 'It brings up sore memories,' he said. 'Losing those I love hits me hard, and Aymer was Aliza's brother and mine too.' He stood up straight and forced a smile. 'Still, I have plenty to keep me occupied.'

William turned to Iohan, who had been a model of good behaviour throughout the ceremony and had shushed his little brother when he had started kicking his feet. 'Your baggage is packed, young man?'

'Yes, sire,' Iohan replied with a proud jut of his chin. He was returning to the de Warenne household to continue his training with John.

'Good, then it is time.'

Iohan turned to Joanna and knelt to her in farewell. She had to swallow a painful lump in her throat, for she had grown accustomed to having him in the household again and parting from him was painful, although at eleven years old he was more than ready. 'I am very proud of you,' she said. 'I shall see you again in the autumn and your uncle John will let me know how you are progressing at your lessons. Be good for him.'

'Yes, Mama.' Iohan rose and regarded her steadily out of the same grey-gold eyes as his father before going to stand with the others of John's entourage.

'Look after him,' Joanna said, and then laughed and shook her head. 'Oh, of course you will. It is just a mother's worry when her chick leaves the nest.'

John kissed her cheek. 'Do not worry. He shall be safe with me and we shall visit soon.'

Joanna waved them off, watching Iohan on his new bay palfrey. Her heart ached, but it was the way of life. William was smiling with the satisfaction of a task well accomplished, but it was different for him.

'He could not be better placed than with John,' he said to her.

'Yes, I know.' She swallowed her tears. 'Come, we should be on the road. We have a long journey to Goodrich and much to do.'

36

Westminster Palace, February 1263

Joanna shivered and pulled her cloak more closely around her for warmth. A bitter wind laced with light snow was blowing off the Thames and through the palace corridors. She and William had not long returned from a lengthy sojourn on their estates and had arrived at Westminster to find the King absent at Merton, but due to return on the morrow.

Joanna wandered through the complex, taking stock and remembering when, twenty-five years ago, she had begun learning the duties of a chamber lady and the etiquette of the court in these rooms. The dangers too, and the constant battles for power, both the subtle and the blatant.

In the great chamber she paused before the figure of Hope and reached out to touch her lavender-blue gown and look into her eyes, wondering at what the painter had seen in them all those years ago. 'My Joanna of the Stars', William called her. The figure stared into the distance while the trampled serpent of Despair glared up at her, striving, refusing to die.

Joanna shivered with cold and turned to the fireplace, rubbing her arms. The hearth had cracked badly while Joanna had been away in exile. During its repair, a magnificent Tree of Jesse depicting the family of Christ had been painted on the mantle with exquisite small images of the people in the holy bloodline, and she recognised many of the mannerisms and faces, including a particular angel with curly hair and a sharp nose. Henry, it seemed, unable to have his own family around him, had compensated in other ways.

England was still in turmoil. Henry had overturned the Provisions of Oxford and the barons were more ambivalent about Simon de Montfort, but concord remained elusive. Each side had a staunch core while those in the middle swayed in the wind. Everyone wanted peace, but everyone had a different notion of what that peace might look like. Their own uneasy rapport with de Montfort had not lasted and Joanna feared it would again come to blows. At least de Montfort was absent on business in France, although still determined on reform. There was endemic skirmishing in the Welsh Marches and the death of Joanna's cousin Richard de Clare had left his volatile nineteen-year-old son up in arms because he had been refused permission to inherit his father's earldom until he came of age. Edward and Henry were not on the best of terms just now either and William was having to thread a delicate and difficult path between them, often acting as an intermediary.

A servant brought a fresh load of dry, seasoned wood into the great hall and arranged it ready for burning. The fierce heat had begun to burn her cheeks, and with a last look at the Jesse tree, she stepped back and returned to her chambers.

William sat with Agnes, Margaret and William, toasting small pieces of bread and meat on skewers at their own central hearth. Earlier he had taken the children skating on the frozen river, the shin bones of oxen and sheep strapped to their feet by leather thongs. Joanna smiled to see the firelight on their faces and went to answer a few queries from her clerks and chaplain who were working by the last of the good daylight near the window. She spoke to her almoner about the provision of food and coins for the poor and arranged to return the travelling cart she had borrowed from the Bishop of Hereford together with a thank you gift of some candied peel. And then, with a sigh of release, she joined the family at the fire and gratefully took the cup of spiced wine William handed to her. Moments like this were few and far between and she treasured them amid the turbulence. She tried to imagine her husband with angel wings, but could not quite fit the reality to the image.

'Can we go skating again tomorrow?' Margaret wanted to know, her cheeks as red as apples in the firelight. 'Can we, Papa?'

William chuckled. 'Was today not enough for you, young mistress?'

Margaret shook her head, making her thick curls ripple. 'Today was just a taste, Papa.'

'Well, sometimes a taste is better than a full feast,' William replied, amused, 'but I promise you we shall go again. Perhaps we shall bring your mother as well this time.' He cast a sparkling glance at Joanna and offered her a piece of toasted bread.

She made a face at him, and taking the bread, bit into the crisp brown crust.

'No, I am serious.' He paused, raising his head and sniffing. 'What's that smell?'

Joanna lifted her head and inhaled. 'Burning,' she said. It wasn't from the fire, nor from the candles and lamps that had been lit as dusk descended.

And then came the shout of 'Fire!' The door burst open and two of Henry's clerks shot into the room. 'Fire! The King's great chamber is ablaze!'

Joanna gasped, and William leaped to his feet.

'What?'

'The chimney, sire, the chimney is on fire and the flames are engulfing the room!'

'Right. Get the barrels of water from the kitchen and the buttery. I'm coming.' He left in haste with the men, beckoning to his retainers and servants as he ran.

Fear surged through Joanna as the smell of smoke intensified. Fire was a deadly hazard that would cause massive destruction around the convoluted chambers and corridors of the old palace where she had just been walking, including the King's great chamber. The heat had indeed been intense over the mantel.

'Stay here,' she told the children. 'Nicola, Mabel, look after them. If you have to leave, put on their cloaks and hoods and take them to the abbey.'

'But, madam—'

'Do as I say – and don't forget Weazel!' Joanna snapped, and hurried after William, grabbing the household's water pail on her way out. She could be another pair of hands in a bucket chain if nothing else.

Even before reaching the King's chamber she saw the smoke billowing from the windows and the smell of burning was now a stench. Entering the hall was like standing in the antechamber to hell, and she gasped. The flames had reached out from the cracked chimney and were already gorging on the roof beams. The King's great bed was a roaring conflagration. William was directing bucket chains, using barrels of drinking water from the stores, while others beat at the flames with cloaks and blankets and brooms. Sparks showered upwards like vicious fireflies amid the billows of smoke, and William stepped back, choking, but darted in again to bat down the flames with his drenched cloak as they surged again.

Joanna grabbed his arm. 'What can I do?'

Coughing into his sleeve, eyes streaming, he choked at her, 'Take the furniture and objects – anything that can be salvaged.'

She darted away to her task, determined to do her part, fiercely glad that William had not ordered her back to the chamber.

Some items had already been moved, but Joanna organised two men and a serjeant's wife to carry out anything portable from the chamber and deposit it on the yard outside the porch. She fetched and carried with them – candlesticks, chests and coffers. Rolls of precious textile. A sodden colourful rug, charred at the edges. The items from the chapel. Sooty smuts bedaubed her gown, and water soaked through her clothes to her skin, but she had no time to notice.

Finally, the desperate firefighters brought the fire under control and the last stubborn licks of flame were beaten into the ground and stamped out. William stood, chest heaving, amid murky, stinking chaos. Smoke layered the room in oily grey veils. People were coughing, clutching themselves, stooping over. Joanna joined him, took his arm and saw the raw burn blistering his wrist below his singed sleeve.

'You should have this seen to.'

He looked down, noticing for the first time, and shrugged. 'Later,' he said.

Someone brought candles back into the room, which seemed like sacrilege given the amount of damage, but they needed light.

'Dear God,' Joanna whispered, gazing at the blackened ceiling and the destroyed décor. Henry's bed was a charred lump in one corner; the painted soldiers guarding the area were scorched beyond recognition, as was the figure of Edward the Confessor. 'What is the King going to say?'

William shook his head. 'I thought at first it was a good thing he was not here, but if he had been, the fire would have been spotted straight away.' He pushed a sooty hand through his hair.

'Done is done. We must send him word, and in the meantime clear this up as best we may.'

He turned and began giving orders, clear and concise, but she saw his despair. The damage was catastrophic. The King's red lions above his chair were bubbled to ruination. The chair itself, borne outside in the nick of time, had suffered scorching, as had the royal cushion, which had been stitched by the Queen in the early, happy days of their marriage.

William doled out more instructions and then paced the room for another assessment, stopping before the figure of Hope. Joanna, walking with him, covered her mouth in dismay for Hope's face and upper body were no more than a dirty shadowy outline under the searing smoke damage. It felt as though a part of herself had been obliterated.

'I should have been more vigilant,' William said in a grief-filled voice. 'I should have been on my guard.'

'How was anyone to know?' Joanna replied, turning to the practical because it was the only place left where she was able to move. 'It has happened. You might say that if I had lingered a moment longer I might have seen the smoke. It was God's will. Clean what can be cleaned, shore up the damage, and wait for Henry.'

'I will send word now.'

'At least no one has died, or been hurt beyond a few burns,' she said. 'We stopped the fire before it could spread. It could have been much worse.' It was true, but the words felt like nothing – like ashes and dust.

'Yes,' William said bleakly. 'But it is bad enough.'

The morning's stark winter daylight revealed the true terrible state of the King's chamber, the walls, textiles and artefacts ruined by smoke, flame and water, although the motto over the doorway had survived with its ironic declaration that he who desired something must first give everything away.

William had stayed up throughout the night, writing letters and organising the clean-up as best he could. Joanna had made him bathe and had tended his burned wrist with unguent and bandages, but he was ashamed at receiving succour, because he deserved the pain.

Looking at the wreckage in cold daylight, it seemed to him almost symbolic of his brother's reign. So much promise and beauty, not fully destroyed, and yet utterly ruined.

Henry arrived back from Merton shortly after noon, pale and grim-faced, having received news of the fire from William's messenger. Filled with trepidation, feeling sick, William waited for him at the gates.

'How did this happen?' Henry demanded as he dismounted. 'Tell me!'

'I was waiting for you so that I could show you rather than tell you, for a picture is worth more than I could write.' William could barely meet Henry's bewildered, furious gaze.

Stripping off his gloves, Henry strode into the chamber that had been his pride and joy, and then stopped and stared in shock. Turning and turning, he looked around at the devastation.

'The fire started in the repaired chimney and spread fast,' William said. 'We were hard-pressed to contain it, but by God's grace we succeeded. If you wish to blame someone for this, then blame me, for I was not swift enough to act. The first anyone knew was when the flames began to spread. I organised a bucket chain and beaters and we managed as far as this.'

Henry shook his head. 'It is ruined.' He drew a deep breath that sawed over his larynx with a sound of anguish, and his mouth stayed open.

'Sire, if I could mend it for you I would. I am very sorry; I know what this chamber means to you.' And to himself. He studiously avoided looking at Hope. 'We can rebuild.'

Henry closed his eyes briefly, blotting out the sight, but had to reopen them. 'Perhaps indeed it is a portent from God.' He went to look at the lettering over the door, blistered and smoke-scarred but still legible. 'I love this chamber.' His voice cracked with emotion. 'This is the heart of my home when I dwell at Westminster, part of my life that I had kept whole for myself, and now it is destroyed.'

'It can be restored, sire,' William said, and pressed his hand over his bandaged wrist deliberately to feel pain.

'But it will not be the same.' Henry shook his head. 'I need time to grieve my loss before I can think of restoration. But I am glad you were here, for if not, the entire palace might have burned to the ground.' His gaze met William's with more than one nuance – a silent exchange of reality and metaphor – and then his gaze dropped to William's wrist. 'You have been injured, my boy.'

'Sire, it is nothing – a hot spark I did not notice in the thick of things. Joanna has tended to it and it will heal.'

Henry opened his arms and embraced him. 'You remind me that I have a great deal more than nothing, and much for which to be grateful, even now.'

'I shall always serve you faithfully,' William replied, chagrined and offering the only thing he could.

'I know, and it is one of my solaces. We shall speak later, but for now, I wish to pray alone.'

William bowed and watched his half-brother walk away in the direction of the chapel, his figure stooped and dejected, his head bent, and he realised anew and with a jolt that Henry was becoming an old man.

37

Windsor Castle, October 1263

Joanna picked up the little girl tugging insistently at her skirts, and swung her into her arms for a cuddle. The child giggled and put her arms around Joanna's neck. Edward and Leonora's daughter Katharine was not quite two years old, with fluffy chestnut curls and wide brown eyes. Joanna already loved her dearly. She had been at Windsor for two weeks, visiting Leonora while the men were occupied at a parliamentary gathering between the lords loyal to the King, and Simon de Montfort and the barons dedicated to reform.

'A messenger arrived from Edward today,' Leonora said, her eyes sparkling. Her accent was less strongly Castilian these days.

Joanna smiled. 'With good news I hope, madam.'

'The best! He is paying us a visit and says to make ready!'

Joanna loved to see Leonora so animated. She and Edward doted on each other.

'When will he be here?'

'Tomorrow morning, he says. Come, we must prepare food and chambers!'

Joanna threw herself into preparations for the rest of the day. She oversaw the brushing of the colourful woven rugs in Edward and Leonora's chamber, and ensured that fresh sheets, pillow cases and coverlets were aired and the bed dressed fittingly. Joanna noticed that Leonora was brighter and more on edge than usual. Not by nature a butterfly, today she seemed distracted and almost flighty. It could, of course, be anticipation of Edward's arrival after a long time apart. He had been away in the field and at the counsel table, dealing with the continued rumblings of civil war. De Montfort had been in France earlier in the year but had returned in late April, had revived the Provisions of Oxford against foreigners, and taken to the field. The Burgundian Bishop of Hereford had been seized from his church and thrown in jail. Gloucester, Worcester and Salisbury were all in de Montfort's hands.

The King and Queen had retreated to the Tower of London for safety, and de Montfort had promptly occupied their home at Westminster, although not the great chamber, which was in the midst of renovations after the fire. Joanna was glad for she could not bear to think of Simon de Montfort sleeping in Henry's place or using his chapel.

The Queen had attempted to leave the Tower and join Edward in Windsor, travelling by barge, but had been attacked by the citizens of London as she passed under London Bridge. The Londoners, firm supporters of de Montfort, had pelted her with rotten fruit, stones and mud and she had fled back to the Tower, humiliated and fearing for her life. Eventually, having no other choice, Henry had been forced to make peace with de Montfort, part of that peace being to surrender Windsor into his hands and agree to reconsider the Provisions of Oxford. Windsor had been under de Montfort's control since August, and Leonora was, in effect, a hostage for Edward's obedience, although it had not been said in so many words.

Joanna could feel the inexorable march into armed confrontation. They stood on the brink of war and she could not see how it would be avoided.

Edward and his entourage arrived at Windsor early the next morning. Riding among them, William drew rein and gazed at the ghostly outlines of the keep emerging from the pearly morning mist. The damp curled his hair and dewed his cloak. So many times he had ridden up to the gates as a welcome guest and entered to take his ease. A family home, but a formidable fortress too, currently garrisoned by de Montfort's men.

His belly sparked with anticipation and he glanced round at the others, all robed in finery and wearing their swords in full view. Edward looked magnificent – a young man coming to visit his wife with peacock feathers in his cap and a smile on his lips. Indeed, they were all smiling, but some with tension. It all still might go badly wrong, but William hoped the bribery in which they had engaged beforehand had done its work.

The gates opened on oiled hinges and they rode into the courtyard and dismounted. Grooms came to take their horses, although Edward kept hold of one particular pack horse laden with leather sacks.

'Your weapons if you please, my lords,' demanded the senior serjeant, his gaze flicking to the sacks and then to Edward, who inclined his head.

Everyone unbuckled their weapons and handed them over, as well as hunting knives and personal daggers. The sacks were unloaded and distributed among Edward's men. Each one resounded with a musical jingle of coins. The guards exchanged glances but Edward remained bland. 'I think the sun will burn off later,' he remarked with a glance at the sky as he and his small party were escorted from courtyard to hall. He walked with nonchalance, his body relaxed. Once inside, he turned towards Leonora's apartments. 'I can make my own way,' he said cheerfully. 'I want to surprise my wife.' He completed the statement with a suggestive wink and a broad grin, before continuing on his way, running eagerly up the stairs to the royal apartments with his men following.

When he opened the door, Leonora shot to her feet with a gasp, and dropped the book she had been reading. 'Edward!' She ran to meet him and flung her arms around his neck.

He swung her round exuberantly, kissed her soundly, and set her down. 'Business first before pleasure,' he said. 'We have come to take back the castle.'

She took in the situation immediately. 'How many men have you brought?'

'Enough,' Edward said, 'and more are coming; it is all in hand.'

One by one his men put the sacks of coin on a trestle table standing at the side of the chamber.

William deposited his own burden and briefly embraced Joanna, suppressing a chuckle at the sight of her astonished face.

'What is all this?' she demanded in bewilderment.

'There are more ways of taking a castle than using a battering ram,' he said. 'Not every man has his price, but fortunately the majority do. The garrison is about to depart. I doubt any will wish to stay and dispute the issue, especially when offered a fortnight's wages to leave. The ones loyal to de Montfort won't remain and fight when they realise how few of them there are.' He tipped up her chin and kissed her. 'Windsor is about to become ours.'

*

Joanna ran her hand over William's smooth bicep, admiring the candle sheen on his skin and the way his hair glimmered with twists of gold. In his mid-thirties it remained as thick and springy as ever, although it badly needed cutting. She would see to it before he had to leave. Today's mission to take the castle had been a triumph, and reinforcements would be arriving at dawn.

'How long can you stay?'

'That depends on the King and the lord Edward,' he replied, 'and what is decided, although I shall mostly be riding at Edward's side – Henry asked me to.' He put his arm around her. 'Edward's flirtation with Simon de Montfort is over, for he has learned what he needs from him. It is like a stable yard. You see one pile of dung and it is not so bad and you even think you can make use of it, but when it becomes a mountain, then you notice the smell and the mess and it has to be dealt with. Edward has matured. No one holds his rein – unless it be his wife.'

'She is a very resourceful and unusual young woman,' Joanna said. 'The Queen lost control of Edward several years ago, but Leonora has power over him. He is besotted with her body, but they talk together long into the night too. You and others might advise him during the day, but not in bed at night, or in tender letters.'

He grunted with amusement. 'I can think of another woman with such skills very close by.' He leaned over to kiss her and pulled the cover over her shoulder where it had slipped down. 'The lady Leonora will be staying to defend Windsor while we are in the field. I want you to stay here with her. It will be the safest place for you and the children, and Leonora values your advice. We shall have our own garrison of trustworthy men by morning, and the castle is strong.'

'As you wish.' Joanna yawned, feeling sleepy, replete and

relaxed. 'I am fond of Leonora. But I do hope there will be peace soon.' *Hope, there was always hope.* Her mind filled with the image of the damaged portrait in the King's great chamber as William reached out and snuffed the candle.

38

Windsor Castle, January 1264

The children were playing in the snow that had fallen overnight. Squealing and laughing, they were moulding snowballs and throwing them at each other. Leonora's little daughter, Katharine, looked on, held by her nurse and all wrapped up in warm furs. Joanna folded her arms inside the layers of her cloak and watched the sport, although her mind roved elsewhere.

William was currently occupied in the Welsh Marches with Edward but messengers brought her and Leonora frequent news. Some of the Marcher barons had united with the Welsh causing a more vigorous than usual state of flux and skirmish along the borders. Simon de Montfort was an absentee general. He had been unable to sail for France for King Louis' arbitration on the dispute between him and the King. Nor had he been able to take to the field because he had broken his leg in a fall from his horse in early December and was laid up at Kenilworth, conducting operations from there.

'You were sick again this morning,' Leonora said knowingly.

Joanna made a face. 'I have missed two fluxes now,' she admitted. 'I am almost certain I am with child.'

Leonora folded one arm companionably around Joanna's. 'We must take care of you and make sure you rest then.'

'He or she will be born in high summer,' Joanna said. 'Men come home in autumn from their wars, and the next year there is a harvest.'

'Not yet for me,' Leonora said, touching her own waist. 'The time was not right, but I shall see Edward again soon enough.'

'There is so much pressure on us to provide heirs to dynasties.'

'It is our duty,' Leonora said.

'Yes, but the expectation is weighty.'

'A king must have an heir, and more than one. And daughters too, to make strong marriage alliances.' Her gaze turned to Katharine, who had left her nurse's arms and was touching the snow in wonder. 'Edward and I will make some glorious sons and daughters between us, God willing. You do not need to comfort me with sympathy, though I should thank you for it. You are a good friend and companion.'

Joanna's heart expanded with love for this extraordinary young woman. She would be a great queen, God willing, and she was the perfect consort for the headstrong Edward – a steadying hand on the rein.

A robin flitted on to a branch, sending a spray of snow to the ground. The nurse picked up Katharine again. The children were becoming cold and the sky had started to cloud over, threatening more snow, and the group turned to go inside to the comfort of a warm fire and hot wine.

As they were crossing the courtyard, a messenger arrived – one of Henry's. Leonora and Joanna looked at each other. Leonora bade her usher have the man brought straight to her chamber and the children were sent off with their nurses to drink hot milk and warm themselves by their own fire.

'It will be news from France,' Leonora said as Joanna took her cloak and hung it on a peg. Leonora's breath was short and her face flushed as much with anticipation as from the cold. 'This will be the judgement of King Louis on the King's right to choose his own advisers.'

Joanna's stomach churned with tension. Simon de Montfort had sworn to abide by the ruling of King Louis, but whatever happened, there would be dilemmas. If Louis ruled in de Montfort's favour, then she and William would face further exile and the loss of their lands. But if the judgement went to Henry, de Montfort would not accede with grace, whatever he had sworn to do beforehand.

Ushered into the room, the messenger knelt. He had a wind-burned, ruddy complexion and shrewd, bright blue eyes, cornered with deep weather lines. A dewdrop hung from his beaky nose. He blotted it on the cuff of his tunic and removed his cap to reveal receding flaxen curls. Kneeling, he presented Leonora with a sealed letter.

She took it from him, opened it, and as she read the contents, a triumphant smile broke over her face. 'King Louis has ruled in our favour! That is great news!' She looked to the messenger. 'Does the lord Edward know of this?'

'Yes, madam, riders went out to him also.'

'Nevertheless, I shall write to him. I take it the King is still in France?'

'Yes, madam.'

'Go and eat and rest, and be ready to ride again shortly.'

He bowed and departed.

Leonora read the letter again. 'There is nothing here for any of the reformists – nothing,' she said to Joanna in a wondering voice. 'All is to be restored as it was. The King is to have free rein to choose his own advisers as he wills.' Anxiety tinged the pleasure in her voice. 'A papal legate will be appointed to restore order in the Church, and excommunicate those who do not obey.'

'Simon de Montfort will never accept it,' Joanna said. 'He will reject the findings, I know he will.' The hot wine was like boiling lead in her stomach and she had to run to the latrine to be sick.

When she returned, Leonora gave her a sympathetic look.

'It will pass,' Joanna said with a grimace. She sat on Leonora's day bed, feeling heavy and unwell. 'There is going to be war. Even if de Montfort is laid up at Kenilworth, his leg will soon mend and he still has allies.'

Leonora's young face grew hard. 'But fewer allies than he did before, and many of them Churchmen. Even the ones he does have are unreliable.' She rose to her feet to unwind her thoughts, and looked at Joanna over her shoulder. 'The only thing that will end this is Simon de Montfort's death – and Edward will see to it. He used to admire him – I believe he still does. He learned a great deal from him, but it is like playing chess with a skilled and dangerous opponent. If you want to survive you have to out-think your enemy. Edward has no softness in him that way, and the way he saw de Montfort changed for him when he saw his father belittled and his mother pelted with rubbish by Londoners. He will not stand for it. I saw what was happening when you were exiled, but the Queen was involved and Edward was younger then. Now he is a leopard full-grown.'

'William has learned by this too – as have I,' Joanna said. 'I agree with all you say.'

Leonora looked at her. 'I trust you with my life, and I hope you trust me with yours.'

'That is a given, madam.'

'Then even as men swear brotherhood on the battlefield, so should we be sworn sisters.' Leonora came to Joanna and, taking her hand, gave her the kiss of a lord to a vassal. 'We shall defend and protect each other and we shall not fail.'

By February royalist forces packed Windsor to the rafters, new men riding in daily as they gathered for war against Simon de Montfort. On a bright, cold morning, still clad in winter but with a pale blue sky between the ragged banners of cloud, Joanna was busy liaising with the stewards and helping Leonora find sleeping space for everyone who considered themselves entitled. The King and Edward had their apartments, but dealing with the other lords and ensuring that no one's dignity was slighted called for bushels of tact and diplomacy.

'Mother?'

She looked up at a tall, handsome youth with glossy brown hair and a soft moustache smudging his top lip. He wore a quilted tunic with the de Warenne badge sewn on the sleeve, and a dagger at his hip. A minor flourish of adolescent blemishes sprinkled his cheeks, and his nose was becoming William's, chiselled and sharp.

'Iohan!' She rose, and threw her arms around him. 'Oh, I vow you have grown again! When did my boy become a man?' She held him away, laughing, and tearful. 'Hah, you make me foolish because I am so proud!'

He flushed at her praise. 'It is good to see you, my lady mother,' he replied, very much the courtier, before turning to greet his sisters and youngest brother. He was uneasy at first, a bit embarrassed, not so much at the age gap but at the distance between them of children living in the household and a young adult in the world.

John de Warenne arrived, and Joanna embraced him too. 'Thank you,' she said, indicating Iohan.

'He's a good lad,' John replied with a smile. 'He works hard and is swift to learn; I have only good to report of him.' Iohan's ears reddened, and John chuckled. 'Well, to report to his mother anyway.'

'I have things to tell both of you,' she said, 'but I need to speak to William first.'

John raised his brows and gave her a quick assessment from crown to toe, but the loose cut of her gown gave nothing away. 'Well, William and Edward will be here very soon, before dark I expect. Come,' he said to Iohan, 'we have baggage and armour to stow.'

William stared at Joanna. 'With child?' he said.

She nodded at him. 'He or she will be born in high summer. Our time together in the autumn has proved fruitful. As our eldest son becomes a man, we have a new life to nurture, God willing.' She stroked his face. 'But you must take care of yourself because this child will need its father.'

'I have every intention of keeping my hide intact,' he answered with determination. 'You are safe at Windsor with Leonora, and it will be well defended by loyal men – not the kind who may be bought for a handful of silver.'

She pressed her hands over her skirts, exposing the early swell of her womb. 'I do not fear for myself,' she said. 'I know I am safe here, and by the time the child is born let us hope we shall be at peace again.'

That night the men gathered in the hall to discuss tactics and plans. The fighting talk and bullishness increased as the wine barrels emptied, and men made expansive toasts filled with bravado but holding a steely core of serious intent to bring Simon de Montfort to battle and finish him, especially from Edward, who was adamant.

Henry unfurled his new war banner and raised it beside his chair – a great dragon with rubies for eyes, a snarling open mouth, and claws fashioned from shards of polished jet. Twists of red and gold paint decorated the banner pole, and William could almost detect a visceral glint in Henry's eyes. The King was no warrior and had long eschewed the training to arms he had received as a youth, but with the fire upon him he could inhabit a dramatic role with conviction. He also had some courageous, stalwart men at his back. De Montfort might be a talented and experienced commander, but the lord Edward was coming into his own and he and John de Warenne were skilled and battle-hardened men, well able to stand hard against anyone. This was do or die, for the dragon banner meant all-out war and death to the enemy. As the cheers resounded around the hall, William punched his cup into the air and roared with the rest of the men within the firelight and under the dragon.

39

Windsor Castle, May 1264

Joanna put her hand on her belly as the baby kicked vigorously. He or she had been active all night and had kept her awake until the dawn had gilded the eastern skyline. Probably another one like its father that needed to be constantly busy, although she acknowledged that the baby's restlessness might be caused by her own worries.

Since leaving Windsor in February, the King's forces had secured Oxford and successfully taken Northampton. Prisoners from that particular skirmish had been sent to Windsor, into Leonora's custody. De Montfort had besieged Rochester, but John de Warenne, who had taken the position of constable there, had resisted him until relieved by royalist forces. But sooner or later it would come to a pitched battle. Joanna tried her best to conceal her fear for William and Iohan. Leonora was focused and calm, certain that Henry and Edward would carry the day, and Joanna tried to follow her conviction. Their numbers were greater and de Montfort at a disadvantage.

Joanna was sitting in a sun-splashed corner of the Queen's chamber, teaching a group of girls different stitches. Agnes was playing the harp, her fingers delicate on the strings. Already an accomplished embroideress at thirteen, she needed no extra tuition today. Her sister Margaret had talent too, and a way of blending colours that showed a pleasing artistic eye. Joanna was thoroughly proud of her daughters. Their brother Will was more of a scape-grace, always into mischief. He had boundless energy from dawn to dusk, and even when asleep he kicked and tossed, rather like this child in her womb. Just now he was at weapons practice with the other castle boys and they had a moment's peace.

Leonora was busy dictating letters and dealing with adminis-tration matters but had paused to listen to the rills of the harp, a smile on her lips.

The morning duties were interrupted by the arrival of a steward leading an unsteady, travel-stained soldier. The smell of hard-ridden man and horse was immediate and pungent. Joanna gasped as she recognised Luke de Sandal, one of John de Warenne's men, who had helped move the cartloads of wool when she had gone into exile. Flushed and red-faced in the late spring warmth, he knelt to Leonora and bowed his head.

'Madam, I bring grave news,' he said. 'There has been a battle close to Lewes Castle and our forces have been destroyed and scattered.'

Leonora became very still, her face an expressionless mask. She drew a deep breath and ordered him to rise. 'And my husband and father-in-law? What of our men?' She held her voice firm and steady, although she had turned as pale as alabaster.

'Madam, the King, the Earl of Cornwall and the lord Edward have all been taken prisoner by the Earl of Leicester – but they are alive and unharmed, thanks be to God.'

Leonora gave a very small but perceptible sigh of relief.

Joanna's heart kicked in her chest. William would have been fighting in the thick of the fray. Perhaps the child's constant churning in her womb last night had been a premonition. And what of Iohan? She turned frightened eyes to the messenger.

'What of the King's brother? What of my lord?'

'Madam, I believe he managed to escape with the Earl of Surrey and the Earl's brother, the justiciar. Your son too. They are bound for the coast and will go directly to Queen Alienor and seek to regroup.'

'Then God grant them swift horses and a safe passage,' Leonora said, still remaining calm and collected.

Joanna's knees buckled, and for an instant the world darkened. She heard Agnes cry out in consternation and strove to rally for the sake of her daughters. Leonora's ladies helped her to sit down and one of them rushed to bring feathers to burn under her nose. Joanna waved them away and, summoning her will, straightened up. 'That is not necessary,' she snapped. 'My womb has not gone wandering around my body, it is here and full of child. It was the relief of hearing that my husband and son are not dead, and the grief that my liege lord the King and his brother and son have been taken.'

The women retreated, but one of them brought her a cup of wine, from which Joanna took a swallow for form's sake. Leonora commanded the messenger be given a drink and bade him wait while she summoned the knights and commander of the garrison so that he could repeat the story to them.

Joanna tried to concentrate through her worry. She prayed desperately that Iohan and William had managed to cross the sea. How could it have come to this when they had far greater numbers than de Montfort and had been so confident of bringing him down? Instead the opposite had happened, and therefore it must be God's will.

Listening to the messenger, she gleaned that the defeat had largely been caused by a tactical error made by Edward. Part of de Montfort's army had consisted of levies from London, among them the very people who had hurled abuse at the Queen from London Bridge. Edward had attacked them ferociously with the cream of his knights, William and John among them. Determined to teach them a lesson and hammer them into the ground, Edward had become carried away, and when the Londoners had broken and fled from the onslaught he had given chase and taken his eye off the bigger objective. He had encountered some senior London officials hiding among the baggage carts and the ensuing fight and plundering had further diminished his grip on the business in hand. By the time he returned to the main battle, the opposition had gained control and trapped the King in the Priory of St Anne's. Henry's brother Richard had fled the field and taken refuge in a nearby windmill, and it was all over. Edward had joined his father to protect him, and those who could had fled for the coast.

Joanna listened with dismay. It was not, then, the will of God that had ruined them but the distraction and carelessness of men. Edward's impetuous nature had gone unchecked by others who should have been cooler and wiser, her own husband among them. The only ray of comfort was that William and Iohan had managed to escape into exile – again. All the promises, all the talk, had come to naught.

Leonora rose to her feet. 'It is in our hands,' she said, staring round fiercely. 'We must help the King and the lord Edward in any way we can. We must be here for their return, and they will return – I do not doubt it.' She looked at Joanna to include her in the conversation. 'Perhaps we shall have to yield Windsor in the future, but they shall pay a price and they will want the hostages from Northampton intact. We have to be the lords of this fortress as well as its chatelaines.' Leonora swept a wide gesture with one smooth young hand. 'The lord Edward entrusted his authority to me, and I shall carry out his wishes, with the advice of all. We must craft the best of what we have, and that means making it into something greater in the eyes of others. We have to be united and strong, and we must be each other's support. This is merely a setback. We are safe here and no one will dare to harm us.'

Joanna was not so sure about that, remembering how those Londoners had pelted Edward's mother from the city's bridge, but Leonora had such determination and conviction in her eyes that she tried to believe her.

Sitting on a barrel, William listened to the thrum of the waves under the ship's keel. The stars were white sparks in the deep sky and a steady breeze bore the remnants of Edward's army towards the French coast. He put his head in his hands, feeling sick, mortified and full of self-disgust. In becoming carried away by Edward's zeal he had made one of the gravest errors in his life. He had been like the tail of the comet as they chased the Londoners and seized the baggage carts. The sheer joy of the chase and the kill. The satisfaction. But that loss of wider awareness had allowed de Montfort to take the day. He did not know if Edward and Henry were safe, or even if they were alive. And Joanna and his children, stranded at Windsor. The thought lay in his belly like hot tar. He was to blame if any of them died. He had failed everyone, most of all himself. He hadn't felt as bad as this since the tourney at Newbury when he was a youngster, but this time the stakes were disastrous and no one could tell him all would be well.

John de Warenne gripped his shoulder. 'We are alive,' he said. 'We have escaped with our horses and our arms intact.'

William shook his head. 'We abandoned Edward and Henry.'

'It would not have done any good to have stayed and been captured ourselves. It is what it is.'

'We should never have chased off the battlefield with such reckless abandon.'

'True, but we must own our mistake and not let it clog our thinking now.'

William palmed his face. 'We have to go back and put it right.' He punched his clenched fist on his thigh. 'We had de Montfort for the taking and we let it run through our hands like water – and I was most to blame.'

John shook his head. 'All of us were, but we have to move on. You taught me that.'

'I did?' William looked at him in surprise.

John produced a wine flask. 'Yes. Whatever happens, it is not the end while you still have breath in your body. No matter what, you pick yourself up and you learn from your mistakes – you do not let them drag you down.'

William put the flask to his lips. The wine was sour, but he could still taste the grape as it stung the back of his throat. John's reminder brought him back to himself, and created a breathing space to process the utter shock and horror of their defeat. The knowledge that while he was alive there was always a next time, and he would not make the same mistake again. He was not looking forward to reporting to the Queen, but he would do it.

'You are a good friend,' he said to John. 'And my brother.' He stood up and gave him a hug, feeling the dull ache of bruises and strained muscles after the fierceness of battle and the bitter hard riding. 'I stood in danger of self-pity, but you have rallied my wits.'

He returned the flask to John and went to speak to Iohan,

who was slumped on the bench near the prow, head bent. The youth was holding a pendant from a leather breastband enamelled in the de Valence colours, and turning the piece over and over in his fingers. He had not been involved in the fighting – his task had been guarding William and John's baggage – but he had still been a witness to battle and massacre and been engaged on the periphery when they had had to run. There had been some skirmishing at their own lines as they loaded the sumpter horses and one man had taken a deep sword cut and had died on the race to Pevensey. They had laid his body in a nearby church, but there had been no time for the proper observations due to him.

William crouched to the youth's level. 'You have done well. You kept up with us on a difficult ride and you never complained. I am proud of you – prouder than I am of myself.'

Iohan lifted his head and gave him a look so much like Joanna's that William almost flinched. 'What is going to happen now?'

'We are going to the Queen, and we are going to regroup and return with an army to finish what we did not accomplish this time.'

'Will . . . will my mother and sisters and brother be all right?'

'Yes, of course they will,' William said steadily. 'Windsor is a powerful fortress and the lord Edward's wife is accomplished. You know how strong and formidable your mother is. There is nothing she cannot do.'

Iohan's nod was subdued, but after a moment he gave his father a rueful man-to-man smile. 'Yes,' he said. 'I know.'

William pulled Iohan towards him and kissed his brow, and swallowed the knot in his throat.

Two days later, William knelt at Queen Alienor's feet and told her all that he knew. Emotion welled up inside him – that hot tar feeling of shame and sorrow, molten and fierce. A few hours ago another ship had arrived from England with news that Henry, Edward and Richard of Cornwall had been taken prisoner but were unharmed.

'Madam, there was nothing we could do. The lord Edward instructed us to come to you and regroup. With your permission I will go to Bordeaux and recruit troops. And I shall do so on Joanna's lands in Ireland too. I will not rest until my brother and my nephew are free. I remain loyal to the very marrow of my bones.'

Alienor regarded him with her lips primly set. Fine spider lines had begun to form where she had so often pursed them. 'This is a grave setback, but as you say, we must now rally for the next attempt and there is no point in recrimination here. In truth, my lord, we have had our differences and they have created chasms between us, but whatever I have laid at your feet in the past, I have never doubted your loyalty to my husband and to my son – and I hope we can build bridges across those chasms.'

'Yes, madam, it is my dearest wish and purpose.'

She paused to compose herself, and William admired her tenacity and the steel in her spine. 'Madam, I have never been your enemy,' he said quietly. 'We shared true family friendship when I first married Joanna. Whatever has happened in the past, I ask you the grace to put it behind you, as I shall put it behind me and close the door. We still have allies in England and we shall free the lord Edward and the King – I swear it, madam, on my life. The Earl of Leicester stands condemned for what he has done.'

Alienor looked at him fiercely. 'Simon de Montfort will die for this – and you will make sure of it.' Her glance flashed around the gathering with narrow, hard intent. 'All of you. That is your sacred trust.'

*

In the hot June evening, Joanna's womb was as round as a full moon and she felt heavy and tired. The child remained vigorous, so she knew it was healthy, but what it was going to be born into frightened her.

Leonora sat by the window in the last of the light, reading letters that had recently arrived from Henry. A month after the disastrous battle at Lewes, Windsor still held out against de Montfort and his faction. As yet they had not been besieged, but messengers arrived daily, bringing threats, demands and intimidation, all of which Leonora ignored.

At least they had received solid news that Edward and the King were safe and that William, Iohan, John and his brother Hugh had reached the Queen in Flanders. William had written to say he was heading to Bordeaux to recruit troops, and would return as soon as he could. Realistically that would be months, and the sudden turns of Fortune's wheel could spin from top to bottom in a heartbeat.

'The King has a message for you,' Leonora said as she perused the last sheet of parchment. She rose from her seat and came to Joanna, at the same time ordering the servants to light the candles. 'I think perhaps the time has come.'

Joanna took the letter. Henry called her his dearest sister. He said he understood the predicament of her advanced state of pregnancy and was worried for her welfare since Windsor must yield to opposing forces and it was no fit place for a gravid woman. He had arranged for her to leave under safe conduct and go to either a convent or one of her manors to give birth. He guaranteed her safety and that she would face neither persecution nor molestation.

'It is a good offer,' Leonora said. 'The King has no influence in great matters of state for the moment, but he does have power to grant a safe conduct for our wellbeing. They will not dare to harm us.'

Joanna smoothed the parchment under her fingertips. 'No, but they might take us hostage.' Her heart filled with fear, for herself, for her children, for the baby. Whatever Leonora said, murder was common coinage these days.

'We are prisoners here anyway,' Leonora said. 'We have held out and bargained for the best terms we are going to receive, but it is now time. It would seem that I too am with child after February, and I do not want to continue dwelling here while Edward's son grows in my womb.'

'I am glad for your news, but not our situation,' Joanna replied.

'I have done what I can. The King has summoned me to go to him at Canterbury. I shall bolster his determination and raise his spirits and he shall do the same for me. But you should prepare to leave very soon. Your confinement is almost upon you and you must have somewhere peaceful and close to bear the child. I would not want your travail to happen at the road-side.'

'I would not want it either,' Joanna said fervently. 'But I must have that safe conduct before I stir from this place.'

'You shall have it. I will write back immediately.'

'The nunnery at Cookham is only half a day's journey; I will go there.' She shook her head. 'Dear God, if you had told me this would be my lot when I was a girl, I would not have believed you.'

'I would not have believed it of my own life either, but when you are an old woman with grandchildren playing at your feet – God willing – just think of the life story you will spin for them.'

Joanna gave a mirthless laugh. 'Perhaps, but it will be dark at times.'

'The best tales always are,' Leonora replied. 'But if you are there to tell them, then you will have won through, and they will be there because of your strength – yours.' She added the last word with emphasis and her cheeks grew pink. 'This much I know.'

'Not mine alone.'

'No, but your part in it is as bright as anyone's – perhaps brighter for what it has endured without being sung as a great deed.'

Joanna stood up. Her chest was full, swollen with emotion. 'You will be a great queen,' she said.

Leonora's flush deepened. 'That remains to be seen. For now, I am doing what I can with what is possible. I will have my scribe write to request a letter of safe conduct, and you must make preparations to leave.'

A week later, Joanna set out with her children for Cookham Abbey with a safe conduct tucked in her pouch, bearing Henry's seal and approved by the council of barons. Leonora remained at Windsor, awaiting her own escort to Canterbury.

'Take care and may God protect you,' she said, embracing Joanna as they said their farewells in the courtyard.

'And you.' Joanna hoped she would see Leonora again, but nothing was certain.

Trying to quash her fears, she settled in the cart, adjusting the side cushions to support her spine. The journey to Cookham was only half a day, but far too long when being escorted by men who, while professional in their duty, bore no love for her husband. She felt as vulnerable as a hermit crab pulled from its shell. As the cart rolled away from Windsor, she realised that Agnes was watching her with knowing eyes.

'All will be well,' she said, too brightly. 'Your father will be home soon. He just has things to do elsewhere first.'

Agnes said quietly, 'Mama, I know the truth. I am old enough to understand, and sensible enough not to say anything to the others.'

Joanna gazed at her eldest daughter with an aching heart, reminded of herself at that age. 'Yes, I know, sweetheart, and I am not hiding anything from you, but it is true that your father will soon be home.'

'How soon? A week, a month, a year?' Agnes jutted her chin.

'Whatever time it takes, but sooner than never.' Joanna's tone sharpened. 'Do not look at me like that. Truly there is nothing I know that you do not. Your father will return as swiftly as he is able but at the right moment, and until that time we must husband our resources and take each day as it comes. You are almost a woman grown, and brave – I know you will help me in this.' She put an arm around Agnes and hugged her narrow shoulders.

After a moment, Agnes hugged her back, adding an extra-tight squeeze at the end by way of affection and apology. 'It is so hard, Mama.'

'Yes, I know.' Joanna kissed the top of her daughter's head. 'And I am proud of you.'

In the courtyard of his keep at Bellac, William sat at a table under an awning in the hot late August sunshine. A few clouds drifted across the blue, insubstantial as ghosts. His shirt sleeves were pushed up, revealing long forearms glinting with gold hair and smattered with freckles. On the dusty ground to his right, the squires were at arms practice. The thud of blunt weapons on shields and yells of profanity and encouragement filled the air. A pair of grooms rode past, leading horses to the river. William briefly admired a handsome bay before returning his attention to the matter in hand. The scribe at his side was tallying a list of names on a wax tablet.

Recruiting men to fight in England had not been difficult in these parts where men reviled the name of de Montfort with a passion as deep as the blood they and their families had shed during the religious wars of a generation since when de Montfort's father had been the scourge of the region.

William had limited finances to recruit troops, although he had received donations from many who had long memories, and William was one of their own. He was looking at one such man now – Raoul de Barret, whom he had known since childhood. Raoul was an acquaintance rather than a close friend, but William knew he could fight and had a good horse and armour.

Raoul slapped a coin on the table in front of William. 'Here is my token,' he said, his brown eyes full of fire. 'I will come with you to England and fight. I will be avenged for what the de Montfort family has done to me and mine.'

William picked up the coin, a gold bezant. 'You do not need to resort to such, but it is welcome,' he said, 'and so are you.'

De Barret nodded brusquely. 'He burned my lands, he hanged my nephew,' he said. 'I want a part in bringing him down.'

'And you shall have it.' William indicated acceptance to his clerk, who added de Barret's name to the list and took his pledge.

William then dealt with three men whose village had been plundered by de Montfort's troops. A father, son and uncle, all wanting to do their part and each possessing some skill in arms. And then a group of peasants who had heard that William was recruiting and had turned up in the hope of wages and gain. William was less keen on them, for they were armed with pitchforks and clubs, and there were only so many places on the ships he was hoping to land at Pembroke. Such men could be recruited more locally, or from Ireland.

'I am glad you have come,' he told them, 'but I need to know how well you can fight. You are welcome to test your mettle against my serjeants and see if you can match their standard.' He gestured to a roped arena a short distance away, where hopefuls were going up against his experienced men. A few were waiting in line. Others had hastily changed their minds. It was a good way of sorting wheat from chaff, and the determined from the hangers-on.

They went off in a huddle to confer. William stretched his arms above his head and left the table for a short while, putting his knight Geoffrey Gascelin in charge of the recruitment. Impatience burned inside him. He had to constantly curb his eagerness to return to England; the time had to be right. This recruitment was but a preliminary and much more had to be done. He had dreams of sinking a sword into Simon de Montfort's chest, and seizing back all that had been stolen, but dreams they remained for now even if he was grounded and driven forward by a heavy, determined energy. Every act, every deed had to be considered and measured against the penalties. He had learned it the long way, the hard way, but he had come to maturity, even if he was still becoming accustomed to its weight.

His chaplain, Peter, was waiting for him, holding a letter. 'This arrived with today's messages,' he said. 'It bears your lady's seal.'

The letter had been tampered with and badly resealed, but William expected nothing less following his previous sojourn in exile. It amazed him that it had arrived at all. Written by Joanna's scribe, the letter informed him that she had retired to Cookham Abbey with a safe conduct from the King and there been safely delivered of a daughter, baptised Isabelle after William's mother, and her own grandmother. Both mother and child were safe and healthy. Once churched, Joanna intended moving to Bampton. She would write again to let him know how she fared, and hoped he was in good health and that they would be together as soon as God willed.

'I have a daughter,' he told his chaplain, his heart flooding with joy and wonder. 'Born the second week of July and named after my mother.'

'God save you, sir, and the lady and the child,' Father Peter answered with a smile. 'I will say prayers and light candles for their continuing safety.'

'I want you to arrange for twenty paupers to be fed tomorrow and the day after in honour of the news – and give alms to the poor today, whatever we can spare.'

He went to his chamber and prayed his thanks at his portable altar for Joanna's safe delivery. He imagined her cradling their new daughter in her arms and a frisson of anxiety shivered through him at what might happen without him there to protect them. Again, he had left her to cope alone in precarious circumstances. Knowing her capable did not assuage the hurt, frustration and guilt that he could not be there to fulfil his role. He had to succeed this time; there would be no more mistakes.

40

Manor of Bampton, October 1264

It was market day at Bampton and under a sky the same strong blue as the banding on the de Valence coat of arms Joanna had come from the manor to visit the stalls, where people from the surrounding area had gathered to buy and sell their wares – butter and cheese, eggs and poultry, rope and baskets, pottery and nails.

She had come on foot, walking with her children, ladies and guards. Mingling among people bustling about their business, she appreciated the normality of their daily life in the midst of turmoil. To them it mattered not who governed the land, only that they should have a roof over their heads and food in their bellies. She prayed that Bampton would be safe and that its small but thriving centre of trade would not attract unwarranted attention from their enemies.

She had a little coin to spend at the stalls and a modest amount to give in alms from her carefully husbanded resources. She knew her duty to provide and to be a benefactress to the people. She had employed one of the young village women as a wet nurse for Isabelle and taken on two others to serve at the manor during her stay. She had employed the miller's brother, Thomas, a retired soldier, to act as her escort in the village and her usher in the hall.

Accustomed to the big markets in London and to sending out her factors to obtain anything she wanted, Joanna found it a novelty to walk among these rustic stalls and tables, set up for a day. She bought a roll of wool braid with an unusual pattern to trim the girls' dresses. A local potter had a jug with a face on it; the sharp features reminded her of William and, amused, she bought it. Another rustic jug for flowers, glazed in a wash of pale gold, caught her eye, and she added it to her purchases, thinking how cheerful it would look in her chamber.

Thomas's older brother, the miller, was florid and plump with flaxen-white hair and bright blue eyes. He greeted Joanna with a bow and she dipped her head to him, but before they could engage in polite formality they were interrupted by a disturbance over at the squared-off area where two men had been wrestling for the prize of a pig and now a more general brawl had broken out. The miller, very much head of the community, strode off to deal with the matter. A knife flashed, but the miller disarmed the offender with swift efficiency and knocked him to the ground where he gave him a hefty kick, before hauling him back to his feet by his scruff and shaking him as if he were a rat discovered in a sack of grain.

'Do you want to return to the manor, my lady?' asked Thomas, fingering his stout quarterstaff.

'No, I will deal with this.' She stepped forward with regal dignity. 'Who disturbs my peace?' she demanded in a clear, strong voice. 'No one shall draw weapons in this place of trade.'

The offender, belligerently drunk, sneered at her. 'I'll do what I want – don't have to listen to the word of a hoity woman.'

The miller drew back his fist and punched him to the ground again. 'You'll mind your mouth, or I will stuff it with stones.'

'Put him in the stocks and let him stew,' Joanna said curtly. 'I will deal further with him in the morning when he is sober.'

The miller and his burly oldest son dragged the troublemaker roughly to the village stocks and locked him in while he proceeded to curse and revile the bystanders incoherently from his bloody mouth, uttering curses in English that were an education to Joanna. Small boys were already gathering with their slingshots ready to torment him, and Joanna did not prevent them.

Although shaken by the event, she stayed a little longer at the stalls to show she was not intimidated.

'He's not one of ours, my lady,' the miller said, solicitous and angry at having his village shown in a bad light. 'I have seen him here before, but he comes from over Buckland way. I am sorry for what he said.'

Joanna shook her head. 'It is not your fault and I am grateful for your intervention. In every place there are those who live their lives well, and those who do not. A night in the stocks will either bring him to his senses or herald his downfall.'

On her return to the manor, Joanna discovered that a messenger had arrived from Leonora, and her body tightened with new tension.

'Madam, I am sorry to bear sad tidings,' the man said. 'The little lady Katharine has died of a fever and is among the angels in heaven.'

'No!' Joanna's mind filled with the image of the beautiful little girl and her eyes brimmed with tears. Dear God, poor Leonora and Edward.

'The lady Leonora said to tell you that although she is grieving, she is in good health in her condition and that she hopes for better news soon. She bade me give you this and say she keeps you in her thoughts.' He presented Joanna with a small purse embroidered with the arms of England. Inside was a brooch in the shape of a golden heart with the motto 'In place of a friend'.

Swallowing on tears, Joanna thanked the messenger. 'Take time to eat and care for your horse and I will send you back with a reply.'

He bowed from the room and left her with the letter. Leonora had written the sad news of the infant's death without elaboration. Joanna went to look at little Isabelle, slumbering in her cradle, her cheeks rosy with life, and wiped away a tear for Leonora's child. Her own offspring had survived illness and danger thus far, but she knew the grace and fragility of life and thanked God daily. The little brooch pinned to her gown, she wiped her eyes and read the rest of the letter.

Leonora said that the King's health was reasonable but his spirits were heavy. She hoped to hear from Edward soon in his own captivity. Joanna wondered if the statement held a hidden meaning, but everything was vetted and it was difficult to tell. Leonora added that even while grieving she had put her trust in God, and she asked Joanna to write back to her.

Joanna summoned her scribe and dictated a letter of condolence. She sealed it and gave it to the messenger, together with the little golden jug from the market, protected in a nest of straw. 'Tell the lady Leonora that I hope to see her before too long,' she told him, 'and that I pray she finds solace and comfort in God as she wishes.'

That evening at dusk as Joanna played with Isabelle in her crib, she was interrupted by a commotion at the manor gates. Her heart began to pound. She gave Isabelle to the wet nurse to tend and threw on her cloak. Thomas hurried to find out what was happening and swiftly returned with news. 'There's a band of ruffians in the village, madam. They have sprung today's drunkard from the stocks and are assaulting the mill.'

Joanna compressed her lips at this challenge to her authority. 'Summon the household,' she said, 'every able-bodied man who is capable of carrying a cudgel or handling a weapon. Send them straight to the mill. Apprehend the ill-doers and bring them straight to me for judgement. You know your business.'

'My lady.' Thomas saluted and left.

Joanna swallowed her fear and rallied. Bidding the children remain in the upper chamber with their nurses, she went down to the hall with Robert her cook and her groom, Joli, for protection. The folk at the manor and the villagers were far stronger together than any band of chance-come ruffians. She just prayed no one of her affinity was injured.

Night had fallen by the time the party from the village returned, dragging with them the corpse of the man who had been sprung from the stocks, who had died on the edge of Thomas's sword. The miller sported a shiny blue egg of a bruise on his temple and his knuckles were scraped and swollen. Another ruffian had fallen into the mill leat while trying to escape and had drowned. He too was laid out before Joanna.

She gazed impassively at the corpses and then raised her head to the villagers, all full of themselves but anxious and a little overblown too. She ordered cider, bread and cheese to be brought from the stores and doled out to everyone, and commanded the two dead men to be taken out and hanged on the gallows as a deterrent.

'For a month,' she said firmly, 'until after the next market day, and then let them be taken down for burial.' The approval on people's faces told her she had done the right thing. 'I want to thank you all for your stout defence. I am in safe hands, and I value all of you for your service and protection. Please, eat and drink at my board and then return to your homes.'

The villagers sat down at three hastily erected tables and shared drink, food and talk of the moment. Joanna watched them and felt a warm surge of affection. No one would harm her here, and she was equally determined that she would let no one harm them.

Eventually they took their leave, some carrying extra bread wrapped in cloths. When the last one had departed through the gates, wobbling slightly, Joanna looked up at the star-scattered sky. 'Oh William,' she said softly, and rubbing her arms, returned inside.

Three weeks later, Joanna was in the mews inspecting her hawks and falcons when she heard horses in the courtyard. With her female peregrine on her glove, she went outside and found the space full of big, glossy horses, and dismounting from one of them her second cousin Gilbert de Clare, who was in Simon de Montfort's camp. He had the beacon-red hair of his father's family, a freckled complexion and sharp green eyes. A stocky young man, in his early twenties, he was dressed for hunting but his accoutrements were very fine and as much for show as for the field. De Montfort referred to him half disparagingly as his 'red-dog'. William said he was an entitled brat who would change allegiance on the turn of a coin to further his cause, or just because he happened to have woken up in a sulk that morning. But he possessed strategic lands and held the balance of power.

Although astonished to see him, Joanna put on a warm smile. 'Cousin, you are welcome, even if it is an unexpected pleasure.'

'Thank you,' he said. 'We are travelling to Gloucester, but if you have some wine, it will serve to break our journey.'

'Of course.' She started to give the peregrine to her falconer but Gilbert stepped in. 'May I?'

Joanna gestured, and her falconer handed the Earl a spare gauntlet. He pulled it on to his fist and took the bird. 'What a fine creature.' He gently stroked the back of the falcon's head, while it stared round with fierce black eyes. 'Is she your lord's?'

'She is mine,' Joanna replied. 'Would you like to see the mews?'

'Indeed!' His face lit with enthusiasm as he returned the peregrine to her.

Joanna took him and his entourage to the mews, and as they looked at and remarked upon the various hunting birds on their perches, she pondered what they were really doing here. Gilbert was no ally, nor, although her kin, did she like him, but she prepared to be diplomatic.

He examined the birds with a covetous eye, especially another peregrine. 'I shall send you this one if you wish,' she said. 'Or if you want to take her with you, I can arrange that too. She is fairly advanced in her training and swift as an arrow.' She gestured, and her falconer unfastened the falcon from her perch and placed her on Gilbert's fist.

'You are most gracious, cousin,' Gilbert said, giving her a vulpine smile. 'I shall be glad to take her now. How fortunate that I should happen by.'

Joanna inclined her head, and behind her agreeable expression felt bitter. De Montfort had taken her best horses from Westminster. Now de Clare was appropriating a costly falcon in which she had invested much training. However, this was no chance visit; something was afoot. Better to grease the wheels than break them. 'Fortunate indeed,' she said drily. 'Come and have some wine.'

'I noticed the corpses on the gallows as we rode in,' he remarked as they entered the manor.

'It's a deterrent. They caused a disturbance on market day and then tried to rob my mill. I have no desire to see bodies hanging in the wind, but it sends a message to others who would disturb my peace, and the villagers approve. They are loyal people, and loyalty matters these days.'

He flushed. 'Quite so.'

She ordered the best wine to be brought from the cellar, together with bread, cheese and dried fruit. Weazel arrived to inspect the visitor and then sat on the sill in the sunshine to wash his paws. De Clare eyed the elderly cat sidelong with a fastidious grimace.

'How is your wife?' Joanna enquired pleasantly, his wife being William's niece Alais, daughter of his oldest brother. 'And your daughters?'

'Alais is well enough,' Gilbert said gruffly. 'And the girls are in good health, although it is a pity neither of them are boys. Alais has been recently churched and hopes for a boy next time.' He spoke indifferently, stating the details to get them out of the way and making it clear he had no interest in pursuing the subject. The marriage had been arranged when he and Alais were children and no love had grown from it. 'Have you heard from your husband?' he asked as they sat down.

'Communication is difficult, but I understand he is busy on his estates in the Limousin,' Joanna said, immediately on her guard. She pushed the platter of cheese towards him. 'Of course, you must know this, so forgive me for being curious.' She spoke courteously, and managed not to imbue her words with scorn or venom.

'There are certain matters of diplomacy I want to discuss with him. Matters pertaining to the future, and where a man might fix his gaze and where he might not.' He cut himself some cheese.

Joanna raised her brows. 'What are you saying, cousin? Let us have this clear between us.'

He paused for such a long time that she wondered if he was going to reply, but at last he looked at her. 'I have been having second thoughts of late. You speak of loyalty, but what do you do when you find that your loyalty has been ignored or misplaced, or paid back in false coin? Do you stay in that position and watch it grow ever more stained and corrupt, or do you step back and admit that you were wrong?'

Joanna's heart began to beat swiftly. 'I would do as my conscience bids me.'

Gilbert de Clare's position in de Montfort's regime was pivotal, and his Marcher lands of strategic importance. If he changed his allegiance then the whole balance of power would alter. However, his loyalty and conscience were both attached to his own gain. He might be disgruntled by de Montfort at the moment, but it could not be taken as carved in stone. It was, however, an opportunity worth a prized falcon.

She met his gaze, and to his credit he did not look away. His eyes were a striking shallow green with brown flecks, and he had thick eyelashes as gold as straw stubble.

'Pembroke,' he said. 'You are lady of Pembroke, but it is in my custody as matters stand.' He refreshed his cup. 'However, if my attention lapsed, and if I were to leave the castle unmanned, then who knows what might happen.'

'You would do this?' Her piece of bread almost stuck in her throat and she had to swallow hard.

Gilbert drank again. 'I have debated long on the matter. I would not have visited you otherwise.'

'But even if Pembroke lacked a garrison, your other lands still stand between it and England.'

'But I might not be there either to prevent anyone from

travelling across them. Of course, it is late in the year now, and much may happen before the spring, but you remain my dear cousin and neither you nor your husband are my enemy.'

Joanna dipped her head. 'That is reassuring indeed, but I will not mince words with you. We have been enemies in the past and until recently I did not have reason to believe otherwise.'

He smiled thinly. 'We have seen things differently, it is true, but we are kin and times have altered. Changes are afoot, and I wanted to assure you that you are my dear cousin and I desire to become better acquainted with you and your lord in due course to our mutual advantage. I shall send messengers to him, but I wanted to let you know also.' He drained the wine and stood up. 'Your subterfuge with those carts of wool – it was talked about for a long time at court.'

She lifted her brows. 'The duplicitous cunning of women no doubt.'

His lips curled with reluctant amusement. 'It may have been remarked upon.'

She suspected that despite his apparent humour he agreed with the statement, but she said nothing as she accompanied him back to the mews, to arrange the handover of his new falcon.

'Look after her well,' she said as he took the young peregrine on his wrist and covered her eyes with a plumed hood.

'Indeed, I shall, and I thank you for your generosity. I hope we shall hunt together in better times.'

'Indeed, my lord,' Joanna said, hoping no such thing.

She waved him and his troop on their way and then returned to the manor to write to William and Leonora.

41

Pembroke Castle, Wales, Spring 1265

A thick sea-mist shrouded the outline of Pembroke Castle as William and his soldiers approached the gates in the chilly April morning. The four ships that had slipped into the dock overnight had now disgorged their cargo of fighting men and horses. More were due from Ireland within the next few days once the castle had been secured.

A porter and his lad stood beside the open castle gates. Apart from a handful of servants, they received no greeting beyond that of the gulls wheeling over the buildings. The great domed tower built by Joanna's grandsire, William Marshal, rose out of the mist in a blunt cylinder at the heart of the solid defences, but it was a place of ghosts, the sounds muffled and hollow. The back of William's neck tingled. Although Pembroke belonged to him through marriage, he had never set foot here before.

John de Warenne joined him as the troops marched into the deserted stronghold. 'My mother told me that when she was a little girl she used to drop her toys off the top of the tower,' he remarked.

William stared around the defences. 'It is a mighty fortress.' He suppressed a shiver. 'But on the edge of the world.'

'It is,' John replied. 'You cannot get much further from the court than this, although of course it is a good launch point for sailing even further into the outreaches – to Ireland. My grand-sire dwelt there for many years.'

William went to explore the castle, and climbed the great tower to the battlements. The mist had begun to dissipate and the seagulls wheeled and screamed in the blue, grainy air. A weighty sense of destiny settled on him even though he could not imagine living here for any length of time. Pembroke was the first stage of the road to return. He could sense the endurance and power in the stones, and the close connection with Ireland was strategic.

Some months ago he had begun receiving messages and coded overtures from Gilbert de Clare via letters from Joanna. De Clare had intimated his change of political direction and announced his intention of leaving Pembroke undefended should William and John de Warenne wish to take advantage. He had also sworn not to hamper William and John's advance through Wales to the Midlands – the roads would be open for them. Everything thus far had been accomplished in secrecy, but de Montfort had his spies and would find out. Still, he would not come to Pembroke for he could not afford to be tied down in South Wales. Providing de Clare held to his word, William was safe, and could establish a base here while waiting for Irish troops, and for the next part of the plan which involved the lord Edward. It was his final chance. He would either survive and return to his lands, or die fighting, and that knowledge was as heavy and solid as the stones of the great tower on whose battlements he stood.

*

In Hereford, Edward was kicking his heels and trying to conceal his impatience. The May morning was as bright and fair as it had been yesterday and the day before. He had been waiting for a sign all week. He knew his uncle William and John de Warenne had landed at Pembroke and were making preparations. Word had come too from Roger Mortimer and Gilbert de Clare that everything was ready.

During his imprisonment, Edward had come to hate Simon de Montfort with a fury that burned beneath steely control. Conscious of what was at stake, he dissembled and was sociable with the servants appropriate to their rank. He rewarded people with what he could give and when funds had run out he had promised future rewards. He had moulded the situation, behaving as an honoured guest rather than a prisoner, always presenting a debonair front, lulling his gaolers and laying a false trail. He took great satisfaction in playing with them and turning them to his will, even while they thought they were controlling him.

If his mind turned to his wife and the loss of their daughter, the ice-burn inside him became almost unbearable. He had been forced to borrow money to pay for Katharine's funeral and had been denied the comfort of grieving at her bier. For that alone Simon de Montfort would die, but he tried to avoid those thoughts, for they led him into darkness, and he had to keep everything light and allow those around him to relax, especially his chief gaoler, his cousin Henry de Montfort.

He was permitted to go out riding, but he was always well guarded. The forays and the chance to exercise his healthy young body and stretch his mind were what kept him from insanity. He had recently received a letter from his aunt Joanna at Bampton wishing him well and sending him a box of sugared marchpane balls. She said she remembered how much he had loved the confection as a little boy, and her cook Robert had made some to raise his spirits. His aunt often wrote to him. She had sent her condolences and some candles when Katharine had died. In January, a letter had arrived with an exquisitely embroidered napkin. At Easter there had been a palm cross and a little psalter. Ostensibly her contact consisted of social and family matters, but hidden in all these tokens and among the letters were other gifts – small coded pieces that told him what was happening beyond his prison.

The most recent letter, concealed in the box lid containing the marchpane balls, had given details of the planned escape and his part in it. He was to watch for a Welsh horse trader arriving with some new coursers and he was to select the black one. The rest was up to him. He had burned the parchment to ashes on the small altar in his chamber and in the morning had sent a messenger to Joanna, thanking her for the gift and saying that she always knew what would please him. That had been three days ago.

Edward had visited his palfrey in the stables and remarked that he thought it was going lame. He made a point of having the groom examine the horse and expressed his concerns, saying that he needed a replacement.

Thomas de Clare put his head round the chamber door. 'Sire, the horse trader is here.' He was flushed and breathing swiftly. 'He might have something to suit you.'

'At last! I had better come and see.' Edward plucked his cloak off its peg and steadied his breathing. He tugged on his riding boots and fastened his spurs.

Thomas, younger brother of Earl Gilbert de Clare, was one of his guards, and had become a clandestine ally in the changing tides of allegiance.

The trader stood in the yard, talking to Henry de Montfort. Edward immediately noticed the large black courser. It had a deep chest, powerful quarters and long legs and was looking round with pricked ears and flaring nostrils. Edward dropped his gaze from the horse and looked at his cousin instead. 'Fine weather for a try out,' he said. 'Let's see if there is one suitable among this lot, although I will be hard-pressed to replace Bayard.'

Henry raised his brows. 'I would go for the black,' he said. 'He looks the likeliest.'

Edward shrugged and smiled. 'I agree with you, but I'll leave him until last. I want to give the others a chance first and enjoy myself.' He approached a rangy chestnut and stroked its nose. 'I shall try this one,' he announced. 'Who will race me to try its mettle. Tom? Your roan is strong and fast.'

Thomas de Clare grinned. 'Rufus has never been beaten.' He patted his chaser and gave Edward a meaningful look.

As soon as the chestnut had been saddled, Edward mounted and trotted him about, warming him up, then moved to a canter, and then with a look and a shout to de Clare, spurred to a full gallop. The chestnut had a rapid turn of speed but was no match for de Clare's Rufus and was easily beaten by several lengths as it ran out of stamina.

Edward tried a grey next and encouraged three of his guards to race with him. The grey, flat out, won by a neck, but Edward complained that the others had not been trying hard enough to overtake him.

'I like this one here.' He indicated another chestnut with a golden sheen to its coat and a flaxen mane and tail.

Henry de Montfort shook his head. 'Not enough power at the back.'

'No harm in trying, is there?' Edward responded. 'Come, all of you, race with me again.' He fixed Henry de Montfort with a challenging stare and a sharp grin.

Henry reined his bay to face the field. The group set off at a hard canter which soon increased to a stretched gallop over the firm ground. Edward rode the chestnut hard, forcing him to work, spurring him when he flagged, and he stayed in front. Thomas de Clare was riding Rufus again, but the palfrey had lost his edge following the first race, and this one was harder still. Not to be outdone, de Montfort forced his bay, and beat Edward and de Clare by a head. By the time Edward pulled up, all of the horses were blowing and sweating.

Edward's squire arrived, mounted on Bayard, Edward's usual horse, the excuse being he was gently exercising him despite the suspect lame leg. The young man was leading the black and had harnessed him with a spare saddle and bridle.

Edward dismounted from the heaving chestnut and approached the black. He offered him a piece of apple from his belt pouch and rubbed the horse's muzzle as it crunched the treat. 'So,' he said. 'We are friends.' The black pawed the ground and butted Edward's hand, seeking more. He gave the horse another piece and scratched its forehead, then set his foot in the stirrup and mounted. He gathered the reins and walked him around a little, warming him up to a trot, then a short canter, before returning to the knot of guards and companions.

'Another race?' he asked. 'Henry, your bay is still fresh and strong.'

'I think you would beat me, cousin,' Henry said, looking a little resentful.

'But still, come, race with me,' Edward cajoled. 'You have a head start back to the stables, and see if I can catch you.' He waved his arm to show that they should all join in.

Thomas exchanged looks with Edward and fretted his roan, before turning to urge Henry de Montfort into the race with him. A spark of competitive annoyance lit in Henry's eyes and he spurred his bay, stealing several yards on Thomas, who gave a yell and set off in pursuit with the others, except for Edward's groom. Edward immediately reined the black around and spurred him in the opposite direction, riding for freedom, although after the first spurt he controlled the horse to a steady gallop, knowing he must not spend the horse early when speed might be useful later. The black's gait was economical and ground-eating. The groom rode behind on Bayard, now miraculously cured and showing a clean pair of heels.

They heard the sudden shouts behind them and Edward urged the black to a faster pace but still not a flat-out gallop. Exhilaration burned in his chest at the joy of the steady speed and the wind in his hair. Freedom held the scent of summer grass, of sunlight, of the working horse beneath him, of warm leather. He let out a triumphant whoop and the stallion's ears flickered. Risking a glance over his shoulder, he laughed, for their pursuers were pulling up with the gap too wide to close, and lengthening all the time. Edward eased the black down again, not wanting to founder him or risk him putting his hoof in a hole.

A couple of miles further along their road, trotting briskly, they saw horsemen riding to meet them, wearing the blazons of Mortimer, de Valence and Warenne. 'Hah!' Edward kicked on towards them in triumph, and then drew the sweating black to a halt. 'A fine day for a ride, gentlemen!' he cried, his face alight and exuberant. 'I hope you all have horses as fast as mine!'

Amid laughter and back slapping, someone tossed Edward a costrel of wine and he caught it and drank. 'To freedom!' he toasted. He looked round at the gathered, jubilant knights. 'When my great uncle Richard Coeur de Lion was liberated from wrongful imprisonment, his enemies received warning to beware, the devil was loose. Now I say that the lion has been unleashed, and let my enemies tremble in fear!'

*

Joanna took Isabelle's hand and walked her across the chamber. Her daughter had begun taking her first steps a fortnight ago and, although unsteady, was improving daily. As though her name was a portent, she had her grandmother's golden fair hair and blue eyes. None of Joanna's other children had blue eyes, all were variations of hazel or brown. What would William say when he saw her for the first time?

The July morning grew hot as the sun climbed in the sky. Joanna had received several letters from William in the field informing her of progress. She had replied, sending him sacks of flour from Bampton mill. Edward had been free since May and men had flocked to his standard. Gilbert de Clare had honoured his word and William had occupied Pembroke unopposed. The Irish mercenaries had arrived and William had moved out across Wales. Edward had taken both Worcester and Gloucester, but where William was now she had no idea. She was terrified that de Montfort still might prevail, as he had done before against the odds, but comforted herself with the thought that William too had survived against the odds and so had she and their children.

Hearing horses in the courtyard, she handed Isabelle to her nurse and hurried to the window. Two serjeants wearing the livery of de Warenne were dismounting in the courtyard, and they had Iohan with them. Joanna's heart began to beat in hard, swift strokes, and with a soft cry she sped down to greet them.

Iohan turned and dropped to one knee. 'My lady mother,' he said.

She lifted him to his feet and abandoned formality to throw her arms around him and kiss him soundly. 'It is so good to see you! What are you doing here?'

'My father and the Earl de Warenne have sent me to protect you and my brother and sisters.' His tone was neutral, but she could tell from the look in his eyes that he was not pleased to be here.

The serjeants bowed and led the horses away to the stables, except for the sumpter which Iohan's servant was unburdening.

'Come within – have you eaten?'

He shook his head. 'No, but we haven't ridden far.'

'Still, you will be hungry; young men of your age always are. You have hollow legs. I swear you are as tall as your father now.'

'We are of a height,' he said.

Agnes and Margaret came running to him with squeals of joy and he hugged and kissed them. Will arrived on their heels – ten years old and shiny-eyed at the sight of his manly big brother whom he aspired to be. He wished he had whiskers and a deep voice.

'And this is your sister Isabelle.' Joanna took her youngest daughter from the nurse.

Iohan squatted to a level with the fair-haired, blue-eyed infant and hugged her too. 'Strange,' he said, 'to meet a sister and already it is a year since her birth.'

'Yes, so much time has been stolen from us by this war – your father has yet to see her too.' She forced a smile. 'How is he?'

'He is well. I have a letter for you in my baggage.' His tone held a vestige of irritation.

The wine arrived, and Joanna sent the younger children off to play.

'They sent me away,' Iohan said in an aggrieved tone. 'Protecting you and my siblings is an important task, but it is not the main reason I am here.'

Joanna waited for him to speak, not prompting him. The servant returned with a platter of small tarts filled with marrow and dried fruit. Iohan took a napkin and devoured a couple at speed.

'There is going to be another battle,' he said between mouthfuls. 'Without quarter. The lord Edward has given orders that Simon de Montfort is to be brought down and killed whatever it costs.'

Joanna shook her head. Matters had been leading to this for a long time, like a gathering storm that had to disperse its energy before the sky would clear. Nothing would ever be the same again. At least if de Montfort was brought down the rebellion would be cut off at source, but at what price? She looked at little Isabelle in her nurse's arms. William had to live because he had never laid eyes on his daughter.

'The lord Edward is right,' she said as Iohan claimed a third tart. 'Nothing will stop de Montfort save death. I am very glad your father sent you here.'

Iohan continued to look disgruntled.

'No, my son,' she said. 'You are too young for the kind of battle they anticipate. You are your father's heir and fifteen years old. You will have time to learn your craft on fields that will not involve such desperate stakes. You are swiftly coming to manhood, but it should not be like this.'

He nodded stiffly but she could tell he was still annoyed. But better that than being caught up in violent bloodshed. Even if he did not have to fight, he would still be a witness, and baggage lines were dangerous places during a battle.

'I will get you my father's letter,' he said and, wiping his hands, went off to his pack.

Joanna took the letter away to her chamber to read, for she did not know its content and she needed to be strong and composed in front of her family. Sitting by the window, she broke the seal. Inside, folded into the parchment was a gold ring set with an amethyst that fitted her wedding finger perfectly, and she had to wipe her eyes. William had written the brief message himself rather than using a scribe, and touching the words made her feel closer to him. He addressed her as his dear love and companion. He missed her and the children and hoped to be with them soon. He was sending her Iohan for safe keeping. This coming battle would be all or nothing, and if he did not return from it, then he knew she would cope and do what was best for the family. He had lodged his will with the monks at Westminster. He asked her to pray for him and hold him kindly in her thoughts.

She pressed her lips together and her chin wobbled, but then the letter's tone changed at the end. He said he would bring victory home to her and that, God willing, he would win through and they would be together very soon.

Joanna wiped her eyes and drew a deep breath. So be it. She was proud of him and she would be fierce in that pride. Kissing the letter, she placed it on her small chamber altar.

When she returned to the hall, Iohan was playing chess with Agnes while Will and Margaret watched them. 'I am proud of you,' she said to them clearly. 'I am proud of all of my children. You are a credit to yourselves, and to your family names. I need to say it now, because perhaps I have not said it often enough. I love you with all the blood in my heart.' She went to the cradle where little Isabelle had been put to nap. Gazing at the sleeping, rosy infant, she vowed that God willing she would be there for every one of them while she breathed, whether they were little babies or grown men and women. It was for ever.

William dismounted from his palfrey and had his squire bring up his destrier. He checked his armour again, adjusting his shield strap, making sure his sword drew cleanly from the scabbard. He had checked several times already, but it was part of his detailed preparation for battle. Everything had to be right; there were no more chances. They had been riding through the night to get into position, ready to intercept Simon de Montfort's force as he tried to break through towards support from the Londoners.

In the early daylight birds were singing, and the leaves hung heavy and limp on the trees, dark-green and weighted with summer. The weather had been as hot as a dry cauldron over a fire for several days, but now the air had grown sticky and humid. He was sweltering in his armour and minute black flies crawled on any areas of exposed skin, and itched like the devil.

The dawn had risen with a gleam of gold on the horizon but that had gone now, leaving the sky bruised and oppressive. God's wrath was waiting, and he harboured no doubts as to where that wrath would fall. He could not afford to be anything but convinced in his belief.

Two days ago, Edward had held a commanders meeting of the joined forces, and had given Roger Mortimer and a dozen others the task of bringing down and killing de Montfort. That was their sole objective, and it was a sacred trust and a holy thing. A crusade against a man who had overturned the natural order. A man whose supporters had insulted Edward's mother, imprisoned the ailing King and compelled him to their will. De Montfort had dragged Henry all over England, forcing him to confirm his every command. Edward had told everyone to watch for his father lest he was among the combatants and had assigned Roger de Leyburn to seek him out and ensure his safety.

The sky continued to darken, and thunder grumbled in the distance. The first drops of rain spattered, heavy as silver, and twisted veins of lightning forked the sky. William's destrier tossed his head and sidled. William kept him reined in and gripped his lance. A rumble beyond the thunder heralded de Montfort's arrival. William's heart quickened as he gazed upon the ranks of horsemen and foot soldiers. He drew a long, steadying breath, for now they came to it. The moment between living and dying, when all still had life, but when many soon would not.

He gave the signal to his knights and pricked his horse with his spur. From a walk to a trot to a canter, steadily increasing speed. The rumble of thunder was echoed by the pounding hooves of the destriers as they gained momentum towards their quarry.

The rain increased and started to drive down. De Montfort's centre hurtled at them, the slope barely diminishing their impetus. William chose his target, a knight astride a bay destrier with a white snip, and adjusted his lance. The thunder crashed overhead and the lightning ripped and flickered. William felt the impact, the scrape of steel on mail, and then the punch through into flesh. Casting aside the lance he pivoted, his sword drawn.

The fighting was hard and close and bloody. Horses plunged and shied, slipping and falling on the wet grass, screaming as they were injured, the din of the battle and the torrential storm melding into one tremendous cataclysm. Blood and water streamed over the trampled ground like channels in a slaughterhouse and churned to crimson mud, and the air stank like a city shambles of blood and bowels and shit. William's breath sawed over his larynx as he parried and slashed and bludgeoned. He killed in order not to be killed, and gave no quarter. Each blow he struck avenged his exile, the insults, the scorn and contempt. It was for Joanna, for his family, for Edward and the King. It was brutal slaughter and mayhem through a hammering curtain of rain and, as the thunder rolled overhead, William knew that God was directing his sword.

To his left, through the torrent, a knot of men surrounded something on the ground, their arms rising and falling in a flurry of dull mail. A dead white horse lay in the mud, blood streaming from savage blade wounds. Close by, Roger de Leyburn, his sword raised, approached a horseless, unarmed knight clad in common armour screaming for mercy and crying in cracked anguish over and over that he was Henry of Winchester. William recognised the voice, as did Leyburn. 'The King!' he roared. 'It is the King!'

William spurred to join Leyburn, dismounted and frantically unbuckled the knight's helmet to reveal Henry's white, tear-streaked face and wild eyes. Blood was trickling from his shoulder where an arrow had pierced his mail, but the wound was slight and the point easily plucked out.

'You are safe now, sire,' William said. 'Come, messire Leyburn and his men will take you to safety and tend to your wound behind our lines.'

Henry responded with a terrified wail, and Leyburn had to manhandle the King away to his escort for he was rooted to the spot and crying like a rabbit in its last moments. Rage and pity burned in William's heart at the agonised bewilderment contorting Henry's face. It was not the look of a king but of a wounded, traumatised child.

De Montfort's levies were fleeing the field and the de Montfort lion banner had fallen, trampled in the bloody murk, its shaft snapped off. A group of knights on foot had surrounded de Montfort and were hacking and stabbing with their swords in an act of filthy raw butchery and dismemberment. William's lip curled. It was not enough. It could never be enough to wipe away that look of tearful terror on Henry's face. What kind of man would do this to a king who was not a warrior and who abhorred violence? What kind of arrogant cruelty? Attempted murder, too, in cladding Henry in plain armour and leaving him to take his chance. Some might call Simon de Montfort a devout Christian and a great man, but William had no such scales covering his eyes. He knew de Montfort for what he was, and he hoped his soul burned in hell for eternity.

Sword drawn, William walked over to the group of men. He looked at the hacked and mutilated body and, raising his arm, added another slash to the torso in a single blow. 'For Henry,' he said, his voice raw and breaking. 'For my wife, for my children. For all that you took!' He wiped his reddened sword on the tatters of de Montfort's surcoat and turned away before the rage and grief overwhelmed him beyond control, and before he was sick. De Montfort was down and dead, butchered in the mud. Now it was time to move on, to salvage and rebuild.

He went to find Henry and discovered him at the nearby priory being tended by Leyburn and the monks. William left his sword outside the door. His hands were dyed with blood and his surcoat saturated and streaked with mud and gore. He washed his hands and face in a bucket of water by the trough and tipped it out when he finished, his stomach burning at the sight of its discolouration. Crossing himself, he entered the monastery guest house. Henry sat on a bench before the fire, which had been lit despite the oppressive heat of the day. He was bare to the waist and a monk was tending to his shoulder wound. William swallowed, moved to pity to see Henry's torso, the ribs showing through the flesh. He was shuddering and glassy-eyed. Small whimpers escaped between his teeth, and William remembered that another of his half-brother's morbid dreads was thunderstorms.

'Sire.' William knelt before him. 'Sire, Simon de Montfort is dead on the battlefield and his forces are scattering in disorder. The lord Edward has carried the day. You are safe now.'

Henry nodded, but his gaze was vacant and William did not know if he had absorbed the words.

The monk stepped back for William to see Henry's wound, which was a flesh cut and barely seeping, although it would require a couple of stitches. Henry would live, providing he did not take the wound fever.

'You will be sore for a few days,' William said, 'but you will soon mend.'

Awareness glinted in Henry's eyes. 'But it will always be with me,' he said, shivering. 'I thought I was going to die.' He swallowed. 'De Montfort put me in ordinary armour. He said my name was Henry of Winchester, because it was my only entitlement in this world, since I was born there. He intended me to die – to have my own men kill me.'

'But you are alive and he is dead,' William said with icy anger. 'He has paid the price. You can put it behind you, even while never forgetting. You have survived, and the victory is yours.'

Henry did not answer. Two tears rolled down his vein-spidered cheeks and he whimpered again.

William kissed him, gripped his hands briefly, and left him. There was much to do and, in the meantime, Henry needed to rest and hopefully recover his wits. He detoured briefly into the church to thank God for the great victory, and then went in search of Edward.

Three days later, William stood before the dark marble tomb in Worcester Cathedral and gazed on the effigy of Henry's father King John in the majesty of a scarlet robe with a gem-set neckline of sapphire, emerald and ruby glass. John's hair lay in wavy ripples to the level of his beard and his eyes were open, staring into eternity. His white gloves were gilded on the backs and so were his spurs. Either side of his head sat protective images of St Oswald and St Wulfstan. From everything William had heard, King John had not been particularly religious, but prudence said a man should store up insurance in heaven and invoke protection in the afterlife.

Henry joined him. 'I have been looking for you,' he said.

'I was paying my respects to your father,' William replied.

He glanced at his half-brother. Although still gaunt and pale, Henry's shoulder wound was healing well and he had recovered a little of himself. His hands still trembled and he was skeletal under his robes, but he had been able to go through the day and sit in council, although Edward was doing most of the organising.

Henry touched the side of the tomb. 'It resembles him a little,' he said. 'I remember him wearing those scarlet robes on great occasions, and that jewelled collar. Your wife's grandsire once told me that if ever I should grow up to be like him, then he wished me an early grave.'

William raised his brows. Henry had spoken of the incident on another occasion, many years ago, and clearly the Marshal's words had cut deeply.

'I tried not to be,' Henry said wearily, 'but my barons still rebelled against me and hated me as they did him. If you are a king, some things are cast in stone.'

'Not everyone rebelled,' William said. 'And many love you.'

Henry grimaced. 'All I have ever wanted is peace, but it seems that so many men prefer war as a means to an end.'

'But there is hope,' William said. 'I was thinking of your great chamber and how it is being restored and made new, even if it will never be the same. Things can be made better than they were.'

Henry nodded, and his eyes were wet. He embraced William affectionately, then drew away. 'I came to tell you that some prisoners have arrived, including your wife's half-brother, Guillaume de Munchensy. If you want custody while we negotiate his ransom and reparations, he is yours.'

William puffed out his cheeks. He had no desire to see his

brother-by-marriage, but he had a duty towards him, and there was the matter of Swanscombe. 'Thank you, sire, I will attend to the matter.' What a pity Guillaume had not died in battle, he thought. The way he had turned to de Montfort and scorned his family was an insult hard to forgive.

Filled with distaste, William returned to his lodging and sent for the young man. In the meantime, he had James bring a flagon of wine and a platter of crisply fried pastries – he might as well be comfortable while he dealt with the youth.

Guillaume arrived, escorted between two of William's knights. His clothes were creased but decent; the dagger sheath at his belt was empty. An angry scratch swiped his face from temple to jaw and the look he shot at William held bitter hostility, and also fear.

William directed him to a bench and, dismissing everyone, poured wine. 'I am not going to gloat,' he said, 'nor am I going to dwell on past harms and insults because it does no good beyond satisfying an appetite for vengeance, and for now I am staying my hand.'

'What are you going to do with me?'

'That is not my decision, although as a favour because you are kin I have influence to mitigate some of the consequences. I can plead your case and say that you were young and easily swayed, that you have seen the error of your ways and deeply repent supporting Simon de Montfort. Whether either would be true is another matter.'

Guillaume thrust out his bottom lip and scowled.

William sighed. 'I am trying to help you for your sister's sake. Not for your own or mine, but for Joanna's.'

'She would not care if I died,' Guillaume said roughly.

'You are wrong, which shows how little you know of her. She may have no love for you, but she has never sought to do you ill even if you have been less discriminating with her. For my wife, it is a matter of duty to you, and to God. Certainly, I would not care if you died, but I will not actively seek your demise. If you have survived thus far, it must be for a reason.'

Guillaume shrugged. 'Let us get on with it then.'

William took a drink, feigning indifference. 'You are to be released on bail into the custody of your mother for the time being. I shall be administering your lands while matters go forward and England is restored to full and proper rule. You shall have an income on which to live – dependent on me. Once that has been settled and you have proved trustworthy, you shall receive a full pardon from the King and be restored to your inheritance. Until you have proved your loyalty and worthiness you will not be permitted the use of your estates. However, you will not be a prisoner and your mother will go surety for you.'

Guillaume regarded him with loathing. 'Am I supposed to thank you for this?'

William shrugged. 'Do as you wish. It matters not to me.' His irritation increased. 'I have no need of or requirement for your gratitude. If you are nothing to me, then you become an irrelevance. If I objected to your attitude, it would imply that it mattered enough for me to care, and I no longer do. I would say, though, that if you wish to have your lands returned, you should be more amenable, since I am your road to the mercy of the King and the lord Edward – as is your sister. I leave it to your common sense to decide which road you will take.'

Guillaume's jaw worked. He picked up his cup and took a drink.

William helped himself to a pastry. 'It is your future.'

Guillaume cleared his throat. 'You give me no choice,' he said, scowling. 'It is not palatable, but it seems I must eat what is upon my trencher.'

'Now you understand.'

Guillaume put down his cup and stood up. William looked at him, for although very different from Joanna, something in the set of his shoulders when facing a challenge reminded him of his wife.

'You may go,' William said, 'and I hope to talk to you again before you are given into your mother's custody. I shall organise that exchange once we reach Gloucester. For now, you will be kept under house arrest – although not in my household. I shall arrange for you to join the Earl of Gloucester – it will suit both our purposes better. I hope you will accept the terms of release by giving your word as a knight. I would hate to see you back in fetters.' He indicated the red bracelets of chafed skin on Guillaume's wrists.

'You have my word,' Guillaume said stiffly.

William gestured for his knights to escort Guillaume out, and when he had gone he heaved a deep sigh and, leaning back, raked his hands through his hair. Then he poured another half cup of wine and ate a second pastry because doing such mundane things put normality back in the world. He would never come to any sort of friendship with Guillaume de Munchensy – there would be friction even in times of peace – but for now it was settled.

He still had so much to do. De Montfort was dead but pockets of rebellion remained and nothing would be untangled in a day, or even a month. Everything had changed. Like Henry's great painted chamber, the fabric might remain, but recovery from fire meant what was laid over that fabric would be very different.

42

Winchester, August 1265

Sitting on a window seat in the great hall of Gloucester Castle, Joanna had never seen such a bustle of industry at a court gathering, as though Simon de Montfort's death had torn open a sealed-up beehive. The place thronged with nobles and officials, with hangers-on and servants and supplicants. William had yet to arrive and the waiting made her stomach churn with tension. They had been apart and in peril for more than sixteen months. Isabelle had been in her womb when they parted; now she was walking and saying her first words.

To meet him, Joanna had donned the best gown of those she had left – the blue silk with the embroidery of ruby martels – but the hem was dusty from all the bustle in the courtyard and hall. She kept searching for him among the crowds in the hall, and Iohan had gone to look for him outside.

Five days ago she had learned of the victory at Evesham in a letter from William filled with relief and thanksgiving and telling her to come to Winchester with the children. She could barely come to terms with knowing it was over and that Simon de Montfort was dead. She had feared him since her childhood, and now he was gone. She ought to be dancing with triumph, but she kept thinking of Eleanor de Montfort as a wife and mother and how devastated she must be. They had been enemies, they disliked each other, but they shared the common ground of family and motherhood. It could so easily have been her in Eleanor's place.

Arriving at court, Joanna had been appalled to see Henry's gaunt frailty, his trembling hands and drooping eyelid more pronounced than ever. He had made wrong and foolish choices, but to drag him into a battle, unmarked, unknown, certain of death, was unforgiveable.

Without warning, as she was craning her head one way, William arrived from the other side, and the first she realised was as he knelt at her feet with head bowed. 'My lady wife,' he said. 'My heart, my reason, my hope.'

Her own heart turned over and melted. He was wearing his heraldic surcoat over a plain blue tunic and his Limoges enamelled sword belt, every inch the supplicant knight to his lady. She gasped and put her hands in his hair, just to feel the luxuriant curl. The familiarity and the relief were like gold within her. He looked up and they searched each other's faces.

'I trusted you to come through, and you did,' she whispered, 'but oh, I have missed you and prayed for your safety.'

She laid her palm against his cheek and he moved his head sideways until her hand was upon his lips, and he kissed it. Then he sat beside her on the window bench and drew her into his arms as though they were alone together and not in a crowded hall.

'And I trusted you too,' he said. 'You are so brave and capable – but to see you now and touch you, and know you are real when you have only been in my mind for all this time. That is all I can think of beyond anything . . . and that I really do have a family, and it is not in my imagination – that I do have something to be proud of. I can begin to believe that everything is going to be all right.' His voice wobbled, and as he kissed her again, she tasted his tears.

'Oh, William,' she said softly.

Iohan arrived and loudly cleared his throat. 'I see you have found each other,' he said.

William rose from Joanna's side and clasped his son in an emotional embrace, man to man. 'You have done a fine job keeping the family safe,' he said. 'I am proud of you.'

Iohan flushed with pleasure, but he was frowning too. 'I wish I had been there.'

'No, you do not,' William answered quickly, with a shudder of revulsion. 'Why would you go to hell if you did not have to? I would not wish such a thing on any son of mine. There will be times in your life when you will have to fight and attend your lord in battle, but what went forth at Evesham was something you would never want to witness.' With hands either side of Iohan's face, he kissed his forehead in blessing. 'The Earl de Warenne is outside; you had better go and see if he needs you for anything.'

'He has grown again,' he said to Joanna as Iohan shouldered his way through the busy hall.

'Yes, there's not a pantry big enough to feed him at the moment.'

He greeted the other children, marvelling at how they too had grown, and his eyes filled at the sight of Agnes. Fourteen years old – almost a woman, with a willowy figure and his own steady grey-hazel eyes.

'My lord father,' she said with a smooth curtsey.

'Are you not glad now that she is not yet wed?' Joanna asked.

'Yes, you were right,' he answered gruffly. 'Plenty of time for that later.'

He lifted Agnes to her feet and hugged her, then turned to embrace Margaret, stroking her tumbled curls with warm affection. He admired Will's new knife and exclaimed on his growth too, saying he would soon be old enough to become a squire. And then Joanna presented him with their youngest daughter.

'This is Isabelle,' she said. 'Almost born on the road to Cookham Abbey, but none the worse for her ordeal, save that she has a penchant for wandering!'

William took her solid weight in his arms and gazed at her rosy cheeks, her whorls of golden hair and bright blue eyes. He held her close, inhaling her infant scent, so different and healing after the stenches of the battlefield. He looked at Joanna again. 'What you had to do,' he said hoarsely. 'What you had to endure. Yet you have come through it all and kept the children safe and increased their number. You truly are a remarkable woman.'

'I do not feel remarkable,' she answered with a tremulous laugh. 'I did what I had to do, and you the same.'

Isabelle demanded to be put down and was immediately off, toddling like the wind, and Joanna had to run to catch her.

'Hah, she is just like you!' she declared.

William was called away then on a matter of business, but promised to return later.

In the castle, packed to the rafters, everyone had to find sleeping space as best they could, but Joanna's servants had managed to secure a small lodging house near the castle wall, and when William finally escaped his duties, he came to her.

The children had retired to the loft room above to sleep, and they were alone. He sat on the bench beside her with a sigh of relief and took the cup of wine she handed to him. Weazel was curled up on a cushion at Joanna's side, an old cat now, battle-scarred, skinny, with patchy fur, but surviving and content to sleep by the fire.

'I have been given the wardenship of Winchester Castle,' he said, 'but I also have to go with the King, so I am afraid that the custody falls to you until I can deal with it. Your rule is mine, and mine is yours. I will give you documents in the morning.'

Joanna was briefly taken aback, but then pleased, for she could do this and do it well, and it was a recognition of her abilities. 'Of course.'

'I have something for you.' He put down the wine and left the bench, returning moments later with a roll of cloth from his baggage pack. 'I had this made while I was in France.'

Filled with curiosity, Joanna unfastened the ties and unrolled the fabric to reveal a second roll within the first. Inside that was a length of linen, and pricked out upon it in charcoal a replica image of the figure of Hope from the King's great chamber in Westminster. To accompany the roll, he gave her an exquisite Limoges enamelled casket filled with richly coloured embroidery silks and a case of silver needles.

'I thought you might like to stitch this to hang in our chamber for the times we can be together. The King is having new figures designed for the great chamber, and this is not part of his design, but it shall always be ours. The face is not as exact as I would like it, but it still looks like you.'

Joanna's eyes filled with tears and for a while she could not speak. Then she swallowed and looked at him. 'I would have no other for my husband but you, even if I were offered the choice of the world,' she said, her voice hoarse with emotion.

'And I no other wife. We have come through this. We have many more battles to fight and seas to cross, but for now we are here, together, with all our children safe abed.'

He poured more wine and they touched goblets together and drank. When they had finished, he gathered her in his arms and took her to bed, drawing the curtains around them, and shooing Weazel back to his cushion by the fire.

Joanna turned in his arms. Even in times of great change, some things were sewn indelibly on the heart. She would cherish every stitch she made when she began work on the image of Hope among the stars – triumphant over Despair.

Author's Note

My novels always stem from personal curiosity. I want to know who my characters were, what their daily lives were like, their thoughts, motives and emotions – what they did and why. When I start asking questions, the answers lead to more questions and a deeper dialogue. I become increasingly intrigued, and at some point these people from the past will enter the present, come to me and tell me their story.

I first met Joanna de Valence in a biography written by historian Linda Mitchell who had set out to document and champion this little-known granddaughter of the great magnate William Marshal (see my novels *The Greatest Knight*, *The Scarlet Lion* and *Templar Silks* for his tale). Mitchell regards Joanna as 'a figure of substance, of importance, of significance to her age' and believes she has been overlooked and misrepresented on the rare occasions when she is mentioned in historical works. The same can be said of her husband, Henry III's half-brother William de Valence, who has also, Mitchell believes, been wrongly maligned and dismissed by historians. De Valence's steadfast support of his brother the King, his absolute loyalty and his refusal to back down to Simon de Montfort have either been ignored or distorted by modern historians. Spin and lazy research have led to his portrayal as a greedy, grasping and unscrupulous 'foreigner'. As yet no historian has explored beyond the superficial his role at the core of thirteenth-century diplomacy, warfare and politics – a career in royal service spanning almost fifty years where his unswerving loyalty to the Crown echoes the values of his wife's more famous grandfather. It is astonishing how many biographies of Simon de Montfort exist, but not one that follows the career of William de Valence. It's like having the pepper on the table without the salt!

As I read Mitchell's biography, I wondered about Joanna de Valence and who she was. A woman who had risen from run-of-the-mill aristocratic beginnings to become the sister-in-law of Henry III. A woman of resourceful intelligence who ran rings around the men who tried to seize her rights and property. A woman much loved and treated as an equal partner by her husband – and I knew I had the subject for my next novel.

The first we know in history of Joanna is her marriage to William de Valence in the summer of 1247. We don't have secure birth dates for either of them, but they would have both been in their late teens. Joanna had not been destined for great things at her birth. Her mother, the youngest daughter of William Marshal, had made a respectable marriage to Warin de Munchensy of Swanscombe, a safe but routine match. She bore her husband two children, John (Iohan) and Joanna.

Historical novelists are always faced with dilemmas when it comes to names. Although medieval people, like us, had their flights of fancy when it came to naming their offspring (I have come across a thirteenth-century 'Snow White', for example, and a 'Teffania', or Tiffany), the majority of them took a traditional approach. I found myself laden with an over-abundance of Johns and Eleanors who were often interacting with each other in the same scene. That is why Joanna's brother and son became Iohan (a medieval spelling of the name). They did not share the same stage at the same time, which made it easier. With Eleanor, I have used the French spelling Alienor for Henry III's queen, the anglicised spelling for Eleanor de Montfort, and Leonora, the Spanish version, for Edward I's wife Eleanor of Castile.

At some point in Joanna and Iohan's childhood, their mother died and their father remarried and had another son, William (given the French spelling Guillaume, again to avoid confusion in the novel).

It is very likely that Joanna was educated at court from late childhood. Noble families would pay for their daughters to be raised in a high-status household as it increased their prospects and standing. We know she was tutored by royal 'governess' Cecily de Sandford, who had taught the King's sister Eleanor and had been her close companion between marriages.

Through a series of tragic but unfortunate deaths, including that of her brother Iohan, Joanna became, in the spring of 1247, a major heiress with lands in Ireland, Wales and England, including Kilkenny, Pembroke, Tenby, Goodrich and Swindon. From having nothing, Joanna suddenly became a highly valuable marriage prospect.

Henry III had recently invited several half-siblings to the English court from their native Limousin in France. They were the children of his mother Isabel d'Angoulême's second family after she had remarried following the death of King John, Henry's father. Henry's invitation to his brothers and sisters followed on the heels of their mother's death, and was probably a combination of Henry's desire for family supporters at court, a useful means of remaining connected with his volatile lands in south-west France (centred around Bordeaux), and complex emotional ties.

To provide for these half-siblings, Henry arranged wealthy marriages, wardships, ecclesiastical appointments and gifts of land and money. Aymer was to be educated for a bishopric, Geoffrey and Guy were given monetary rewards. Aliza married John de Warenne, young heir to the prestigious earldom of Surrey, and William, for whom Henry developed an especial fondness, was paired with Joanna de Munchensy.

The marriages themselves were highly successful in terms of personal compatibility. William and Joanna were married for almost fifty years until William's death in 1296. In the one surviving letter we have between them dating from shortly after the Battle of Evesham, eighteen years and five children into their relationship, William addresses Joanna as his 'Dearest Friend and Companion' when asking her to take charge of Winchester Castle for him. In their mid-forties they were still adding to their family, with little Joanna and Aymer being born somewhere in the early to mid-1270s. In the novel I have William saying to his wife that they will always make time for each other if they can, and we have evidence for this from their lives. In January 1296, Joanna left her family to go specifically and indi- vidually to meet William and spend two days with him in Dover before he embarked for campaign duties in France.

The marriage of John de Warenne and Aliza de Lusignan ended in tragedy, however, when Aliza died bearing their third child. John never recovered from her death and did not marry again, although he was still under thirty when Aliza passed away. Given the high childhood mortality of the period, having only a single son might suggest he would marry again, but he chose not to. He maintained strong ties with William and Joanna throughout their lives. Perhaps his wife's tragic early death contributed to the reputation he acquired in later years for being difficult and bitter.

Henry III's reign is an incredibly rich and detailed period and I have had to cherry-pick and streamline my narrative and remember that I was writing a novel, not a text book. When I write about the people of the best part of a thousand years ago, my interest is in who they were at the personal level. For the purposes of keeping the story on track, I have had to miss out episodes involving several personalities. There is a lot more to be said about Henry's relationship with his brother Richard, for example, who in many ways was more suited to be King than Henry himself, but fitting his story into the work would have made the novel unwieldy and three times as long. There are also portions of history I have omitted to keep the storyline moving, but I have included a bibliography for anyone wanting to read about the period and get to grips with a more in-depth view of the politics and other personalities.

William de Valence and Simon de Montfort clashed during their involvement in a complex and often vitriolic territorial dispute over the land rights of Simon's wife, Eleanor, the King's sister. Before marrying de Montfort, Eleanor had been married to William Marshal the second Earl of Pembroke, and when he died she was entitled to a third of his lands. The Marshal family disputed the vast sums involved and Eleanor agreed initially to a cash payment. Later, she was to say that she had been exploited in her widowhood and was entitled to far more. Naturally, the other Marshal heirs, including Joanna, who were numerous, did not agree and a long, often bad-tempered legal wrangle ensued. Following his marriage to Joanna, William de Valence became tangled up in the dispute. The de Montforts resented him in particular because of all the extra favouritism and gifts that came his way from Henry III.

Simon and William also clashed on the matter of the reforms. I have not gone into details in *A Marriage of Lions* regarding the said reforms – again, the bibliography suggests useful further reading on the subject. Reform was certainly required, but the men took a very different stance on the matter. Simon de Montfort is often fiercely lauded as the father of Parliament, and a sword of justice, but if the matter of the Marshal estates had been settled early on in his favour one has to wonder if history would have taken a different road that did not lead to the Battle of Evesham.

William de Valence remained fiercely loyal to his brother King Henry and Henry's son Edward, the heir to the throne. In his youth William was impulsive and rash and frequently paid the price. His immaturity caused countless difficulties and he was his own worst enemy. The raid on the Bishop of Ely's wine cellar is well documented, as are William's forays into tournaments. He also got into various sometimes disgraceful scrapes with his brothers, especially Aymer, that do not cover him in glory. However, he steadied down as he matured and the once 'wild youth' developed into a trusted and talented military commander and diplomat.

William de Valence is buried in Westminster Abbey. He lies on a pillow decorated with exquisite medieval Limoges enamelling, and despite the vagaries of time, the effigy shows a stylish, sharp-featured man, with the hint of a smile on his lips. A man who was sufficiently valued to be granted a tomb in the Plantagenet family mausoleum, as were several of his children.

The story of Joanna and the wool carts is true. It is mentioned in passing by the most famous chronicler of the day, Matthew Paris, who gives the basic details in his work the *Chronica Majora*, here translated into English from Latin. Note again, too, the mention of the love Joanna had for William.

> The King's brothers whom fame had aspersed . . . had to the great loss and detriment of the kingdom been enriched by a large sum of money, thanks to a woman . . . Joanna wife of William de Valence, who left England with a large sum of money, instigated by love for her husband to follow him. According to report, the aforesaid Joanna with womanly ingenuity, procured a large quantity of wool, which she caused to be securely packed up in sacks. Amongst this wool she hid a large sum of money. Then placing the sacks in some strong carts, as though it was only wool, she sent it into Poitou at a convenient opportunity. Therefore, although it was stated by many that the money belonging to the aforesaid William was confiscated wherever it was stored up, it was evident from this proceeding that no reliance could be placed on such a statement.

Joanna was courageous, resourceful, intelligent and loyal, and probably more mature than her husband in the early days of their marriage. After William had been threatened with beheading by Simon de Montfort and fled for his life, she had to cope in a hostile arena, and keep herself and her four children safe. She played her part to perfection and succeeded in exporting the family wealth right under de Montfort's nose. Prior to joining William in exile, Matthew Paris tells us Joanna was in dire straits and struggling to make ends meet, but clearly she was working very hard under cover. It is likely that she had some assistance from allies within the court, including her cousins Hugh Bigod and John de Warenne.

Joanna was also left to manage alone in difficult circumstances when William once again had to flee following the disastrous Battle of Lewes in 1264. On this occasion she was heavily pregnant and locked up at Windsor with Edward's young wife, Leonora of Castile, under the threat of siege. Joanna was granted a safe conduct to depart to bear her child elsewhere and may have gone to one of the manors that this time she was permitted to use to support herself and her family. One of the likely manors was Bampton in Oxfordshire, today famous as the village used to film the TV series *Downton Abbey*.

During the period between the battles of Lewes and Evesham, Joanna bore her fifth child, a little girl christened Isabelle. If Joanna was at Bampton during this time, she would have been living there when the mill was raided by outlaws. The entire village turned out to deal with the thieves.

Joanna in later life is particularly associated with Goodrich Castle in the Welsh Marches, for which we have some of her household accounts and the names of her staff and servants. She seems to have been conscientious, and constantly busy, but had time to socialise too. She held a feast for all her lady friends one Candlemas, for example, and was a close friend and confidante of Joan of Acre, a daughter of Edward I and Leonora of Castile. Goodrich Castle has a very special atmosphere. It is tranquil today, and set in glorious Herefordshire countryside. In its heyday it was clearly a dwelling of comfort and magnificence that welcomed Joanna's later years and became her favourite residence, particularly during the ten years of her widowhood.

I was sorry to discover that two of Joanna and William's children who feature in the novel died young. Margaret and John (Iohan) died in 1276 and 1277 in their twenties and were buried in Westminster Abbey. William and Joanna's son William died in battle as a mature adult and is buried in the church of St Peter and Paul in Dorchester, where his knightly effigy can still be seen. Their last son, Aymer, born outside the scope of this novel, succeeded to the inheritance but produced no heirs of his own. He too is buried in Westminster Abbey with his father, brother and sister. Joanna and William's other daughters, Agnes, Isabelle and Joanna, all went on to marry and have descendants.

Joanna de Valence's burial place is unknown. Her biographer Linda Mitchell strongly suspects that it was Dene Abbey (also known as Flaxley Abbey), a short distance from Goodrich Castle. The abbey has since disappeared, and Flaxley Hall, a private residence, now stands on the site.

With regard to William's brother Aymer de Valence, he did indeed die suddenly in Paris at the end of 1260 on the cusp of returning to England to take up the post of Bishop of Winchester. He had been Bishop Elect for some years, and was close to William in age. He was heartily disliked by Queen Alienor and her faction, and indeed his reputation has been tarnished by the chroniclers of his day. For example, he is blamed for kidnapping and beating up the official of Boniface of Savoy after being denied the right to approve his own incumbent for a vacant post, but it isn't mentioned that Aymer's incumbent had been arrested and beaten up first by Boniface, who was not above violent sharp practice himself.

The King's great chamber at Westminster, known as the painted chamber in later centuries, no longer exists, although we do have illustrations of some of the décor from sketches, drawings and paintings made in the late eighteenth and early nineteenth centuries. A fire destroyed the chamber in 1834 – it seems to have been prone to such accidents. The blaze I mention in the novel in 1263 began in a chimney, which had been repaired in 1259 and quickly spread, causing extensive damage. The chamber, always a work in progress, was repaired and restored but with a different series of wall paintings, some of which survived to be recorded, including the figures of the Virtues and Vices. My choice of Hope trampling upon Despair is my artistic licence, but within the context of the chamber, and as one of the medieval Virtues itself, is thoroughly plausible, and we do not know the exact composition of all the figures prior to the 1263 fire. We do know, however, of the motto Henry had painted above the great gable in the room next to the entrance: *ke ne dune, ke ne tine, ne prent ke desire*, which translates to 'he who has and does not give, will not, when he wants, receive'.

Writing *A Marriage of Lions* has been an enriching voyage of discovery and I am so glad to have encountered Joanna and William de Valence and have them welcome me into their fascinating lives. I hope readers enjoy their story too.

Bibliography

Ambler, Sophie Thérèse, *The Song of Simon de Montfort: England's First Revolutionary and the Death of Chivalry* (Picador, 2019)

Armstrong, Abigail Sophie, *The Daughters of Henry III* (Canterbury Christchurch University – thesis submitted for Doctor of Philosophy, 2018)

Baker, Darren, *Henry III: The Great King England Never Knew It Had* (The History Press, 2017)

Bémont, Charles, *Simon de Montfort, Earl of Leicester* (Oxford University Press, 1930)

Binski, Paul, *The Painted Chamber at Westminster* (The Society of Antiquaries, 1986)

Binski, Paul, *Westminster Abbey and the Plantagenets: Kingship and the Representation of Power 1200–1400* (Yale University Press, 1995)

Brooks, Richard, *Lewes and Evesham 1264–65: Simon de Montfort and the Barons' War* (Osprey, 2015)

507

Carpenter, D. A., *The Reign of Henry III* (The Hambledon Press, 1996)

Carpenter, David, *The Battles of Lewes and Evesham 1264/65* (Mercia Publications, 1987)

Carpenter, David, *Henry III 1207–1258* (Yale University Press, 2020)

Church, Stephen, *Henry III, A Simple and God-Fearing King* (Allen Lane, 2017)

Cockerill, Sara, *Eleanor of Castile, the Shadow Queen* (Amberley, 2014)

Davis, Paul R., *Three Chevrons Red: The Clares: A Marcher Dynasty in Wales, England and Ireland* (Logaston Press, 2013)

Harding, Alan, *England in the Thirteenth Century* (Cambridge University Press, 1993)

Howell, Margaret, *Eleanor of Provence: Queenship in Thirteenth Century England* (Blackwell, 2001)

Jobson, Adrian, *The First English Revolution: Simon de Montfort, Henry III and the Barons' War* (Bloomsbury, 2012)

Maddicott, J. R., *Simon de Montfort* (Cambridge University Press, 1994)

Mertes, Kate, *The English Noble Household 1250–1600* (Blackwell, 1988)

Mitchell, Linda, *Joan de Valence: The Life and Influence of a Thirteenth Century Noblewoman* (Palgrave Macmillan, 2016)

Morris, Marc, *The Bigod Earls of Norfolk in the Thirteenth Century* (Boydell, 2005)

Powicke, F. M., *King Henry III and the Lord Edward: The Community of the Realm in the Thirteenth Century* (Oxford University Press, 1966)

Prestwich, Michael, *Edward I* (Methuen, 1988)

Prestwich, Michael, *English Politics in the Thirteenth Century* (Macmillan, 1990)

Remfry, Paul Martin, *Goodrich Castle and the Families of Godric Mapson, Monmouth, Clare, Marshall, Montchesney, Valence, Despenser and Talbot* (Castle Studies Research and Publishing, 2015)

Ridgeway, Huw, 'William de Valence and his Familiares 1247–71' (*Historical Research*, vol. LXV, no. 158, 1992)

Rothwell, Harry (ed.), *English Historical Documents 1189–1327* (Eyre & Spottiswoode, 1975)

Shoesmith, Ron, *Goodrich Castle, its History and Buildings* (Logaston Press, 2014)

Steane, John, *Archaeology of the Medieval English Monarchy* (Routledge, 1993)

Vincent, Nicholas, *The Holy Blood, King Henry III and the Westminster Blood Relic* (Cambridge University Press, 2001)

Wilkinson, Louise, *Eleanor de Montfort: A Rebel Countess in Medieval England* (Continuum, 2012)

Woolgar, C. M., *The Great Household in Late Medieval England* (Yale University Press, 1999)

Online sources

https://archive.org/details/matthewparissen01parigoog/page/n9/mode/2up (Matthew Paris, *Chronica Majora*)

https://www.oxforddnb.com (*Oxford Dictionary of National Biography*, for snapshot studies of all the main players)

Acknowledgements

I would like to say a quick thank you to the people behind the scenes without whom this novel would never have seen the light of day.

My gratitude goes out to everyone at the Blake Friedmann literary agency for their friendly professionalism and for keeping me solvent by their joint efforts around the globe, and an especial thank you to my dear friend, poet and agent Isobel Dixon, who keeps me on track and always fights my corner.

I have been with my publishers at Little, Brown for many years and although a few faces have changed, the team always remains strong. I want to thank Cath Burke, Thalia Proctor and Millie Seaward for their time and effort, and also my editor Darcy Nicholson who has been a pleasure to work with and given me many valuable insights and food for thought while working on *A Marriage of Lions*. For the final edit before proofs, I owe Dan Balado-Lopez a big thank you for picking up on some of the dodgy dates and timelines that successive drafts had left in their wake. Any errors that remain are mine alone.

My thanks as always to my husband Roger who has been my rock since we were teenagers, and is always on hand with mugs of tea to keep me fuelled at my desk. And to my dear friend and historical time traveller Alison King, who I have to thank for showing me Joanna and William in their true light.

Last but not least, my thanks to my many dear friends and readers online who light up every day with our exchanges on all manner of subjects. I've come to know your lives as you have come to know mine, and our interactions have become such an enrichment and life enhancer, never more than in the strange days of 2020 when I was writing this novel and we were spending a lot of time in lockdown – but not isolation. It would take several pages to mention you all, and I would still be afraid of leaving one of you out, but just let me say an especial thanks to Marsha Lambert, who has been unfailingly supportive for many years, and although I have never met her, is the kindest, most genuine person anyone could know and a most important part of the glue that keeps us together.

Thank you all.

New York Times bestselling author Elizabeth Chadwick lives in a cottage in the Vale of Belvoir in Nottinghamshire with her husband and their three dogs. Her first novel, *The Wild Hunt*, won a Betty Trask Award and *To Defy a King* won the RNA's 2011 Historical Novel Prize. She was also shortlisted for the Romantic Novelists' Award in 1998 for *The Champion*, in 2001 for *Lords of the White Castle*, in 2002 for *The Winter Mantle*, in 2003 for *The Falcons of Montabard* and in 2021 for *The Coming of the Wolf*. Her sixteenth novel, *The Scarlet Lion*, was nominated by Richard Lee, founder of the Historical Novel Society, as one of the top ten historical novels of the last decade. She often lectures at conferences and historical venues, has been consulted for television documentaries, and is a member of the Royal Historical Society.

For more details on Elizabeth Chadwick and her books, visit www.elizabethchadwick.com, follow her on Twitter, read her blogs or chat to her on Facebook.